EVEN AS YOU ARE IN ME

THOMAS CURTIS

outskirts press

ACKNOWLEDGEMENTS

My gratitude embraces Bridget Olson who taught a fourteen-year-old boy with wavering self esteem that he had an inquisitive voice and a talent for turning a phrase. Bridget, you transformed my life.

John Judson further encouraged me at university, informing me of my progression beyond just the mechanics of writing. I played the game. I remember your explanation of how literature informs us better than anything else that we are not alone. Thank you, John.

I thank the people at Outskirts Press for their friendly and professional treatment of this project. Whereas I did not agree with every suggestion given by the editor, it was so much fun to learn. Some suggestions with which I disagreed nevertheless prompted me to research further and find something better. It is how I arrived at the word, "ha'adam." A discrepancy was identified about the technology of Israel's car in chapter two, that such technology was not applied to personal vehicles in 2009, to which I responded the technology was discrepant also with that of the same car in chapter one and was purposeful. Knowing then that I needed to make it clearer that it was intended, another technological inconsistency was added in chapter four. Now it is for readers to decide what they want it to mean. This is among a multitude of considerations made after the diligent editing for which I am thankful.

Similarly I am joyfully pleased with the cover. It is lovelier than I had imagined before working with Outskirts.

My brother, Stan, a retired Methodist minister, has influenced my spiritual growth from when we were kids and quibbling siblings. We have differences of understanding about the structure of it all, and occasionally we still debate within a spiritual atmosphere of love. Stan, in this story the protagonist's brother is named Jeff. You will find multiple contributions you have made. Thank you.

My sister, Bev, was the oldest of us three kids in my family of origin. In 2008, the ravages of aggressive dementia took her from this physical plane of existence. Bev, I miss you. Thank you, for participating in the development of who I am and therefore this story.

Harold and Alberta Curtis made me. I miss you. Thank you, Mom and Dad. It is not by coincidence that there is a character we first meet at the end of chapter fourteen who is named Tom, son of Harel.

My three children are Christoffer, Joshua, and Stella. What wonderful people you have become! You have enhanced my understanding of the world, even as I have contributed to yours. This book will be one of the ways by which you remember me after I have moved along to the next adventure. Christoffer, thank you for the gorgeous photo of Mount Rainier that we put on the cover. Joshua, thank you for pointing out that the word, "daddy," now has acquired a sexual connotation I want to avoid. Was it just a coincidence that I happened to read that part of the story to you, just a coincidence that you corrected my looming error? Stella, thank you for being a star in my life; your influence added to the personality of this story.

Thank you, all who have read my story at any time from its rudimentary beginnings to now. Your recommendations and encouragement have been most valuable.

This is a work of fiction, and it does not in any way reveal the lives of real people, resemblances to whom are coincidental. Ideas came from everywhere. Some arrived from radio and television, speeches, books, conversations. If any reader thinks they recognize an acquaintance in this story, you don't. Imagination is sometimes startling and mysterious, and if we are insightful and honest, we admit that everything we know and work with has come from somewhere else. We become a bud on a tree, building new fruit with nutrients pulled from our foundation.

Thank you, all the authors of books I have read that explain physics for those of us with limited mathematical background. Thank you, all the authors of books I have read on the historical Jesus.

Edward K. Rynearson, M.D., is a psychiatrist who has devoted his life to the psychological care of people who lost loved ones to violent death. Ted, you impressed me strongly with your insight of stories people tell themselves over and over about how they might have done something different to change events and save the person who had been ripped from their lives. Thank you, also for sharing over lunch one day the delightful story of your father's definition of idiopathic.

I am grateful for and humble in a realization that every part of existence was caused by an entity I do not fully understand. I was pushed to write this story by something inside that said it was a purpose of my life, and my response is that everything I am or have done has been a gift from something greater.

I hope you will enjoy and want to talk about it.

There are more things in heaven and earth, Horatio,
Than are dreamt of in your philosophy.

—William Shakespeare, *Hamlet,* Act I Scene V

I made both light and the darkness.
I caused both prosperity and disaster.
I who am, did all these things.

Isaiah 45:7

The soul is immortal . . . which means if I will live forever, then I also
have lived before, lived for the whole eternity.

Leo Tolstoy in the voice of Natasha Rostov,
War and Peace, Volume 2, Part 4, chapter 10

"A purpose of human life, no matter who is controlling it, is to love
whoever is around to be loved."

—Kurt Vonnegut, Jr., in the voice of Malachi Constant,
The Sirens of Titan

Love is eternal sacred light
Free from the shackles of time . . .

Paul Simon in his song, "Love Is Eternal,"
on his album, *So Beautiful or So What*

The mind is its own place, and in itself can make a heaven of hell, a hell of heaven.

John Milton in *Paradise Lost*

"That they will be one, Father, even as you are in me, and I am in you, so that they also will be one in us."

A prayer of Jesus
John 17:21

Chapter One

LIGHT IN THE HEAD

I f this story began at its beginning, at the Big Bang moment, so to speak, it might have been when Israel Newman first tried on the now-beacon helmet, a yellow monstrosity with a big green *G* on each side, with lots of wires sticking out and leading into a collage of electronic boxes in Professor Hannity's laboratory, but would that really be the beginning? Perhaps the beginning was that one September morning in 2009, but then I'm getting ahead of myself.

It will help to know a bit more about Israel. His father was named Jacob, and it was because Jacob struggled with his belief in God that all along he had been thinking about naming his first son Israel. He would paraphrase the thirty-second chapter of Genesis, saying, "Jacob wrestled God to a draw! God kept trying to escape, and Jacob wouldn't let him go. They wrestled all night long, and in the morning God gave Jacob a sucker punch, hit him hard, smack in the sciatic nerve; hit him so hard it dislocated Jacob's hip, and he never did stop limping after that. Still Jacob wouldn't let go of God, not until God blessed him, and He did. God said, 'Your name no longer will be Jacob. Instead you will be called Israel, because you have been strong against God.'"

On the day before Israel's birth, his father strained his back while helping with chores at church. It was a burst of awesome and inspiring sharpness, as though God had punched him from the inside, charged him with divine electricity running down his right leg. He limped with excruciating reverence. "It's a sign," he announced.

Israel's father died before his mother, but then she died too, and her death is connected to why the beginning of this story might be the one September morning. Israel bumped his forehead while getting out of the shower, maybe because he was distracted by thinking too much about Einstein's Theory of Relativity. He was getting out of the shower and toweling himself at the same time, and while his head was too close to a safety grab bar mounted on the wall, the mind inside his head was light-years away. Also, and this is just one of those niggling little things, his balance was off because of motor neuropathy that caused him to limp mildly, not too much, maybe something like the limp of Israel in the Bible.

Bang! It happened. He studied his forehead in the mirror, gently touching the red lump. *Damned grab bar!*

He had installed the bar when his mother was unsafe without it, but now there was no practical reason to keep it on the wall any longer, or maybe there was. She had been afflicted wickedly by a combination of weak bones and dizziness, and the bar provided support for her. When she finally fell and broke her hip, it hadn't been in the bathroom, no. It happened when she got out of a car, twisted her leg, and down she went. At the hospital several days later she suffered her life-ending stroke.

The grab bar remained on the bathroom wall, a monument to her once having lived there, and it gloated, *I kept your mother from falling in this bathroom.* Israel kept it, telling himself there would come a time when maybe he would need it for himself because of his own neuropathy, mild but slowly and relentlessly progressive. *I would have kept it anyway. Damned bar.*

Did his mother also have neuropathy? There was a good chance of it. Motor neuropathy like his, an illness of nerves causing weakness of calf muscles, tended to be either inherited or idiopathic.

Idiopathic! That's a word for you. It means that the cause of an illness is unknown. Israel was a doctor, and sometimes when he told his patients about the word *idiopathic,* he tried to amuse them by saying, "It means the doctor is an idiot, and the patient is pathetic." If he was convinced they could handle adult language, he'd then tell them another humorous definition given by an endocrinologist at the Mayo Clinic whose wonderful lectures he had been privileged to hear. Dr. Edward Rynearson would explain, "Idiopathic is from the Greek. *Idio-* meaning I don't know, and *pathic* meaning what the fuck it is." That got a laugh.

Israel was married once to Sonya. They had a son, Markus. As college sweethearts having no premonition of the intense strain medical school would have on their relationship, they believed that once Israel became a doctor they would sail with following winds from then on. People warned them, but Sonya and Israel nevertheless expressed confidence they would flourish. Israel always was at school, and later, when he continued a pattern of always being at work, Sonya became increasingly aloof. The marriage lasted twelve years, about average for those that end in divorce.

When Sonya left Israel, he knew she had to have her reasons, but for the life of him, he didn't understand completely why. For him the breakup was idiopathic. He had become established in his practice; money finally was flowing in, and he was home more than before. Life was supposed to get good again, and besides, wives with three-year-old kids don't just pick up and leave their husbands. She said she had been chased away by his jealousy.

Jealousy! He explained it to himself as a combination of nature and nurture, to which genetic factors were added the influences of experience. His father had been jealous, and to hear it from his mother, it was hard on her and challenged her happiness, but she adhered to her marriage and loved him.

It is fair to admit that with evolution of societal relationships and despite promises made in front of God and congregation, marriage bonds had changed over time; attitudes and opportunities for a woman did not used to be what they were becoming. The courses of his and other lives were therefore not determined just by genetic inheritance and psychological nurturance, but also by the shifting landscape of the world itself, the foundation upon which a person relies.

Although he was aware women found him attractive, he was shy nevertheless. He kept himself trim with regular exercise, and women complimented him for his svelte torso and broad shoulders. They appreciated his politeness, laughed at his gentle humor, and soothed themselves in the warmth of his eyes. One woman had touched her fingers to his mouth without realizing what she was doing, entranced with desire; she had even whispered "those lips," before removing her hand almost with embarrassment. Often it was the woman who made the first move rather than Israel, reverse from the traditional man-pursues-woman stereotype, and not all of the women who seriously flirted were single, which eroded his trust. Married women pressed their legs against his under the table, and the honest truth was he enjoyed it. It excited him. Later, when he was married and his own marriage was strained, when Sonya was flirtatious at a dinner party, he wondered what was happening under the table.

Sonya left then, and took Markus with her. If that had been all there was to it, Israel would have endured it, but one evening he received a fateful telephone call. Sonya sobbed uncontrollably, hysterically and he couldn't understand a word she said. A nurse explained how a car parking brake had failed on a sloped driveway, and the vehicle rolled down the hill just as Markus tumbled forward. The car ran over his head, and that was the end of him. That was the end of him!

It ended the life of Markus, and it also ended Israel's life as his life had been, an event demarcating what had gone before from what came after it, a continental divide between eons of a lifetime. The death of his son had stopped the relentless progression of time, had pinned it in place, and had cheated him out of his right to fulfill an obligation to protect his son. Markus died on February 12, the anniversary of the birthdays of both Abraham Lincoln and Charles Darwin. Maybe that was the beginning of this story, the day Markus died.

Israel took leave from work for several months because he couldn't link any two thoughts together. Corrective rewrites of the nightmare kept interrupting him, kept knocking him down to his knees, kept playing in his mind over and over how Markus still would be alive if he had found some way of making his marriage work or some way of prying Markus out of Sonya's possession at least for that one day.

Many times he drove out to the scene of Markus's death and memorized it.

His pain was physical, in his muscles and joints. He couldn't move without hurting, and headaches were torture. Maybe they would go away if he could bring himself around to thinking correctly again. He needed time away from work to focus on coping without resorting to the opioid medicine upon which he relied for a while, and then he became dependent on them, needed them. At first he didn't care how much he used.

He himself was a physician, a pain specialist, fully aware of the relentless allure of these drugs, even as they sometimes destroyed souls, but for a while he didn't care. Pain also destroyed souls.

Pain! It was a foundation of western philosophy. Three hundred years BCE, Aristotle did not regard pain as a sensation, not like touch or taste, not like smelling or hearing. He described pain as a passion of the soul, and modern studies of brain activity in response to pain retrieved Aristotle's insight from the trash bin, resurrected and elevated it with a theory of patterns weaved in a tapestry of nerves. Every region of the brain connects, and every part participates in the formation of myriads of patterns representing what a person is, what type of pain prevails against them, and consequences of pain, various responses that reach into the very heart of a person, becoming that passion of a soul. The heart indeed! Pain influences the heart rate, the size of an eye's pupils, blood pressure, and the amount of sweat pouring from a tormented forehead. It triggers anxiety and delusions of dread.

Pain touches every part of a soul as a composite that cannot be separated into what is physical and what is psychological, because as it continues without end, a person's neural structure changes, reorganizes itself, and becomes sensitized. The subconscious brain increases its surveillance of the dangerous world around it by discarding its damaged self and replacing it with another more miserable, more easily startled apparatus that feels its surroundings more pointedly and with curious combinations of numbness and irritation, as though every day begins and ends with sunburned skin and arthritic joints, a soul that regards the world with apprehensiveness and avoids life with all its little triggers that make it unbearable.

Medicines against pain, the little uniformed soldiers swallowed over and over, ultimately never win their war. Every time they numb the nerves in futility, like Hercules severing the heads of a Hydra, the neural monster that in fact is us, the neural system increases its sensitivity still more, resoundingly reasserting its need to be aware of the threats of life.

For a while Israel didn't care; he took the medicines anyway. And then he did care. Gradually he realized he wouldn't be able to restore himself until he stopped the anguished struggling over and over in his mind to be an angel stopping the hand of Abraham against Isaac on the altar, until he ceased the impossible quest of saving his only son. He meditated often, finding comfort in attempts to escape his own ego, and gradually he decided he still wanted to live, even if it was living without his son. Finally he quit taking opioids, all at once, recognizing that if he let himself take only a little, he ended up taking a lot. It was too difficult to draw a line between four tablets and twenty, so he just quit.

He returned to work half time, and he kept it that way. He needed time more than he needed money.

It was at a time in the life of America when opioids had been a primary strategy for treatment of pain, a perspective on the cusp of reversal, and his job compelled him to prescribe opioid medicines for people with chronic pain. He labored toward persuading them to embrace lifestyle strategies as well. He coached people about what he called the Big Four: daily exercise, good nutrition, restorative sleep habits, and taking care of psychological and social needs. But he prescribed opioids as well and decided it was best to remain abstinent himself to sidestep the conflict that might arise if his own mind became distorted by collusion with those drugs.

He had attended a psychology support group for about a year. He was making progress. He wrote in a journal.

It annoyed him when people broadcast the old insanity that God never gives more burden than a person can bear. The statement bruised his common sense and rang cruelly in his ears. *Are they saying that if I had been weaker and couldn't handle as much, Markus would still be alive? People who say this are full of shit.* He was barely getting by, and some of his patients hadn't coped at all; frankly had been unable. Life had bitten them off, chewed them up, and spit them out of its carnivorous mouth. Two of his patients had committed suicide with medicines he had prescribed, and he felt those patients had betrayed by them. One man managed to taper completely off his drugs and then chose a different way to end his torment. He bought a gun and shot himself to death.

People do not agree about heaven. Is it a place to be found only in a spiritual realm, or is it physically palpable somewhere in our universe or another? Is it a place or a state of mind? Does a person experience heaven only after dying, or can it be experienced here and now? Does it exist at all? Are heaven and hell separate from each other? Are some people rewarded with the one and some punished with the other? Or are heaven and hell just two different names for the same place, the contentment or horror determined by a resident's interpretation of it? Does a person earn heaven, or is it a gift freely given? Is it a place that just exists, neither given nor earned? Must you believe that there is a heaven to go there?

Israel was certain that to be a holy place, a place truly of goodness, heaven had to be a physical realm because how else could he hold his toddler son in his arms again? Heaven wouldn't be heaven without that, which also meant that time could not intervene. Heaven had to be a very real, physical world in which time never would run out for holding his little son.

On that September morning, just after he bruised his forehead, Israel stopped in the kitchen for a cup of chocolate milk and a single tablet of aspirin. He swallowed some vitamin D as well, and some fish oil. *They'll love my breath today.*

He heard a thud on the living room window. *Not again!* The room had large windows on opposing walls, and birds tried to fly through from one side to the other. It was the third bird to hit the invisible wall that summer. Sometimes they survived, and sometimes they died. Israel went out to look at the bird on the porch lying on its back, stunned but still breathing. He turned it halfway over onto its belly thinking that if it managed to revive, that position would be the easiest for it to get up onto its feet. It was a pretty bird, gray-brown, a pale yellow breast, a brighter horizontal yellow stripe on its tail, and a black head and beak.

He went back inside to write about it. He had time.

> *I think the sonnet died a year ago.*
> *Or was it two? Or three? A century?*
> *Oh, please do tell me that it isn't so,*
> *for I may die myself if dead it be.*
> *But yes, the sonnet died a while ago.*
> *Who killed it? No one knows or cares to tell,*
> *for mum's the word in circles who might show*
> *they cared. They don't. They say they do. Oh well.*
> *The sonnet's pretty body like a bird's*
> *that flies into a window pane, may be.*
> *When thinking it could take to flight with words*
> *got sorely broken, stunned, its soul set free.*
> *Or might it wake again to fly, and hence*
> *will sing its song anew with audience?*

When he returned outside half an hour later the bird was gone, and in its place remained a tiny pile of dark blue poop, the color of blackberries. *Shit in its wake.* Either the bird had survived or a cat had gotten it, one way or the other. He looked around. No loose feathers.

As he walked to his car Israel enjoyed the glorious late summer day, and it wasn't just the colors. The air smelled like memories of childhood when a person paid more attention to such things, and every once in a while a September morning punched him in the nose with it. It punched him in the nose, and pain was felt in the heart. *Why can't there be enough time for life always to be like this moment? Isn't there a place in the mind where it is always late summer? Isn't there a place in the mind where it is exactly this moment always?*

He climbed into his small sports utility vehicle, inserted the key, and turned it. The radio blasted to life, and the engine purred. In the morning he listened to talk shows, news, and commentary.

Sally stood on a platform at Coffee-On-The-Go's drive up window, just high enough that Israel could see her bottom, and she wore short fitted pants, tight but not too tight. He liked her pants. When she leaned out the window to hand him his drink, he imagined she wanted him to admire her cleavage as well.

She flirted. "Just drip coffee, Israel? Really, this is something you could do all by yourself." She smiled.

"I know, Sally, but some things are better when somebody shares them with you."

She pressed a heart-shaped chocolate into his hand. "Is it as good for you as it is for me? See you tomorrow, sweetie."

Driving away Israel couldn't help thinking, *Isn't there a place in the mind where Sally's boobs are always dangling right in front of my eyes? Isn't there a place in the mind where I'm always telling myself she dangles like that for all of her customers? Don't take Sally seriously. She's just marketing, like everybody else. Everyone has something to sell; the question is, what is Sally selling?*

He escaped again into Einstein's light and time. He could pretend the physics of light and time was important enough to spend treasures of his time, even though it wasn't, not really, not for him and his life. It was so much bigger than he was, bigger than life. It was as big as the Big Bang itself, but since it never would affect his personal life, the challenge of understanding it was safe. Sensible people escaped into sports or stories that way. Israel escaped into Einstein's Theory of Relativity.

He tantalized himself with a brainteaser. How could space get both bigger and smaller at the same time? As he understood it, if light were emitted from a source somewhere behind him and he were moving away from it, then space would get smaller. But if light came from in front of him while he was moving toward it, then space would get larger. What, then, would happen if a beam of light came from behind him at the same time that another beam of light came from in front of him? How could space both shrink and expand at the same time? There was more to the issue than that. Time would go slower if he moved away from the light source, and faster if he moved toward it. *This is a crock. Where is Einstein when you most need him? Dead! There is no promise of immortality.*

Damned handle.

He looked back and forth from cars in front of him to cars reflected in his rearview mirror, and he imagined himself getting larger and then suddenly smaller. He imagined getting jerked back and forth from the past into the future.

He burped and tasted fish.

On Wednesdays he didn't have to be at work until ten thirty, and he puttered away many of these mornings. His home was on the north end of Queen Anne Hill, and on this particular day he decided to stop at Kerry Park along Highland Drive on the south end of Queen Anne. In 1927, Mr. and Mrs. Albert Sperry Kerry, Sr., donated a small parcel of land to the City of Seattle so that anybody who wanted would be able to enjoy this most magnificent view of the city with Mount Rainier behind it, sixty miles farther to the south.

It was at this park on this particular day that Israel Newman's world completely and forever changed. It was here that another point in time might be considered by some readers as the true beginning of this story. On this spectacularly clear day something was different about the scene before him, and not being able to put his finger on what it was, he searched for it, finally giving up, and he started walking back to his car. It then struck him like a bolt of lightning. He froze for a moment and then turned and studied Mount Rainier. *Where's Tahoma Peak?*

Little Tahoma Peak was a satellite peak of Mount Rainier, visualized just to the left of the mountain's main bulk when looking southward from Seattle. It was an unstable volcanic remnant, and in 1963 some of it eroded and crashed down upon the lower section of Emmons Glacier. *Has the rest of it fallen? Why wasn't there anything on the radio about it?*

He hurried to his car and turned on the radio, expecting to hear something about this extraordinary event, but there was nothing other than the usual chatter, lots of enthusiasm for what looked like a hopeful year for the Huskies. *What the hell?*

On his cell phone he punched the speed dial for work. "Hello, Mary. This is Israel. How are things? I should be there real soon. Say, that's really something about Mount Tahoma, isn't it?"

"Mount whatzit?"

"Tahoma Peak on Mount Rainier, how it finally crumbled the rest of the way. That's something, isn't it?"

"Oh, I don't go hiking in the mountains. I wouldn't know anything about that kind of thing. Listen, there's a problem with Freddy Salazar. Late last night he left a message on our answering service that his wife got angry and stole his medicines and threw them away. They're not doing so well."

Too many things going on. Stay focused. Hold it together. "He knows our policy, doesn't he? No replacement of lost or stolen opioids."

"He's hoping you'll make an exception for him because he's never given us problems like this before. He's always been reliable, always on schedule."

Medicine is like money, and patients need to be responsible with it. Once it's gone it's gone. They wouldn't leave five hundred dollars just lying around for someone to pilfer. How can I know for sure Salazar is telling the truth? Is he selling?

"Mary, I'll look through the record when I get there. When's he coming in?"

"Ten thirty. He's your first."

Great. That will put me behind schedule for the rest of the day.

"Okay, Mary. I'll be there soon."

He sat in the car and wondered. There still was no commentary on the radio about Tahoma. *Should I drive in to work and continue my day as though nothing happened?* Something was amiss with either his perception or his memory, or maybe something was wrong with the world itself. *Am I going crazy?* He felt himself about to tremble. *No! Yesterday there was a Tahoma Peak, and today it's gone. What the hell?*

He got out of the car and walked to see Mount Rainier again. It was as though the rules of the physical world were thrown away like so much rubbish. A few moments passed before he was able to register what he saw. At first Tahoma Peak was back where it belonged, but after only a few more seconds it disappeared again. After a few more seconds it reappeared, and then instead of being on the left of Rainier, it was on the right side, and in fact the entire scene before him was reversed left and right, a mirror image of what it was supposed to be. Puget Sound was on the east side of him instead of the west.

He wasn't dizzy. The ground did not shake. He did not fall.

Again the topography of the world returned to normal. Completely normal!

He dropped to his knees and gently covered his eyes with his hands. *Holy Christ! I'm going crazy!*

Two

AT THE CLINIC

Still shaken by having witnessed an impossible event and by having been alone in it, Israel drove to a parking lot near his clinic. A worthy question pummeled his mind. How would one share this experience with someone else, a prodigious event that could not have happened? But it did happen. He was lonely in a world where there should have been hullabaloo, but where instead there was silence.

He recalled another episode when his senses had been assaulted by a similar feeling, long before, when he was a boy daydreaming in the dining room of his family's house while everyone was still together, Mom and Dad, Jeff and Bev, a time when everyone called him Izzy. There and then, in the dining room, he realized the lamp hanging from the ceiling was different from what he clearly remembered it to be. It was a small and simple chandelier with a circle of metal beneath a glowing globe, and Israel had remembered that this metal ring was corrugated, but the one he was looking at was smooth. When his mother told him the lamp ring always had been smooth, his astonished disbelief upset him so much that he searched the entire house relentlessly, from attic to basement, trying to find the discarded lamp. He interrogated every member of his family, certain that the old lamp was not the new one. Somebody had to have changed it. He had sought validation of his memory and never found it.

Now the same feeling haunted him, a craving for validation of his memory, but this time he realized he lacked sufficient energy to launch a quest that he already knew would yield no answers. How would a person solve a problem like this one?

Acceptance is the path to happiness. This Buddhist admonition counseled him, and he decided to accept what he didn't want to accept, that he would be stuck forever with another unanswered question teasing him. Was his memory fractured and unreliable, or were time and space unreliable, tracking inconsistently from one moment to another? He looked around and found nothing else amiss; everything was faithful to his memory, unchanged. Walking across the parking lot toward the medical center, he took special notice that the ground was solid, and the sky was complete from horizon to horizon; there were no rifts in the firmament. The sounds, smells, and sights of late summer were intact. *On a more-probable-than-not basis, the explanation is that my mind was interrupted by a cognitive glitch. The change was in my head, not the world around me.*

When Markus died my world was torn apart. This is nothing compared to that.

The sounds, smells, and sights of late summer were intact except for one eerie thing. Everything seemed exactly how he remembered it from a long time before, as though he had been away for a while. *Déjà vu, or déjà vu's second cousin.*

Perturbations of the soul may be soothed or even supplanted by routine activities of everyday life, and we should welcome gratefully any employment that demands our devotion.

Israel specialized in the management of pain. Of course his patients would have preferred to have their pain whittled away rather than to be besieged by a need to endure it, but sometimes the whittling could not be accomplished, and the management of pain became an acceptable alternative, better than succumbing.

The most healthful treatments focused on lifestyle strategies, on doing what keeps a person healthy, even if pain made it more challenging. Quit smoking; exercise every day; get good sleep and good nutrition. These were the easy lifestyle strategies because they could be accomplished by diligence and willpower. More difficult was the solving of psychological and social problems that required the cooperation of others.

Not all but many patients preferred the easy way, the passive treatments of massage or manual therapy or taking medicines, particularly opioids or benzodiazepines. Some doctors eschewed the prescription of opioids, and a few even looked disapprovingly at the dependency of patients who took them, as though it demonstrated a weakness of character. Some of these doctors considered Israel an enabler for his weak patients.

Maybe I'm weak too.

At the time of this September day in 2009, our society was in a transition of realization and policy concerning the dangers of opioid medicine, progressing from a generosity of compassionate use to a more informed reluctance to contribute serious risks to individual patients and society. Certainly medicines could be dangerous if used without a reasonable understanding of how seductively they could coax a person to ever higher doses until they stopped a breath or crashed a car or pushed an impaired user over the edge, whether it was the edge of the mind or the edge of a precipice. The medicines could ruin relationships, could destroy a life even without killing.

But they relieved pain, for a while anyway.

Some pain specialists preferred injections or pumps, electrical stimulators, or other devices. Often they justified the expense of these procedures by the extent to which they reduced a patient's reliance on opioid medicine. Each of these approaches had a place, of course, and many of Israel's patients had tried them, but even when the devices were effective people usually still wanted to continue opioid medicine. Patients depended on opioids as though they were friends upon whom they could depend, assuming opioids were friends that would not be deceitful. They were tried and true, trustworthy.

People also wanted to talk about struggles in their personal lives, and Israel listened to their frequently twisted and harrowing histories. The desperation of their pain might diminish if somebody cared about them enough.

Mary informed Israel that Mr. Salazar was in room six. "He's really upset," she warned.

"Mary, you know that I want each of my patients to feel at least just a little bit loved when they leave our clinic, but I'm tired of love meaning eighty milligrams of extended-release oxycodone. I'm not so comfortable with it anymore, trusting people, trusting medicines."

Freddy Salazar was an average-sized man with large calloused hands and a gentle handshake. He fidgeted a little as he told his tale. "Ya know, Doc, I don't want to go into withdrawal off this medicine you been givin' me. I don't like that I take it, but I need it. I really do. It's the only thing that gives me any kind of a life."

Israel reviewed the medical record: lumbar stenosis with postoperative scarring, not operable. In other words, Freddy's back already had been operated on, and scar tissue had formed with such exuberance that the major nerves to his legs were being squeezed. It could not be corrected with another operation because the scar tissue would only grow back again, maybe with a vengeance. Freddy also had diabetic neuropathy, illness of his nerves, and he had small vessel circulatory insufficiency. The tissues in his lower legs were not getting enough blood to keep them healthy and happy. This condition could be very painful.

"Freddy. Are you having any problems controlling your bowel or your bladder?"

"Only stuff that's been goin' on for years. I have to pee a lot of times, and then it only comes out a little bit at a time, but that's been goin' on forever."

The record showed he had an enlarged prostate. Blood studies were normal for his prostate, kidney, and liver.

"Do you have any numbness in your private areas?"

"You mean can I get a hard-on?"

"That's a different thing, no. I mean do you lose feeling down there?"

"No. I got none of that."

For a few moments the two men just looked at each other. Freddy did not avoid Israel's gaze. His pupils were small, probably from having taken opioid.

Israel sighed. "Look, Freddy. I've got to show that I'm being responsible here. Somebody who doesn't know you might look at the record and wonder what's really happening to those drugs. I'm not accusing you of anything. I do believe you use your medicines the way you're supposed to. I believe you want to do the right thing, but if using this medicine is hurting your relationship with your wife—"

"She don't like me. That's all there is to that. If it wasn't the drugs it would be something else. She wants to get rid of me, see? That's what this is about. I can't keep up with her anymore. I can't work, and she says she's scared I'm going to die. Disability don't pay enough." He paused. "Besides, I think she's found herself another guy. These drugs are just her excuse for dumping me."

Freddy was taking nine hundred milligrams of gabapentin three times a day, as well as fifty milligrams of amitriptyline at dinnertime. He also was taking forty milligrams of extended-release oxycodone every eight hours. That medicine was the one his wife had stolen, a narcotic with street value.

"Did she really throw it away, Freddy?"

"That's what she said."

"For nerve pain like yours, methadone might be a better choice."

"No. I don't want that crap. That's the stuff drug addicts take, isn't it? I'm afraid of it."

"Yes, it's the medicine doctors give to heroin addicts so they won't go into withdrawal. It calms their craving when they're trying to quit. Doctors use methadone because it's longlasting. Since they can't trust an addicted person to use the medicine honestly, they don't give them more than one dose at a time. They can give methadone once a day and watch it being swallowed right then and there. Methadone lasts long enough so the doctors can administer it that way. And it's good for pain too, for the same reason. It lasts a long time, and with pain like yours, pain that starts in the nerves themselves, sometimes methadone works better than oxycodone."

"I was doin' fine with the oxy. All I need is more."

Israel sighed again. "Okay. I still need the record to show that I'm being responsible. If I prescribe the medicine just one week at a time, it will limit how much your wife can hurt you if she steals it again, and it will be easier for you to stay in control."

"My insurance pays for only one prescription a month, and this stuff's expensive. I can't afford it all by myself."

Good sign. He probably isn't selling his drugs. He wouldn't complain about the cost if he were, unless he's cleverer than I think he is. "Okay," Israel said with a tone of resignation. "I'll prescribe the medicine for you, but here are some things I want you to do. Put your medicine in a safe deposit box in a bank vault. Go to the bank once a week and take out only what you need for that one week. Get a solid safe for at home too, not one of those skimpy ones. Get a hefty one, a safe that takes two men to carry. Put your medicine into that safe, take out only what you need for one day, and keep it on your person. Don't let it sit out where others can get it." *And get a divorce.*

"One more thing," Israel added. "Take this sheet that describes how these medicines can be dangerous. Use them safely. Oh, there's one more thing after that. Mary will give you the prescription after you give us some urine."

Israel's next patient, Patrick Palin, surprised him with the first good laugh of the day. "Tell me, Doc; when the medicine makes the pain go away, where does the pain go?"

Alan Hanks came in, one of Israel's favorite patients because of his extraordinarily good sense of humor. He laughed easily. Alan had diabetes with painful legs, and one of his legs had been amputated when it no longer got enough blood and oxygen to keep it alive. Alan began by saying, "I tried to stop taking the morphine, but then I got diarrhea, and it wouldn't stop until I started taking the morphine again."

"That was withdrawal, Alan. If you think about what opioid

medicine does, then withdrawal does about everything opposite of that. Morphine tends to constipate you, so withdrawal would be diarrhea. Morphine reduces pain, so withdrawal increases pain. Morphine calms your nerves, so withdrawal can cause anxiety."

"Of course! I knew that."

Israel suggested, "If you taper your medicines slowly, you probably won't have any of those problems. Let's do that. Let's taper you slowly." Israel decided to tease. "Then there's another thing, and I want you to take me seriously here. You've got to stop encouraging the Diarrhea Fairy. I know you have compulsive tendencies, but please stop putting laxative suppositories under your pillow at night. You're just asking for trouble. Maybe you think the Diarrhea Fairy will exchange them for money, but it's not going to happen."

Alan laughed.

As the two of them stood up and Alan struggled with his prosthetic leg, Israel noticed something awry. "Alan, I thought your amputation was on the right leg."

"No, it's always been on the left. Can't change that."

"But I distinctly remember you telling the surgeon over and over, 'Right is right, and left is wrong.'"

"No, no, no." Alan laughed. "I'm a Democrat. That's what I told Dr. Green. I told him, 'Remember I'm a Democrat, always have been. So left is right and right is wrong.' He got tired of me saying it, I think, and then before surgery I even wrote it on my legs." He paused and then said, "You're just tired, Dr. Newman, and you've got a lot of patients. Nobody expects you to remember all the details."

All the details. Back at his work station computer, Israel pulled up Alan's history. It was his left leg that was amputated because of diabetic circulatory insufficiency leading to gangrene. *Left leg. But if the universe is playing tricks on me, it would make all the details consistent, wouldn't it? It isn't possible to figure this out.*

He saw a couple more patients and just before noon he received a call from one of the neurosurgeons.

"Israel," said Dr. Primus, "I just saw that guy you sent me, Farrow. Remember him? He's the one who had the upper thoracic pain, and he was lucky enough that the MRI picked up the huge disk higher up at C6-C7, pressing on the cord. Remember him? I took out the disk and fused him two weeks ago, and he's still complaining about pain. His x-rays look good. There's nothing there to operate. He was just here with his wife, and he looked strung out. I think he's probably drug seeking. Anyway, the two of them are coming down to your clinic right now. There's nothing for me to do surgically."

An add-on. There goes lunch. "Okay, David. I'll talk with him. Wouldn't it be something if this whole thing were just a drug seeking scam and we just happened incidentally to find a serious problem in his neck? I'll take care of him."

Denny Farrow's clothes were rumpled, and he hadn't shaved in days. With red, glistening eyes he looked worried and agitated. "I haven't slept in three days," he said, "since my meds ran out, and they won't refill them. They said you would take care of that." Though he wasn't pacing the room, the subdued tension of his posture, trembling hands, and dilated pupils reported his predicament of opioid withdrawal.

Sitting in a chair close to Israel, Denny's wife couldn't have looked any more different from her husband. She was resplendent, with clean, tailored clothing and subtle makeup well applied, a crisp appearance, fresh and pretty. Her plaintive eyes reminded Israel of a puppy as she quietly pleaded. "He's been miserable. The pain hasn't let him sleep at all. We used to go out for walks, and we're not doing that anymore."

Israel pulled up the preoperative MRI images onto the computer screen. A large, pea-sized area of the spinal cord stared back at him with a shading much lighter than the rest of the cord. Clearly the spinal cord had been injured, myelomalacia. This could cause considerable and persistent pain. As a construction carpenter, Denny wouldn't be going back to that kind of work any time soon. The injury wasn't work related either, so he wasn't eligible for Worker's Compensation. Applying for disability would take time, and the family's income would depend entirely on Denny's wife, maybe for a long time. They were in trouble.

Israel looked at the two of them. She was alluring and Denny was a mess.

"Denny. Look at this," he said. "This was the injury to your spinal cord that we saw before your operation. Dr. Primus successfully took the pressure off your cord, but the injury is still there. Healing will take time." *Even with healing there's no guarantee that the pain will go away.* "I do believe you are having pain, and I will prescribe pain medicines for you."

The pretty wife said, "I want to hug you."

Israel continued, "I'll prescribe the oxycodone in the same amount you were taking before surgery, but I'd like you to try something else." He explained why methadone would be a good choice for Denny, but the man was in too much pain to think straight and kept talking about oxycodone. "Yes, you're going to get the oxycodone. I'm not taking that away from you, but let's start this, very low dose at first, one tablet in the morning, five milligrams; that's all."

The pretty wife understood the counseling.

Israel turned toward her. "Explain this to him later when he's able to understand."

She nodded.

As they were leaving, the woman came to Israel with open arms and again said, "I want to hug you."

Israel was holding paperwork in one of his hands and put his other arm lightly around her shoulders, trying to maintain his professional distance, which was not enough for her, and she pulled him closer. He resisted a full body press but felt each of her breasts individually touch his chest. The competing energies of intimacy and distance caused the touch to be discretely and ironically even more sensual. He worried about Denny's feelings then, *but these thoughts are just a dance in my own mind. This is my own obsession.*

After he signed the prescriptions he looked up and saw the couple holding hands. "Do a lot of that," he advised. "It helps to get rid of the pain. Start taking those walks together again."

A pile of paperwork beckoned him, and there were only fifteen minutes left of a lunch break before his next patient.

Mary asked, "Would you like me to run out and get you a sandwich?"

He looked into the top drawer and saw a bag of dark chocolate Crunch bars. "No thanks. I'll get by." He asked, "Mary, I can't believe you've never heard of Mount Tahoma."

"What are you talking about? Of course I know about Mount Tahoma. Didn't I tell you that last year my brother climbed it? He got some gorgeous photos. He said it wasn't a very difficult climb until close to the summit, where the ice gets steep. It's good to know how to use an ice axe."

Israel was stunned. *I'm going crazy.*

Mary said, "You look like you're not all there. Are you okay?"

"Did I say that out loud?"

"Say what?"

"Oh, nothing. I'm going out to eat tonight, and I don't need to eat a lunch. Maybe I'll enjoy the dinner more if I'm good and hungry. I'm okay." *I'm not okay.* He couldn't focus his mind on the paperwork, and he felt rescued when the next patient was ready for him in the exam room.

She was a long-time patient, a woman with chronic pain and a remote traumatic brain injury that caused some loss of her behavioral control. She tended sometimes to act in ways that were way over the top. She liked to flirt with Israel.

On this September day she wore a white page boy cap and matching white denim jacket that was open in front to reveal a fitted pink top and a trim waist. The pink matched her lipstick. "You know I'd do you right here," she said.

Israel talked gently. "You see this room? This room is my temple. It's holy. We solve problems in this room. We don't make more."

Back at the work station there were a turkey sandwich and a bottle of iced tea. "Thank you, Mary. Or should I suspect that you just don't want my being hungry to make me irritable this afternoon?"

Mary smiled.

Later in the afternoon several patients with back pain needed to hear his well-rehearsed lecture about how medicines, all by themselves, would never give satisfying relief as long as there were mechanical problems aggravating the pain. "You've got to exercise. It's the only way, and not just any exercise either. You've got to do exercises that are directed specifically at correcting your particular problem. Everybody's different." He referred them to physical therapy, hoping they would take the therapists seriously.

Bob Gentry came in, a fifty-nine-year-old man with back pain and sleep apnea, a condition that causes people to stop breathing while they sleep, for maybe only a few seconds at a time, but they do it over and over until the oxygen in their blood gets low enough it can hurt their nerve cells.

Bob was one of his patients in the work-conditioning program, so Israel pulled the physical therapists' notes onto the computer screen. "Bob! You fell asleep while walking on the treadmill?" The note described how the sleeping Bob, still standing as he slept, had ridden the conveyor belt backward and gotten spit out the back end. He awakened when he landed on his feet without falling down. It was a comical scene to imagine, except he sustained strain of a ligament in his right knee. *And the sleep apnea!* Israel shook his head. "You're not using your mask, Bob." The CPAP (continuous positive airway pressure) was a device that kept oxygen flowing into his lungs while he slept. "Why not?"

"I get pimples on my belly whenever I use it. Dr. Kirkland told me the mask has nothing to do with the pimples, but whenever I use the mask I get the pimples. So something happens that nobody understands, but it still happens."

"Bob, this is a matter of life and death. Your sleep apnea is severe enough it's going to kill you if you don't treat it." The medicine list showed that three weeks earlier in the emergency department Dr. Masters wrote a prescription for oxycodone, twenty tablets. "How many of those pain pills have you been taking?"

"Not every day, just sometimes, maybe one tablet every three days or so."

Israel put on a stern demeanor. "I'm sending you back for an urgent consult with the sleep-disorders clinic. Maybe there is new technology that will make the mask more tolerable, okay?"

Bob nodded.

"And Bob. You are not going to take any of the oxycodone right now. Until you get your sleep apnea treated, that medicine is poison. Do you understand? And don't drive a car. How do you get here to the exercise gym? Do you drive?"

"No, I take the bus."

"Good. Do you drive your car to the park-and-ride?"

"No. The bus stops just two blocks from where I live."

"Good. Don't drive." Israel put his hand on Bob's shoulder. "You're going to feel a lot better when you start treating this breathing problem. Your pain probably will be less too, and for sure you're going to have better energy. You'll be happier."

The second-to-last patient of the day was Roger Roust, whom Israel had followed for several years, a man with trigeminal neuralgia. The fifth cranial nerve was called trigeminal because it had three major divisions. The upper part provided sensation to the forehead and eye; the middle part to the cheek, nose, and upper teeth; and the lower part to the lower teeth and jaw and the inside of the ear. Roger had severe pain in all three parts.

Roger had survived a horrible, abused childhood, and residuals of the horror still tormented him. Once his crazy mother tried to burn the house down with the three kids sleeping inside. Roger just happened to awaken in time to rush his siblings out of the house. He was a proclaimed hero. After Roger 's mother died he still heard her voice talking to him.

He was out of his medicines three weeks early. Roger told the doctor, "You know my brother; he's a crackhead, never made anything out of himself. But he got this job taking care of this old man, Edmund, who couldn't take care of himself anymore. So my brother got some money, and what did he do with it? He bought drugs and got himself messed up again and couldn't take care of Edmund for a while, so he called me up and asked if I would help out and take care of him. I went and got the old man and brought him home to my place. Then I went out for a while, and when I came back the old man was dead. He stopped breathing." Roger stopped talking for a moment and studied Israel's face for a sign of how all this information was sinking in. He continued his story. "I know Edmund wanted to die. He told me so before. He's wanted to die for a long time, but when my brother found out about it, he was mad at me. He was so angry that he took my pain medicines away. He stole them, and he said he never should have let me use that shit. Anyway, my brother had some methadone, and I took some of that until I could get in here and talk with you about it."

There was silence.

Addicts are most afraid of the pain of withdrawing. Read between the lines! Israel said, "With a story like that, I can't prescribe narcotic medicines for you anymore. With this information in the medical record, for me to continue prescribing narcotics would put me at risk of losing my license."

Roger looked at the sheet of paper on which Israel had been jotting. "Then tear up your notes. You don't have to put any of that in the medical record."

No. I just have to live with myself.

Israel prescribed a three-week taper, completely down and off the pain medicines. While he typed the prescriptions into the computer, Roger said, "I'm not angry. I'm scared. Three weeks is too fast."

"I know it is. I agree with you, but it's what I can do."

Out of the exam room, Israel asked Mary to give Roger a list of detoxification centers.

After Roger left, Mary commented, "He was really angry at you. He said you strung him out on these drugs, and when he tried to get off them you said it was okay that he was taking them. Now you're cutting him off. He said he was going to get a lawyer."

Israel had heard this accusation and threat from other patients. He wasn't concerned about a law suit, but it still bothered him. It stung. It was an outrageous breaking of trust, the natural consequences of which included irrational and accusatory speech. It was like a divorce.

At the end of the day a woman came in with back pain. She was forty-two, quite pretty and intelligent, a put-together master-piece. She had elegant hair and wore clothing that either was silk or looked like silk. It fit loosely enough that it allowed her to move well, so Israel told her, "You can leave your clothes on for the exam. I don't need to see skin. I just need your limbs to be able to move freely. Besides, that's such a beautiful outfit, and you look so good in it that it would be a shame for you to take it off."

She smiled at him. "I'm wearing good-looking underwear too."

Dodge the bullet. "Oh no," he laughed. "Now I'm tempted."

At the end of clinic hours Israel looked at the paperwork on his desk, and he couldn't find the initiative he needed to get it done. *Tomorrow is soon enough. I've got disappearing mountains to think about.*

When he walked out to his car in the late afternoon he saw a long scratch and a dent along the middle of the passenger-side front door. He couldn't recall having seen this damage before, but it clearly wasn't new. A thin film of rust indicated that it had been there for some time. *Why haven't I noticed this before?* He ran his hand along the scratch. *I'll be damned.*

He climbed into the car and pressed his thumb against a thumb-print reader on the steering wheel, which triggered an invisible flash of infrared light that measured the iris of his right eye. The engine roared to life. *It's so nice not to have to carry car keys in my pants pocket anymore.*

Three

PROFESSOR K. MICHAEL HANNITY

S ome people differ from the group and don't fit in. People with differences so extreme they fall far outside the borders of a graphed normal curve of the population are designated outliers. Professor K. Michael Hannity was an acquaintance of Israel's, another participant in a psychology support group they attended on Wednesday evenings.

Dr. Franklyn Linder, the host psychologist, a tall, portly man who possessed stunning blue eyes and a warm smile and demeanor, worked on the second floor of a building on First Avenue, just a few blocks north of Pike Place Market. His comfortable office sported a subdued liveliness of colors balanced by the complicated pattern of a large Persian carpet.

Frank began the session by introducing a new member. "As you recall, last week Dave decided he would move on and not come to our weekly meetings anymore. Today we welcome a new person to the group." He reached over and placed his hand on the hand of a woman sitting to his right. "This is Monica Morales."

The woman smiled briefly and nodded her head. She was middle-aged with petite features and blond hair. She appeared almost frail.

"Monica has had some struggles in her marriage, and after talking with her I thought she had insights that would contribute nicely to our group, and I'm sure we can help her too. Since this is her first time here, and this group can be a little intimidating for newcomers, I thought it would be a good idea to introduce ourselves by going around the group and sharing our names and then a brief rundown of what we ourselves are struggling with. Let's start on my left and then go around the circle. Susan?"

Susan Carter, a woman in her twenties, said her entire family would have nothing to do with her because she was a lesbian. "They're religious freaks," she said, "Old Testament freaks. They're Leviticus freaks, and they say it's because they love Jesus. Do you know that in Leviticus it tells you how you're supposed to kill and burn animals as a sacrifice? It's a horrible book. Well, about homosexuality, do you remember when that poor kid in Wyoming got tied up to a fence and beaten just because he was gay, and then he died? My family said that people end up reaping what they sow. That's what they said about murder. They're ignorant! And then what finally got me completely kicked out of the house was when I pointed out to them that Jesus spent a lot of his time living in Capernaum and teaching people there. That was a city on the shores of the Sea of Galilee. It was heavily influenced by the Greeks, and there was homosexuality going on there. I asked my parents why Jesus didn't ever say anything about homosexuality. I told them that it just wasn't a big deal with him; that's why. But they said, 'Jesus had bigger fish to fry than preaching against them homos. He was busy saving the world from the devil.' They're so ignorant! They kicked me out.

"Now I'm trying to learn what's the right amount of shutting-up to do and when it is safe to speak my mind. I fell in love with this woman at work. I hinted about being attracted to her, and she seemed to be flirting back, but when I got the courage, I asked, 'What would you do if I kissed you right now?' She giggled in a kind of way I knew was not the kind of giggle I wanted her to make, and she said that if I did she'd probably try to avoid me from then on, so I didn't kiss her, but she avoided me anyway.

"I live up on Capitol Hill, and you might say something like, 'Aren't there lots of gay people up there?' There are, except I'm talking about love, you know. So maybe I tend to fall in love with straight women. I'm just lonely, and I worry about what people have said behind my back at work. It's not always the friendliest place toward me. That's all I have to say." She looked to her left where a bespectacled, fifty-five-year-old man was sitting, leaning forward with his elbows on his thighs and resting his chin in his hands.

He shifted to a more upright posture and pushed his glasses a little farther up on his nose. "Suzi," he said, "If I may be so familiar as to call you that cutesy name, because let's face it, you are cute, you know, and I'm just trying to be friendly here; that's all I'm trying to do. If I were a woman I'd kiss you. I'd have no problem with that.

"The Wyoming boy you talked about, his name is Matthew Wayne Shepard." He looked at the floor and shook his head. "Horrible. Did you know when it happened there weren't any Wyoming state or federal hate crime laws that applied to violent acts against homosexuals? That's a problem. It looks like President Obama will be signing the Matthew Shepard and James Byrd, Jr., Hate Crimes Prevention Act next month. We move ahead slowly. We'll take care of things like that in the future. We're driving toward it in a golf cart.

"About the Bible, you're right, and it wasn't just Capernaum. The whole Galilee region was swarming with Greek homosexuals. Jesus maybe went to Capernaum for the first time after he turned baptismal water into wine at the wedding party in Cana; that story's in the book of John, chapter two. But he went to Capernaum a lot, back and forth. He must have liked it. I like the story in the eighth chapter of Matthew, the first chapter of Mark, the fourth of Luke and the sixth of John. Don't mind me; I just remember this sh—, this stuff. Excuse me. So like I was saying, Jesus came to Capernaum for a day that time, and on his way there, it was on the Sabbath, he cured a centurion's servant, and then he went into the synagogue and cured some people there, and he drove a demon out of a guy, and then after that he went to Simon Peter's house and cured Peter's mother. All in all it was a pretty busy day, and at least that time he might not have noticed any homosexual horsing around. He was just too damned busy. Anyway, and I say this only to make the story complete, according to Matthew, Mark, and Luke, he then had to leave Capernaum the very next day because there were too many people in the crowds wanting him to perform miracles. I imagine that was hard work to do that. He had to move on, and those three books said it was because the important thing he wanted to do was to deliver his message.

"The John story is always a little different. Have you noticed how different John is? He said that the people of Capernaum, at least some of them, were outraged that Jesus was talking about people needing to eat his flesh. That must have grossed them out. See, that was his message to them, the one he had to get out of town because of, and it was somewhat grosser than homosexuality, you might say. The crowds in John's story were more threatening than they were in the other accounts of Capernaum, so Jesus had to skedaddle."

The bespectacled man looked at Susan, paused, and then said, "But your point is good; I got that. I'm sure your parents are ignoramuses, and I don't mind at all that you're a lesbian; just want to be clear about that. If I were a woman I'd kiss you."

He looked around the room at the others who quietly looked back at him. He ran the fingers of his right hand through his curly gray and auburn hair. It then seemed as though he suddenly remembered to be polite. He looked over at Monica, the new woman in the group, and he said, "Hello, Ms. Morales. I'm Michael Hannity. I apologize for myself. I'm kind of a horse's ass, and that's why I'm here. Excuse me. I'm not supposed to use that kind of explicit language here unless it's explicitly necessary. That's what I'm trying to learn here, how to talk without using ejaculatory speech. Damn it! It's not as easy as you might think. I'm sorry; really I am.

"I have Tourette's syndrome, and that condition comes with uncontrolled behaviors called tics. For me it means sometimes uncontrolled dirty speech. Most Tourette's people don't have that one, but I do. We have neurological tics, movements our bodies make even without our permission, and the dirty words are neurological tics too, the same way. The brain has a mind of its own, you might say. I can suppress those behaviors most of the time if I'm vigilant, but if I relax even for a moment my default behavior is to be rude and sometimes in the rudest sorts of ways. The problem is that just like everybody else, I like to relax once in a while, and then the tics kick me in the ass. Excuse me."

He turned again to Susan Carter. "Suzi, Jesus came back and stayed in Capernaum, and he spent a lot of time there sitting in a boat and preaching to all those Greek homosexuals who lived there. I think maybe he sat in the boat out in the water so they wouldn't eat his flesh. It wasn't time for that yet."

He turned back to the group. "Tourette's is not just about my potty mouth. Actually it started when I was a kid with motor tics, weird movements I would make. One of them was I'd swallow air for no good reason at all, and my belly would blow up like a balloon, and it hurt. Maybe I started doing that because my brother told me that was how to make a fake burp. He could swallow air only half-way down, and then he'd release it and make a belch. But I couldn't do that. The air would go all the way down into my stomach and stay there until my belly was so distended it made me cry, and then I'd burp. Oh, what heavenly relief! But then after the first time, I did it again and again and again.

"The next thing was maybe my shoulder movements. It was way back in the sixties when the Green Bay Packers were trouncing the rest of the league. They had this halfback who I thought was the best player of all time. He was my hero. His name was Paul Hornung, number five. After he was tackled, every time when he was walking back to the huddle, he would sort of shrug his shoulders and tug on the front neckline of his jersey. My brother said he did that because he had a trick shoulder, so I started doing that too. I wanted to be like Paul Hornung, so I picked up on that habit of his. At least I could say I had something that was the same as him, right? But after I started doing it, I couldn't stop.

"The next thing was I started blinking my eyes, but blinking isn't the right word for it because I squeezed them shut with so much force I could hear it in my ears, and somehow that relieved anxiety I was having, except it made me even more anxious because I was self-conscious about it. I'm glad I don't do that anymore, but I still do the shoulder thing.

"None of those things got me into trouble, though. It was the words that did. I'm a smart guy, a genius, and I don't say that to brag. It's just the way it is. Some things come easily for me, just like other things are not easy, like the neurologic tics." He sighed.

"The unauthorized authorities in my life recognized my genius and my affliction at precisely the same time, give or take a few years. I remember vividly a time in preschool when our teacher, Miss Priscilla, was trying to figure out how long to draw the wings on a picture of a damsel fly, you know those little things that look like miniature dragonflies. Miss Priscilla mumbled, 'Hm-m-m-m-m, they go back a little bit more than two-thirds of its body, but not quite three-quarters.' I was watching her. I was a little four-year-old kid, and I immediately said, 'You mean seventeen twenty-fourths.' She looked at me, first kind of startled, and then with a look of realization. Then I said, 'Or you could say eight-point-five twelfths, but then everyone would know that you're a shit-turd.' I noticed how startled she was, and then I said it again, a couple times half under my breath. 'Shit turd. Shit turd.' Actually it was probably a little while after that the adults started putting all the information together, when the motor tics started, but I'm just saying the clues were already there when I was in preschool.

"A guy can say *shit* only so many times, and I'm using the word this time only because it's explicitly necessary to get my point across. You can talk like that only so many times, and a physics department at a major university will send you packing. What got me canned was the one time I felt a tremendous urge to write something dirty in a scientific article, something about my department head. I had talked myself into thinking nobody reads that crap anyway. Excuse me. Nobody reads those articles because they're too dry and boring, so right in the middle of my paper, buried in the most boring paragraph, I wrote 'Doctor Melvin Manheim eats shit turds for breakfast, with marshmallows between graham crackers; shit s'mores.' Writing that in the report relieved my need to write it. Does that make any sense to you? They fired me for it." He shook his head. "Actually let me be honest. Saying Manheim ate shit s'mores really had nothing to do with Tourette's; that was just my excuse. It had to do with me being an uncontrolled jerk.

"Now I work on my own. I still get grants occasionally, but nobody wants to work with me." He looked at his shoes, and as if talking to himself he said softly, "Maybe that's a good thing. They'd end up arguing with me, and that would slow me down."

Still looking at his shoes, he continued. "I'm here in this group because," and then he looked up, squarely at Monica Morales, "because I'm a lonely old fart. I don't keep any of the friends I make. Something always happens to screw up my friendships.

"I'll give you an example. I was going pretty well with this woman for a while, Jessica, and she had some friends. I got along with them okay too, for a while, but there was this summer party in the backyard of a couple of her friends. These friends told us about how their two-year-old son had gotten up on the window sill in a bedroom on the second floor of their house. The boy stood there and pressed on the screen. The screen popped out, down it came, and the little boy too. The thing about it was the boy was okay. He cried and they took him by ambulance to the emergency room, and there was nothing seriously wrong with him. I saw him right there in the garden playing with all the other little kiddies. He was a normal boy. Sigh of relief, right? We were at this backyard picnic, and I was trying to keep the conversation light with a little humor, and I said this stupid thing. I said, 'The important thing is, because I'm a physicist and very interested in this sort of thing, and I hope you noticed this when you saw him land on the ground,' and I paused then for effect; timing is everything with humor, and then I asked, 'Did he bounce?' They didn't laugh at my joke, and after that Jessica wouldn't go out with me. She said it was the last straw. Come to think of it, that's what the university said too. The last straw gets around. It makes its appointed rounds in every aspect of my life. Here a straw; there a straw; everywhere a straw-straw.

"So there you have it, except I've kept thinking about the parents of that little boy who fell out of the window. After a crisis like that, from which tragedy is averted, isn't it natural to take a sigh of relief? Laugh a little? But some people don't do that. They are either unwilling or unable. So it was with these people."

Sharon Ingle, another member of the group, could hardly contain her emotion. "Michael, those parents were scared to death. They must still have been worried about the consequences of that fall. They probably wondered what kind of serious injury might have happened that nobody's discovered yet, something that might show up later, like maybe the boy will have trouble in school. I hope you said you were sorry."

"Yes, well, you're right. I was a schmuck. The thing is, I had a hard time knowing I was going to be a schmuck before I said the schmucky thing." He looked over at Frank. "Is it all right to say schmuck?"

"I think that's allowed."

"Because you know its original meaning in Yiddish is the foreskin of a penis, the part that gets thrown away after a bris, a circumcision."

"Then no; it's not allowed."

"Okay. Then I want to say that I don't want to be a discarded foreskin of a penis. I don't want to be discarded. I'm a guy. I'm a guy, and I have feelings."

Israel commented, "Michael, I like you. I want you to know that. I think the reason the little boy's parents couldn't tolerate your joke was that they felt guilty. They couldn't laugh at their own guilt over not having watched their son closely enough. That story might have turned out horribly, like my own. When you joked about it, you gave them an opportunity to direct their anger at you. You hadn't taken their guilt seriously enough. This is one of those things you'll just have to chalk up to experience and move on."

Michael twisted his mouth and shrugged his shoulders.

It was Israel's turn next, to explain his own grief over the loss of his marriage and the death of Markus. He told the story briefly, and then he said, "My mind's pretty screwed up right now." He looked around at the faces. "And then these things happened today that are eating me up. This afternoon one of my patients told me a story that makes me suspect strongly that he used his medicines, the ones that I prescribed, to help somebody else commit suicide. I feel betrayed by him. I've got to wonder what the hell I'm doing in my practice.

"Even more unsettling was this other thing that happened this morning, and it makes me wonder whether my own senses are betraying me. Maybe I'm going crazy. I was up on Queen Anne Hill looking south over the city, and I noticed that Tahoma Peak wasn't there. Then it was there, but it shifted back and forth from the left side to the right side of Mount Rainier. It went back and forth like that."

Frank asked, "Have you been getting enough sleep lately? The combination of stress and not getting enough sleep can do that to you. This is not so unusual. It's probably something akin to slumber-related hallucination."

The others of the group got into a pleasant argument about which side of Mount Rainier the Tahoma Peak was supposed to be on. Someone said the east and another said the west. Michael Hannity didn't say a thing. He just looked intently at Israel.

Finally Frank turned to Michael. "You know the answer to this, Michael, don't you?"

This was like Frank. Israel was quite certain Frank knew the answer already, but he preferred for the matter to be settled by one of his patients. He chose Michael because even though Michael was irritating, he also was absolutely trusted by every member of the group. Professor Hannity was an authority on all topics except interpersonal skills. He knew almost everything, and when there was something he didn't know, he was comfortable saying so. Frank asked, "Michael. Where is Tahoma Peak? What's the answer?"

Michael Hannity quietly said, "The answer is in Matthew seventeen, twentieth verse. 'If your faith were the size of a mustard seed you could say to this mountain, "Move from here to there," and it would move; nothing would be impossible for you.'"

Four

PERMANENCE

Immediately after the meeting Professor Hannity tugged on Israel's shirt sleeve and asked, "How do you do that?"

"Do what?"

"How do you remember things from one time thread to another?"

"What are you talking about?"

"The mountain! You saw it going from not there to there and from left to right and back again. You were shifting back and forth from one time thread to another."

Israel stared at Michael Hannity's rust-colored eyes.

The professor continued, "You really don't understand what I'm saying, do you? I'm fairly certain that people do this sort of thing all the time, but they don't remember it. Their minds are waterlogged. Except you! You do."

Israel noticed a peculiar fleck of blue in Michael's left eye, at the bottom of the iris in the six o'clock position. It was shaped like a tiny heart.

Michael announced, "You can help me immensely with my research. You're the one. You can do it."

"Do what? What are you talking about?"

"I'm talking about traveling across time."

"Time travel? Are you serious?"

Michael stared back with motionless features, intense eyes. *He is serious.* "Why me?"

"Because you remember, and others don't. I tried it myself, but I don't remember either."

"Do you mean I remember what happens to me when I've been in another time period?"

"That's exactly what I mean."

"What makes you think I'm time traveling?"

Michael almost shouted, "Are you listening to yourself? Today you saw a mountain disappear and reappear. You saw it jump from one location to another. That's not a psychological blip. It's not something that has psychological meaning. Think about it. What kind of hallucination is it that doesn't have a psychological meaning? That wasn't your imagination causing that mountain to jump back and forth. It really happened."

Israel felt lightheaded. "Let me get this straight. You're saying that what happened this morning was that I traveled from one point in time to another point in time? So tell me, when was Tahoma Peak ever on the west side of Rainier? Or forgive me if it happens right now to be on the west side, because that would mean my mind is totally fucked."

Michael smiled. "Your mind is not totally fucked. Right now Tahoma is on the left side of Rainier when you look at it from Seattle, and that's just how you remember it, right? So your mind is not fucked. When you saw Tahoma jump back and forth, you were seeing images of different moments in different threads of time, and that's fantastic because just like lots of other physicists, I believe that different time threads occur, but this is actually evidence of it. You're going to be historic, man." He laughed. "I'm not kidding you. There are different threads of time, and that means there's at least one other dimension of time. And you're not crazy." He put his hand on the back of Israel's arm. "Look. This is going to take a little time to explain. Can I buy you a beer? I'll have to bum a ride, though. I came downtown on public transportation, so I need your kindness on this. Fair trade! I'm buying your beer."

They walked to Israel's car, and Michael commented about the scratch on the passenger side door. "Nasty scrape there. But isn't it amazing how cars don't rust any more like they used to? It's because cars now are made with galvanized steel, and they removed the stainless steel and chrome trimming that used to be on cars. It used to be that different metals touching each other would set up a tiny galvanic current that eventually rusted cars. Not so much any more!"

Israel pulled a key out of his pocket, unlocked the car with radio signal, two beeps twice, and the two climbed into the front seat. He inserted the key into the ignition, turned the key, and the engine roared to life. He drove a few blocks south and parked in a garage below Cutter's Bay House. They took the elevator up to the restaurant.

Cutter's had an atmosphere of brass and glass and class. They got a table in the bar next to a window looking southward toward the market and toward Mount Rainier in the distance. Israel strained to see the mountain, but it was shadowed by clouds and the evening's increasing darkness.

"It's there," Michael reassured him, "and Tahoma's on the left side. Trust me."

Their order was taken by a voluptuous waitress wearing a fitted white blouse and sleek black slacks. After she left Michael said, "She's gorgeous," and then he covered his mouth with his hand and mumbled something.

"What was that?" asked Israel.

Michael said nothing, just shook his head abruptly.

Israel asked again. "No, really, I can handle it, whatever it is."

"It's not something I want to say. Nobody should have to hear this. Cockshitfuck. Damn! I'm sorry."

Israel sat back in his chair. "No, it's okay. I understand. I'll back off."

They sat in silence for a while. The professor leaned back in his chair with his eyes gently closed.

Israel watched people both inside the bar and outside on the grass on the other side of the window. When the waitress brought their beers, Israel thanked her, and Michael smiled broadly and nodded but didn't talk.

After she left Michael carefully said, "I'm attracted to that woman. We should leave her a nice tip. The things I learn in the psychologist's office are sometimes impossible for me to do in everyday life. That's just the way it is."

The beer glowed within tall funnel-shaped glasses, a slice of lime perched on the brim of each. Michael brightened. "Isn't this lovely? I enjoy coming here because they make me feel special." He took an appreciative draft of his beer and then turned to look at Israel. "So instead of asking, 'What time is it?' maybe we should ask, 'Time, what is it?' Most people don't have anywhere near an accurate understanding of time." He took the lime slice off his glass, dipped it in his beer, sucked on it, and then took another sip of beer. "Do you believe the past exists?" He waited a few seconds. "People talk about time travel all the time, but time travel doesn't make sense unless the past exists, right? Or the future. When I've asked others this question, about whether the past exists, usually they give an egocentric answer. They say that the way to get to the past would be somehow to make time run backwards very fast. That's rather amusing to me because it's like they suppose the past can't exist unless they are there to see it. Also, even though there isn't any mathematical or physical law that says time has to move always forward, nobody has ever seen it go backward, except on those days in elementary school when teacher was in a silly mood and ran the movie backwards. Maybe that's why people think that way."

He took another draft of beer. "That's not how time works, though, so that's why I'm asking you, Do you think the past exists, and I mean like right now, someplace else, of course, but right now?"

Israel wasn't ready with an answer. The idea of time had gotten more difficult.

"Well, it does!" exclaimed Michael. "Right at this very moment the past exists. Your son Markus is alive and so are your parents and so is the moment you watched Markus getting born. It's all there; never went away. Drink your beer; it's delicious. And don't get too carried-away happy about this permanence of events, because it also means somebody right now is getting gassed in Auschwitz." He paused for another sip of beer. "Buchenwald," he continued, "is a Nazi death camp where fifty-six thousand people died. The watchtower clock at Buchenwald is set permanently at three fifteen, the time the camp was liberated on April 11, 1945. Time is like that. Every moment stays in its place, just like a point on any other spatial plane.

"So how do I know that? How do I know the past never went away? Simply because of a popular discovery made by a splendid gentleman named Albert Einstein."

Einstein! Time running faster and slower at the same time. Space contracting and expanding at the same time.

Israel interrupted, "I have a question for you about Einstein's theory of relativity. I'm stumped by it. Let's say you're in a spaceship going fast, and light is shot at you from two different sources. One is behind you and catching up to you. The other is coming from in front of you and meeting you head on. Since the speed of light is constant, what happens to time then? How does it get faster and slower at the same time?"

Professor Hannity laughed out loud. "You're a troublemaker, Dr. Newman. Did you know that? That's an outstanding question, worthy of my prospective conspirator in the planned exploration beyond the impenetrable defenses of relentless time." He bit the fruit out of the rind of his lime slice and ate it. He twisted the rind between a thumb and forefinger while he explained. "The way to understand that is when you look at it from your own perspective on the spaceship, space and time don't change at all. They remain constant and reliable from your point of view. But observers in other parts of the universe see it differently. Some of them would say your time is going faster, and some would say your time is going slower.

"Let's talk energy for a moment. This is a little harder to grasp. From your perspective in the spaceship, looking at the light catching up to you from behind, in order for it to sort of catch up to the speed of light in your frame of reference it has to take energy from its frequency, which thereby gets slower, and the wavelength gets longer. We call that red shift, and I'm sure you've read about that before but maybe it was not explained in quite that way. I bet you've never heard anyone say that the light has to steal energy from its frequency in order to speed up to the speed of light in your frame of reference. At first glance that seems to break the law of light-speed constancy, but that's what happens. The same goes for the light coming from in front of you, just the other way around. The light needs to slow down to the speed of light in your frame of reference, so it takes energy from all that extra speed that Einstein's speed limit won't allow, and it puts it into a higher frequency. That's called blue shift. Is this making any sense to you?" He didn't wait for an answer. "This has been a useful tool for astronomers who measure how fast stars and galaxies are moving away from Earth. The point is, from your own frame of reference you don't notice any changes in your own space-time; you just notice the changes of other people's spacetime. That's the answer to your question."

Israel nodded. "Simple as that." *Simple my ass.*

"Yes, as simple as that," the professor answered matter-of-factly and did not pick up on Israel's sarcasm. "So then you have all these different people and groups of people and planets of the universe, all of them moving at extraordinarily different speeds relative to one another, all of them living at different rates of time passing, and that means of course that the past must persist in one place even as the future is springing to life in another."

"Of course," teased Israel.

This time the professor picked up on the sarcasm. "Hey, I can explain it with a metaphor." He held up a finger to indicate a brief pause in the conversation. He took another draft of his beer, and then he said, "I've got a great metaphor for this, and speaking of metaphors, how about let's have some key lime pie. I always tell metaphors better when I'm anticipating or actually eating key lime pie and drinking a cup of coffee, especially after a golden ale like we're enjoying. If we order it now, Miss Beautiful, who makes me

hot and bothered, will have it to us by the time we finish the beer."
He held up his hand to get the waitress's attention, and then he told
Israel, "You do all the talking. I want to make a good impression."
He covered his mouth with his hand and mumbled.

Israel ordered burnt cream custard for himself, key lime pie for
Professor Hannity, and two coffees.

Michael nodded at the waitress and smiled. A few moments
passed after the waitress left, and then Michael said, "I know I can
do this. I know I can, fuckfuckfuckfuck . . ." He covered his mouth
and closed his eyes. After a few seconds he looked at Israel and
held up his index finger, this time meaning he had an idea. With
his other hand he lifted his beer glass to his lips and took a large
mouthful of beer, swished it in his mouth, tilted back his head, softly gargled for a moment, and then he swallowed. "Ah-h-h-h-h-h-h."
He almost gasped. "Medicine to my soul. I had to cleanse my filthy
palate."

Israel looked around to see who else might be watching.
Everyone appeared to be absorbed in their own conversations. He
leaned toward the professor. "Tell me this metaphor that will make
everything clear."

"Yes, I was just getting to that. Back when I was a teenager it
was still safe to walk around Green Lake at night in the dark, alone.
You didn't have to worry about getting mugged, and I used to go
for walks in the moonlight. Oh, before I go further with this, I would
like to let you know that I've decided to tell you my first name, the
one that starts with *K*. Not now, though, because it would interfere
with the flow of my story, but remind me later to tell you. I don't let
too many people know my first name; I want you to know that. If I
tell you, it's because I trust you.

"I was walking around Green Lake one night, and I noticed in
the water this path of reflected light coming from the moon on
the other side of the lake. The reflection came right across the water toward me, rippling and silvery like an inviting mystical path,
and this may sound obvious to you that moonlight gets reflected
by the water, but I was intrigued by it. The path of reflected light

kept following me as I walked along the shore of the lake. It always crossed the water directly between me and the moon on the other side. The part of the lake that used to show the reflection had gone dark, and the dark water in front of me would turn bright with light as soon as I walked by it. I had this glorious realization that at any one moment the entire lake was ablaze with reflected light from the moon. All of Green Lake was ablaze with light; I just couldn't see all of it. I could see only the light on the patch of water that was directly between the moon and me, but if I could have been a thousand different people at the same time, all of us standing in a big line around the lake, then I could have seen the entire lake shining like a huge mirror, a bad mirror with lots of ripples in it. But being as I was only one guy, I could see the light on only one part of the lake at a time." He took a last swig of his beer and set the glass down. "You see, that's how time works. Hold onto that image while I tell you about how time works in the universe."

The desserts arrived along with coffee. "Ah, perfect timing," said Michael, his eyes gleaming. He looked at the pretty server and smiled broadly. After she left there was no funny business with his hand and mouth. He just sipped his coffee and then looked at Israel, who was watching him expectantly. "What?" He laughed. "It's not an all-the-time thing, you know. But I'll tell you something else. This mumbling behind my hand does not really relieve the pressure. When we get out of here I'm going to let loose with one great big verbal fart. I'm just warning you. By the way, that reminds me about getting older. I've discovered there are different phases of aging. During their forties everybody's eyes start going bad. The fifties are different for different people. For me I've been farting and burping a lot, but my eyes and ears are still good enough to enjoy the bubbles in my bath water. I read somewhere that a blue whale can make a fart bubble large enough to envelope a cow." He smiled at his key lime pie, and took an appreciative, small, delicate bite. "Now where were we? We were talking about time and the universe. Can you see things happening in the past?"

"No," Israel answered.

"Of course you can. Every time you look at the stars you're seeing the past. Even moonlight is a little more than a second old. Sunlight leaves the sun eight minutes before you see it. You're seeing the past all the time."

"I thought you meant . . ."

"How about the future?"

"I'd be a millionaire if I could see the future and predict the market."

"Of course you would. Einstein's theory of relativity makes it clear that different ones of us are moving at different speeds through time. That is a remarkable thing. It's more remarkable than most people give it credit for. These differences of time-speed are magnified by distance of space, and don't look at me so dumbfounded because I'm going to explain it to you. Physicists talk about now-moments. If you and I are at exactly the same instant of time, we are in the same now-moment. So imagine that our friend and hero, First Officer Spock, is way the hell out there sitting on a planet ten billion light years away, and we are here eating our key lime and custard desserts. Let's also suppose that for some strange reason with all the movement of the stars and galaxies and the rotation of planets, it just so happens Spock is perfectly stationary relative to us right here in Cutter's Bay House. Hard to believe, I know, but we're just imagining; it's a thought experiment, so come along with me on this one. So we and Spock aren't moving relative to each other. In such a situation Spock's now-moment is exactly the same as our now-moment. He lives and observes at exactly the same instant of time as we do. So far so good. This makes sense, doesn't it?"

He slurped his coffee. "Cup-cup," he said, and he held his cup up for Israel to bump his own cup against. "Here's to First Officer Spock, one hell of a talented guy with a most attractive haircut, not. So let's say Spock decides to run directly away from us at ten miles an hour. Just that little motion, magnified by the distance of ten billion light years, would make his now-moment one hundred fifty years in our past. He'd be living at the time of the American Civil War. We wouldn't even be here." He waited for that information to sink in. He took another bite of pie and another sip of coffee. "So then, let's suppose Spock runs ten miles an hour directly toward us. His now-moment would then be one hundred fifty years in our future. Think about that." Professor Hannity forked off a piece of pure graham cracker crust and savored it.

"You mean—"

"I mean that if anyone's now-moment includes either our past or our future, then those periods of time have to exist, don't they? They are there whether we can see them or not. We just can't see them because they don't happen to be in our own now-moment, but they're there."

"Wait a moment." This concept strained Israel's ability to think, but he thought he had caught the professor in a discrepancy. "If Spock runs away from us at ten miles an hour and his now-moment happens to be one hundred fifty years ago, then it's just that his now-moment hasn't caught up to us yet. It doesn't necessarily mean that our own past is still there in our own timeline, does it?"

"Good boy! I struggled a bit with that once myself. Let's take it back to where Spock is sitting still with respect to us and we're sharing the same now-moment. Got it?"

"Yes."

"Okay, then he runs away from us. At that moment, from his own perspective, is he moving forward or backward in time?"

"Forward."

"Right. So he moves from our same now-moment forward in time to our past. Doesn't make immediate sense, does it? You've got to wonder what kind of universe would allow that to happen. He moves forward in his time to get to our past." He waited for a moment and then said, "The kind of a universe that allows this is one in which time is a dimension of space. Once something happens it is there forever, eternity. It never goes away. We move through it, through the dimension of time. Time doesn't move; we move through it." He sighed and sat back in his chair. "Here's something even spookier. We are not on the leading edge of it. We are not the first ones to travel through this time dimension. Since Spock can move his now-moment into our future by running toward us, our future already must be there; it must already have happened; it's there waiting for us."

"So much for free will."

"Precisely! You're getting it. You can see why Einstein did not believe in free will. Remember that path of light across the water of Green Lake I was telling you about? It's a true story, by the way. At any one time I was able to see only a single path of light across the water because I could be in only one now-moment at a time. However, if I had been a thousand people standing around the lake I would have been able to see light glistening from every part of it.

"Just like that, if we were able to see the universe from every possible vantage point at the same time, especially with relativistic effects magnified by the vastness of space and the tremendous speeds of stars and galaxies and planets, we would be able to see all of history from its beginning to its end. The past and the future would coexist. The past never goes away. And if you want to think about it this way, the future already has happened. It's there too."

"This is interesting."

"Yes, it is."

"No, I mean it's incredible."

"No, it's not incredible. It's as credible as can be. The way to think about time is that it is a true and complete fourth dimension of space, just like the other three spatial dimensions. Time does not flow any more than height flows or width or length. Time just is. Our conscious awareness moves through this time dimension, just as it moves through the other three spatial dimensions. We experience our passage through the time dimension, but the past is still there. It doesn't get erased after we've passed it, and the future doesn't have to wait for our arrival in order for it to be. The past and the future just are, and they always have been, at least from the Big Bang, and they always will be. Of course the future very well could still be growing. I'm still trying to figure out that one."

Professor Hannity took a deep breath in and out. "So then, how would someone travel in time? How to travel in time; that is the question. I think that will keep for another discussion. You'll want to understand it, and that means I'll have to get into concepts of particulate spacetime and what you can do to get around the time barrier. But like I said, enough is enough for one night. I just hope that I've got you interested because I think we can make a serious time traveler out of you."

I could see Markus again, and Mom and Dad.

Five

SUPERMAN

Prescience sometimes resides in the revealing of a name, as though fate itself has been invited or even taunted to test the holder of it, to exact a fee for it, as though the universe remains complacent about a secret only until it is told, and then it rises like a dragon awakened by the rustling of its treasure, intent upon challenging the worthiness of whomever would intrude on what it believes is rightfully its own.

For a while Michael and Israel sat in the bar and talked about the Huskies and Seahawks, and then Israel asked, "You were going to tell me your first name, what the *K* stands for."

Michael cleared his throat, and for the first time Israel realized that Michael cleared his throat frequently. *One of his neurologic tics.*

Michael answered, "Yes. My parents were into the Superman comics big time. Do you remember Superman's first name, the one he was given on Krypton?"

"Hey, yeah!" Israel laughed. "Your name is Kal-El?"

Michael nodded. "My parents were crazy. This next part I don't want you to tell a soul. You're sworn to secrecy, okay? My parents changed their own names."

"You mean . . ." Israel couldn't recall the names of Kal-El's parents.

"My dad changed his name to Jor-El, and my mom's name

became Lor-El. They painted my bedroom with lead-based paint to protect me from stray kryptonite radiation. Goddamn fools." He shook his head. "Don't get me wrong. I love my mom and dad, but as a small kid I had no clue what my name was going to do to me. I just thought it was cool to have Superman's name. Then in elementary school all the smart-assed little punks needed to find out if they could beat up Superman. It gave them one more reason to pick on the Jewish kid." He stirred the last of his key lime pie with his fork. "I learned to fight. I took years of martial arts in so many different disciplines you can't count them all on one hand; two hands maybe. It started making a difference when I finally was able to combine the different disciplines smoothly, but what really made a difference was when I put on a bit of body weight. Kids left me alone when I reached ninth grade in school, but then I was the tough guy. I was still singled out as different, not worth keeping around." He held his fork vertically between his thumb and index finger, and he wiggled it. "They made me a schmuck."

He stirred his pie some more. "Do you know what Kal-El means? It means 'voice of God.' The suffix 'El,' it's one of the seventy-two Hebrew names of God. Lots of Hebrew names use it. Yours has it, Isra-El. It means 'fights with God.' My middle name, Micha-El means 'resembles God.' There are a bunch of names with 'El;' Dani-El, Ezeki-El, Muri-El, Gabri-El, lots of others. It gets silly sometimes when people change the old Hebrew names, when they try to make something new out of them, like Gabrielle. Gabri-El means 'man of God.' Then the French created the name Gabrielle and said it meant 'woman of God,' but if you think about it, they changed the God part of the name. So Gabrielle really means 'man of a girly God.' That's funny, but it's not as funny as Kal-El meaning the voice of God." Then Michael enunciated clearly, "Cock. Shit. Fuck." Each word was distinctly its own sentence, making it unmistakable that this was not a loss of control.

Michael sat back in his chair and looked at Israel. "So what's your middle name?"

"Legato."

"Legato?" Michael smiled. "You mean like the musical directive meaning smooth and continuous without any interruption between the notes, that kind of legato?"

"The very same. So my name's a little unusual too. I think my parents wanted me to be musical and smooth, cool."

"You're not pulling that out of your ass, are you?"

"What?"

"It's awesome. Right now you have no idea how beautifully that name fits you, but you will. Fights with God! Smooth and continuous! Given that you're going to be my time travel pilot, that's a magnificent name. Legato!" He gleamed. "It's like the smoothness of dark energy between particles of spacetime. I'll explain it later."

"And fights with God!"

"Yeah, that too."

They finished their desserts, and their server delivered the bill. Michael grinned broadly, and after she left he mumbled into his hand. He left an enormous tip, and then he and Israel took the elevator down to the parking garage under the restaurant, to level C. On its west side the garage was open to the outdoors, separated only by a chain-link fence from cars racing by on the Alaskan Way Viaduct. It felt open and loud.

Israel nudged Michael. "Weren't you going to let out with a great big verbal fart?"

Michael shook his head. "Don't feel like it anymore. Crazy, isn't it?"

Walking toward the car they heard an excited voice behind them. "Don't turn around. I have a gun pointed at you. All I want is your wallets."

"Oh, shit-shit-shit-shit-shit," Michael muttered.

"What's that? You mouthing off to me?"

Israel said, "He can't help it. He can't control his words."

"Fuck face, fuck face, fuck face, fuck face, fuck face," Michael erupted loudly, seemingly unable to stop himself.

"Shut the fuck up!" the stranger shouted.

Israel yelled, "He can't help it. I'm telling you he doesn't have control over it."

Michael squealed, "Shitfuckface, shitfuckface, shitfuckface." It sounded like he was singing it. He put his hands up into his armpits and waved his elbows like they were wings. He strutted around like a chicken and clucked the words, "Fuck fuck fuck fuck, fuckface, bagurrrrrrrrrrk, fuckface, fuck fuck fuck fuck."

The assailant screamed, "Shut your fucking mouth!" He advanced, pointing his pistol directly at Michael's head.

"Good God," shouted Israel. "Don't shoot him; he can't help it."

The assailant got just close enough, and Michael struck like a viper. The pistol fired just before it flew from the assailant's hand, and the sound of the shot was followed instantly by a loud crack as the man's arm bent unnaturally backward. His knees buckled, and he dropped. The bullet ricocheted off the ceiling and the floor and a rib on the right side of Israel's chest.

Stabbed by startling pain with each breath and aware of a deeper, more dangerous presence growing beneath it, a tightness prohibiting movement of air, Israel's senses rapidly relinquished surveillance of his surroundings. His vision darkened, and he lost consciousness.

There were brief moments of awareness, being loaded into an ambulance and alternating moments of darkness and light, people talking, telephone talk. Finally he awoke behind a curtain in a noisy, brightly lit room. Every breath triggered piercing pain on the right side of his chest and his head pounded with each heartbeat. Both his chest and his head hurt severely; he didn't know which was worse. If either of the pains intensified an iota he knew he would faint. He breathed short and shallow, and trying not to move his head at all, closed his eyes and waited.

A man's voice asked, "Are you awake?"

Israel opened his eyes.

"That's good to see," the man said. "My name is Ross. I'm a nurse, and you're in the emergency department at Harborview Medical Center. Can you tell me your name?"

He whispered, "Israel Newman."

"Good. That's what we thought. Looks like you're going to be all right, Dr. Newman. You gave us a bit of a scare, but you're all right. Do you know what month it is?"

It hurt to think. "September."

Can you tell me what day of the week?"

It was not immediately there for him to recall, and then he said, "Wednesday."

"Wednesday was yesterday. You've been here awhile." Nurse Ross shined a light in his eyes. "Pupils are equal and react to light. Wiggle your fingers and toes for me. Good. Do you feel this?" He touched each of Israel's arms and legs.

"Yes."

Nurse Ross looked at the bag hanging on a pole, a plastic tube leading from it into a vein in Israel's left arm. "We're giving you antibiotics for that open rib fracture you've got. Everything looks stable. You're going to be all right." Nurse Ross smiled. "Is there anything I can help you with right now?"

"Pain."

"Oh! Okay. We haven't given you anything yet because we wanted you to wake up first. Dr. Wilkerson will be right in to talk with you about what's happened."

The pain was still foremost in Israel's mind when the doctor came in. "Good morning, Dr. Newman. I'm Ellen Wilkerson. I'm an emergency specialist. It's good to see you up and around."

"What?"

Dr. Wilkerson laughed. She asked, "Is your vision clear? Do you see just one of me?"

"Yes."

She put one finger up and asked Israel to follow it with his eyes. She checked his other cranial nerves as well. She listened to his breaths with a stethoscope. "You're doing well."

"What happened?"

"Do you remember the scuffle in the garage down there at Cutters?"

"No. I remember burnt cream custard, and I remember that time has a past and a future. I was at Cutters; I know that, but I can't remember how this happened to me."

"Well, as I understand it, you and your buddy got mugged. That guy's got a mouth on him, by the way. Is he your father?"

"No, no." Israel would have laughed except for the pain.

"Anyway, a pistol was fired and it cracked your right sixth rib, and the rib punctured your lung. It sprang nicely back into place, though; looks good on x-rays. You fainted and struck your head, we think on the floor. Your friend, he's one smart guy. He recognized right away that you had a tension pneumothorax, and he treated you right there in the garage before the ambulance arrived. He did a nice job too. With his pocket knife he made a short horizontal incision on the upper border of your second rib, and he inserted the barrel of a pen to let the air out, a makeshift chest tube. My residents couldn't have done a better job. He saved your life."

"My head?"

"Yes, your head. That's okay too. CT scans of your brain and your cervical spine were normal. We're keeping you here to watch your lung get better and to make sure your neurological exam remains normal. So far things look great. I won't say you're a lucky man because if you were lucky you wouldn't have gotten shot in the first place, but if you have to get shot in the chest, this is a very good outcome. I'll give you some oxycodone for your pain, enough to help you take deep breaths, but not a lot of it. We want your mind to stay relatively clear."

The medicine quelled his pain, and Israel's sleep carried him deep into a realm of darker dreams, the often horrible place where dreams are conjured that rarely are remembered. A god hovered over him and rendered inescapable judgment on a universe without color, a masterpiece of black lines drawn intricately upon three-dimensional parchment; a strange, impossible world upon which Israel himself was inscribed. He felt himself pulled across and through this cartoon land toward a brink of despair, a precipice entry into hell, and among other horrors within it he saw the torn face and broken skull of his beloved Markus, Markus the dead, Markus the custodian of his guilt.

"No!" He cried out, and he pointed an accusing finger at the god above him. "You have no right to judge me, even if you created me and all that I am and have done. You have power, but no right! The world is your fault! If we are the story written by you, then you are guilty, and because of your guilt you have lost your righteousness over me."

This god retreated, and Israel no longer was pulled toward the brink. At that moment he felt his ascendance over what he once had regarded an omnipotent god, omnipotent no longer. It was not God. It was Israel himself mired deeply within his own self-absorbed, selfish remorse.

The god into whom Israel had made himself was lonely.

Israel the man and Israel the judgmental god carefully observed each other. Which of them had written the other? Which of them would make the next move, would write the next entry into the inscription of this world?

It was Israel the man. "Come give us a hug," he said.

Six

LOVE AT FIRST SIGHT

srael awoke to stabbing pain with each breath and a headache that pounded with each heartbeat. He pushed the call button and waited.

A nurse named Gina came. "Can I help you, Doctor Newman?"

"I'd like more analgesic if I may, and can you change the medicine from oxycodone to hydrocodone? Oxycodone gives me nightmares."

"Okay." She left.

He waited.

She returned. "I have some hydrocodone for you. One of the residents was up here and changed it for you. Deep breaths, remember." She helped him sit up in bed and adjusted the pillows for him. "A man has been asking to visit you. He said the two of you are close, important to one another. Michael Hannity. Is he your father?"

Israel smiled. "No, he's not my father."

"Your lover?" she asked sweetly. She was pretty.

He laughed, and it pierced like a spear. "Ow!" He chuckled as softly as he could. He looked at Nurse Gina's left hand to see if there was a ring. Her fingers were slender and unadorned. Her skin was olive, Mediterranean. Her hair was dark brown and wavy with a tiny single patch of gray streaked in it. Her eyes were large and green. Her lips were full.

"No," he answered. "Michael is not my lover. He's a funny guy, and yes, I do like him. He's special in a very special way; peculiar. Maybe I should adopt him. He can be my adopted father. How's that?"

Gina smiled. "Deep breaths," she said.

He couldn't quite make out her full name on the tag she wore. "What's your last name?"

"Oh, excuse me. Let me introduce myself. I'm Gina Provetti." She held her hand out to him.

When he tried to lift his right arm, muscles pulled on his chest painfully enough he simply couldn't do it, and after a brief gasp that he hoped Nurse Gina hadn't noticed, he simply brought his hand up by flexing his elbow. She grasped his hand and, not wanting to hurt him, simply held it still. Her hand was soft and warm. Israel said, "Nice hand. It's worth the pain."

She smiled again. "Deep breaths," she said. "Otherwise I might have to stop bringing you pain medicines."

"My clinic?" he asked. "I need to let them know what happened."

"Already done."

"Already done," he repeated. They looked at each other's eyes, slightly longer than was necessary, and then Gina left.

Israel managed to sleep awhile, and upon awakening he had to cough up a choking bit of phlegm that had gathered in his throat, triggering spasms in his chest and head so abruptly intense that he cried out, and then he whimpered almost silently as he attempted not to move, to breathe with shallow breaths that teased with the threatening pain of his broken rib.

He sensed he wasn't alone, and turning his head toward the windowed wall, he saw a familiar man sitting with his elbows forward on his knees, a middle-aged, bespectacled man with curly gray and auburn hair. He was reading *Alice Through the Looking Glass*. The man cleared his throat and remarked without looking up from his book, "Hurts pretty bad, huh?"

Israel cleared his own throat in response. It hurt his chest.

Michael looked up at him. "They say you're going to live."

"Hi, Michael. Yes, I'm going to live. In pain."

"I brought you some flowers and chocolates."

"I just told the nurse that you and I aren't gay lovers. You'll lose my credibility with her."

"You mean that slender Italian model? She's quite a looker."

"I told her I was going to adopt you. You're my adopted father."

"Okay. I'm not looking forward to the paperwork."

"You saved my life."

"What?"

"You put a tube in my chest and relieved my pneumothorax. I would have died if you hadn't done that. You saved my life."

"Yeah, maybe, after I got you shot." They took a long look at each other. "Hey. I'm sorry about that."

"Sorry about what? You saved my life."

"I've got a confession to make. You know that chicken routine down there in the garage? It wasn't one of my tics. I wanted to sucker the guy into getting close enough I could put my hands on him. It worked except he managed to get off that one shot."

"I don't remember any of that. All I know is that the doctor told me you saved my life, and that's the story I want to remember."

"Fair enough. Would you like to talk physics a little? I can teach you how time travel is possible."

"Not now. Later. My head hurts too much to think right now."

They talked about other things for a while, and occasionally Israel took deep painful breaths and shallow painful coughs.

"I drove your car up. It's here in the garage. The health care team has your keys. Get better, or maybe they won't give them to you."

A while after Michael left, Nurse Gina came in with a couple tablets of hydrocodone. "One or two?" she asked.

"Two, please. Thank you."

She waited for him to swallow the tablets. "So how did Mr. Hannity like the idea of being your father?"

"He doesn't want to do the paperwork."

She smiled with her eyes more than her mouth, and Israel wanted to look at her. "How long before you go home?" he asked.

"Soon. Are you doing okay emotionally?"

"Emotionally? Where did that come from?"

"Your friend, Mr. Hannity, filled us in on a few things. He knows you pretty well. We can get a psychology consult, if you want."

"No, I have a psychologist, a good one. I like him."

There was a pause between them. They looked at each other, and it was clear that each wanted to say something but didn't know what it was going to be.

Gina said, "You must be angry."

"I'm getting over it."

"If you want to talk about it, I'll listen."

"I do have a support group, you know."

"Not here. Not now."

"You're about the prettiest woman I've ever seen."

She laughed gently. "Would it be easier to talk about that?"

"Why do people do the things they do? I mean, I know the answer to that already, but I don't, not really. It's like we all are products of the genes that made us, influenced and molded by experiences. There is a cause for every effect, even on a microscopic level, even on a chemical level, even on an atomic level. And then that cause is the effect of some other earlier cause, and you can keep chasing the causes back further and further until they no longer are a part of you. Each of us is the result of a series of events that was out of our control. So who am I going to blame? Who am I going to be angry at? God?"

"That's deep."

"Yeah. That's deep."

"Don't you believe we have free will?"

"I would like to, but I don't know how there is any room for free will. I've learned that everything is cause and effect, cause and effect."

"Maybe there is spirit, and that could be one of those environmental influences. The spirit could have free will."

"Maybe there's spirit. Maybe. Scientifically I have a hard time seeing that. How would it fit into the structure of things? It might be nice to have a spirit, but the world can be explained without it. We're getting a pretty good understanding about the detail and completeness of causes and effects. When I read about this stuff I get the feeling that, in a way, we're just along for the ride."

"What about love? Is that cause and effect too? Is it cause and effect how you feel about Markus?"

"You know about Markus? Damn it! Hannity's got a mouth on him. In more ways than one."

"Doctor Newman, this information is safe with me."

He looked at her. She was beautiful and intelligent. "Call me Israel," he told her. "Please."

"Israel."

"May I call you Gina?"

She thought about it. "Yes."

The next day when Gina came in, the first thing she said was, "Have you been taking deep breaths, Doctor Newman?" She seemed all business.

"Israel."

She looked at him. "I'll call you Israel in quiet times, when I'm not working."

"When's that?"

"Later."

She came briskly in and out of his room during the day caring for him as only one of many people for whom she was responsible, and Israel wondered if there would even be a *later*. He anticipated it impatiently, listening for her voice in the hall, trying to guess whether the sound of footsteps were hers, until late in the day she came to him.

"Busy day?" he asked.

"As usual."

"It's pretty late."

"Yes. My shift's over."

"Your shift is over and you're still here?"

"I'm visiting you. You're not my friend, though; you can't be my friend. There are rules. So how are you doing, in your head I mean?"

"I'm not as conflicted as you are; that's for sure. You want to be my friend? Thank you. You want to be my friend. I can live with that. You're not taking advantage of me. Sometimes things happen."

Gina sidetracked from that discussion. "Israel is an uncommon name. It makes me wonder if you always have to be vigilant against Palestinian terrorists."

"It means Fights with God, so I guess the Palestinians are in good company."

"You don't have anything against Palestinians?" She asked cheerfully, a light stream of banter overlying a deeper current.

"I'm not even Jewish. Funny about names, isn't it? I've got a Jewish name and I'm not Jewish. Hannity is Jewish, but he's got an Irish name. We're all mixed up. I guess that's what happens when the world goes on for a while."

"Causes and effects?"

"Yes, exactly. Christian guy falls in love with Jewish girl. That sort of thing."

"And we're all along for the ride."

"You've got it."

"No choice in it? We just fall in love, have babies, and give them names? We're out of control!" She giggled.

"It's easier to forgive people when you realize that their ability to stay in control is just one of those things. Just like everything else, it's cause and effect."

"I'll admit I don't always feel in control." Their gaze held each other's. "You don't think people need to be held responsible for their behavior?"

"Of course they do. Responsibility is part of the cause and effect."

"Oh," she said with a pensive heaviness, and then she lightened up again. "I come from a long and pure line of Italians. My ancestors must have remained uncontrollably attracted to Italians. I don't suppose you're Italian?"

"Not the name anyway, and so you're probably Catholic too."

"I probably am."

"It's the most beautiful religion. I wish I could believe what Catholics believe. Then I wouldn't feel so much an intruder when I go to Saint James Cathedral on Christmas Eve."

"Ha! That's very Catholic. We're famous for guilt, and by the way, we Catholics are overjoyed when intruders choose to visit our places of worship. From now on feel invited. People believe what they believe, don't you think?"

"Cause and effect."

"Do you have a girlfriend?"

"Where are we going with this, Gina? I'm not the one at professional risk here, and I'm not the one who feels conflicted and guilty." He watched her shift her weight uncomfortably and look downward. Not wanting to block an avenue he wanted just as much to explore as the woman in front of him seemed to, he opened a door for her. "My problem is that I don't trust people."

"Cause and effect?"

He nodded. "In fact, I don't even trust the ground we walk on."

"Things happen?" she asked.

"Things happen."

"Israel, I want you to remember that you said that." She paused. "Things happen." She reached out and squeezed his hand. "I've got to go. I'll see you tomorrow. I'm not your friend, and I'm guilty as sin."

Their conversation stayed in Israel's mind, and that evening he wrote a poem about not being in control, about things happening.

That night he dreamed of reclining with Gina, talking with her in quiet words, short phrases. Their lips softly touched, relaxed lips wanting to remain intimately close.

The following day, as Gina cleaned around his chest tube, he felt physiologies dancing inside him. *I seriously like this woman.* "Do you like your work?" he asked.

She smiled. "Yes, I do, some days better than others."

"Will you be coming in to visit me later?"

"Don't ask me that question."

"Okay, I respect your professional boundary. Your conversation with me yesterday was therapeutic. Get it, Nurse Gina? You've got a way about you that's helpful to my working through a grunt load of burden. You're a bit like a gentle, guiding light. I'm sorry you feel guilty, but I understand."

"It's not your responsibility to maintain boundaries. You can relax in all of this; I can't."

"We argue well together."

"Yes."

"Yes what?"

"I'm going to visit you later."

"Good. I wrote a poem. I'd like you to look at it."

"You're a writer?"

"You didn't know that? So Hannity didn't tell you everything about me, only the juicy stuff. Yes, I'm a writer. Sometimes I describe myself as a writer trapped in a physician's life."

"What do you write about?"

"Anything. Last night I wrote about what we were talking about."

"One thing leading to another? Stuff just happening? I look forward to reading it."

They looked at one another, and again it was longer than people usually look, and it felt like they were negotiating a slender isthmus of comfortable foundation between stormy seas on either side of it. For the first time Israel studied the complex texture and colors of Gina's green eyes, and then she looked down at his right hand, squeezed it with hers. "I'm looking forward to it. Got to work now."

At the end of her work day she came to him with a cheerful smile and asked, "Okay, so show me your poem."

He handed two sheets of paper to her. "Sorry, it's a little bit long. It's iambic pentameter, like a sonnet; kind of gives it a majestic flow, but I didn't rhyme it because when you rhyme a poem the meaning can get twisted around so much."

Gina read the poem.

I wonder if behavior tells it all
about us, who we are; or whether we

are more than our activity declares.
If we are more than our behavior says
we are, then what ingredients complete
the recipe? Perhaps our looks? Indeed!
A face has launched a thousand ships of war,
and multitudes of men have bent their knees
with passions pounding in their chests to beg
for love. Perhaps our thoughts as well, the ones
not acted on and not immediately
apparent to the world, perhaps these thoughts,
along with acts and beauty, make the whole
of us. I laugh at this because I'm sure
we do not really think. We only think
we do! If one event must cause the next,
and so one thought the thinking next, it follows
that effects and causes order what
our next will be, and we are left without
the prideful claim of being in control.
If this is all there is to it, then let
us laugh, for laughter is the best response
to things that we cannot control. Complain?
Okay, for all the good it does. Complain
a bit, and laugh some more. It entertains
us. Life is entertainment? Yes, of course!
Then what has this to say about the maker
of this mess? Is he a jerk? A joke?
An irresponsible, uncaring God
inflicting mayhem on his unsuspecting
mass of sorrowful humanity?
Or is there more, and if there is, then don't
you think it would be right the great creator
of it all would play a role in it
himself and feel the agony with us?

"Wow! Israel, this is good. I especially like where you say to laugh about life. Laughter is good. You are a writer, and your message, it's Christian."

"Almost. I was brought up Christian. It's hard to escape."

Gina smiled, and her face became the most beautiful in the world.

Israel remarked, "A face can launch a thousand ships," and again they looked at each other quietly, enjoying each other's face. Israel broke the moment by saying, "Mark Twain wrote, 'If Christ were here now there is one thing he wouldn't be—Christian.' Sorry. It's just where I'm at right now. No offense intended."

"No, it's all right. People believe what they believe. I'm okay with that. You're a caring man. That's what I . . . I like that about you; it's important to me. You actually remind me a bit about my mom; she's a heretic too, very spiritual though, always talking about the deeper meanings."

"I'm certain I'd like her."

The seemingly innocent comment pierced too intimately. "Israel, I've got to go now. This is just a little too much for me at the moment. I'm thinking I'm the vulnerable one here and the responsible one, and it's just a bit much." She sighed and then spoke sharply. "You had better be legit, Doctor Newman, because otherwise I'm going to kick you in the balls." She turned and walked to the door, pausing for just one more comment. She softly said, "I don't smoke. I thought maybe you'd like to know," and then she disappeared down the hall.

During the following days Nurse Gina remained completely professional. When she looked at Israel it was not for too long or too short. She called him Doctor Newman. She sounded mildly irritable when each day she declared, "No, I'm not going to be visiting you after work today." She did not elaborate. Daily she repeated, "We want you to use that arm, remember. I'll sic the physical terrorists on you if you're not doing your exercises."

It took five days altogether until x-rays and bedside examination looked reassuring enough for the chest tube to be removed and for Israel to go home. He was told to keep his wound covered

Thomas Curtis

for a couple of days and then keep it clean. He was told to breathe deeply.

Michael visited each day, and each day they talked about all kinds of topics other than physics.

Each day Israel's infatuation with Gina clawed at his heart, but never again did he explore the possibility of a lasting and intimate relationship with her. Over and over he reminded himself that it would be professionally wrong for a nurse to get involved with her patient.

He would keep her face locked in his memory.

On the final day of hospitalization, Gina brought him a present. "It's a cross pendant," she said. "It's a Celtic cross made of silver, plated with gold. It looks like knots made of rope, and each of its four arms is the same length. That's the way the Celts designed their cross before St. Patrick made them Catholic. It's like a pre-Christian cross. That fits you. You once were Christian, and honestly, Israel, you still are and hide it beneath all the baggage you're carrying. Life handed you a lot to carry, so here; carry a little more." As she put the chain over his head, her fingers touched his neck. She pinched the skin of his neck, and without saying another word she turned and walked away.

66

Seven

PARTICULATE SPACETIME

On his way home Israel stopped at his clinic to reassure Mary everything was okay. "I just need another week before returning to work. We've been through this before, right? This is mild in comparison. It's just physical pain. I'm good."

He exchanged greetings with other doctors and other office staff and hauled off a pile of unfinished paperwork to do at home.

His house sat behind a white picket fence on a plateau of land on the north end of Queen Anne Hill, a short walk away from Seattle Pacific University. He enjoyed its view toward the north, over the locks between Lake Union and Puget Sound, the neighborhoods of Ballard and Freemont, even Wallingford and the University District. Only on the clearest of days would the white cap of Mount Baker peek out from its vast distance far to the north. The lawn was neatly trimmed by contracted professionals and adorned with rhododendrons, azaleas, a camellia, and Israel's favorite dogwood tree.

The mailbox welcomed him with a handful of delightful recyclable items, including advertisements from real estate agents, an envelope full of coupons and ads, and there were utility bills and a request for a donation from Northwest Harvest. Among it all was what looked like an invitation to a birthday party sent to him from Professor K. Michael Hannnity, inside of which resided a rather long note.

Dear Israel,

One of these days you will learn that time travel isn't what you might have expected. Physical matter cannot make such a journey. It would be like trying to squeeze one more drop of water into a bottle that's already full. For any one instant of time, space is exactly one size. You can't add or subtract anything from it. Yes, of course, with the expansion of the universe there is room for the addition of mass and energy, and we pretty much are certain that sort of thing happens, particularly at the event horizons of black holes, but the addition of mass or energy is accompanied by progression of time with addition of now-moments, much or all of which already has happened. For any one static instant of time, the size of space remains constant, fixed, and finite. It cannot be changed. No mass or energy can be added to or subtracted from any one instant of the past or future, except maybe at the leading edge of the future, and I'm not really so sure about that. So even with ingenious attempts we never will be able to squeeze your body into another instant in time. To do so would violate laws of thermodynamics, and it's just not going to happen; not now, not ever. No way, no how.

Therefore the kind of time travel you're going to do will be of a different sort altogether. Your body will stay put in my laboratory, and I'll take excellent care of it while you're gone. I can hardly wait to see your surprise when I tell you all about my ideas.

Sincerely from your trusty friend,
Michael

"Scary," Israel heard himself say.

He sat down at the kitchen table to pay bills, but a recurring thought pestered him. *Markus.* Another thought nagged him. It was an adage of the ancient Greek city-state of Sparta. *Go to meet the enemy at once, for every day he gets stronger.*

It would be interesting to learn about Hannity's invention. *I can at least investigate it without actually committing myself to doing it.*

After he was home only two hours, his telephone rang. "Hello," said a familiar voice. "Israel, you're in no shape to prepare your own dinner, so I'm inviting you over for a dinner that I personally am preparing for you." Michael gave his address on Capitol Hill. "If you would be so kind to your dear old Professor Hannity, you might stop at Dilettante Chocolates on the way and pick up a few truffles for dessert. Choose whatever you want for yourself. Get me anything Ephemere. Hey! I've got a special treat for you. After your second glass of pinot noir, I'll show you my laboratory, or as we soon may rename it, Mission Control Central." He hung up.

Israel was about to embark on a date with Professor Hannity who didn't have a clue how much it hurt for him to drive a car. He steered with his left hand as much as possible, drove slowly, and went by way of Highland Drive, hoping to see Mount Rainier, but it wasn't out, obscured by patchy clouds. Driving to Capitol Hill from Queen Anne was a straight shot east on Denny Way, up the hill, and then left onto Broadway. He found a place to park a couple blocks away from Dilettante and walked. *Deep breaths. Don't let anybody bump you. God, this hurts!*

He purchased half a dozen truffles and sat at a table so he could order a shot of orange liqueur. He downed the liquor along with a tablet of hydrocodone. *What a damned fool I am! Take deep breaths. It's a good reason. Damned fool!*

Damned gunshot!

He asked the man who served him, "What's Ephemere? I tried to look it up. It's not in the dictionary."

"It's our trademark chocolate, made with a unique recipe all our own. Ephemere is taken from the word *ephemeral*. Do you like it?"

"It's out of this world."

The server understood the compliment but not the pun.

Mansions perched in rows on the north end of Capitol Hill east of Tenth Avenue, the owners of which either had inherited them and could afford the tax or else they had been extraordinarily lucky in business or investment. For anyone else the cost of those homes was out of reach. This was where Michael lived. On the front door of his estate, just above the mail slot, was a brass plate engraved Prof. Hannity.

Israel rang the doorbell a couple of times, waited, and then he knocked. When he was convinced nobody would answer, he tried turning the doorknob, and the door opened easily with the friendliest of squeaks. The stone-floored foyer was broad, and at its opposite end a grand marble stairway ascended twelve steps to a wall of stained glass windows, where it turned toward both the left and the right, and it climbed still farther. The foyer ceiling towered at least three stories closer to the heavens, adorned with tessellated patterns in gold, cerulean, and white. A crystal chandelier dangled from it. There were grand rooms on both the left and right sides of the foyer. Hallways on either side of the grand stairway ended with elegant wooden doors. It was all very symmetrical, stunningly magnificent.

A sign posted in the foyer read "Hi, Israel. I'm in the kitchen. If I didn't hear to let you in, follow the yellow brick road. Don't stub your toes."

A trail of yellow bricks, placed about two feet apart, led toward the left through a proscenium arch into a high-ceilinged, carpeted room with a fireplace and paintings. The carpet was intricately patterned with various shades of green and flecks here and there of pink and yellow. It reminded Israel of a spring meadow. The walls were sky blue above brown wooden wainscoting.

The yellow bricks turned toward the right and led to a carved wooden door that was as round as a hobbit's hole, and indeed on the other side was a short cylindrical hobbit-like tunnel leading to another wooden door. This one opened onto a kitchen energized with music, The Beatles's *Abbey Road.* "Got to be a joker; he just do what he please . . ."

Complete with white chef's hat, Professor Hannity was chopping a carrot. He looked up and shouted, "Welcome to the Shire. How's my wounded friend?"

Israel smiled. "Managing, a little bit happier just to see you in your natural habitat."

Michael turned the music volume down. "You're going to love this chicken Riviera. *Es muy delicioso.*"

"This is some place you have here."

"Did I forget to mention? I'm fabulously wealthy. Started out with a healthy inheritance, grandparents; then I bought Microsoft, sold Microsoft, bought Amazon, and bought copper mines. Bought this house; it's a plaything. My time travel laboratory is upstairs." He tossed the finely chopped carrot into the tomato sauce simmering on the stove. "Carrot is good in tomato sauce; makes it sweeter. Onions too; sweeter. Garlic too; all kinds of niceness. What you do is first sauté lots of medium chopped garlic and add that to your sauce early on. Gives it a garlic kind of complex sweetness, nice. Then, if you want, just before you serve, it throw in a small amount of raw minced garlic; gives it that pizzazz that will make your sweat stink for days. Oh, mother!" He pointed to a bottle on the counter next to a partly opened window. "That's an Oregon pinot, Willamette Valley, Bergstrom. I've let it breathe now for half an hour. Pour some of it for us."

Next to the wine were two very plain glasses, nothing fancy about them. Israel poured the wine and handed a glass to Michael. "Cheers."

"You're going to love this dish." They watched it simmer. It reduced, and Chef Michael added some water. They watched it reduce again. "This could go on forever; the longer the better, but we have to eat sometime." He layered the sauce onto grilled chicken breasts. "For most things I prefer thighs, because they are moister and more flavorful, but breasts are perfect for this dish. The sauce does all the flavor and moisture, more than enough. Thighs would be too rugged for this sauce." He added some broccoli florets. "Ah, color! We need our vegetables, Dr. Newman."

They took their food and drink to an adjoining room, a richly wooden-walled dining room with a fireplace. The room was smaller and more intimate than Israel expected in the mansion.

Michael explained, "That room you walked through with the green rug, that's supposed to be the dining room, but it's too damned big. That's why I decorated it like the outdoors. This in here is my hobbit hole. It's my home within a house. The rest of this house . . ." he waved his fork like a magic wand, and he shook his head and didn't finish his sentence, and then he mumbled something.

"What's that?" asked Israel.

"I need a fucking gentleman's gentleman to help me take care of this dust bowl."

The delicious chicken Riviera confirmed Michael's ravings about it, and the wine went down easily as well, potent enough that Israel began to believe he would be able to understand and believe whatever physics Professor Hannity wanted to teach.

"It's time for us to get into the nitty-gritty," began the professor. "The last time we talked about time, I think I had you convinced that the past is still there. In a different concept of time, of course, but it's still there. Right?"

"Yes, I think so."

"So tell me. You're here talking with me right now in this moment. Something that is you, something that you identify as you, your consciousness, is inside this body of yours right here and now, yes?"

"Yes."

"Good. So tell me, who is doing the thinking and all the self-awareness business in the Dr. Newman body that right now is eating burnt crème custard at Cutters?"

"Holy shit!"

"Yes, precisely!" Michael smiled wryly. "Hey, look. I'm a Jew, right? But that doesn't mean I don't appreciate some of the things said by Jesus, and one of them was, 'There are many rooms in my father's house.' That's a pretty interesting comment if you ask a time investigator like me. What the hell was he talking about? I've got an idea about the answer to that, and it has to do with . . . No, let me get at it a different way. How many rooms do you think your physical body has had in it while it's been alive? How many rooms for how many souls? A little scary, huh? The number might have to do with the Planck time unit, a very short interval of time, miniscule. If you stacked souls next to one another, each separated by only one Planck unit of time, your body could house every soul that ever lived." Michael flicked a finger against the brim of his wine glass, ringing it like a bell. "And there's a chance each now-moment corpuscle of time is even briefer than that, housing for even more souls. Why Israel, your body is a veritable housing project, voluminous beyond imagination."

Israel tried to focus his mind, but the room had begun to spin slowly.

"So Israel," Michael asked, "do you think your body is a heaven for your partner souls or a hell?" He laughed.

Israel imagined that he must have looked terrified because Michael said, "Only kidding. Nobody says your body has to be either a hell or a heaven. It can be in between. You know, purgatory." He laughed again.

Israel was certain he still looked terrified. "This is terrifying," he said.

"You'll get used to it. Pretty good wine, isn't it?" Michael poured some more in both of their glasses. "Maybe you're worried that somehow some of those many spirits could get mixed up or something, jumbled and out of order. That doesn't happen because time is not continuous. It's particulate, at least the material component of the time dimension is particulate, so that keeps you safe in your own little capsule of cohesive spacetime particles, moving along on your merry way through time. No other soul is going to invade your space. None of the other souls has any interest at all in your particular capsule. You own it. The other souls have their own. There are plenty of other capsules of time for them, and very simply they don't need yours. You're safe there, pardner."

Israel put his face in his hands and rested on his forearms, elbows on the table.

Professor Hannity asked, "You're not understanding, this are you?"

"No."

"Okay. Let's start at the very beginning."

"It's a very good place to start," Israel sang.

"Very good." Michael chuckled. "Maria in *Sound of Music*. Very good, Israel. The beginning would be my telling you how I happen to know that time is particulate, and space also, by the way; material space, that is. Are you familiar with the argument of whether spacetime is continuous or particulate? Do you know what that means?"

"No."

"Okay. Then let's start there. Most people believe that space and time are continuous. This has been called the field concept, and it means that there is no break or interruption of space between any one point and another. We think of time the same way, continuous between points, without interruption; and it has been upon this concept of continuous spacetime that our current understanding of physics has been built.

"Recently however, not all physicists have been so sure. In 1954, about a year before his death, Albert Einstein wrote a letter to his close friend, Michele Besso, and in it he confessed that he found it quite possible that physics cannot be based on the field concept; that is, on continuous structures.

"Nowadays there are physicists who no longer believe that spacetime is continuous. Some of us believe it is particulate, made up like a crystalline structure of miniscule packets of spacetime. We believe that mathematics based on a concept of particulate spacetime will be the only way that there ever will be discovered a unified understanding of the forces of nature expressed by a single equation. I am one of these physicists. I am convinced of the particulate structure of material spacetime.

"When I first learned about this great argument, whether spacetime is continuous or particulate, I couldn't stop thinking about it. I thought about it constantly, and one day there popped into my mind a recollection of a little curiosity I learned when I was a lad first studying algebra. I can't emphasize enough how important mathematics is to our understanding. The structure of mathematics is the way it is because the structure of our universe just happens to be the way it is. The physical universe is so intertwined with mathematics that you should think of them as one and the same thing. They are inseparable. The universe is mathematics."

"Professor Hannity?"

"Yes, Doctor Newman?"

"Would you happen to have some ibuprofen handy?"

"You have a headache?"

"I have a headache."

"Was it the wine?"

"Among other things."

Michael nodded and quickly retreated from the room. Only moments elapsed before he returned with a circular platter on which were two tall crystal glasses of water and four round red tablets of ibuprofen. "Mind if I join you?"

"Not at all."

"Notice the glasses; they're my mother's. They're called tea glasses. I love to drink water out of beautiful crystal like this and wine out of a plain glass."

"Why is that?"

"Crystal contributes a sparkling magnificence to water, but it detracts from the beauty of an excellent wine. Simple as that."

"Simple as that?"

"Simple as that."

"Professor Hannity, that is the most sensible thing you have told me since you were talking about garlic in tomato sauce." Israel attempted to look as sincere as he could while Michael stared back at him with an almost contemptuous expression. Israel could hold it no longer, and a smile erupted on his face.

"Why you little bugger!" Michael laughed. "You had me going. You've got a way of yanking my chain. I thought you were getting ready to tell me that you thought my entire life's work was silly, and I was preparing to be offended."

They laughed, and then Israel asked, "So tell me more about your entire life's work, Professor Hannity, especially the part about why it's not silly."

"Look, I just want you to know a little more about what you're doing when you start being a time travel pilot."

"Time travel pilot. I like the sound of that. Time travel pilot. TTP. In medicine that acronym stands for thrombotic thrombocytopenic purpura."

"Is there anything at all about that disease that is pertinent to what we're talking about?"

"Only that it's frequently fatal."

Michael sighed and put his forehead down on the table. He rocked it from side to side.

Israel said, "I just want you to know a little bit about how scary this is getting to be for your prospective TTP."

Professor Hannity lifted his head and said, "It's safe. It's as safe as can be. I would do it myself if . . . In fact I have done it myself. The problem is that I just don't remember my experiences when I get back. It's safe. Believe me. I know that you are going to be successful."

"It's safe," Israel repeated.

Michael nodded.

"Okay."

"Is the ibuprofen working?"

"Yes, I think it is."

"As I was about to say, when I first was learning algebra as a kid, I noticed something about the number nine that tickled my interest. If you divide the number two by the number nine, you get zero point repetend two. Here, let me write it out for you."

The professor produced a notebook, seemingly out of nowhere, and on it he wrote:

$2 \div 9 = 0.2222222222 \ldots$

"This sequence of twos goes on forever. At least it does in our imagination; not necessarily in reality, but I'll get to that later. It's similar for three divided by nine."

$3 \div 9 = 0.3333333333 \ldots$

"It's the same for all the single-digit numbers until you get to nine."

$4 \div 9 = 0.4444444444 \ldots$
$5 \div 9 = 0.5555555555 \ldots$
$6 \div 9 = 0.6666666666 \ldots$
$7 \div 9 = 0.7777777777 \ldots$
$8 \div 9 = 0.8888888888 \ldots$

"But it changes when you get to the number nine. If it followed the same pattern as the other numbers, you should get nine divided by nine equals zero point repetend nine."

$9 \div 9 = 0.9999999999 \ldots$

"But mathematics teachers tell us that nine divided by nine equals one."

"What's so funny about that?"

"That's exactly the same thing I asked myself when I was nine years old. I showed it to my algebra teacher, Mr. Bensen, and using algebra he showed me that zero point repetend nine actually equals the number one. Here's how he did it." Michael wrote out the equations.

$X = 0.9999999999 \ldots$
$10X = 9.9999999999 \ldots$
$10X - X = (9.9999999999 \ldots) - (0.999999999 \ldots)$
$9X = 9$
$9X \div 9 = 9 \div 9$
$X = 1$

This delighted Israel. "That's clever."

"Yes, it's clever, and that's all I thought about it until I confronted the argument of whether spacetime is continuous or particulate, and then that clever little algebraic exercise became an intrigue. I asked myself what kind of a universe would it be in which zero point repetend nine equals one? Was it more likely to occur in a continuous spacetime or in a particulate spacetime? This is where you'll need to do a little bit of thinking. If the universe were continuous, then zero point repetend nine would continue infinitely. It never quite would equal one. But if the universe is particulate, a point would be reached at which zero point repetend nine has to stop, at least as a real number representing physical spacetime. I assumed at first that the stopping point most likely would be the Planck length, in the consideration of space, and the Planck time, in the consideration of time, but space and time go smaller than those."

"Planck length? Planck time?"

"Doctor Newman, it's clear you're not a physicist. Planck is famous. In 1899 a German physicist named Max Planck introduced physical units of measurement that elegantly simplified algebraic expressions of physical law. These units have been called natural units because they originate from properties of nature, not from any human fabrication. Some physicists refer to Planck's units as God's units because of this. Basically Planck's units make sense of the physical world. They coordinate things like the gravitational constant and the speed of light in a vacuum, and the Coulomb's and Boltzmann's constants. Because of Planck's units, all these other constants work together. Planck units allow us to work with the physical universe in a common language in which everything fits, so you can see why physicists think quite highly of Max Planck. Is this making a little bit of sense?

"Yes, it is. How small are we talking?"

"Quite small. A Planck length is roughly 1.6 times ten to the minus thirty-fifth power, meter. That would mean you would move the decimal point thirty-five places to the left. A Planck time is roughly 5.4 times ten to the minus forty-fourth power, second."

"Okay."

Professor Hannity kept talking. "I won't bother you with the values for Planck mass, charge, and temperature because I'm not trying to make a physicist of you. I'm just trying to get a concept across. The universe is built with finite units."

"And that's all I need to know?"

"Yes."

"Okay."

"Let me write it out for you. Planck's unit for space would look like this."

0.00000000000000000000000000000000001616252

"A Planck unit of space is that much of a meter. A particle of space is at least that small, and a bit of mathematical physics called the Lorentz factor tells us that probably space is smaller still . Now I'll write it for time."

This explanation gave Israel time enough to swirl his wine around in its simple glass, and he took another simple swallow while Professor Hannity scribbled another number.

0.0000000000000000000000000000000000000000539124

"Ah. It's beautiful, isn't it? A Planck unit of time is that much of a second. A particle of time is at least that small."

"That's pretty small."

"Yes, it is."

"How can the size of a space particle be different from the size of a time particle, if they're the same particle? Because that's what we're talking about, right? We're talking about a particle of space-time, right?"

"Is that the wine talking, Dr. Newman? Your question is like asking how a pencil can be longer than it is wide. It's simply a different dimension. A particle of spacetime is a four-dimensional structure."

"Okay. I get it."

"If spacetime is particulate, then there is a digital position in the number, zero point repetend nine, far to the right of the decimal point, at which zero point repetend nine no longer can continue as a real number. Of course it can continue infinitely in our imagination, but not as a number having meaning in spacetime. At that very next digital position, the position immediately following the last real-world digital position, the universe has to make a decision. It must decide what number in the real world is closest to the most accurate. I'm going to write it out again."

Israel drank some more wine, anticipating that it would take some time for the professor to scribble out a bunch of nines.

0.9999-----9999

"Those dashes there, they mean that there are a lot of nines in between. That last nine I wrote on the right; that's the last possible real-world digital position toward the right. You can't go any further than that in the real world. If we add one more nine to the end of this chain, it becomes imaginary. Therefore, in the real world and at that minuscule level, the universe is forced into a decision about what is the most accurate number for the real world. The number has to be rounded either up or down, based on the value of the number in the next digital position, the first imaginary digital position of repetend nine. If that first imaginary digit is a five or higher, then the universe would round the number upward. And that is the case. Putting nine in that first imaginary decimal position causes the whole kit and caboodle to be rounded upward to one. Voila!"

"Voila!" Israel repeated. "Michael, could I explain to you that right now I'm a little tipsy, and could you just tell me in layman's terms what this means?"

"It means that material, four-dimensional spacetime, is particulate."

"Okay. So what difference does that make, exactly?"

"Would you like some coffee?"

"Yes, I would. Thank you."

"As I recall, you like it black?"

"Yes."

Eight

CONTINUITY

With the professor away conjuring up coffee, Israel looked around the room and discovered on the wall behind him, where he hadn't noticed it earlier, a large photo of a little boy wearing a Superman outfit, and on either side of him stood a woman and a man who must have been his parents. The parents were dressed in normal garb of the fifties, and Israel smiled as he imagined how they might have appeared sporting costumes from Krypton. Here they were, Jor-El and Lor-El.

From the kitchen came the shouted words, "Fuck! Shit-shit-shit-shit-shit-shit. Fuck! Crap!" *The voice of God.*

Atop the mantel of the fireplace in the room sat three sculpted busts. One of them was Albert Einstein, and Israel tried to guess which of the other two might be Max Planck. He looked at the nameplate on its base. James Clerk Maxwell. *That must be the physicist who's on deck, the one who's up to bat next. Maxwell was all the rage with light waves in the nineteenth century.* The third head on the mantel was indeed Max Planck.

Michael came in. "Aha! Caught you exploring. I knew you were a curious person."

"Are these your parents?"

"No. Those are busts of famous physicists," he deadpanned and then relented. "Yes, they are."

"If you don't mind my asking, where are they now?"

"Well, it's very possible they are bowling."

"Bowling?"

"You know I grew up in Wisconsin; don't you? We lived there when I was just a wee tot and before we moved to Seattle, to escape the cold, I guess. You know what they say about Wisconsin? They say, 'Many are cold but few are frozen.' When you go outside in January and the temperature is minus ten degrees and it hurts your throat to breathe, you think, 'Man, I could die out here!' We lived in Milwaukee. Bowling and beer were a lifestyle there. They went together like a horse and carriage."

"What would these stereotyped Wisconsinites say if they heard you talking like that?"

"I'm certain they'd be okay with it as long as they know I'm a Green Bay Packers fan. But you're right. Wisconsin is more than beer and bowling and the Packers. Make it bowling and beer, Green Bay Packers, and cheese. They go together like a team of four horses pulling a stage coach, or like Polish sausage in a smorgasbord at a German wedding."

"I never would have thought you were the kind of guy who thinks in stereotypes."

"You're right. I shouldn't stereotype. Not all Wisconsinites like snowmobiling and hunting. You can find some who love to dance and to sing. I once knew a lady who blew the trumpet like nobody's business. It's true that Wisconsinites aren't all like each other, except for one thing. Each and every one of them has shoveled snow at least once in their lives.

"My parents are bowlers. There is something wonderfully powerful about rolling a heavy ball and knocking down all ten pins. My parents enjoy that. Maybe it makes them feel . . . super." He raised his eyebrows.

"So right now your parents are where?"

"Knocking down pins. They're in their late seventies, and they do what they want. I'm pretty sure that when they die it will be a bowling accident. Sometimes I amuse myself by thinking about what that might be." He smiled. "Right now they're in Wisconsin visiting friends, but they'll come back here before the Wisconsin turf freezes."

"So they live here with you?"

"Yes, but only when they want to."

They sat and sipped coffee and began to eat their truffles. Israel's chest began to hurt again, but not severely. *Ibuprofen works pretty well against pain. What's the real reason I take hydrocodone?*

Professor Hannity said, "If spacetime is particulate, made up of all these minuscule units of spacetime, then maybe there is something between the units, something in which the particles float, but we have to be careful about such a thought, because that's a spacetime concept, and we're talking about something outside of material spacetime. Is there something that resides beyond the realm of material space and time, and do particles of spacetime flow within it?

"There are some clues. When we look at sound emitted or reflected from turbulent water at the bottom of a waterfall, the sound waves are all broken up and scattered. This happens because sound moves through the medium of the water, and so turbulence of water in a waterfall breaks up the sound.

"We used to think light was different. We thought light could travel in a vacuum of continuous space; it didn't require a physical medium for it to travel, and so it was independent and unaffected by any such turbulence in the physical world. But then some upstart astronomers discovered that around structures of tremendous gravity, like stars and black holes, light signals get broken up just like sound gets broken at the bottom of a waterfall. So I'm telling you that these tiny units of spacetime are able to flow something like water. Admittedly spacetime particles do cling together. They flow sort of like almost-solidified Jell-O. The question is this. If they flow, is there something in which they are flowing? Is there something between the particles?"

"Is there?"

The professor nodded. "It's pretty much like raw energy, or it is made of particles that are way smaller than we can measure, and at this level the universe might indeed be continuous, at the level of universe beyond spacetime. Mystics call it spirit. Some call it the Akashic record. A lot of physicists call it the bantering and wishful thinking of an old crap. Ahem, carp!" He sipped his coffee. "The old crap-carp is me. But these same scientists also talk about dark energy that accounts for seventy-four percent of the universe's mass energy. We've never actually observed dark energy. We suspect it's there because of how the universe behaves, but it's hidden away from us, out of sight. Take it from me on this one. The difference between scientists and mystics on this issue is mainly semantics and approach, mathematics and philosophy. Thank you for the truffles. I never get tired of Ephemere."

"So you're a scientist who believes in spirit?"

"Call it whatever you like. Call it spirit if you want. Some smug pseudo-scientists call it crap. They call me an old carp. So maybe it's just crap from a carp," he chuckled. "Call it what you want, but it's there. The energy is there."

"Does this energy interact with spacetime?"

"It is the energy bank that feeds the quantum wave nature of particulate spacetime."

"Um . . ." Israel drew a blank. He asked, "So it does interact?"

"Yes, it does, but in all honesty we are talking mostly philosophy in this realm that is beyond our technological ability to test scientifically. This realm is beyond spacetime, smaller than particles of spacetime, between them, interwoven within them. Spacetime does not move. It is solid like a block of wood. The smaller particles form structures that you have liked to call spirits, and these move. They move along the space axis of time, and they read the changes between one moment and the next. They constitute consciousness. Without movement there is no consciousness, and these so-called spirits are the entities that move."

"You're telling me that you have found a way to prove that there is a spirit world, and you can describe it, and this isn't making headlines all over the world? This is monumental!"

"No, it's the bantering and wishful thinking of an old carp . . . with Tourette's syndrome."

"But you've got the mathematics to show it."

"Most of them."

"Most of them? You're planning to send me on a spiritual time travel wild goose chase, and all you've got is some of the mathematics?"

"Well, you know: nothing ventured, nothing gained."

"This is my life we're talking about."

"It's safe."

"With only some of the mathematics it's safe?"

"Yes, it is. I'll show it to you first with my pet rabbit if you want, Fuzzball. I'll show it to you with myself. I've done it before. It will be a blink of an eye and I'll be back, because I'll return to exactly the same point in time that I left. It will seem like I haven't even been gone at all."

"You have a pet rabbit named Fuzzball?"

"No, I was lying."

"What does James Clerk Maxwell have to do with all this?"

"Maxwell? Not much, except let me tell you something spooky about one of his discoveries. Nobody ever has found a mistake in his mathematics about light, by the way. He showed mathematically that light has another component that has been ignored for the most part, because nobody understands it. He showed there was an advanced wave of light that travels backward in time. It gets to its destination before it is emitted from its light source. Fathom that!"

"It goes backward in time?"

"And at the level of the universe beyond spacetime, at the so-called spiritual level, this consciousness is not confined to the unidirectional character of observed spacetime. It can go either forward or backward, unrestrained."

"Damn!"

"Most physicists are compelled by the comprehensive studies of Richard Feynman showing that light moving backward in time probably has to do with antimatter electrons."

"You're going to make me into antimatter to send me backward in time?"

Michael laughed. "The neighbors wouldn't like that. It would be an explosion like the end of the world."

"Yes, I'm feeling really safe right now."

Michael looked squarely at Israel, and in the meeting of each other's gaze, Israel once again noticed the tiny heart-shaped fleck of blue at the bottom of Michael's left rust-colored eye.

Michael said, "This is not about turning you into antimatter. This is about something that is not matter at all. It is outside the world of space, and it's outside the world of time. It just is. And since there is no time in this world where you are going, you will be able to select . . . " He stopped. "You will be able to encounter any location in the entire history of space and time, past present or future."

"This is god-like."

Michael nodded and shrugged his shoulders in a gesture that revealed not just a curious combination of his pride and humility, but also of his awe for the universe, both what he knew of it and what he did not. "Maybe."

"And I'm not supposed to be scared?"

"Okay, be scared, but mystics have been saying for millennia that they do this very same thing using meditation. I've just made it easier."

"How?"

"Do you meditate?"

"I used to meditate a lot."

"Good. That will make this all that much easier. The body has electrical polarities. Different parts of it are positive or negative relative to its other parts, and these polarities change amplitude with different states of consciousness. These changes are subtle but easily measurable."

"Like a lie detector."

"You say the damnedest things sometimes. Yes, it's like a lie detector but much, much more sophisticated. If that's how you must think about it, then it's a very sophisticated and expensive lie detector that measures your state of consciousness. And it interacts with it. When your state of consciousness reaches a threshold of readiness, the time machine submits the subtlest of changes in the electrical polarities of your body."

"It electrocutes me."

"God Almighty, Israel. Will you just listen?"

"I'm not as scared when I make light of it. You're going to have to learn how to get along with your test pilot. This is my way of coping, Michael. By the way, 'God Almighty?' You are a spiritualist, aren't you?"

"I'm a Jew. I'm not orthodox. Science is my way of studying God. Can we go on now? These subtle changes in the electrical polarities of your body make it uncomfortable for the consciousness to remain in the body. It doesn't exactly get booted out, but it decides to leave of its own accord. It joins the mother energy of the universe."

"What kind of changes does the time machine make?"

"What normally is slightly positive is made slightly negative by the most miniscule of amplitudes."

"Okay, so then I'll be freefalling in an ocean of dark energy, and how do I get to where I'm going?"

"That, my friend, is what will make you an explorer of the highest order. I want you to help me learn exactly that. You will figure it out."

"I'm being thrown to the wolves! How do I get back again? How do I find my way back into my own body?"

"After your consciousness has left, the time travel machine detects that, and immediately it reverses polarities again and makes your body most attractive to your consciousness. It is a beacon that will guide you back."

"Won't other consciousnesses want to enter my body?"

"Your consciousness is like a fingerprint. There is no other like it. At the particular now-moment you leave, you also will return. You alone. Other consciousnesses within your body would choose different now-moments."

"This is scary."

The professor nodded nonchalantly. "And yet it is very safe. It's not really anything new at all. It's very much like meditative escape from ego. I've just made it easier." He squared himself toward Israel and put his hands on the upper arms of his young apprentice. "Legato! Your name describes the continuous energy within which you will travel to different places of the staccato, particulate, material spacetime of our universe."

Markus.

"May I see your laboratory?

Nine

THE NOW-BEACON HELMET

Climbing stairs to the mansion's second floor and feeling the sharp crescendo sting in his right chest, Israel put his left hand into his front pants pocket to remind himself of the security promised by the bottle of hydrocodone.

They entered a room that sang the music of Mozart, a room clad in a bank of electronic instrumentation along one wall, lights and screens, a community of interconnected computers. At the center of the room was an overstuffed recliner on top of which rested a yellow helmet with a large green *G* on either side of it. Dozens of wires emerged from different sites on the helmet, and they were tied together into a long Rapunzel braid leading to the electronic wall.

Music played softly.

Michael remarked, "In this room there is never-ending Mozart. He never dies, you know." He walked over to the chair in the center of the room and with an air of reverence hoisted the helmet. "This once belonged to Paul Hornung. I paid a pretty price for it." He put it on his head, and then he put a wired strap around each of his wrists and ankles. Up from the floor he picked up a remote control. After collapsing into the recliner, he paused and looked around the room and then stood again. "Just a moment." He removed the helmet and wrist bands and directed Israel's attention to a drawer in a long counter at the side of the room opposite the electronic wall. "Top left; there's a green jersey in there. Fetch it for me."

Israel brought a Green Bay Packer jersey sporting the number five to Michael who, after pulling it over his head and reattaching the wrist bands and donning the helmet, chirped, "I'll be back in a moment." He pushed a button on a remote control, and a soft hum played from the electronic bank. He closed his eyes and remained silent.

Israel watched.

After about ten minutes there erupted a quiet buzz and then a ringing like the sound of a dinner bell. Michael opened his eyes, sat up, and looked at Israel. "You still here?" He chuckled. "It seems as though I've been gone quite a while. I've just lived a segment of a life somewhere else and in some other time."

"How do you know?"

"Snippets. I remember snippets, but that's all. I wish I could remember more about the back seat of that car." He raised his eyebrows. "Then there was a kiss, and I went off to war. Don't remember much about that, but I think that was the end of it." He paused with furrowed brow. "And now I'm here again. What do you think?"

"This is weird."

Michael sighed. "Yes, it certainly is."

"May I try?"

"Be my ghost."

Israel stared at him.

"Just kidding," said Michael. "Be my guest." What happens is the helmet and straps measure electrical parameters of your brain and body. They give micro-current electrical feedback that helps you relax in a meditative sort of way, and when the time is right it boots your energy right the hell out of there. Then at the very next instant, it calls your energy back."

"How do I know where I'm going and how to get there?"

"Just think about what you want, where you want to go. Maybe you'll get lucky."

"Is this like I'm a body snatcher? Am I going to be stealing somebody else's body?"

"No, not at all. Remember, 'My Father's house has many mansions in it.' You're not going to steal anybody's body. You're merely going to be sharing it with them, separated, of course, into a different time capsule, so to speak, a miniscule fraction of a second away from the other spirits."

Israel stared at him.

"Look," said Professor Hannity. "It's no different than what's happening in your own body right now."

"Holy Christ!"

"Okay, I'm a Jew, remember? But that being said, yes, Holy Christ indeed!"

Israel looked at the inside of the helmet. The padding was stained with water marks. *Paul Hornung's sweat!* He put the helmet on his head. Ear pads filtered out the sounds of the room. Professor Hannity put the cuffs on Israel's wrists and ankles, making sure that the little embedded metal disks were on the palm side of his wrists and on the midline side of his ankles, and then Michael held up a sign that read Sweet Dreams.

Israel tried to relax, at first hampered by a tremble of excitement, but it subsided. He tried the meditation technique of focusing on one part of his body at a time and then forgetting it, first his legs, then his arms, then his head, finally his heartbeat. When he no longer felt attachment to his body, all there seemed to be of the world was a soft hum inside the helmet, and he focused on that. Time seemed to pass.

He fell asleep.

The professor awakened him. "Too much wine," he said. "Too much wine to travel in time; too much wine to drive a car. You can stay in a guest room, and we'll have another go at it in the morning."

The next morning Israel awakened early with the right side of his chest scolding its very existence, reminding him of bruised ribs he had sustained in high school football. For the moment his pain was tolerable, the excitement of what was about to happen suppressing at least the hurt of it. Reaching toward the bottle of hydrocodone on the bedside table but not wanting to spoil his chances at time travel, he realized it would be a balancing act, how much analgesic medicine to take. Pain would distract him from his meditation, but too much medicine would dull his mental clarity, and he might fall asleep again. He took half a tablet and then showered.

Down in the kitchen he found cereal and orange juice, and after a sugar-poison breakfast he climbed the stairs again to the Mozart laboratory.

Michael was sitting in lotus position, meditating, quietly intoning his unusual mantra. "Shi-i-i-i-i-i-i-i-it. Shi-i-i-i-i-i-i-i-it. Shi-i-i-i-i-i-i-i-it."

Israel waited until Michael was finished and then cheerfully greeted him. "Good morning, Dr. Hannity."

Michael nodded. "Good morning, Dr. Newman. Did you sleep well?"

"Yes, I did. Why do you use 'shit' for a mantra, may I inquire?"

"Sometimes it makes sense to accept who you are. I'm embracing my inner Tourette's. You've got to know when and where to do that sort of thing. If you fart around a campfire, then the whole world farts with you. Fart in synagogue, and you'll have a pew to yourself." He smiled. "Are you ready to travel in time?"

"Yes, I am."

Israel donned the gear and again meditated. *Escape ego.* It did not take long. There was a soft buzz and a bell ringing, and he was wide awake staring at the ceiling. He sat up and looked at the professor. "Where am I? Was that it?" He felt dumbfounded.

"What do you remember?" Michael asked excitedly.

Images erupted within Israel's mind, memories. "Oh, my God!" He waited as the realization congealed. "I don't remember much, but there are some things. I remember riding in a train, an old fashioned train with a steam engine. Smoke billowed out all over the place, and we rode over a trestle bridge. On the far side of it and on our right we passed by a plantation. That was my home. I owned slaves!" A look of horror stopped his talking for a moment. "Oh, no!" He closed his eyes in reflex, not able to shut out from his vision a gruesome memory. Words thickened in his dry mouth, mechanical impedance to match the friction in his consciousness. Why did he feel such oppressive guilt? Wouldn't sadness be enough? No, because it was him. He had been himself, and there was no way of divorcing his conscience from it. "I was in a barn," he whispered, "and one of my slaves, a woman, was angry and coming after me. I had had relations with her, and she was pregnant. Oh, my God! Michael, I don't know if I can do this. I don't know if I can even say this."

Michael put his hand on Israel's shoulder. "It's okay. There have been all varieties of happenings in the history of humankind, both good and bad. You've read enough, haven't you, to know that Emerson's Over-Soul has been bloodied mercilessly in every generation? Don't put a millstone around your neck by thinking you can change all of that. Are you God? No. You are not God. The past was then, and the past still is, and it forever will be. It doesn't change. You lived what you were given to live." With a gentler voice than Israel could remember ever having heard before, Michael reassured him, "You can tell me what happened, Israel. I won't dislike you for it."

Israel closed his eyes and rocked backward. "I stabbed her in the belly with a pitchfork. I killed her."

"Cockshitfuck."

"What?"

"Oh, I was just saying that's really something, a bad trip, you know?" Michael looked up at the ceiling and then back at Israel. He put a hand on his shoulder. "What a blasted shitty kicker for the first experience. Better luck next time. You know what I mean?"

"I want to be able to control it better." Israel felt tears welling in his eyes. "I need to go back to Markus and hold onto him. I don't know if I can do this again."

"It will take practice, but not a lot of practice. It will come to you. Be patient."

"Michael, was I there for only those few scenes I remember? I remember only bits and pieces, but was it just for that short time, or was I there longer, like years or a lifetime?"

"I don't know. It sounds to me like you probably were in it for a little while, anyway, and then something booted your spirit out of it, maybe the anguish you felt about the murder."

"Murder, Michael! It was murder. Forever I'll remember this blood on my hands. This is horrible, scary."

"Don't be scared. You've discovered something about eternity and your involvement in it. There will be good moments too."

"When will I be the woman whose belly I just stabbed?"

"I don't know that you ever will be her."

"But that's karma, isn't it? I deserve it."

"Deserve? No. You don't deserve it, not any more than she did. Nobody deserves it. You will learn that your spirit is not the same as the material body it inhabits. If you study it you'll find people disagree on this point and argue a lot about it, but I can tell you what is consistent with your experience. This is the hard problem of trying to answer what consciousness is. I'm sure in your studies of biology and medicine you've been taught that the mind is a function of the physical brain, and we just have to figure it out. The promise is that someday we will. I'm going to give you a different perspective, not inconsistent with the mind and brain being the same thing, just a different perspective. If you don't understand it today, you're going to understand it later. Okay?"

Michael waited for Israel to answer, but he didn't. "Are you following me on this? Do you want me to tell you what's going on?"

"I want to know how you can say I don't deserve it."

"We'll get there, my man."

"Aren't you at a place where you say cock-shit-fuck or some such?"

"I don't do that much when I'm fully in my own element, Israel." Michael rubbed his hands together thoughtfully, searching for the right words, trying to be the voice of God. "You already know that the past still exists and the future already exists; they coexist."

"Okay."

"That means the physical world is static; it doesn't change. Each now-moment is completely still, motionless. But. Each motionless now-moment is just a little bit different than the one preceding it, and it's a little bit different from the one that follows it, even though each now-moment is completely motionless. What we've been calling spirit is something that moves through time, and by moving through time it gives us an illusion that the material world is moving. It is composed of a substance so small we can't measure it, so of course people without imagination refuse to consider that it even exists. They limit themselves to the boundaries of technology. But this movement of whatever it is we call spirit, through the dimension of time, is what causes consciousness. Whatever it is, it reads the differences between one now-moment and the next, and that is consciousness. Think of it like a player piano reading the holes in a roll by which it plays music, or a music box. Think of old movies made with film, pictures one at a time, shown in sequence so fast that we see an illusion of movement, but each picture is completely still. Do you understand what I'm telling you? Don't make the mistake of thinking your spirit actually causes events happening in the material world. It only reads them, registers them. How can you blame your spirit for reading an evil story it had nothing to do with writing?"

"I've got to think about this."

"Yes; we both do; me too."

"I've got to go now. Thank you for talking me down."

"It has been my pleasure. Thank you for listening."

Ten

GINA

The sun still was ascending the morning sky when Israel left the professor's house.

Michael said, "See you tonight at support group." While Israel nodded, Michael added, "Maybe it's best that we not say anything about all of this. We might get expelled."

"Yeah, I was thinking the same thing. They're going to ask about moving mountains, though. And I can't be talking about murdering a pregnant woman with a pitchfork."

"You'll think of something to say."

"Yes, something to do with brain games and craziness. I have no idea what I'll tell them."

A clear sky welcomed him as he drove past Kerry Park on Highland Drive, and Israel appreciated Mount Rainier's splendor. Tahoma peak asserted its existence where it was supposed to be, on the left; all was correct in the moment. He drove home.

He sat down to his computer and signed on to Facebook. There was a friend request from Gina Provetti and a message. *Hi. I'm not your nurse anymore. I like you. And I'm angry about it because this isn't what is supposed to happen, but it's real, and I'm not denying it. There is something about it that's causing me to break rules, and you had better respect that, Doctor Newman. I'm counting on you to treat me right, and then the anger will dissipate. I'm not angry at you. I'm angry at God for allowing this to happen, but I'm also in love with God. Both. My mother taught me that knowledge sometimes comes to us without having been invited. We recognize something truthful within us even though we have no idea how that knowledge occurred. We can't explain it.*

Israel typed a response. *I like you too, a lot. And I can't explain it either. Things happen.*

He accepted her friend request, and then, while he was reading posts, the chat window popped up. *How's your chest?* It was Gina.

Hurts like hell, but I'm managing. How's yours?

Do you really want to go there? That was quickly followed by *I mean is that really what you want to talk about?*

Sort of. The wait for her response was a little bit longer than he would have liked and made him wonder if he'd gone too far with the flirt.

There's no pain in my chest, she wrote.

Israel wondered if she might be annoyed with him.

She was writing more, and then her message posted. *No lumps. No axillary nodes. Pretty!* A pause and then she wrote, *Something's come up, and maybe you'd like to see a play with me.* Wicked. *It's at the Paramount, but you have to decide fast, because my tickets are for tonight.*

Instantly he decided to skip his psychology support group that evening because he damned sure wasn't going to miss an opportunity to spend time with this beautiful woman. He typed, *Who got sick?*

That's for me to know and you to find out.

Yes, I'd like to go.

It must hurt to drive a car, so I'll pick you up. I'll come early and we can eat dinner at Ayutthaya. It's close to the Paramount. You do like Thai, don't you?

Yes, very much.

Good, because that could have been a deal breaker.

I would have learned to like it.

Gotta go.

They exchanged addresses and agreed on a time. Israel signed off Facebook. He looked around at his house and decided that for a guy's house it wasn't terribly messy, but the thought struck him that she wanted to pick him up just to uncover how much of a pig he might be. *She wants to see my digs. The pig's digs!* Despite the pain in his chest he was going to clean house. He swallowed a tablet of hydrocodone and two of ibuprofen, waited fifteen minutes for the medicine to start working, and then tackled the chore of making his home most sparklingly presentable to Gina. Clearly the bathroom had to be spotless, had to gleam. She might never go there, but she might. Other than that it was a matter of washing dishes and picking up. Anything that didn't have a defined place he would throw into a back room where nobody ever needed to go; nobody needed to know the room even existed.

Cleaning the bathroom tortured him. As excruciating as it was to scrub using his right arm, he tried scrubbing with his left, and though it hurt less, it took longer, and he didn't have time. He found himself sitting on the floor, slumped against a wall, and looking upward.

It stared at him.

Damned safety bar!

Washing dishes also tested his pain tolerance. Another hydrocodone and two more ibuprofen made him sleepy, dulled his enthusiasm, and he decided to let it rest, let the house show itself for what he was. *The pig's digs.* He invigorated himself with a shower, protecting the wound by standing sideways and covering it with a plastic seal. He shaved with splendid, awkward technique. For the most part he held the razor still in his right hand, supporting it with his left hand on his right elbow, and he dragged his face across the blades by turning his head. He nicked himself a couple of times before recalling he wanted to maintain range of motion of his shoulder. *This is my physical therapy session.* He forced himself to shave normally, with winces. Shaving became for him like a hike up an icy mountain. *I can do this.*

He donned his shirt by putting his right arm through its sleeve first, knowing he wouldn't tolerate donning his right arm second.

He looked at the clock. Gina was five minutes late at a time he realized he needed to relieve himself on the toilet. He pulled down his pants and sat down. The doorbell rang! After wiping himself hurriedly with his left hand and then pulling his clothes together, he was washing his hands when the doorbell rang again. "I'm almost there," he shouted and then gasped from a flash of lightning in his chest. When he answered the door, the left side front of his shirt was untucked.

Gina was stunningly gorgeous. He hadn't imagined her wearing lipstick or heels or a leather jacket or fitted jeans.

"Hi, Gina. Would you like to come in?"

"Yes, I would, but not for very long; we don't have a lot of time. Besides, you're a man, and I already know you need to hire a maid service. Tuck in your shirt, and no, I'm not going to help you. I'm not your nurse anymore." She smiled and put her hand on his chest. "You're wearing the cross I gave you."

"Yes, thank you for that. Your gift sits over my heart."

She patted his chest. "Maybe just slightly too romantic at the moment. Things get connected, don't they, Israel? Don't forget your jacket," she said. "It's getting chilly."

She drove a pristinely clean Toyota Corolla. It rode smoothly and was quiet.

Her perfume stirred feelings inside of him, a wave of emotion, a slight tremble, a sexual arousal, something familiar but entirely new. He could feel her even though they were not touching. Perfume or not, he would feel this way. *Things get connected, don't they, Israel?*

"You look great, Gina. Beautiful."

She turned to look at him. "Thank you." She almost laughed. *Those lips!*

"I very much like your fragrance. What is it?"

"You really are a guy, aren't you? Maybe if we're still holding it together after a sixth date, I'll tell you so you can give it to me for Christmas. And then again, maybe not. Maybe I'll never tell you; you never can tell. There are everyday fragrances, and I guess I wouldn't mind you knowing what I wear for everyday. But if I wear a distinctive fragrance for special occasions, that might be a mystery you'll never solve."

"Special occasions?"

They were silent for a minute, and then Gina asked, "Do you know anything about *Wicked*?"

"It's about the Wicked Witch of the West, isn't it? From *The Wizard of Oz*."

"Yes, from her point of view. I read the book, and I've been looking forward to seeing this musical. Everybody says it's fantastic. I'm pretty certain it's mainly entertainment, but if there's a message in it, then I guess it would be that whatever looks benevolent on first glance might not be benevolent. And whatever seems wicked on first glance might not be wicked. It's about appreciating people for who they really are instead of what they seem to be."

How does a woman drive a car with high heels?

Ayutthaya was perched on the southwest corner of Pike and Harvard, just a block west of Broadway. It had started as a hole in the wall, one of the first Thai restaurants in the city, with food so delicious that for the first year after it opened people would wait in lines out the door. Gradually the décor became more upscale, with wooden paneling and three small chandeliers with alabaster glass, but the place remained quaint. Now that Thai restaurants had sprung up all over the city, a table usually was available without a wait. There was a small parking lot in back, but the hill was steep.

How does a woman walk downhill in high heels?

She seemed to read his mind. "Strong legs," she said. "A girl's got to bend her knees more when she walks downhill in heels." She looked askance at him. "It also takes flexibility."

Was that a flirt?

Almost immediately after they sat down, a small bowl of soup was set in front of them.

Gina ordered a Singha. So did Israel.

"You like beer," he observed.

"Yes. Only with Asian food, though, light beer. Otherwise I prefer wine."

"You know this place," he said. "How about you order for us?"

The beer came. Gina ordered pad thai with shrimp and a two-star-spicy Thai special salad, a cooked salad of green beans, chicken, and peanut sauce.

As they looked at each other, their pupils got slightly larger, their hearts beat slightly faster.

Gina asked, "What do you like to do in your spare time?"

"You mean when I'm not getting shot in the chest? I'm a time travel pilot." He chuckled and watched her beautiful face patiently waiting for him to say something more meaningful. *Don't tell her about that.*

"I like to write, for fun mainly, for myself, and also I'm thinking about writing a book on back pain." He waited for Gina to reply, but she smiled at him and waited quietly.

He said, "This past summer I did a lot of hiking at Mount Rainier. Usually . . . I used to go with other people, but the last two years I've mostly hiked alone. There's something about being alone in all that vastness. I've done a lot of thinking up there." Without knowing where the words came from, he said, "Sometimes when the path is narrow, with a wall of granite on one side and a steep precipice on the other, you think about how your legs aren't as certain as they'd been a decade ago. Maybe you look back at where you've been, and you know you're not returning, so you move ahead mindfully, not worried so much about a misstep and fatal fall, but enthusiastically interested in what meadow of flowers may await you around the bend."

Gina and Israel looked at each other quietly.

"Of course on the main trails you meet people all the time and talk. They come from all over. Every time I go there I see something new. The mountain keeps surprising me." He thought he saw Gina glance at his lips and then back to his eyes.

"You seem like a social guy," she said.

He nodded. "I also like theater. Thank you for inviting me."

She looked pleased.

He asked, "What do you like to do?"

"Different things. I like to have fun, and I don't mean that in a frivolous way. Fun often requires planning, and I don't want to ruin my future by being stupid about it. There are so many people who are just plain unhappy, and I'm not going to be one of them. I can feel sorry for them, sure, and I can help them, yes, but I don't have to be one of them. Does that make any sense?" She leaned slightly closer toward him. "I give money to charity and I volunteer sometimes, but I don't get involved in causes much. That's my mother; she does that over and over again. She says she doesn't want to be a person who weeds her garden once and then thinks the job is done. I'm glad she and other people do that, but it's not me; it's not what I do." She sat backward with an abrupt smile. "I believe God wants me to be happy, darn it. Somebody has to be happy, for God's sake. I think being happy is a way of being nice to God, so I do things to have fun." She giggled. "And I knit."

"You knit?"

"Yes. It's cuddly, you know. And it's creative and colorful, and it goes well with watching movies at home." She asked, "Have you ever gone on that giant slingshot ride at the Puyallup Fair? It's awesome! I did it this year. You've got to try it. Wow! Put it on your list of things to do. What kind of music do you like?"

"All kinds, as long as it's good."

"That's a cliché answer," she teased. "Everybody says that. Do you have an iPod?"

"I've been thinking about getting one."

"Catch up with the times, handsome. What CD do you have in your car right now?"

"I've got a six-CD changer. Rock and pop mostly, but a little of everything. Beatles, Led Zeppelin, Rush, Rodrigo y Gabriela. I've got a more classical bent, too. I like Yoyo Ma. How's that? What kind of music do you like?"

"A little bit of everything, as long as it's good. Okay, so I'm a cliché answerer too. I like classic rock, lots of different things. Carole

King, Pink Martini, The Celtic Women; sometimes I like soft and beautiful. Luther Vandross! Nobody sings like Luther Vandross. What's in my car right now? Paul McCartney. I like him because he's both masculine and sensitive, has a sense of humor, and he's deep. I like that. And he loved Linda so much, remember? I think he got into a mess with Heather, but with Linda, they had something special. Someday I'd like to have something special like that."

"My ever-present past," Israel said. "If I only had one love, yours would be the one I'd choose. Do you think he was talking to Heather in that song? The ghost of Linda! Or go back a few years; remember his song "Wanderlust?" I bet there were struggles between him and Linda too, but they stuck it out. That's the thing. They stuck it out." Israel locked on Gina's eyes for a moment. "Listen to this." He smiled. "This is precious. My brother's daughter, she was only two years old at the time, and right after my brother and his wife went to a Paul McCartney concert, my niece says, 'Paw Cotny cute.' So where did she get that? From her mother, of course. Women bequeath their Paul McCartney infatuation to their daughters; it gets handed down from one generation to the next. It's almost a genetic thing, a genetic attraction. I guess that's part of what makes him a legend. Sometimes I think every female in the world is infatuated with Paul McCartney."

"Maybe." She almost sang it, and then with a stricter voice she announced, "Except Heather Mills."

"Except Heather Mills." Israel found comfort thinking that even a man as attractive as Paul McCartney could run into marital problems.

A moment passed, and then he said, "There's no way anyone could compete with the greatest songwriter who ever lived, but if it's masculine and sensitive and deep that you want, lots of men could play that role. I could play that role."

"I know. That's why I asked you out."

They looked at each other.

The food came and they shared it, got silly, and fed each other with chopsticks.

Walking to the car afterward, Israel took Gina's left hand with his right. It was his painful arm, but he wanted to walk between Gina and the street, to be a gentleman. He opened her car door for her.

They drove the short distance to the Paramount Theatre on the corner of Pine Street and Ninth Avenue. "We could have walked," Gina said.

"Yes, but then your car would have been towed."

"That wouldn't have been so great, huh?"

They laughed.

The Paramount Theatre enshrined a colorful portion of Seattle history. Its construction had been funded by Paramount Pictures. The Rapp brothers designed it, and it first opened its doors on March 1, 1928. It was intended for showing movies and vaudeville. It was remotely located some distance away from the main theater district at the time on Second Avenue, so the team of investors countered the disadvantage by constructing the largest, most spectacular and opulent movie palace Seattle had ever seen. The golden walls and ceiling were intricately and lavishly decorated.

The seats were comfortable enough but without enough leg room for Israel, who was forced pleasantly to decide whether to sit with his knees pressed against the seat in front of him or to let his left leg relax toward Gina's. Partway through the first act their legs touched, and then Israel pressed his leg gently against hers. Gina pressed her leg hard against his, and she put her hand on his thigh. He put his hand on her hand. Their legs relaxed.

Wicked entranced its audience. At the end of it Gina said, "It's happier than the book and not as complex, but it really couldn't be as complex in just a couple of hours. I think they did a good job of implying complexity. It's like a first date." She laughed. "Implied complexity."

They got into the car, and Israel waited for Gina to look at him, and then he quickly and softly kissed her lips.

"Oh, Israel." She smiled.

She drove him home and walked with him to the door of his house.

He asked her, "Are you coming in? We could get wicked ourselves."

"No, not yet."

"Why did you walk me to the door then?"

She kissed him. They kissed for a long time, at first gently, moving their lips and softly sucking. She nipped him, and the kiss became passionate. They pressed against each other, and their teeth bumped. Time stood still.

Gina broke away. "Call me. Don't wait very long to do it." She looked at his lips and kissed them again for just a couple of seconds, and then she turned and ran to her car.

How does a woman run in high heels?

Eleven

WHERE HAVE YOU BEEN?

srael went to his computer, logged on to Facebook, and sent a private message to Gina. *Awesome evening. Thank you. Sweet dreams.*

There was a message from Michael. *Where have you been? People asked about you at group. I had a hard time shutting up. Are you okay?*

Israel answered. *Yes, I'm okay, except I think I'm falling in love. With Gina, that Italian nurse at Harborview who looks like a model. I don't want to fall in love.* He logged out.

He sat back in his chair and stared at the computer screen. *Markus!* With softly sonorous sobs he wept.

Grief distinguishes itself from depression in several ways. It assaults its victims in episodes, harassing them with abrupt, unexpected challenges to their feelings of cheerful normalcy, plunging them into agony, and then it relents for a while. At first grief's campaigns against the soul seem to endure forever, separated by only brief, tantalizing periods of optimism about the chance of becoming happy again. Gradually over time grief decides to attack less frequently, as though it gets bored with itself, or maybe its victims learn to construct barriers and detours around deep emotional regions of their minds. Grief's episodes shrink, and normal periods lengthen, but grief never completely relinquishes its purchase. It never goes completely away and may assail a mind's decorum unexpectedly even years later. Every time it ravages a soul it brandishes its ferocity with intensity equal to the very first time.

What triggered his grief this time? Was it the depth of a life murdered, followed closely thereafter by the passionate emotional peak triggered on his date with Gina, left lonely after her departure? Israel felt as though his life could crumble at any moment, like Mount Tahoma, an unstable volcanic remnant of a greater mountain. After the tears stopped he wrote a poem.

particulate reality!
a nodular complexity
of energy that's bound,
and when it breaks my soul and heart,
and when my mind's bereft, apart,
where is the schism found?
where is the break in who i am?
in spirit deep or in the man?
and how can i rebound?
if broken man, could i exchange?
if broken spirit, rearrange?
a tragedy profound!
can i as mass, as man survive?
can i as spirit yet revive?
can i again be sound?

Reading through the poem a few times, he regarded it too cerebral. *I should have poured out my guts. This sounds like a philosophical hypothesis. Why the hell is that? It's a crappy poem, not my best effort at writing.*

He saved it to read another time.

The right side of his chest ached and pierced like a biting drill, and the skin felt scalded. He swallowed a tablet of hydrocodone, and, knowing it was unwise, he also poured himself some tequila and went to bed.

He fell asleep quickly, after just his second sip of tequila, and at some time during the long night, at some location in the vast depths of his consciousness, he found himself crawling on his belly through a narrow tunnel, leading his family away from Nazis, hiding from them. He was given only a glimpse of that tale, for his dream did not recall the music recitals and the parties, the hikes in the woods. It did not recall for him the love he had made with his wife, the mother of their two children, all of whom were hiding with him in the tunnel. Together.

The dream abruptly ended when Nazis discovered them and burned a fire at the mouth of the tunnel, consuming all their oxygen with its flames. Smoke wafted into the tunnel, suffocating them, and there, in the tunnel in his dream, Israel died with his family. At the very end he heard a peep, like the sound of a smoke detector when its battery has gotten weak, and the peep awoke him. Unlike his usual response to nightmares, after which he often awakened cold, sweaty, and anxious, this time he was calm and dry, but also sorrowful and lonely. He looked at his bedside clock. It was 3:16 in the morning.

He wanted to get up for a cup of water, but pain in his chest immobilized him. *Dear God in heaven!* It pierced when he tried to sit up, stabbed when he attempted to roll over, and he could not tolerate rolling onto his right side. After he managed to roll onto his left side it was prohibitively painful to sit sideways up toward the right. *I'm stuck. Note to self: keep water and hydrocodone on the bedside table.*

His telephone rang across the room where it was plugged into its charger. *It's the middle of the night. Who in their right mind?* He ignored it and decided just to lie still for a while. *Go away, world.* He felt like the personification of a whimper. *This life!*

He managed to fall asleep again.

When he next awoke, his mind erupted with thoughts about the life he supposedly had visited while hooked up to Dr. Hannity's time machine. He had killed a pregnant woman. *God!* A tear formed at the corner of his left eye and then swelled over the brim of the lid and down his cheek. One thought connecting to another. He recalled a story his brother once told him, Jeff, who claimed to be psychic, a story about remembering a past life in which Jeff was a small boy, a slave, out in the fields picking cotton with his mother. *Jeff remembers!*

Israel needed to call Jeff, needed to get up out of bed. He prepared his tortured tissues by stretching, slowly reaching his right arm up over his head, and then out in front of him. This movement was tolerable if he did it slowly, and then, with his left hand he gently stroked and massaged the right side of his chest, trying to desensitize the complaining nerves, quiet their strident screams. After all that, and then a count to three, he pushed up onto his left elbow while doing his best to relax the right side of his body. He put his left leg out over the edge of the bed, shifted his weight a little, and pushed with his left hand. His body rocked upward. Voila! He sat upright. He scooted forward to the edge of the bed so that he could place his feet almost directly beneath him, and then he stood up without having to bend his torso. He walked to his hydrocodone bottle in the bathroom, swallowed one tablet, and looked in the mirror. *Good morning!*

He listened to the message on his phone. It was Michael Hannity urging him to come over and time travel. "Practice makes perfect."

Actually, thought Israel, *practice does not make perfect. Perfect practice does. That's from Vince Lombardi. Michael ought to know that.*

He called Jeff and got his answering service. He said, "Hi Jeff," trying to think how to phrase his question. "You know that story you once told me, your memory of a past life as a little slave boy? You told me spirits tend to stick together through many lives through the ages, and you told me it was our mom, yours and mine, her spirit that was in the slave woman you were with in that previous life. Do you remember that? I want to talk with you more about that. I've got questions. Give me a call, would you?"

He slumped with his eyes closed, fighting to keep his responses in check, struggling for shelter in an emotional storm that pelted him. *Deep breaths; thoughtless mind.* Moments passed, or were they minutes?

He went to his computer and opened up Facebook to write a message.

Gina, I'm messed up. Really I am, and I'm thinking I'm not ready for us. You're beautiful. You are so very beautiful, but I'm not ready to get close to anyone right now. Love has always demanded a little too much from me. He thought about whether he really wanted to use the word *love* in the note and decided to leave it in.

While Israel drove to Professor Hannity's home, his awareness once again was pinned by pain to a normal world focused on the ever-present now, normal but not normal, because however familiar the foreground of the experience appeared, it was displayed prominently against a dramatic backdrop of events about which he could not claim understanding. Proximity of pain and solid reality clutched him to the here and now, but he realized he could not deny another world existed. More than that, there were worlds without end, and he was connected to them.

Just as he pulled over to the curb in front of the mansion his cell phone alerted him. "Hello, Jeff?" he answered.

"Hey, Izzy, what's up?"

"Um . . ."

"Are you okay?"

"Yeah. Jeff, I'm okay. It's just that . . ."

"You don't sound okay."

"I'm okay, really. I'm fine." There was silence while Israel gathered his thoughts on how he wanted to ask his revealing question, and after a few seconds that seemed too long, finally he said, "Do you have any memories of past lives in Nazi Germany?"

"Where'd that come from? Are you suffering, Iz? It hasn't been that long since all the crap happened to you. I'll fly out there if you need me."

"You're always welcome, Jeff, but I'm okay, really. I'm just working through some stuff. No memories about living through the Holocaust?"

"No. Why are you thinking about the Holocaust?"

"Just a nightmare."

"Not all dreams are dreams, Izzy."

"Yeah. I'm starting to believe you about that."

"Ha! A convert."

"A convert."

"Why'd you ask about my previous life as a slave boy? Did you have a dream about that too?"

"No, that's not it. I was just wondering, you've told me souls tend to stick with each other through multiple lives. Was I in that life with you and Mom? Do you remember me in that one?"

"Oh God, Israel!" There was silence from Jeff's end.

"I was?"

"God! Israel, why do you think I never told you about that part of it?"

"I never asked."

"Yeah, and I was glad you never asked."

"I'm asking now."

Silence. "Yes. You were in that lifetime with Mom and me, sort of."

"Sort of?"

"Mom was murdered, Israel." Silence. "While she was pregnant with you; you died too, of course. You never got born that time, Iz."

"How'd she die? How was Mom murdered?"

"Don't know. I was just a little kid, and they wouldn't tell me; they protected me."

"But when you grew up you would have investigated."

"Probably. Don't remember that part. Israel? You okay?"

"Yes, I'm okay, Jeff. Just thinking about karma."

Twelve

A HAPPY DAY IN A LIFE

There was a new contraption on the wall beside the front door of Michael's mansion and a sign, "Ring the doorbell, and hope for the best. If you're Israel, press your thumb against the reader, and the door will open." He pressed his thumb against what looked like a tiny television screen. It turned green, and the door clicked.

The foyer was filled with music of the Beach Boys. "I wish they all could be California girls."

He stood awhile and listened, reassured there was happiness in the world, but happiness caused an ache in his heart, incongruent with losses he must endure. His eyes puddled, and when he closed them, a tear on each cheek streaked down to his chin, where they tickled, a familiar sensation, reminding him of all he knew in life that he cherished and all he knew that he mourned, and in the balance of it he realized he could not escape. Not even in death could he escape. *Life has no foreseeable ending.* Gina came into his mind, accompanied by hope that anything was possible, even Markus, and for the first time he recognized his feelings for these two people intersected, something he did not yet understand.

He climbed the stairs to the second floor laboratory with its eternal Mozart and found Professor Hannity at his desk studying a letter. Upon seeing Israel, he snapped the letter into its envelope and into the top drawer of his desk. "Good morning, sir," he said.

"Good morning to you."

"What a splendid morning for a jaunt in the past!"

Israel nodded and asked, "How do I go to a specific time and place? How do I go back to who I was in February a year and a half ago and change things? I want to save my son."

"The answer is that I don't know. If you did that, you maybe wouldn't come back here. By doing that you would branch off into another time thread."

"I figured as much. It would be a better time thread for me."

"I'd miss you."

"Yeah. I'd miss you too."

"No! Actually we won't miss each other because for me, your body will still be here with the same personality and all. I'll be hard pressed to recognize any difference. You won't miss me because when you do it, when you go there, you'll never meet me. There will be no painful separation from your son; no support group; no me."

Michael talked as though he knew it was going to happen. "What would happen to my body here then?"

"It will go on living. The energy source is infinite, or nearly so. There are 'spirits,'" he gestured with his fingers like quotation marks. "There are 'spirits' everywhere."

Israel sighed. "That's good."

"Do you want to get started?"

Michael strapped Israel's wrists and ankles, and Israel donned the helmet. It was with some trepidation that he meditated, this time keeping in his mind only the image of Markus; nothing else existed. There was a buzz and a ring, and the trip was complete, but within that infinitesimal stretch of time, between the heralding buzz of its beginning and the seemingly instantaneous ringing announcement of its finish, there could be inserted all of eternity, not that all of eternity had been inserted, but it could have been, and in that fragment of a moment the spirit of him, who in one world called himself Israel Newman, became a spirit of another, a young man who stood puzzled before a mirror in the morning.

I, Steven Connor, am twenty years old and just finishing my junior year at the University of Wisconsin in La Crosse, in the year 1973. I won't be drafted to fight in Vietnam because my birth date bestowed upon me the draft number of 332. There are so many my age who are being forced to go and risk their lives. Questions of moral purpose become more boldly expressed by those whose lives, or the lives of loved ones, are at stake. Anti-war demonstrations are happening all over the place.

Some of my friends decided they had to sign up voluntarily in order to have some choice about which branch of service they're going to be assigned.

I won't be going to Vietnam at all, don't have to delay the progress of my very well-planned life. Uncle Sam won't yank me out of school in the middle of a semester.

Today while looking in a mirror, a crazy thought comes to me about spirits. Having been brought up Lutheran, I know that Lutherans might like to talk about a soul that inhabits each person, but usually the pastors don't. Lutheran pastors are almost Catholic this way, although you can hardly tell by listening to them. There's a lover's spat between Lutherans and Catholics. Strictly speaking, to either a Catholic priest or a Lutheran pastor, Jesus arose bodily from the grave, and that is soul enough for them. There's nothing ephemeral about a soul. A soul just means a person, and that's all it means.

Maybe that's what the shepherds think, but it's not what their sheep think. We sheep who go "Bah," we believe in something spiritual, deep inside us, something that kind of drives the system. We're more than just bodies, and that thing inside us is a soul.

My reflection stares back at me from the smooth silvery surface of the mirror. How do I know the soul inside me today is the same soul who was in me yesterday? The brain is physical and goes on thinking the same thoughts it always thinks, and different souls can come and go as they please, can't they? And a guy will have no idea it's happening.

There's a jabbing pain on the right side of my chest, and then it's gone, except for a lingering tenderness, completely unexplainable. Where did that come from? A word jumps into my head, *Israel*. Goofy! Jews and Muslims! Ongoing tensions between Jews and Muslims in the Middle East. What do I know about that? Not much.

Christina Cantor comes to mind, my blond beauty! My heart flip-flops, and so does that little guy in my pants. All I have to do is think of her.

She's devoutly Catholic, and that's why I know quite a little bit about how Catholic all us Lutherans are. She's also earnestly private about things she regards intimate. She allows few to call her Christy, me among them, so I'm special. To most people she remains Christina.

With Christy and me, sex has meaning that connects us to each other and even to something greater, as though God is with us when we enjoy sex. God is love, or whatever God is, he wears the name of love, and I love Christy.

Her boyfriend before me went to Vietnam. How am I not supposed to feel guilty about that?

Deep within my mind, far into the bleak depths of it, a voice remarks, "Gina." And there are other names in heretofore unrecognized recesses, every so often emerging to the surface of my ocean of thoughts, and all the names are associated with this feeling of love, each enriching the power of this emotion I feel for Christy. It's a complicated emotion, and I'm not in control of it.

She attends school in Winona, Minnesota, at the College of Saint Teresa, and now I'm driving up the river road on the Minnesota side of the Mississippi River, admiring the beauty of the panorama on my right. One might encounter grander scenes elsewhere in the world, but none of them is any more beautiful than this one. It is a splendid drive for half an hour, and I'm distracted only a little by a soreness lingering on the right side of my chest.

Christy captured me with intelligence and warmth, playfulness and grace. She wants the world to see her as a rule follower, even though she breaks rules. Sometimes she breaks rules. She chooses which ones to break, and she's more likely do it when it involves romance. For example, Saint Teresa's is an all-girl's school, and the curfew for first-year students is 11:00, but Christy's dorm room is on the first floor, and after hours I once hoisted her into her room from outside so she wouldn't have to awaken the guard on duty. I climbed into her room myself, and we kissed awhile. It wasn't anything more than that, but it was illegal and could have made trouble for her, gotten her expelled. It pleased us to do it.

I'm bringing a poem for Christy because we've been together two years.

> *I've known you nearly all my life,*
> *two out of twenty turns around the sun;*
> *but who can say I did not dream,*
> *for every birth must be conceived;*
> *and out from God's eternity,*
> *cannot I've loved you always?*

I'm ticklish inside and can't determine whether it's more from hormones or nerves, but of course it's both because the entwinement of these two systems of anatomy and physiology can't be separated. They are a marriage of lovers constantly at play with each other.

Christy's dorm, Lourdes Hall, has a spare, elegant look to it, and I admire the stone floor one more boring time while waiting for her. I've gotten accustomed to her almost always being late. Finally she walks out with her smile, wearing a top that shows off her figure. Her breasts are perfect, not too large or small, and she has every right to display them like that. I like when men turn their heads. She told me that she never notices other men looking at her, that she dresses this way for me. I believe her when she says this, because I need to believe her. It's what makes her beauty bearable for me, and sometimes I find it necessary to think about the proximity of agony and ecstasy. Here she is, and I want to touch her.

She asks, "Would you like to go see *The Sting?* Everybody's raving about it."

"Sure."

I put my arm around her waist and pull her close. She puts her arm around me, and we walk with our thighs happily brushing against each other. I kiss her as sweetly as I can.

"Are you hungry?" I ask. "There's time before the movie."

"I could eat a little something."

We drive over to the Country Kitchen, and she orders a salad. I order a patty melt.

I want to touch her. I want to bury my face in her.

In the depths of my thinking, an image appears of which I'm only marginally aware, beneath the surface of the ocean of my thoughts, at the border between what can be seen through the transparency of intervening awareness and what can't be seen at further depth, something strange. It seems there are two, or maybe more than two, minds inside my head. One of them is up front, alertly dealing with my tangible world, thinking what it needs to maintain my attachment to it. Another mind, or another part of my mind with an independent life, is deep and thinking something entirely different. I'm looking at Christy, who has blond hair and blue eyes, but also this other part of my mind is looking at a woman with black hair and olive skin, and this is crazy because I love this other woman too, the same feelings I have for Christy. This woman is completely unfamiliar to me, and in the depths of my mind I'm kissing this other woman.

Later when we walk back out to my car, I forget to open Christy's door for her, and she waits until I come around and open it. I know she regards her participation on a date as being worthy of my jumping through the hoops, which I'm happy to do. It has always been like that, even after two years. She responds to politeness and gallantry.

We drive to the theater and watch *The Sting* featuring Robert Redford.

Around Christy's shoulders I put my arm until it goes numb, and then I put it down. A little later I put it back around her, and it goes numb again.

After the show she tells me about the music. "Don't you just love Scott Joplin?"

It is the first time I've heard the name Scott Joplin, and I answer, "Yeah! Scott Joplin's something, isn't he?" I've heard the music before, of course, because with the popularity and marketing of this movie radio stations are playing "The Entertainer" almost nonstop, but until this moment I never connected the name Scott Joplin to it.

Christy instructs me, "He was tremendously influential on American music. Did you know George Gershwin admired his music and incorporated many of his techniques? If you listen you can easily hear similarities."

"Wow!" I wonder if Christy has known this awhile or just studied about it before this date. Maybe that's why she was late.

We drive out Prairie Island Road to a place where there is privacy, more or less. A few other people are parking there too, but there is space to be far enough apart so that lovers can be alone with just themselves.

I show Christy the poem.

"It's beautiful," she says.

We kiss, and the olive-skinned woman is in the depths of my mind again, almost in my awareness during moments when I'm not entirely focused on the inside of Christy's mouth. The presence of this other woman enters the stream of those many causes of my arousal. Into my mind a name emerges, Gina. What is that about? Don't call Christy "Gina." Holy Christ! That would be bad.

We touch each other and kiss. I reach under Christy's top, and she says, "It's a little chilly." I pull a blanket off the back seat of the car, and she removes her top. I take off my shirt. Her hard nipples feel cold against my chest, and we cuddle to warm up under the blanket, kissing and touching, teasing and giggling.

I stop kissing Christy for a moment, suddenly more aware of the olive-skinned woman named Gina. What is going on in my head?

Christy's voice beckons me back. "I want the rest of my clothes off."

Off comes our clothes, and we cover ourselves with the blanket.

I kiss her sensitive places, enjoying her soft remarks, "Oh, honey, that's wonderful!" Her body relaxes. When I get down on the floor in front of her, she moves toward the driver's end of the seat and reclines with her back against the door. I kiss her tummy, slowly moving downward, telling myself to go slowly; don't be in a hurry; make it last for her.

She shouts excitedly, "Steve! Get up! It's the police." She points out the back window. About fifty feet behind us a policeman is shining a flashlight through the front side window of one of the other cars.

"Christy, get dressed." I start the car and drive while Christy puts on her clothes. I look over at her, and she's smiling broadly, clearly amused by the situation and relieved. I'm driving down Prairie Island Road completely naked, still hard, with the flagpole standing erect and waving with gentle movements of the car.

Christy begins to laugh. "You're truly a gentleman, Steven Connor."

I laugh. It really is quite funny, and I know I've scored points with Christy by protecting her from embarrassment. I'm pleased with that but also disappointed because on this night I'm not going to experience more of the pleasures of her most intimate touches.

She dresses and then helps me put on my shirt while I'm driving. I pull into the driveway of a private house with dark windows. I put on my jeans and shoes.

I hear an unusual sound, thinking it's in the car's idling motor. "Do you hear that?" I ask.

"What?"

"That sound. It's a very soft ringing." A pain jabs my chest again.

Thirteen

ENOUGH IS ENOUGH

I t took a moment for Israel to make sense of his surroundings. A curly haired, middle-aged man wearing glasses sat across the room, putting some paper into the top drawer of his desk. He turned to look at Israel. "How was your trip? Did you get to see Markus?"

Israel then recognized Professor Michael Hannity. "No, not this time."

"Anything horrible this time?"

Israel smiled. "No. As a matter of fact I'd have to say this was a good trip. I wish I could remember more of it. I was in love, Michael. It was a love story. She was beautiful." In Israel's memory were confused images of Christy and Gina. "But it was like having a dream and waking up before it gets to the best part. I liked it, though."

The professor laughed. "Good. How much of it do you remember?"

"Not much, just one day, part of a day, a very nice day." He smiled. "I can do this time travel again."

"Yippee! Victory is ours! But not any more today. Enough is enough for one day. I'd like you now to go home and write everything you can remember about living in this other body. Do that after every trip, and I think a time will come when you're better able to remember from one life to another."

Those instructions reminded Israel of the technique used to

develop the ability to remember dreams, even to realize while in a dream that one is dreaming, to dream lucidly. He asked, "Was it a dream?"

"Do you think it was a dream?"

"It was more vivid and detailed than a dream, most dreams. Dreams can be quite detailed sometimes."

"It wasn't a dream. It was the real deal, Israel."

Israel shuddered, rethinking his previous travel, the woman, the pitchfork, the murder. There is not a single moment of one's experience that does not in some way affect every other, the total being. In this moment he touched a connection between love and joy with distrust and dismissal. It did not seem right, but there it was, a complication of his existence, a sobering step that might one day lead to gratitude, a gracious acceptance of what has been given.

At home Israel logged onto Facebook to see if there were any messages, and there was one from Gina.

Dear Israel,

Of course you've got to do what you've got to do, but let me tell you something that I hope has meaning for you. Life isn't perfect, but don't you think perfection would bore us? Perfection wouldn't be heaven. Let the world be imperfect and enjoy it just the way it is. Sometimes it takes effort to enjoy, yes, but you will enjoy it better if you don't expect it to be any more than it is. That's all I'm saying.

We talked while you were in the hospital, and we got to know each other. I like you enough to wait a little while, but I want a man. I don't want to be alone.

By the way, nobody got sick, and that wasn't why I had tickets to Wicked. *I broke up with my boyfriend because he wasn't the right one. You might be, and I want to find out. You've had problems, but what is past is past. Think about your future. I like you. That's all I have to say. Enough is enough.*

He logged out of Facebook and opened Word to write what he could remember of his time travel. It aroused him.

He decided to clean house a little more, at a relaxed pace. All the rest of the day he contemplated what he would say to Gina, and he recalled a movie he had seen years earlier, *The Unbearable Lightness of Being*. He asked himself if he could live with that kind of lightness of behavior and thought. Could he decide and live for what pleased him today? Could he worry less about the meaning of it all? At the end of the day he opened up Facebook and wrote this note:

Gina,

I've been thinking about your message and how to respond to it. I keep telling myself to keep it honest and simple. Here it is. I want to kiss you again. That's all I have to say. Enough is enough.

Before retiring to bed and into the relaxed escape of sleep, he took a tablet of hydrocodone and this time remembered to put the bottle on his bedside table along with a glass of water, a little more than half full. He skipped drinking any tequila.

He did not remember any of his dreams that night, but when he awoke in the middle of the night he found it curious that the clock on his bedside table again shined its message that it was 3:16 in the morning. *Coincidence.*

Fourteen

HE DESCENDED INTO HELL

srael awoke without the earlier relentless, sharp, searing pain in his chest that for the moment had subsided into more of an ache and tightness. Nevertheless he lay still awhile, intimidated by anticipation of pain. He carefully stretched. He looked at the bottle of hydrocodone and decided to forego the mildly mind-stupefying security a tablet might provide. He would save it for when pain struck severely.

Two different vectors for his future beckoned. Gina enticed him with tangible companionship, beauty, arousal, and cognitive stimulation. He imagined her laughing and her bare body pressed against his own, conversations on who-knows-how-many different topics. But there was no guarantee that she would last more than a little while. Would she truly and enduringly love him?

On the other hand, Markus was a guaranteed, never-ending passion who always would be attached, but he resided in a place impossibly remote.

His expectations of a relationship with Gina demanded her fidelity, whereas his expectations of a relationship with Markus required his own steadfastness. This fact struck him as being a difference between established love with core responsibility and a nascent hope of a so-far-unrealized dream. It wasn't fair to Gina; he knew that, but the conflict of his emotional obsession with Markus needed to be resolved before he could give his best attention to Gina. She deserved that much.

Would a time come when Israel would choose between the two? Would today be the day? Today he might save Markus, and that would put him on a trajectory into an entirely different world, a different future in which Gina probably would remain unknown. There were other women. There was only one Markus. There was only one Gina. Markus. It appeared that either his success or persistent failure would be the event that decided for him. How patient would Gina be? With Gina it was still early. Just as much as he was exploring her, she explored him, and his assumption that Gina was a healthy personality counseled that her confidently independent self would expect only so much of him as yet. He said, "It's not time to decide. I'll be honest with her. Honesty is enough." How would he explain it?

He drove to Professor Hannity's mansion expecting light music again in the foyer, but this time it was the "O Fortuna" movement of *Carmina Burana,* beautiful, raw, complex, brutal.

He marched up the stairs to the Mozart laboratory and found it empty, music playing of *The Magic Flute.* He walked around the room, looking at the apparati. There was a moment when, because the soles of his shoes had worn unevenly and because his neuropathy threw him slightly off balance, he bumped against an instrument and accidentally pushed a button. A tiny light turned off. He pushed the button again, and the light turned back on.

He then noticed a letter on the desk, out of its envelope. A Superman paperweight sat on top of it. He hesitated at first, aware of his inevitable infraction against personal privacy, and then he read it.

Dear Michael,

I am writing to you first, before doing anything else, because I don't know how my actions will change the future. I want you to know that I have succeeded. I have time traveled to where I need to be, and I remember. I remember everything, Michael. It is possible.

You have not yet met me. You will receive this letter before we meet. You and I will meet, Michael. You are instrumental to my having gotten here. We have to meet. Otherwise I wouldn't be here.

My god, Michael, I am about to launch into another timeline. What does it mean? You have successfully made it possible to travel spiritually to different locations within the same timeline, but what about different timelines? It must be the same thing, right? Different particulate timelines would be connected by the continuous energy, wouldn't they?

Thank you

Curiously, there was no date or name on it.

Israel replaced the Superman paperweight atop the letter. He walked to and sat on the recliner in the middle of the room, the pilot seat. He eased back and looked at the ceiling. *It's possible. Michael should have told me this. He's had success before.*

A few minutes later Michael Hannity entered the room while reading a book, walked over to the desk, and sat down, continuing to read studiously. After a brief startle when he looked up and saw Israel, a smile erupted on his face. "Well, if it isn't my dear friend, Mr. Surprise-the-hell-out-of-me. How is Israel today?" Turning back to his desk, he noticed the letter, snatched it up, and put it away.

Israel said, "I was looking at your instruments and accidentally bumped a button." He pointed out which one.

The professor examined it and two other panels as well. He toggled a tiny lever and watched a screen as four different spiral lines coalesced into a single line. "No damage done. Everything looks exactly as it should. I take it you're here to try traveling again. Do you remember any more of your last trip? A day in love with a beautiful woman!" He chuckled and sighed. "I might want to try that life sometime myself, if only I could figure out how to steer this damnable piece of horse shit." Seeing the concerned look on Israel's face, he added, "It's safe! I know that it's safe. Don't worry about it. You're going to be successful. I'm just thinking maybe I can find a way to steer this machine better, so you can be successful sooner. Cockshitfuck."

Israel considered asking about the letter but didn't.

Michael asked, "Have you had any more contact with Gina?

She's a beautiful woman. Wouldn't it be wonderful to send the two of you together on an extended vacation in time? You could live the lives of all the lovers in history. Wouldn't that be astounding?"

"Relationships take time, Michael."

"Yes, of course they do, and that's what I'm saying; all the time in the universe might be yours."

Israel donned the now-beacon helmet with the historical sweat of Paul Hornung, and he sat in the recliner.

Michael strapped Israel's wrists and ankles, and he whispered cheerfully, "All the lovers in history!" His eyes widened.

The instrumentation hummed for a few minutes, and then there was a buzz and a ring, and then there was another buzz and a ring, another buzz and a ring, another buzz and a ring, another and another.

"Flying fucking crap!" cried the professor.

Although we don't understand the vast and complex connectedness of all things, it is reasonable to do our best to describe it, realizing any attempt at explaining what we don't know is limited and inexact, awaiting a future when technology improves to an extent we scientifically can study each important step in our quest for complete knowledge.

Why did it happen at this time, that Israel traveled into segments of many different lives? Was it because of a malfunction of apparatus or something different, something inherent to the structure of his life? Why were each of these several segments of lives connected to horror of one sort or another? Was he to learn from it?

His spirit launched beyond spacetime, and briefly he was aware of existing without ties to material senses with which he had any sort of familiarity. How could he guide his travel without being able to observe and respond to guideposts? He then reentered spacetime as a spirit within another person.

I am Lavern Lamont, and my little house sits alone in a little cut of woods on a country road. Neighbors live behind clumps of trees, so I'm isolated out here unless I go meet someone, but I don't do that often 'cause people take advantage. Once a taxi driver forced himself on me; brought me to my door and pressed his stinking fat body against me, pushed me against the door and kissed me and tried to stick his tongue in my mouth. Should've bit it off. He stunk.

Arthritis deforms my joints, so they don't move the way they're supposed to, and they hurt a lot, so people can take advantage, and they do. Unhealthy-minded people with powerful bodies take advantage of folk like me who can't defend against their terribleness. Ought to be a cosmic rule that people live a crippled life before they get to have power over anyone, so they know better, and then maybe after the powerful life they live crippled again to make up for the crap they did when they were dirty shits.

Tonight I sit alone in darkness, alone except for Whiskers, my cat, in a room at the back of my house, 'cause it's Halloween, and Halloween's not fun. Scares hell out've me 'cause some people go crazy on Halloween, want to hurt you, 'specially if you're weak, and they pick on you. Jerks pick on weak people, so I need to prepare for 'em, not be weak. I shut all the curtains so nobody can see in, can't see me. Got candlelight and a gun, this time a real gun, not pretending.

Not many trick-or-treaters come to my door, and nobody comes at thirty minutes past ten, but a year ago one did. Ten thirty and there was knocking on my door. I'm no fool, so I yelled, "Too frickin' late for trick-or-treating. Go home."

Man's voice answered; gave me shivers. He was taller'n me, from where his voice came in. "Come on," he said. "It's Halloween. Just open the door and give me some candy."

What kind of candy he wanting? I shouted, "Go away. I'm on the phone right now to the police. Talkin' to 'em right now. Yes, officer, he's threatening me, and he's right outside my door. Come quick before I have to shoot 'im. You better get away from here. Git," I said. "Git away from my door." I snarled the words, tryin' to sound heartless, like I was just as dangerous as him, crazy dangerous. "Got a gun." I tol' him. "Go. Git away from here 'fore I shoot through the door."

Went away; at least I thought he went away; at least he wasn't sayin' no more, but there was no way of knowin' if silence meant he went 'round back of the house. Remember wondering which window might break any second. Any minute? Any hour? So I din't sleep that night. Still don't sleep during the nights. No way; no how. Too many windows. Not safe for disabled people to have windows. Board them all up. That's what I'll do; live with peepholes.

Next mornin' after Halloween last year, on the television news they showed the house where my neighbor lives up the road. Maxine got raped and murdered that night. What happened to her was goin' t' be me, 'cept I played my cards right that time.

This is my life I'm s'posed to live now; no fairness in it, 'specially on Halloween when people go crazy, and weirdos come out of the woodwork, but most nights, even. Don't sleep 'cause I can't sleep. Sit in the dark and make like I'm not home. Anyone breaks into my house goin' get hurt. Blow 'em to kingdom come. Doctor tells me get more sleep, but that's not happening. Tonight here, alone again in the blackness of a back room of my house, with all the curtains closed and my candle lit, my gun at my side, and I'll use it, by God. Lord help any shit's comin' in my house.

Wanna go to the toilet and can't see in the dimness; trip over the rumpled edge of a rug; grab for somethin' and jiggle the table where the candle sits; tip it over and set fire to papers there, too many papers. My hip breaks. Goddam hip breaks! Hear and feel it, my right hip snaps. Like a blow torch it sears and stabs me and makes a crunch as my leg twists inward, and I fall down. Hand slaps my cat, Whiskers. She screams and runs from the room like a cat out of hell, and my head hits the corner of the table. Rib snaps. Got weak bones too.

Stunned, I lay here not knowing what's goin' on for a minute, and my head pounds, and my hip don't let me move, and my rib don't let me breathe, all the while flames gettin' more and more. Is it bleeding? My head? Is it bleeding? Stabbing in my chest stops my breath. Awake but just barely holdin' on, keep my thinking goin'. Right leg won't move; won't move 'cause of the violent hurt. Yes, it's broke, gotta be broke.

Cry out as papers blazin' catch a curtain that burns more and more with thick black smoke curlin' up and spreadin' 'cross the ceiling like an impending thundercloud belched up from hell. Going to die?

Where's the phone? Can't reach.

Doorbell rings. My gun! Where's th' dam gun? Next t' me on the floor. Make enough noise, they'll call the police. Shoot things, counting the shots; save one for me, just in case.

What was it that yanked Israel out of this body of Lavern's? He flew beyond the confines of material spacetime and briefly identified as himself before entering spacetime again, into another being different from who he would have chosen. If given a chance, he would have avoided doing so, but into this other person he went for reasons unknown.

I am Cutter of Lives, spilling blood of the unholy, emptying it onto the soil of the Earth. Stories are written about me, both the creator and victim of hell. Before I was born of a mortal woman, the bitch who made me, I was ageless before her evil handiwork. I existed as a thought inside each of you, a being to cut evil out of you. She, my bitch mother, made this body and mind a host for me, made it a house grabbing and pulling my soul into it.

My father worked as a butcher when I was a boy just starting to spurt the fetid-smelling milk from my hardened penis, and what was wrong with this bastard father of mine who tied me to a post in his shop while he killed squealing pigs outside and brought them in and cut them up? I heard them squeal and I saw their silent meat being hacked and sliced. I watched, hearing and seeing and smelling it, and while I watched, my mother bitch sometimes came to me crazy and drunk, with her breasts exposed, and she'd breathe on my face and my neck. She'd rub her hand on my thighs and between my legs, and she kissed my mouth with her wet mouth, with her tongue, and I watched my father cut the pigs. He didn't care shit what was going on. Bitch mother unzipped my pants and stroked me while she kissed my mouth, and when I came, she laughed and scorned me as a sinful boy. My father cut the pigs.

Now I am nineteen years old and ordained to cut evil out of those who sin, God's messenger, Cutter of Lives, spilling sinful blood onto the soil of the earth.

Don't run from me, little boy. I've been studying him secretly awhile. He is about seven years old, often plays alone, and all little boys his age have sin in them. I say to him, "That's a nice stick you're hitting the fence with. Where'd you find it?"

He says, "I can break it." He hits the fence again, and the stick breaks.

I laugh and tell him, "I know a place in the woods where there are lots of sticks that break easy because they've already broke off the trees. Those kind of sticks are brown inside and dry, so they break easy. The green ones don't break. You have to cut them."

He just looks at me like I'm stupid because the evil in him thinks I'm stupid, but maybe I'm interesting to him.

I say, "Yesterday I found a baby fox in the woods. His mom wasn't around. Maybe the hunters got her. So I've been taking care of him. Do you call them pups when they're foxes? Baby foxes, are they like dogs?"

"You got a baby fox?"

"Yeah. I bought a little cage to keep him safe from the other animals in the woods. He's such a little guy. I'm going to go feed him now, soon, anyway."

"What are you going to feed him?"

"Got some leftover chicken from my dinner last night." I show him a bag I have in my pocket with chicken in it. "He ought to like that, don't you think?"

"Yeah. He'll like that."

"Maybe tomorrow I'll buy some Puppy Chow at the grocery store. I think foxes will eat that stuff too, and that will help him stay healthy. You eat good food, don't you? Your mom and dad, they give you good food too, don't they?"

"My mom does," the boy says while looking at his shoes. "My dad went away."

"Oh, that's too bad. But you're getting good food, anyway. That's what I want for my baby fox. Well, I'm going to go now." I walk away, and I look behind and see that he sort of walks along after me. "Where you going?" I ask.

"Can you show me your baby fox?"

I hurry back to the kid and act excited. "You got to keep it secret where I'm hiding him. I don't want anyone to find out where I'm keeping him."

"Okay," he says, and he walks a little behind me, not wanting to get too close because he's got instincts, but instincts or not, this is easy.

We walk into the woods, and I say, "I have to pee," so I take my dick out of my pants and the boy looks away. "Don't you want to see my dick?"

He shakes his head and looks away.

"Does your mom tell you your dick is dirty?"

The boy just looks away and at the ground.

"That evil bitch!" I knock him down on his back and sit on his chest so he can't move. I sit with my back towards his head and I watch his legs kicking, and I see my dad cutting the pigs. It's easy enough to pull down the kid's pants and cut off his penis with the cutters I keep in my pocket. It bleeds and I watch the sin flow out on the soil of the earth. My job is done, and I let the boy go.

In my ears are the tinkling chirps of a thousand times a thousand crickets in a field, like silence that never is silent.

Jarred out of this life, whose thinking disoriented Israel, again he traveled beyond spacetime, confused, not fully aware he existed. He reentered, this time into a young soldier in Rome, about fifty years before the Common Era.

"My name is Aulus Sempronia Tuditanus. I was told to report for duty here, sir."

The centurion's tired eyes look at me from sockets in a grizzly face. "Who were you to report to, soldier?"

"I was told to go to the Porta Esquilina in the Servian wall on the east side of the city and report to Centurion Publius Sulpicia Paterculus, sir."

"Yes, I am that man." The centurion looks at me, up and down. "Yes, you have muscular arms and legs, but the question is whether you have stomach enough for this duty. Do you have the stomach, soldier?"

"I am eager to find out, sir."

"Yes, well, that is the correct answer, son, but how could it be honest? What young kid of a man would be eager for this kind of work?" He scratches the back of his neck and looks away for only a moment, and then he looks back at me. "You are here to replace my man who last week fell ill and was taken away. Have you ever worked a crucifixion detail?"

"No, sir."

"Ah, so you're eager." He chuckled. "Well then, your inexperience explains your eagerness." He motions for one of his soldiers. "Titus Fabia Dorsuo." Dorsuo comes forward, and while the centurion talks to him he is looking at me, directly into my eyes. "This is our new man who knows nothing about what he's about to do, but he's eager. Teach him how to do it without damaging his dignity. I want none of that nailing of men in silly poses. You know what I think of that. Soldiers turn cowardly when they cannot face what they are doing, and they make ugly fun of it to hide their cowardice. Don't let this boy turn ugly. Don't let him be a coward. Teach him to face this with the honor of serving his republic."

The centurion turns to face Dorsuo. "Take the boy out and show him around. Give him a chance to vomit his soul. Then go to a palus that has been made ready. The others and I will bring a man out in not too long. We have another who is condemned for violent action against the state. No details. I don't want details. I don't want you to know details either. He is condemned. That is enough. Go now."

Fabia Dorsuo has very broad shoulders, hence his name, and I'm sure his back has muscles like a bear. I follow him through the gate of the main entrance on the east side of the city, and I am startled by what is there. It is not that crucifixion is new to me because I have seen it before, and I also have seen refuse dumps of other cities but none so large as Roma. It is the size and the stench of it that strikes me. Crucified men line both sides of the avenue, some of them dead and some of them almost dead. Blood and excrement and urine mix in streams down their legs to the ground, some of it dry and some of it wet. Flies are everywhere, flying and crawling. A few of the older carcasses crawl with maggots. Dogs and rats and ravens scatter as we approach and then return to their meals after we pass. The air is not breathable, and I gag. I cover my face with my hand and breathe the air that is in my palm.

"You will get used to it," says Dorsuo.

A crucified man squawks as a dog bites at his leg, but he has not strength enough to scream aloud. He will die very soon.

Fabia Dorsuo points to the land north of the thoroughfare. "That is where we once put waste, but it filled up and got to be too much. The breeze tends to blow away from the city during the day and toward the city at night. People used to work near the wall, but they did not live there, and farther into the city people could sleep at night, ignoring the stink. But then more buildings were made on the wall, and more people stayed close to the wall even at night. It got to be too much for them. They complained about the stench of rotting flesh, so now it has been filled over with soil, and on that side there are gardens and repositories for the wealthy who can afford proper burials, paying respects to Libitina."

Next he points to the right side of the road, toward the south. "After the carrion have had their fill of the dead, slaves throw the waste over there in the puticuli. Be glad you're not a slave. Their job is worse than ours. Come, I'll show you."

I follow him, but now I am certain he wants me to vomit. He wants me to, and I am close to it, but I won't. The puticuli are holes dug the depth of two men's height and nearly as long and as wide. I know this only because the first one we come to is empty. There are many of these holes, and in them are piles of bone and unrecognizable rotting flesh along with excrement and other scum that has been scraped off the streets of the city. I hold my breath as I look into one of them. There is a dead boy lying broken and face down in the refuse, and a dead dog.

Dorsuo says, "He probably was a street urchin they found dead in the street. Nobody knew him, so here he is, thrown away."

We return toward the road and halfway there I retch, and then I vomit, and it comes out forcefully and repeatedly until it is only frothing yellow water. Dorsuo waits patiently for me to finish. He tells some slaves to throw soil in the pit where we had just been. "It's getting ripe," he says.

When I can walk again we return to the road, and along the way I see a dead man whose penis has been nailed, and I ask, "Didn't Centurion Sulpicia Paterculus instruct us not to nail men in silly ways?"

Dorsuo sneers. "That piece of shit was a slave who raped a little girl. He got what he deserved."

Farther down the road we come to a place where slaves are clearing the area around an empty palus, a post set vertically into the ground. On either side of it are two boulders with flat tops, and I wonder what they are for. I saw them next to some of the other posts as well.

"Now we wait," says Dorsuo.

We sit down on a grassy knoll on the north side of the avenue. The day is neither cold nor hot, and I am glad for that. Clouds are scattered in the sky. The breeze is mild. This is the way of the world.

Dorsuo asks, "How did you get your name, Tuditanus?"

I tell him, "When I was little, my father was a skilled craftsman. He gave me a mallet and I loved it. I carried it around everywhere. I hit things all the time, anything, so people would keep track of me and keep me from hitting breakable things. 'Here comes the mallet,' they would say."

"Ah, that's a good name for you then." Dorsuo laughs.

The sun still is on the morning side of the sky when we see Centurion Sulpicia Paterculus and three soldiers walking up the road toward us with a man who carries a large wooden beam on his shoulder. It is heavy enough that the man occasionally grunts, and he sways a little, this way and that. There are six people following behind at a distance, one of them a woman who is crying.

"Don't talk to the condemned," warns Dorsuo, "not any more than you have to for the job to be done. He already is dead. Think of it that way. We are not the ones killing him. He has killed himself, and the judges have confirmed it. You are an instrument of their wills. He has died already, so do not listen to what he says."

But the man is silent when he first arrives.

"Drop the beam here," commands one of the soldiers. The condemned drops the beam. The soldier says, "Take your clothes off now, all of them." A few people on the road stop to watch. "Come here; put your arms around the post."

Stripped of his clothing, the condemned puts his arms around the palus, and while the soldier ties the hands together, the condemned speaks. "Have you no mercy? I am not the one who started the riot; it wasn't me. I was only watching like these people on the road."

The crying woman shouts her pleas from a distance because she is not allowed to come near. "He is innocent," she screeches. "He has children. Do not leave me alone like this. We will starve."

The condemned says, "You can let me go. You are able to let me go. I will run away where nobody will ever see me again. Exile me then. That is what you would do if I were a person of higher birth. It is not because I am guilty that you do this. I am not guilty. You do this because you think I have no worth. I tell you I am not guilty."

The soldiers are deaf to the man's speech. They do not hear these people. With Dorsuo I walk over to the other soldiers, and Centurion Sulpicia Paterculus introduces me. I learn their names. Aelia Paetus is appropriately named squinty, as is Mamilia Licinus, spiky hair. I suppose the third soldier also is appropriately named: Calpurnia Bestia, like an animal. This third one looks unpredictable and aloof. Immediately I do not like or trust him. He is the one who holds a whip, a short whip with a firmly woven leather handle and braided leather lashes into which are embedded fragments of bone and scraps of metal.

Centurion Sulpicia Paterculus tells me, "Today you will watch and learn. Bestia is here today and maybe tomorrow. He prefers this part of the job, and we are happy to let him do it. After he leaves we will take turns at this."

Bestia does not warn the condemned before he strikes with great force, and the lashes tear open the flesh of his back. The condemned screams, and the woman screams, and we soldiers warn spectators not to come close. Dorsua draws his sword to have it ready, and so I decide also to draw my sword. We look for anyone who might gather stones to throw at either us or the condemned.

I hear the condemned scream again. The woman falls to her knees and sobs into the garment she holds to her face. Even from a distance I can see her body shaking. The condemned screams again, and I look to see what his back looks like. It is torn and some small pieces of flesh dangle off. He bleeds freely. After a while he screams no longer; he is reduced to whimpers and groans. I think Bestia would continue until the condemned is dead, but Centurion Paterculus stops him.

"It is enough."

The hands are untied, and the condemned slumps to the ground.

"Come here, Tuditanus," Dorsuo says to me. "See on the cross beam where a hole has been chiseled out? Lay the crossbeam so that the hole points toward the feet when we lay the body on it. That hole will go over the top of the palus so that the crossbeam will stay in place.

Licinus and Paetus drag the body over to the crossbeam, each holding one of the arms. They set the body in place. Dorsuo tells me to hold the left arm in place by pressing down on it with my full weight. Licinus holds the right arm and Paetus sits on the legs, and then with ropes Dorsuo ties the arms to the crossbeam. Paetus ties the legs together.

"This helps us hold him from jerking when we drive the nails in. And we tie his legs together also; don't want him to be kicking around," Dorsuo says. "See here? Look at the lines on the palm where the hand meets the wrist. The lines form a triangle. See? That is where to put the nail. When you pound the nail in there, the hand will lose its feeling and the cords to the fingers get pinned, so the condemned cannot move his fingers. He won't wiggle free that way, but he might pull his arm off using the muscles of his upper arm, so we put this block of wood between his wrist and the head of the nail. His flesh would let him tear free, but this block of wood won't tear. Point the nail slightly at an angle toward the elbow. It will hold better."

I am not certain whether the condemned is conscious or not until Dorsuo pounds in the nail. The condemned shouts, curses, and jerks, but we hold him tightly in place. Dorsuo finishes the left arm and next pounds the nail in the right arm. On both sides it is upon the first strike with the hammer when the condemned flinches and shouts. He moans and cries with tears streaking the dirt on his face.

Licinus and Paetus get up on their feet, and so do I, and then each of them takes one end of the crossbeam and lifts it. Dorsuo and I help by lifting the bloody body. We hoist the beam up onto the shoulders of Licinus and Paetus, and they step up onto the boulders on either side of the palus. With the condemned dangling from it, we work together, the four of us, to push the crossbeam up and over the top of the palus, and with some adjustment it drops into place, stable. The condemned grunts and cries and moans over and over.

"It is not an easy job?" Paetus laughs. The front of me is covered with blood.

"Next the feet," says Dorsuo. At the lower end of it, the palus is fortified with an extra block of wood on each side. "Those blocks of wood can be changed when they become too torn up. Otherwise it would be the palus getting torn up, and we don't want that. We nail one foot on one side of the block of wood on the palus, and the other foot gets nailed on the other side. Just as we did with the arms we put a block of wood between the heel and the head of the nail. That way he won't pull his feet free."

While Dorsuo tells me this, Licinus is winding a rope tightly around the legs and the palus. "You don't want to get kicked," he says.

We also hold the legs, and when Dorsuo pounds the nails through the wood and the heel, muscles in the legs spasm and relax and spasm again. The body tries to move the legs away from the pain, but it can't, and trying to move them must intensify the pain. The condemned screams again.

"That got his attention," mutters Dorsuo. He then nails the other heel in place.

"He's nailed now; take our ropes back. Save them for another day," says Dorsuo.

We undo the ropes.

We step back and look at the condemned. His bowel and his bladder both let loose, soiling the palus and his legs and the ground below him.

"We got out of the way just in time." Paetus laughs.

"What do we do now?" I ask.

"We wait," Dorsuo answers. "We watch. We keep the crowd away. If he takes too long to die we break his legs with an iron club. There's one somewhere around here. One of the other teams must have it."

Centurion Sulpicia Paterculus is on the road, with his right hand on the hilt of his sword, and he chats with passersby. The sun is nearly overhead now, and the day is warming. I want to be somewhere else.

I am Tuditanus, and I have assisted with crucifixion of a man for the first time in my life. Instead of a man, we call him *the condemned,* so that we ourselves feel less of his anguish, but I have not yet rehearsed enough that way of thinking, and it haunts me. He hangs on the south side of the road, quiet and no longer moving much. His blood is on the front of me. I'm glad it has dried because fewer flies bother me. I hope the condemned will die quickly so I may leave and bathe.

Traveling along the road in and out of Roma are many people of different sorts. I do not understand why they haven't chosen one of the other gates, but here they are walking back and forth, and a group of them comes by singing happily and ringing little bells. They do not look at the condemned men crucified on either side of the road; instead they dance briskly along, ignoring the death that surrounds them. This also is the way of the world, the ringing of bells in ignorant happiness.

Israel was jerked again beyond spacetime, and this time, in the brief moment between an episode of one life and the next episode in another life, he began to interpret meaning, origins, and plausibility of hell as a real and exquisitely tangible place. The next episode took place in the person of a little girl.

I am Leslie Stadtler. I'm six years old. My friend Alice told me that her parents told her that hell was a bunch of bunk, and we don't have to worry about it. I like that idea. Alice also takes the name of the lord in vain. She says, "God," when she's surprised or when she's angry; other times too.

I started saying "God" myself.

We have a large sandbox beneath the porch on the back of our house, and we play there, my brother and sister and our friends. I'm playing there now, and Sushi is there in a corner lying on her side. She's our cat. We call her Sushi because she likes to eat raw fish. Sushi has kittens! They are sucking on her belly and making little mewing sounds.

I crawl out of the sandbox and run into the house to tell Mommy about the kittens.

"Oh heavens," she says.

It's later now. I'm hiding behind the door at the bottom of the stairs we climb up to our bedrooms. I'm hiding because Daddy is grumbling in the kitchen, and I want to listen without him knowing about it. He's a minister, and ministers have lots of things to grumble about. He's scary. He says, "Spare the rod and spoil the child." He has caused welts on my bottom, and even though Mommy tries to stop him, he shushes her with words from the Bible. She's supposed to stay in her place.

This time he's grumbling about kittens. "What are we going to do with a litter of kittens? Six will turn into twenty-six before you know it."

Mommy says, "We can give them away."

"Have you ever tried to give kittens away? Wild kittens? To give kittens away you need people who want kittens. Nobody wants kittens."

Sometimes I think Dad acts like he's been drinking alcohol, even though he don't drink at all. He's a minister. I've seen other kids' daddies drink alcohol though. Some of them get sweet and some of them get weepy. Some of them get mean. I think alcohol makes people become more of what they really are inside, the part they keep hid away from the rest of us. The alcohol jagerates it, whatever it is that's inside them. Daddy don't drink, but if he did I would say that he gets to be like the mean ones.

I sneeze. I'm about to sneeze again, but instead I accidentally bump against the door and it swings open. I say, "Oh, God."

Daddy looks at me with those eyes they call scorn, and he says, "Child, are you taking the name of our lord in vain?"

I say, "I didn't mean to. It was accidental."

"Accidental?" His voice is a little louder now, and Mommy puts her hand on his arm. He acts like he don't feel her hand. "Accidental is not a good enough answer. I will not have that kind of talk in my house. Come over here." I walk over to him, but I'm scared because of his scorn eyes. He says, "It's the second commandment, child. Do not take the name of the lord, thy god, in vain. You hear me?"

I nod my head.

"You talk like that, and you'll be on the first bus goin' straight to hell. You want to go there?"

I say, "Alice's mom and dad say that hell is a bunch of bunk," and as soon as I say it I wish I didn't, because his scorn eyes grow big as saucers. They bug out a little and his face gets red.

"Hell is a bunch of bunk?" He says it, and now he's shouting. Mommy looks worried and glances at the window like maybe she's worried somebody will hear. "Go up to your room now," he says, "and don't come down until I tell you to."

I climb up the stairs, and the door behind me closes, and I hear the latch on the other side get locked. Now I'm stuck up here unless I jump out a window or something. I'm not going to do that. I wonder what he has in mind because I think he wants to teach me something, and by that I mean he's going to hurt me somehow, so that I'll remember.

There's more grumbling downstairs, but I can't hear it enough to know what words they're using. I put my pillow over my head and wish I could be somewhere else. I say a prayer. "God, please put me somewhere else. How about Alice's house? I'm happy when I'm with her."

A little later Mommy climbs up the stairs to my bedroom to talk with me. Her eyes are red because either she's been crying or she's about to. She says, "Leslie, dear, come downstairs now." She holds my hand as we go down the stairs and into the kitchen. She sits down and holds me tight, and she's crying.

Daddy has a big bowl, and he shows me that inside the bowl he has Sushi's kittens. He still is wearing his scorn eyes. "You don't believe in the burning fires of hell? Well, you are going to believe before this day is out." He puts the bowl of kittens in the hot oven and closes the door.

I squirm and try to run to the kittens, but Mommy holds me tight and cries. But even if I squirm free it would not be good anyway. Dad would slap me. I scream and cry.

Daddy turns on the oven light so that I can see about the brimstone of hell.

Israel was jerked beyond spacetime and then back into it again.

I'm ten years old now, and I'm still Leslie Stadtler. I'm playing at my cousins' house, running barefoot in the grass. I keep thinking about the fresh batch of cookies Auntie May baked this morning, so I sneak into the house and go to the cookie jar. I'm expert at lifting the lid without making a sound, and that's what I do. I get a cookie.

When I look up I see Uncle Jeremiah looking back at me. He's a minister like my dad, except he's got a bigger belly and doesn't shave his face as often. He doesn't bathe enough either and always smells like old sweat. "Are you stealing cookies, Leslie?"

I'm scared of him just as much as I'm scared of my dad. He says, "Your daddy has told me you have trouble believin' in hell. That's the wages of sin, you know. You know that, don't you, Leslie?"

I'm thinking *Oh no, not this again*. Uncle Jeremiah talks to me sweetly. He says "That's the sixth commandment of God given to Moses that you're breaking, dear." He takes me by the hand and says, "Come over here. I want to show you something." He leads me into their family room where they have an old-fashioned wood-burning stove, and it's glowing orange inside. "Hell is a very real place," he says to me, "just like inside that stove." He pushes the palm of my hand against the burning hot stove and holds it there hard. I have never felt such pain before, and I think I'm going to faint. He says, "Now that's like the burning fires of hell, girl. Imagine that over your entire body."

It's later. It's forever. I don't believe in God because he's evil, but I do believe in hell. My dad showed me. My uncle showed me. They are ministers, and they know all about hell, and they know about their evil god who puts people in hell. Hell is real; no doubt about that. But God is a bunch of bunk. You don't need God in order to have hell. Hell is what people do to each other. Maybe if I hadn't talked to Alice at school or maybe if Sushi didn't have kittens; maybe then I wouldn't believe in hell. Maybe then I'd believe in God. They say people in hell scream for ice cubes, and I get that. I think my ice cubes would be gentleness and love.

Away from the person of Leslie Stadtler, beyond spacetime, and then back into it again, Israel plummeted this time into the long ago reaches of prehistory.

We encounter them in the fallows on the far end of our land, where they lie secretly in wait to ambush us, and we ourselves might have been the forsaken ones, had our spies not made us the wiser. Here we put them to flight, slaughtering many of them. We smear upon our bodies the blood of our enemies, and we revel in our victory over them. As we dance around a large fire I feel the blood dry on my skin, and it cracks and itches.

Quickly Israel escaped the primeval bloodlust by traveling again beyond spacetime and then back into it, perhaps to gain a sense of karma, into a victim of this same conflict.

I never wanted to be a warrior, but it wasn't my choice, especially after enemies blocked our access to the river. I went with others to secure our tribe's right to the waterway for trade and for washing of linens and food. Here we lie down, and wearing dark clothing, we cannot be seen. We plan to surprise them when they walk on the path, but while I am lying with my face next to the moist soil and smelling its fertility, my mind wanders to my newborn son and his mother. I want to return home to them.

Something heavy strikes me in the back, and I can no longer feel my legs or move them. Pain shoots like lightning bolts into my entire body when they roll me over so that I face toward the starry heavens, and with a knife my enemies slice me open from bottom to top and watch my life's blood gush out of me.

Experiencing this death, Israel left his body along with the expelling of the last life-sustaining drop of blood. Again he traveled beyond spacetime and back into it, into his next experience in another life, into another horrible hell, this time about 167 years before the Common Era.

My baby son, Judas, hangs dead around my neck; my heart died with him. No heart. No name. Seleucids desecrate our temple with their many idols, and they wish to obliterate our belief in the one true god. They will kill us all or make us Greek. Antiochus IV Epiphanes dispatches evil on the holy ones. His cowardly army, they are cowards who kill defenseless women. They gathered us together, helpless mothers of baby sons we circumcised after they told us not to circumcise are sons. They killed my son! They killed my son! My baby! My Judas! They cut away his breath with their knife, and they hung him around my neck. He is heavy and does not cry. He does not smile at me. He will not suck my breast.

Other dead boys hang around the necks of their mothers. All of us stand in a line, and one by one they execute us. Miriam screams before her death. Will I scream? A scream with no hope? I will weep as they kill me, and I will weep no more.

Rapidly into and out of spacetime, Israel felt concussed this time. During brief sojourns in the domain beyond spacetime, he had some sense of existence separate from the people, small snippets of whose lives he shared. He prayed for mercy. In his next experience, Israel landed in the person of a naval officer who reflected on events in World War II and contemplated the meanings of war and hell and healing.

I am Lieutenant Ted Coleman, USNR, battalion surgeon for the Third Marine Combat Engineer Battalion, and we're on a float to the tiny Island of Tinian, just south of Saipan. It's late winter 1981, and the day is deliciously warm, suntan weather. Our home is Camp Hansen on the east coast of Okinawa, just outside Kinville, but now we are here on this other historic island off from which the B-29 *Enola Gay* carried the Little Boy bomb that leveled Hiroshima on August 6, 1945. Three days later the B-29 *Bockscar* carried the Fatman bomb that obliterated Nagasaki. These two bombs caused hundreds of thousands of civilian casualties. The Fatman bomb generated seven thousand Fahrenheit degrees of heat and winds higher than six hundred miles an hour. I can't imagine it. It was a whirlwind of hell.

Philosophers and historians have tried repeatedly to justify these bombings. So far the best argument I've heard is that if nuclear bombs hadn't been used to end World War II, they would have been the first weapon used to start the next war. Who knows? Apprehension of horror has its corrective purpose.

Tinian is slightly longer than twelve miles measured north to south, and it is slightly less than six miles west to east at its widest point, roughly in its middle. We have set up our camp on the north end of the island, a little farther north than the two runways that constituted the old Northfield Base during the war when, for a while, a plane took off every minute with ordinance destined for detonation at one or another Japanese target. The runways now are overgrown with jungle. The trees aren't tall, mostly just ten to fifteen feet, but the jungle has grown over the runways, and we are here to clear them, a simple task for exercising our skills.

Field mice squeak and run about everywhere, tens of thousands of them, or more. They have no fear of humans either, to their own demise. They chase each other around even inside our camp. They appear oblivious to our presence, and the ground is thick with them. Our colonel has instructed us to stomp on them, and he's challenged me to do it too. I won't. I attempted to remind our officers that the mice aren't dangerous while alive, but they might become hazardous as dead carcasses strewn in our midst. Preliminary planning for the float did not disclose whether plague is on the island; probably not. The Marines don't listen to me. They like stomping on the mice, and they continue to do it enthusiastically. It's their mentality, and the colonel likes enthusiasm.

We see Saipan from our camp, about three miles to the north and east of us, across some very deep water we are told is filled with sharks. The coast on this northeast part of Tinian is rough, and there are blow holes where the ocean waves press up through and squirt out the top like geysers. It's pleasing to watch, especially since this is the windward side of the island and the spray spreads out in the steady breeze.

Farther to the northwest are two tiny sandy beaches, the White Beaches, where we Americans began our invasion of the island on July 24, 1944. The Battle for Tinian actually began forty-three days earlier than that, on June 11, 1944, with a steadily increasing bombardment by naval support ships followed by relentless harassment from artillery positioned on Saipan and an aerial assault by fighters, bombers, and torpedo planes. Fire bombs were deployed. Some of these were gasoline mixed with oil, but the Battle for Tinian introduced a new weapon about which there was great enthusiasm. It was called Napalm Gel, and it was administered generously. The island was scorched along with some of its defenders, the charred bodies of whom were found during the ensuing invasion. More than eight thousand Japanese lost their lives during the Battle for Tinian, and only 313 were taken prisoner. It is my understanding the Japanese soldiers were told by their leaders we Americans would eat them, so most of them weren't about to surrender. Some of them jumped to their deaths off cliffs on the south end of the island, selecting that short and honorable plummet of one hundred feet onto jagged rocks where the memory of their blood and broken bodies might eternally be washed away by waves of the Pacific Ocean.

First Class Baxter and I explore the island. He's driving me around in a jeep, and we're dressed to kill, so to speak, in our camouflage uniforms with flat black insignias instead of the shiny, pretty ones. We arrive at the southernmost extent of Tinian, Lalo Point, where there is a memorial field on the flat plateau above the cliffs and waves crashing on the rocks below. This memorial field is surrounded by a perimeter of small stones, and it reminds me of a small cemetery, but there are no bodies here, of course, those bodies having been given to the ocean. There are markers with names on them, and a few have flowers.

After our visit there, Baxter and I drive northward along the narrow primitive road, bouncing along pleasantly in the jeep, and at one point we need to drive far to the side to make room for a southbound bus carrying Japanese visitors to Lalo Point.

After that Baxter spots the entrance to a cave in the high ground to the right of us, and he suggests we go up and look for World War II artifacts; of course he's thinking he may find spent arsenal. I think we're unlikely to find anything, because it's been thirty-seven years, and scores of men must already have scoured the entire island looking for such stuff. We go anyway because it's only a short distance from the road and it'll be fun. Baxter parks the jeep, and we hike up to the cave, which turns out to be not much more than a deep hollow in the stone, going back maybe seven feet.

We sift through its dusty floor and find a bone; it's human, a vertebra, and I can tell it's thoracic because there are joint surfaces on both sides of its body and on the transverse processes, articulations for ribs. We look some more, but it's the only bone we find and the only thing of interest in the cave.

We decide to take it to the Japanese visitors, and we drive back toward Lalo Point. We park some distance away and walk respectfully toward the memorial field where they are assembled, quietly remembering their lost loved ones.

Their guide approaches and advises, "Now is not a good time for you to come here."

I say, "We know that, but we also know the Japanese revere the bones of loved ones who have passed away. We want to give them this."

He looks at the vertebra.

"We found it in a cave just a little ways up the road."

He takes it and quietly says, "I'll give it to them."

We drive away.

Half an hour later Baxter and I are parked on the side of the road halfway between Tinian Town and our camp. We are sipping from bottles of beer that Baxter clandestinely brought along. We have only the two bottles, that I know of, and I'm enjoying the beer's refreshing cool bitterness in the heat of the afternoon.

A car drives up and stops. A couple of Japanese men get out with a camera, and they ask to take pictures of us. They ask for our names to write in their newspaper back home.

There is an old saying that time heals all wounds, and maybe that's true. I know enough about healing and human psychology, though, to realize that healing is accompanied by a scar. I hope the cicatrix has been made stronger today. Maybe over time, as is often true of bodily healing, the scar becomes less noticeable, not as ugly. It is not enough to try forgetting about such things because they sit inside us and shape who we are. When planning the structure of our future we need to recognize the ground upon which we build our foundation.

I shall never forget this day.

Israel felt sucked out of this world, into the beyond and back like a conduit, this time into a soldier awakening on the day following the Battle of Gettysburg. "War is hell," is a phrase frequently attributed to William Tecumseh Sherman, a Union general of the American Civil War who, in his famous, ruthless march through the South, made no great attempt to make it anything other than that.

They say it's the fourth of July. How about that! I'm Joseph Tucker, and I managed to survive the last three days. Truth be told, you stop worryin' about death after a while. It's just another step on the way to goin' wherever 'tis you're goin' to. I woke this mornin' behind a rock on the side of the road. My joints hurt like they got glue in 'em. They don't want to move.

Those Rebs; I'd say they underestimated us; must've thought we were still the same bunch they was fightin' two years ago, but we ain't. When you been around war long enough you stop wantin' to run from it. Oh, some still do, but most of us would just as soon accept an end to our misery either way, victory or death. Better to get shot in the front than in the back. Ol' Reb; he didn't know we learned that. Well, now they learned.

Hard to say whether the road is mostly dirt or mostly blood. The battlefield moans with the cries of wounded men who want water or to be put out of their misery. Otherwise the day is not quiet. The Rebel army has moved on, and even though I think our generals want us to chase 'em, it's kind of hard when you ain't got no horses left, and you got all these dead and miserable to take care of. Men shoutin' all over the place.

I run out of shots yesterday. They give us sixty shots, and when that's used up, usually you just hide and pray unless they come running toward you and you gotta use your knife and fists. Last night I was so exhausted I just fell asleep when the noise let down. Nothin' I could do anymore anyway.

Johnson comes over to me and says, "You want some shoes?" He jerks his head toward the battlefield and says, "Lots of dead men don't need their boots no more."

"What about the live ones?" I ask him. "They still got their guns. Maybe they think like heroes, and they don't care if we kill them after they shoot one of us."

"You hungry?"

"Yeah, I'm hungry."

"Maybe they got food in their packs."

As it happens we are assigned to go into the terrain of torn and bloody bodies, and it is our job to loot the dead and bury them. We are to show the ambulances who might be salvageable, so we walk out onto the blood-soaked soil, and we find that we aren't the only ones who've wrapped their feet with strips of cloth. I find some shots for my gun easier than I find any food, but I find a little of that too. Boots are harder to come by, at least ones that fit my feet and aren't already torn up so bad they're useless. A few boots will fit other men's feet. You can cut the tops off 'em and keep the soles to wrap around your feet, but even then the soles usually have holes in 'em. I'm looking for a pair that's intact enough they could keep my feet dry. The skin between my toes is cracked and bleeding, and the softened bloody soil squeezes between them. They fester.

This is what you do in war. You pick up after the dead, and you marvel that you're not one of 'em. You marvel about it; that's what you do. And you live from one small meal to the next and you pick little bits of gravel and grass out of the cracked calluses of your feet. You tell a joke and pretend like the laughter is forever. That's war. It gets exciting once in a while, like the last three days with choking smoke and fire in the air, and then you're weary and excited both at the same time.

Then it's like this.

A man lying on the ground calls to me. He says, "You, man, got some water? I'll trade you."

He's got one arm still on him, and his belly is bleeding. He must have fallen and struck his head too 'cause his forehead is abraded and the skin around his left eye is purple and black.

I ask him what happened to him.

"God if I know," he says.

"Ambulance," I shout and wave my hands.

He says, "You shout like that, but it don't matter. I'm going to die. It's this belly wound; they shot me here, and I can't feel my legs no more or move 'em. Nobody's goin' to fix this one. I'm a dead man. I am waitin' at the train station for my ride to the pearly gates."

I ask him what he wants to trade, and I admire him, because he knows I could just take from him whatever he's got, but that's war too. He's courageous and I'm respectful of that. Some of us, we become gentlemen because there's nothing else that's left of us. We keep that. Not all of us keep that, but this poor dead soul and I do. We keep what's left of us because that's all we really got.

"You got water?"

"Yeah. I got water."

"I got a slice of cheese and half a sausage in my pack, and a cracker."

His food is dry and tough. There's not much of it. We talk. That's about it. He gives me a last letter he wrote for this purpose, and he asks me to put it into the post. I tuck it into a pocket.

The sun climbs to the top of the sky behind darkening clouds, and then just after noon the heavens pour forth a storm the likes of which I've never seen before, with sheets of water plummeting like the purified vomit of a God sickened by the righteous bloodshed of his creatures. Streams appear on the countryside, washing at least some of the gore away like a baptism of holy wrath. This is war and this is God, and it is forever.

Israel felt yanked again, beyond spacetime and back again. Even if hell itself is eternal, one's stay there is not, and there can be many different ways of experiencing hell. One can be in hell while observing the next person in heaven. One can be in heaven while observing the next person in hell. What would a person do if they found themself in heaven next to a person in hell? This, one more of Israel's jaunts, was a reprieve from hell.

There are not many boys named Tom, and I am one of them. My dad's name is Harel, and I am the only boy in Nazareth named Tom the son of Harel. I sit on a grassy knoll outside the village not far from the tomb dug out of the hillside, the one that was built for many. It has a walkway in it, and for prepared bodies there are tunnels on one side and the other, like grapes on a stem. It is a good distance away from the village so that it will not ruin worship, something I do not understand, and I am not expected to understand it because I am still a boy. Yeshua understands it even though he is only a boy, older but still not yet a man. He understands more than others; he understands more than men. I spend a lot of my time with him.

We look at the valley and surrounding hills, and as strange as it seems, I don't know how we came here. I don't remember this morning or what I was doing, not at all. Where did my memory run to? Why am I not troubled by this fact? But I am not. Things happen when I am with Yeshua, things even more unusual than this.

The quiet air is not too cool and not too warm. If there is a lazy breeze at all it can be seen only in tiny movements seldom made by grasses. Today is comfortable, and I bask like a lizard on a rock.

Few boys are named Tom, but many are called Yeshua, so many that boys named Yeshua get called different names to set each one apart from the others. People of Nazareth do not call my Yeshua the son of Yosef. They say, "Yosef is not his father. Yeshua has no father except for our father in heaven." They call him the son of Mary, meaning she came to be with child by relations she had with someone when she was not married, but nobody knows who. "Yeshua is Mary's son." This comment derides her and Yeshua, though they claim they merely describe the situation as it is. Some people accurately describe situations in ways that hurt or cast others away.

They do not cast Yeshua completely out from the community as they would cast away a diseased person, but in their eyes he is not fully healthy either. He is dirty by birth, but because he is not contagious dirt, they tolerate him. Being righteous, they live by rules of righteousness. Maybe it also is because he says delightful things that make them laugh. "It is not his fault he is dirty," they say, but the real reason they tolerate him is that his dirtiness is not of the sort that will hurt them. He comes to social gatherings because of his family. The community cares about Yosef, and the others in his family are pure; only Yeshua is not. They like Yeshua, but he is not pure and never can be because of how his life began. His mother is pure, another curious thing I do not understand. People say she sinned, but because her own birth was pure she can atone for sins that are not a part of her substance; this is what makes her pure and not her son. There is nothing Yeshua can do to become pure, and although they do not blame him for it, they think his existence is shameful. Paying the debt of his mother's sin, he can become righteous but never pure.

She tells him he is the son of our father in heaven, and Yeshua stubbornly answers he is the son of a man, not meaning to be hurtful, but his mother's face shows pain when he says it. He wants truth and is courageous enough to confront it without pretending things are different from what they are, making this one of the ways his mother atones over and over for her sin. Hers was a curious sin because without it there would not be Yeshua, and he is worthy of her sin.

I am glad my parents let me be his friend.

He sits now, drawing with his finger on the ground, a thing he does. Sometimes he draws pictures and sometimes symbols, but usually his mind is in another world when he does it, when he thinks, and he always thinks, remembers everything, and makes it all fit together better than grown men do. He asks questions that stump them.

His curly dark-brown hair hangs down to his shoulders, and with his face turned downward and slightly toward me, I see his large brown nose poking just beyond it. He has taken the sandals off his feet as it is not a hot day, and the ground is cool enough. I take my shoes off as well, a simple pleasure.

He asks me, "Do you remember the Pharisee who comes preaching here sometimes? The one named Simon?" Yeshua still looks at his finger scribbling on the ground. "This morning I asked him if a child was starving, what would be more sinful, to let it die or to feed it a fish without scales." Yeshua looked up at me and started laughing. "He was unable to answer. Imagine that! Truthfully, that is not exactly what stumped him. He answered we must follow the law even when we do not understand why it is what it is. He could not give a good answer for why a loving god would demand from us such a hurtful thing. He had no explanation."

I notice his hand trembles, and words pop into my head that I do not understand. *Benign familial tremor, associated with long life.* Without any idea why I say it, I tell him, "Yeshua, you are going to live a long life."

While he is still looking at me, his expression changes, and he says, "Ah Israel! You've come to visit. Laws are made to serve humans, Israel, not the other way around." He calls me Israel. His eyes look at me with warmth that is strong and deep. For the first time I notice there is a tiny fleck of blue at the bottom of his brown left eye. I cannot remember seeing this spot before, but it feels familiar, as though I should remember it.

"Why do you call me Israel? I am Tom."

"Israel! Is this your first visit? Yes." He pauses and smiles. "Of course you are Tom, and you are many. You always are Tom, and I love you, my friend. I speak to you, Tom, and I speak to the many because this is one of the ways they come to me. Do not struggle against it; it is as it is. Do not struggle to understand because soon it all will make sense to you, like notched wood falling into place, and you will understand."

He puts his hand on the side of my head and says, "You have been through a lot just now, Israel." He frowns briefly. "Never again will you believe those who say there is no hell, for you have witnessed it. But there is heaven too." He smiles. "And heaven waits for you. Heaven wants you. Do not be afraid of it. Do not let hell stand as a wall between you and heaven. Remember I am always with you, even in hell."

My mind fills with visions of bloodshed and suffering; my heart fills with loss; I become sorrowful.

"Heaven and hell," Yeshua says. "Do you think you have control of it? What you do unto others, do you think it will return to you? You have heard that the greatest of all commandments is to love our heavenly father with all your heart, mind, and soul, and you have been taught what Hillel told us, that all of the law is contained in the simple admonishment to love other people as you love yourself. This is how to make heaven, Israel. One person makes heaven for another. Does heaven return to him?"

He looks away from me and toward the hills in front of us. "You come at different times, Israel. This is the first time in your life that you come to me, but not your first visit in my life. I tell you that your journey is one that others do not know they enjoy. Their minds are closed to it. You must tell them. Tell them how to make heaven."

I ask him, "Why did you bring me here?"

"Ah! Look at this day! Here it is heaven, don't you think?"

I am about to answer, but Yeshua quickly adds, "And it always is here, Israel. This never goes away. I am grateful for this beautiful day and this moment with you.

"Days will arrive when you ask, 'Is there heaven and is there hell?' You will ask friends precisely, 'What would you do if you were in heaven and the person sitting next to you were in hell?' This is a good question, Israel. Some people will tell you that people in heaven and people in hell cannot see or hear each other, that communication is lost between them. From your travels you know that they are mistaken, and they will not understand if you next ask what has made them blind. This is how they defend themselves against the anguish of others. They make heaven and hell into abstract places where they can design their own rules.

"You will like other answers better. A woman named Shanta

will remark, 'Many of us see this every day; maybe we just don't realize it. Always the option is to help our fellows as much as possible. What other choice is there, to watch them suffer? That's not heaven.' She understands this is how to make heaven out of hell.

"Another of your friends, John, will write to you about gratitude. 'I've stood on a bluff over a wilderness of heart-stopping grandeur, heard coyotes sing and the howl of a wolf, the drumbeat of a herd of wild horses running across a valley in the Sierras. I have seen kindness and snuggled with a grandchild and a puppy. I've listened to inspirational speeches and beautiful music, seen art and dance. I have tasted the magic of slow-cooked brisket and a glass of wine. I have made love with a woman who trusts me. I believe heaven is here on Earth.'"

Yeshua winked at me. "This is the heaven of gratitude. It is a reason for existence. Another reason for existence is to teach different spirits that they are not separate from one another. This will take time to understand."

He then said, "A minister of a curious religion called Christianity will write to you. Stan will say, 'Hell is here on this planet. Humanity could make it like heaven, but instead, with all the violence and bloodshed, this is a hellish place. Lynn and I are involved with homeless people; we have become friends with them.' Stan understands heaven and hell. You will not escape either one of them. This world is a union of spirits."

Yeshua smiles broadly at me. "Soon I will visit you on your Mount Rainier, at the place called Sunrise. You and I will sit and look at Tahoma Peak together. That will be heaven, yes? It will be the heaven of gratitude. We will eat something, not cheese and grapes, not figs. Enough of healthful things! How about those things called Twinkies? We will eat those and drink a bottle of micro-brewery ale. This is the world, Israel. Appreciate it, and when it offers you heaven, enjoy it."

"When you visit me on Mount Rainier, will your spirit be in another person? Who will it be?"

Yeshua erupts in laughter. "Israel! Does it matter? It will be me."

I start laughing, and every time we look at each other we laugh some more; we cannot resist laughing because we realize how I have just learned the beautiful silliness of existence, how serious and silly it is, and the whole thing strikes us as funny. We laugh because now I see it through his eyes, and it becomes lighter, even delightful.

When we stop laughing we look at the hills and valleys, and I think of Markus. "Yeshua, how do I steer my travels better?"

"You will learn; be patient. Remember to tell people how to make heaven."

"How to make heaven," I say to let him know I have listened, and I pause, but I want to be certain he has heard me. "Yeshua, I want to save my son, Markus."

"Yes, Markus. Does he need saving? Where do you think he lives now? He lives, of course. Maybe he is in me. Could that be? Is he here right now?" He puts his hand on his chest over his heart. "Markus lives, Israel."

"I want to hold him in my arms."

Yeshua nods. He says, "To travel within the spirit you must lose your ego, and without ego you have no need to save Markus or to hold him in your arms. You will be able to steer your spirit when it is about what Markus needs rather than what you need."

He says nothing for a while. Instead of looking at the hills and valleys, he looks at the still grasses on the hill where we sit. We pass through time together.

After a while he says, "You will kill me, Israel."

"What?"

"It is okay. I tell you this because I want you to know that it will happen and you are forgiven. It is the way this world was made. I love you."

"No, I will not do it, Yeshua."

He continues. "You will deceive my whereabouts to the priests, doing as I have instructed, and you will take them to a garden where I will wait for them."

"Yeshua!"

"And you will scourge my back and you will drive the nails in here." He points to the triangle on the palm side of his wrist. "And here." He points to the sides of his heels.

His behavior outrages me. "No! These things I will not do."

"Israel, my friend, you will not remember not to do them. These are things that are done in this world, and afterward you and I will talk more about it. It will be as it will be." He leans over and kisses my cheek. He puts his arm around and holds me. After a while he kisses my cheek again and says, "Now go and enjoy Father's kingdom. Teach others how to make it heaven."

Fifteen

HE ASCENDED INTO HEAVEN

Israel opened his eyes to a familiar feeling; everything around him was exactly as it should be, remembered from long before. It took a few moments to focus on the face of a middle-aged, bespectacled man in front of him who was staring with intense interest. "Are you all right?" the man asked, but Israel couldn't hear him.

He became aware of a helmet on his head and pulled it off. "What's that you said?"

"Are you all right?"

Israel did not quite understand where or who he was, did not recognize the man with a familiar face. There was time enough to take time. Slowly pieces of his life reassembled, and finally he answered, "Yes, I am. I'm all right. You are Michael Hannity, Professor Hannity."

The man studied him. "You are all right?" he asked again.

Israel began to understand his surroundings. "Michael."

The bespectacled man sighed and looked relieved.

"Michael, it isn't so much a question of whether I'm all right. I'm all. Right? I'm here. That's enough. I'm here." Seconds passed slowly. "I'm not there."

Michael took a deep breath and then swallowed. "You've been in several lives, I take it."

"Yes."

"Tell me about them."

Israel shook his head. "I don't know that I can. Not now. I can't."

"But you're all right?"

"I never believed in hell before this."

"Hell?"

"I do now. At least I understand how there can be a hell." He paused. "Or a heaven. Not much heaven in these lives, this time. I think there was purpose in this prolonged jaunt. I lived terrible moments in people's lives, just so that I would know."

"Purpose? What are you supposed to know?"

"There's a hell. Lots of hells."

"Do you need to see a doctor?"

"No. I'm all right. There is heaven too. There must be. Heavens! More than one, many." He looked at Michael. "I met Jesus."

"Jesus!"

"Yeah. Yeshua. He was just a boy, a young man, maybe twelve years old, but he talked like he was much older than that; we talked."

"Who were you in that life?"

"I was a boy named Tom. No, I was in Tom's body, but Jesus talked to me, Israel. He talked to me, Israel, even though I was in Tom's body."

Michael appeared to be taken aback. "Pause for comic relief," he said. "Fuck dammit. What did he say?"

"He wants me to tell people how to make heaven. It's an assignment." They looked at each other's eyes. "There's nothing wrong with me." He laughed a little.

Michael asked, "How do you make heaven?"

"Be grateful. Be good to one another. Treat each other with love and respect. Behave toward other people as if they are you because—"

"Because they are you," interrupted Michael. He nodded with a knowing smile.

Israel said, "I have some ideas for the next time I travel."

"Yes?"

"I'll tell you later." He stood up and shuffled out of the laboratory into the hall above the foyer. Music of *Carmina Burana* still plundered the space. Israel turned to Michael. "How about the next time I come over here you play some Burl Ives songs."

"Hmmm. I'm sorry. It's got to be Mozart. I have this thing about eternity and Mozart, and only Mozart gets played in the lab."

"No, I mean out here in the foyer."

"You want me to start playing music out here in the foyer?"

Israel stared at Michael. "What are you playing right now?"

"Here in the foyer? Nothing."

Israel no longer heard *Carmina Burana.* He heard the soft tones of Mozart escaping the laboratory and realized that, for some unexplained reason beyond his understanding, the foyer music originated in his own mind. He moaned. "How many times are my thoughts going to play tricks on me?" He sat down on the top step. "Did I actually live in those lives, or am I crazy? Are these dreams? Is my mind just fucked and I'm imagining all this?"

"You lived in them."

"I lived in those lives?"

"Yes."

"Whose lives were they then? They were somebody else's, right? And I was just visiting. It wasn't really me, right?"

"They were everybody's lives. Let me reword that. They are everybody's lives. They haven't gone away." Michael said it with gravity. "Time is eternal and there is room for everybody's spirit in every body that ever was or is."

They looked intently at one another, and once again Israel noticed the peculiar heart-shaped blue fleck at the bottom of Michael's otherwise rust-colored left eye.

"Everybody?"

Michael nodded. "More or less. At least an extreme lots of souls, would be my guess."

"Holy shit!"

"Holy shit indeed."

"Even Jesus?"

They just looked at each other. *Rhetorical question.*

On his way home Israel drove to Kerry Park again, on Highland Drive, parked his car and walked over to appreciate the spectacle of Mount Rainier and Little Tahoma Peak on the left of it. "You fucking mountain," he said. "I'm going to beat this thing."

At home he encountered a pile of clinic paperwork, and he was lagging on dictations as usual. He recalled little or nothing about patients he had treated a week earlier, but having compulsively written detailed notes, dictating was easy enough.

He called his office and left a message for Mary, requesting her to find out if he ever had seen a patient named Lavern Lamont or a Leslie Stadtler. *Why? Why did I live in those particular lives? Maybe there's something I can do to help them.*

His computer beckoned him. Logging onto Facebook he saw a message from Gina, and he stared at her picture a long minute. *What a beautiful woman!* Her message responded to something he had written before it, and he oriented himself by reading his own note first.

I want to kiss you again. That's all I have to say. Enough is enough.

Above this was Gina's answer. *We're going to have to do something about that! But I've got to tell you that when it comes to kissing, I'm not sure enough is ever enough. There's always room for a little more. Or a lot more.*

"Gina Provetti! You're a gorgeous woman. I could use a little heaven right now." He called her on his cell phone and got her voicemaill. He said it to her just like he thought. "Hi, Gina. You're a gorgeous woman, and I could use a little bit of heaven right now. It would be enough just to sit and talk with you. I want to look at you again. Call me, or I'll call you; either way."

What day is it? The computer told him, Friday. It had been eight days since he'd been shot in the chest. At the moment his pain was intensifying. He took a hydrocodone tablet. *What the hell.* He looked at a second tablet. *What the hell, indeed.* He put the second tablet back in its bottle.

He wrote in his journal, *I find it curious that after having lived*

*through these gruesome moments of other lives (and I cannot dis-
tinguish them from my own, not completely, except they seem long
ago, thank God), what I now want most to do is to kiss this beautiful
woman. It would be like escaping hell and entering heaven. These
lives loom in my memory, parts of them, brief parts I shared, but
they also retreat from me and seem remote. They are my lives; I
remember them as my own, not somebody else's. Yet none of these
lives is a person who thinks with a mind like mine, like the one with
which I now think. I am different, but I am the same as them. I am
them! I am protected by my mind of here and now, the tangible
stability of a physical world in front of me; these things shield me.
What influence, I wonder, will these memories have on my future?
Will they fester inside me, connecting me to an experience of humanity I would prefer to forget but can't? They have become me.
Maybe kissing Gina will protect me from them. Kissing her will anchor me here.*

Gina called later that evening. "Heaven, huh? You don't expect
much, do you?"

"Gina, it's good to hear your voice. I . . . eh, really I don't expect much. I just want to be with you. It's been two days since our
date, and two days can be a very long time. It seems like a long
time, Gina. I've been thinking. Remember what you said about having fun? I think you're right. If there's a god, he must like it when
people have fun. That would be his heaven, us sharing our fun with
him. We share it with each other, and we share it with God. Or the
cosmic energy or whatever it is that's out there. You know what I
mean?"

"Aren't you going to ask me how I've been?"

"I'm sorry, Gina. I'm full of myself at the moment. How have you
been? It matters a lot to me."

"I've been great. So you want to have some fun?"

"I think you know how to have fun better than I do."

"Do you want to kiss?"

He waited for her to say something more, but she waited for
him. "Of course I want to kiss you." He sighed. "Yes, I most certainly

do. I keep thinking about kissing you. You knocked me crazy off my feet with that kiss. I want kissing to be a part of it, part of something more than that, though. I want to enjoy life again. I'm ready to do what it takes to make it happen. Wednesday night when I was with you, I was happy. It was joyful, Gina. I wish I could say it better than that."

"You said it pretty well. So when do I start calling you 'Darling?'"

His penis moved. He said, "You're not shy at all, are you?"

"Actually, Israel, sometimes I can be very shy, and other times it's different. I'm not always cautious. There is something about you, and I don't feel shy. I like that something about you, and I'm going after it. Damn the torpedos; full speed ahead." She laughed. "Maybe it's because you're a good kisser too. It's got to be balanced, of course; I don't want to scare you away. Am I scaring you?"

"Not at all. Right now you're turning me on."

"That's enough phone sex for you then, this time."

"What are you doing tomorrow?"

"Funny you should ask. I just happen to have tickets to the game between the Trojans and the Huskies."

"You have tickets to see the Huskies and this is the first you're telling me about it?"

"I was waiting to find out if you really liked me or just wanted to jump my bones. You're a guy, remember?"

"I like you."

"Yes, you do. Would you like to go? You know the Trojans are probably going to win."

"What if they do? It's the Huskies. I haven't been to a game in years."

"You're having fun already." She laughed.

"I'm having fun already."

"Do you have a flak jacket to protect your chest? It's going to be bumper to bumper people."

"Do I have a flack jacket? No, I don't."

"Good. That will give me a chance to protect my new honey. I'll just have to stay on your right side, and close."

"What about tonight? What are you doing tonight?"

"Tonight?" She laughed. "Tonight I'm getting ready for tomorrow. Anticipation, Israel. Enjoy the anticipation. It's part of the fun. Kisses!" She hung up.

Israel retired to bed early, wanting the morning to arrive as soon as possible. He fell asleep among memories of hell and hopes for heaven, and then he awoke trembling after an unusual dream in which he walked past a yard surrounded by a picket fence that curiously divided light from darkness, with everything on his side of it visible, warm with sunshine. Nothing on the other side of the fence could be seen, and out from the darkness beyond came the growling of an angry dog, a dog that wasn't a dog. What was it, this terribly fearsome thing that growled ferociously? Fear swelled within him but did not overcome him. *I am always with you even when you are in hell.*

He awoke trembling, and the bedside clock told him it was 3:16 in the morning.

On that September Saturday morning, Gina drove her Corolla, and Israel rode. Her fragrance teased him, caressed his desire. Operant conditioning could work fast. He smelled her perfume and his heart melted. She wore jeans, a white jacket over a soft-golden-yellow T-shirt, and athletic shoes.

"There's a present for you in the back seat." Her mouth was beautiful when she smiled.

As he twisted to pick up a purple cap with a gold *W*, it felt like a spear had pierced his chest, and he winced with an audible grunt.

Gina asked, "Oh dear. What's it been now, nine days?"

"Yeah. It's getting better, though, slowly. I get by with a little help from my friends."

"Friends? Who are they?"

"Ibuprofen and hydrocodone."

"Still need that stuff?"

"It's only nine days. Deep breaths, remember?"

"Oh yes, deep breaths. And today we're going to work on your twisting range of motion. You can do it." She giggled playfully.

He carefully retrieved the cap. "I'm all set now."

They parked far north of the stadium, across from University Village. "Let me carry that for you." Israel took Gina's bag with his left hand, and he grasped Gina's hand with his right. "You were going to protect my right side."

"Yes, I was." She squeezed his hand and put her other hand on the front of his arm, pulling it close to her. She embraced and pressed herself against his arm.

He felt one of her breasts on his arm. "As it turns out," he remarked, "getting shot was entirely worthwhile."

"Don't do it again."

"No, I don't plan on it."

After about a hundred steps Gina said, "You really need to stretch this arm out from time to time to keep it limber. Maybe it would hurt a little, but I think putting your arm around me would be a great idea, therapeutic."

"But you're not my nurse anymore." He put his arm around her, and his hand felt the lower border of her ribs beneath a thin layer of softness. She put both arms around him and pulled herself closer. He didn't mention the silent scream of pain she caused. Their legs grazed each other somewhat clumsily. He said, "It's going to be a long walk like this."

"That's a good thing. We've got time."

They strolled like infatuated teenagers, and Gina said, "We're getting to know each other. I bet we'll have this walking side-by-side down pat long before we reach the Hec Ed Pavilion."

They made it nowhere near that far before pain put a stop to it. Next to the tennis courts Israel suggested, "How about not so tight?"

"Oh! Okay. I'm sorry." She relinquished her grip on him and looked concerned.

Israel turned to face her directly. "Gina, I am so happy to be here with you." She smiled. "Your eyes are green," he said.

"Your eyes are brown."

"We're getting to know each other." He kissed her. He loved the look on her face afterward.

As they turned to walk again he put his right hand between her shoulder blades and then stroked upward to the back of her neck and gave it a gentle massaging squeeze.

The crowd thickened. Once through the gate Israel asked where they were sitting.

"That's a surprise."

They entered the stadium at its west end, the horseshoe section behind the end zone with its vista down the length of the field, the huge screen scoreboard on the other side and Lake Washington beyond that. They were surrounded by people wearing the cardinal and gold of USC.

"Surprise!" Gina said. "It's my alma mater." She unzipped her jacket to reveal the cardinal letters of USC. She took a Trojan cap out of her bag and put it on her head.

"You set me up!"

"Big time." She giggled. "Come on, smile. You're going to have fun."

"Honest to God, I have never liked USC."

"Today you are going to learn all about what gracious winners Trojans are."

"Listen. It's not in the bag for you. Sarkisian and Holt know the Trojan system; they know how to play against it. Your quarterback, Matt Barkley; he's out with a sore shoulder. Taylor Mays, your star safety, is out with an injured knee. He grew up in Washington, by the way. Besides, the Trojans are cursed. Last week they beat Ohio State, and so this week they're going to let down, and they'll lose. That's the way they've done it in the past, and that's the way it's going to be today. If you've got any prayers to pray, you'd better start saying them."

Gina enjoyed his bluster too much. She laughed and poked him on the left side of his chest. "Hey! We're getting to know each other."

He sat as a lonely and subdued Husky wearing a purple cap in a sizable bay of Trojan fans wearing cardinal. Ahead and on either side of the field the grandstands rose to the sky like purple tidal waves. On the left they roared, "Go," and then the fans on the right bellowed, "Huskies." Back and forth, right and left. "Go, Huskies." It was glorious. Husky hospitality! He hummed along when the Husky band played "Tequila." On third downs he stamped his feet along with everybody else, anticipating the fateful snap of the ball.

From time to time he put his hand on Gina's thigh. She smiled. They teased each other. He looked at her lips as much as he looked at her eyes. He looked at the soft contours of her yellow shirt and her jeans. He tried to think about football as much as he thought about her.

He hoped the Huskies would be able at least to keep the game close. They had not won a single game the season before, had not won a game against a rated team for six years, and the Trojans were ranked as one of the best teams in the country. USC was favored by nearly three touchdowns, so he would be satisfied with just a good game.

It was a defensive battle and close. In the fourth quarter the Huskies incredibly were ahead thirteen to ten. With six minutes left a fumble gave USC the ball deep in Husky territory, and it looked like the end of a Husky joyride against a superior opponent. But the Dawg defense rose to the occasion. Before the game its defensive coordinator, Nick Holt, had described his team as having personnel deficiencies, but there were no deficiencies on this day and especially on this series of plays. On third and six, with seventy thousand fans pounding their feet, Donald Butler stopped Stafon Johnson, and the Trojans were forced to settle for a field goal, tying the score at thirteen. Four minutes remained.

On that final Husky drive it looked like the Trojans would stop them, but on third and fifteen, Jake Locker connected with Jermaine Kearse for twenty-one yards, and then Locker ran for another third down conversion. He passed to Kearse again to put the Huskies on the USC sixteen-yard line with less than a minute to play. For the rest of his life, Israel Newman would remember his exuberant and incredulous thought at that moment, *We're going to win this game!* A roughing-the-passer penalty put them on the eight. A running play took seconds off the clock and set the ball nicely in front of the goalpost. Washington called time out with seven seconds left. Israel was electrically plugged in, connected with the rest of the Husky fans. The cardinal and gold people around him were quiet. Eric Folk kicked the game-winning field goal of one of the most memorable victories in Husky football history, and Israel erupted with the rest of the stadium.

He stood and watched as fans swarmed onto the field. Elation!

Sitting next to him, Gina put her hand on the back of his thigh and then moved it to the inside of his thigh and stroked gently upward. Israel looked at her.

"It's nice to see you happy," she said.

He sat down and put his forehead against her forehead. "You really like me, don't you?"

"I really like you."

"Later, when it's quieter and we're alone, I want to understand better why you like me. I've been so glum. I'm really kind of a boring guy. You and I are so different."

"It's about balance. And I know you don't see it, but you're beautiful."

He kissed her softly. "Things are moving fast," he said.

"Kiss me again."

He kissed her. Elation!

It was a long walk back to the car. Gina leaned against him and his chest hurt, but he didn't care.

Heavy traffic was directed northward by the police, and for a while they drove in a direction different than they wanted to go. Israel said, "A friend once told me that a happy man is one who enjoys the scenery on a detour."

"I like your friend," Gina answered.

"She was a good kisser too."

She slugged his left arm.

"We're getting to know each other."

They turned left onto Roosevelt Way and drove southward again. They stopped at Red Robin just across the University Bridge over Portage Bay. The restaurant was packed with exuberant Husky fans, but they were in large groups and a table for two was immediately available. They ate light. Each of them thinking about the sweetness of the other's lips, they skipped dessert.

Gina asked, "Do you have a fireplace in your house?"

"Yes."

"Sounds nice."

They drove to Israel's house.

"Not bad," Gina observed. "You're not as cluttered as I thought you would be. Flowers would be a nice touch, though. I'll bring you some. Where's your bathroom? I'll be right back."

Israel readied the fireplace. He took from the refrigerator a bottle of dry Riesling wine and managed to get the corkscrew embedded in the cork. It was one with handles that pulled the cork out most of the way. The final pull was challenging, though. Instead of pulling up with his right hand he tried to pull the bottle down using his left hand. That method didn't work. He wiggled it and pulled and shouted with pain as the cork popped out. He carried the bottle and two glasses into the living room and set them down on a table by the fireplace.

He took half a tablet of hydrocodone, anticipating pain if they made love. He suspected Gina was in the mood. He hoped.

After lighting two candles on the mantel, remembering *no papers near, no curtains,* he lit the kindling in the fireplace.

He poured wine into the glasses, three-quarters full, and wondered why Gina was taking longer than he expected. He imagined maybe she would emerge with red lipstick and wearing a sexy camisole.

Gina came into the room. "Is everything all right? I heard you shout."

"Everything's all right."

She was still wearing her USC shirt, and she had washed her face clean of makeup. "How do you like me in the raw?"

"You're beautiful. You're amazing. You keep surprising me."

"Well, don't expect that to go on forever."

Israel handed her one of the glasses of wine, and they sat next to each other on the sofa. She wiggled closer to him and put her head on his shoulder. "Hold me."

They sat and talked.

"It doesn't bother you that I'm a boring guy?"

"You're not boring."

"I've never gone on the slingshot ride at the Puyallup Fair."

"There's always next year, and before that you'll volunteer to take me on a parachute jump; just wait and see. Maybe para-gliding over in Issaquah. That would be a charge."

"Parachute? You've done that before?"

"Nope. Never had a partner I really wanted to share the possibility of sudden death with before."

"You want to share it with me?"

"You and I are going to take some memorable risks, darling."

"Is there anything that scares you?"

Gina took her time to answer. "Oh my god, yes! I'm afraid of everything. Mostly I'm afraid of sorrow."

"You're surprising me again. The last couple of years I've had nothing but sorrow, and you say you're attracted to me. What sense does that make?"

"You're successful at sorrow. You are a survivor, and I believe I'm . . . I feel psychologically safe with you around. I'm not really a risk taker, you know. Maybe it seems like that, but everything needs to be planned. If I jump out of an airplane, I need someone like you to catch me. Does that make any sense to you?"

For a while they were quiet and enjoyed each other's warm body relaxing, soft, and unguarded.

Gina said, "Life is like a sea with all sorts of different currents pushing this way and that. It's nice to have an anchor; I need to have an anchor. I'm thinking you could be a good anchor for me."

"Lead weight?"

They laughed. They cuddled and talked, occasionally stroked each other. After they finished their glasses of wine Gina pulled her hair away from her face and asked, "You wanted to kiss me?"

He put his lips close to hers, paused, and then touched his lips to hers as lightly as he could. He opened his mouth a little and closed it, stroking her lips with his. They pressed against each other softly and then harder, and soon the kiss became deep. Time stopped as they flirted with eternity, and Israel was not sure whether they were his lips or Gina's, his tongue or hers. It was one kiss, one soul. He rested a hand on her tummy and then under her shirt and toward her breasts. She kissed him more ravenously. He stroked over a nipple one finger at a time. Israel savored her mouth as she followed his lead, like a dance. When he pulled his mouth away and kissed her neck and shoulders, she sighed with a breathy moan. He pulled her shirt up and kissed the side of one of her breasts, sucking and nibbling it up toward her chest and shoulder. He put his mouth over a nipple and made circles around it with his tongue, pressed it with the flat of his tongue, teased it with the tip of his tongue, and then he sucked on the nipple, pushing it in and out of his pursed lips. He bit it once, then a second time harder, wanting to learn how forceful a bite she most enjoyed.

"Darling, that's wonderful."

I love you. It was only a thought, but Israel wondered if maybe the thought had appeared in both of their minds at the same moment. *I love you.*

"Let's get closer to the fire." Gina pulled her shirt off over her head and kneeled by the fire.

Her body silhouetted against the fire behind her, the light flickering on her olive skin, through her hair like a halo, on the outline of her body.

"What are you looking at?"

"You. You're gorgeous . . . outrageously gorgeous. I want to remember what I'm seeing right now. *The heaven of gratitude.* Israel took off his shirt.

"You still have your bandage on."

"Yeah well, you know there's been so much going on I didn't think to take it off."

"Come here and lie down so Nurse Gina can take care of that for you."

"You're not my nurse anymore."

"But we can play nurse." She giggled sweetly. "Come lie down here by the fire."

He lay on his back in front of the fireplace, and Gina knelt beside him on his left, between him and the fire. She reached across and tugged at a loose corner. "Here it comes." She yanked the dressing off.

"Ow," he said matter-of-factly.

"It looks good. You're healing just fine." She gently touched the skin around his wound, and then she brushed her fingers over his right nipple. She kissed his other nipple and then quickly sucked it hard. It startled him and hurt wonderfully. She kissed his neck and then his lips. Time went away again.

She lay against him, her left thigh crossing over his left thigh. He was aware of his hand on her back, stroking her smooth skin warmed by the fire, the contour of her shoulder blades, the small of her back, the roundness of her buttocks. He wanted her jeans off. He pulled her toward him, pressed her against himself, but however close he could bring her, it wasn't close enough. He pulled her thigh against his penis and wanted his own jeans off.

She kissed his neck, and he sighed.

"Gina, I want you."

She stopped and propped herself up on an elbow, smiled at him, at his eyes, at his lips. "You want me?" She looked amused. "Darling, if what you mean is that you want your cock inside my special place of holiness, then I must tell you that you'll have to wait until later."

"Later?"

She nodded and looked at him lovingly and spoke with a soft voice. "Yes, sorry to disappoint you. It's just that so far I've taken you out on two dates, and you have yet to ask me out even once. I'm expecting something more out of you before I go all the way." She kissed his neck again.

"But don't you want it too?"

"Oh yes, I want it too, and I'm looking forward to it." She stroked his hair and kissed him briefly on the lips. "Hey, I've got an idea." She sounded gleeful. "Pull down your pants."

"What?"

She raised her eyebrows and smiled.

He pulled his pants down.

Gina said, "Wow! Israel's happy." She grasped his penis and put her lips on it, slid it into her mouth.

Israel felt the presence of God's spirit moving over the surface of the deep. After fifteen seconds he gasped. "Oh, God! That's wonderful."

That's when Gina stopped.

"You're stopping?"

"Yes. Let's have another glass of wine." She got up and poured wine into each of their glasses, and she sat down on the sofa.

Israel said, "You are the biggest tease ever."

"Yup." She patted the sofa seat next to her and said, "Come sit next to me."

He sat next to her with his penis pointing straight up at the ceiling.

Gina spoke with a sincere crispness in her voice. "Sex is like drinking alcohol. Either you have control of it or it controls you. I want you to know that I'm in control of it. If I have sex with you it's not because sex is so all-important to me that I search it out like a junky seeking a fix; got it? If I have sex with you it's because you're my guy; got it? And I'll break it off with you long before I have sex with any other guy. Got it? Put your pants on. I'd rather look at your face while we talk some more. When I think you're ready for it I'll fuck your brains out, but tonight's not the night."

"How will you know when I'm ready for it?"

"We'll know about it together. It won't be about sex. It will still be sex; in fact it's going to be great sex, but it will be about our real feelings for each other. It won't be selfish."

Sixteen

ISRAEL'S DILEMMA

On the next day, when Israel visited Michael again, he put his thumb against the reader next to the door, and not only did the door unlock but it also opened automatically. Burl Ives music played in the foyer, interrupted by Michael's voice announcing, "Dr. Newman is here. Jeeves, my man, please meet Dr. Newman and bring him to the dungeon."

A man appeared neatly dressed in dark blue trousers, black shoes, white shirt, and a golden brown corduroy vest. "Good day, Dr. Newman. I am Professor Hannity's newly acquired valet. It's a pleasure to meet you. Professor Hannity is in his robotics laboratory downstairs. It is my understanding you've not been there before." The man smiled. "Please follow me."

The man was about to turn, but Israel stopped him with a question. "Jeeves?"

The man's eyes subtly looked first upward, then downward at the floor, and then to the right. He took a breath large enough to be noticeable and responded, "My name is Reginald."

"Reginald? You've got to be kidding. And your last name is Jeeves? Like the Wodehouse stories?"

"No." The man shifted his eyes upward and to the left, pursed his lips briefly, and then said, "It is a peculiar quirk of your friend, the professor, to call me by this outlandish name. He gets a kick out of it. Please follow me." He took a small backward step with his right foot behind his left and made a crisp military turn, with his feet twisting on the floor in a precise dance step, and then he marched briskly toward the wooden door on the right side of the grand staircase.

Israel followed in quick step, through the door into a short hallway behind the grand staircase and another door that opened to a downward narrow stairway bordered on either side by rock walls bearing sconces with oil-burning lanterns. Jeeves said, "He has a flare for the ridiculously dramatic, don't you think?"

Israel started laughing. "Jeeves, I'm going to like you."

"You may call me Reginald, thank you."

They came into a cavern that was lit with overhead flood lamps so bright that at first Israel needed to put a hand above his eyes like a brim of a cap.

"Helloooooo, Israel." Michael was in a chipper mood. "Pretty damned bright down here, isn't it? Need sunglasses. There's a pair over there on the bench if you want them."

Israel donned the sunglasses and looked around the room at its orderly clutter of mechanical and electronic parts, and there also were remarkably realistic artificial body parts, arms and legs. Michael was working on the torso of a robot.

"She's a woman," Michael said."

"A robot woman?"

"No, a real live woman. Bwah-ha-ha-ha-ha-ha. Of course she's a robot." Michael looked up from his work. "You've met my man, Jeeves."

Jeeves was looking around with both a supercilious air and an accompanying keen interest like a boy from a prudish family visiting Victoria's Secret for the first time.

"Yes. Seems like a very nice man." Israel smiled. "Reginald. You must have a nickname, don't you? Do people call you Reggie?"

"Doctor Newman, I do have a so-called nickname that people who grew up with me use, but not Reggie." He paused. "You may call me Reggie." He smiled.

"What was your nickname, Reggie," asked Israel, "when you were a kid?"

"Ahem. More when I was a young adult. Prick. They called me Prick."

Israel forced himself to avoid looking at Jeeves's crotch. "There must be a reason for that," he queried.

"Yes, more than one reason. It had to do with my prickly personality, or so they tell me. People will tell you whatever it is they want to tell you, and of course there's my last name."

"Which is?"

"Pear. My nickname is Prickly Pear, PP for short."

Israel restrained his laughter. "Glad to meet you, Pee Pee."

Michael burst in with, "Jeeves it is, then." He beckoned to Israel. "Come over here, Dr. Newman. I'd like to introduce you to my lady friend."

"Lady friend?"

"Yeah well, you know."

"I know?"

"Yes, you know."

"I know what?"

Michael put his left hand on Israel's right arm and held if firmly.

Israel asked, "What are you doing?"

"I'm going to slug you really hard right now."

"Wait a minute." Israel pulled away. "What's this all about?"

"Women don't much care for me," answered Michael.

"Actually you're not bad looking, and you're smart."

"Yes I'm smart, and I manage to have a few dates with them until they find out what I'm really like, and then they don't like me so much anymore. I'm making a robot woman who happens to have a preference for quirky men." He whispered loudly, "She's going to think Tourette's mannerisms are hot."

"No kidding! That's awesome." Israel smiled and then noticed, on the other side of the lab, Jeeves rolled his eyes upward, shook his head a little, turned, and marched toward the stairs.

Michael called out, "Jeeves, I'll be needing your services later."

"Yes, Professor Hotness," came the reply.

Israel noticed a worn spot in the valet's trousers. "Reggie, your pants, low on the right buttock, you've got a hole."

Jeeves reached around and then danced up the stairs with his right hand on his right buttock.

"What do you need a valet for?"

"Just because. That's a good enough answer. I can afford a valet, so I'm going to have a valet. It's something I'm doing for myself."

"Good!"

"Now look at this here." Michael handed Israel a silicon breast. "Isn't that nice?"

"Yes, it is." Israel enjoyed its viscous character and massaged it longer than the professor liked.

"Set it down now. She's *my* robot."

"Of course." Israel hurriedly set the breast implant down.

"Gently!" Michael snapped.

They looked at each other and laughed.

"Someday," Michael said, "robots are going to be perfect. You won't be able to tell them from the real thing, except they'll be perfectly programmable."

"Makes you think."

"Yes, it does." Michael held up a sheet of pliable, elastic material. "Skin," he said. "I've been following the research at Stanford on this. Incredible things are happening there. The world is going to be turned upside down by them. Mark my words. This skin will be more sensitive than yours or mine. Not only that, but it will absorb energy from light, energy that can be used to power the robot."

"Wow!"

"Yes, wow! So what does it make you think?"

"Remember the movie *Blade Runner?* A perfect robot; would it have a soul? I mean, could a time traveler like me enter a robot body, for example?"

"Good question. I don't know. Maybe someday you'll be able to tell me." He tapped a tiny screwdriver on the tabletop. "Some things aren't so easy, though."

"Oh? Like what?"

"Getting a robot to walk like a person is pretty damned difficult. For a while my lady love is going to be wheelchair bound. The other thing is her mind; that's just a matter of time."

"What about her mind is giving you the most trouble? Can't you just program her to be what you want?"

"I want her to be unpredictable. That can be done, of course, with a bunch of nondeterministic programs, some for mood, some for time of day, time of month. I'd like to use quantum computing for this, and that will happen someday. Already I've increased the complexity of her mind by building a larger computer outside of her, communicating with her by radio waves. You know what's awfully challenging? Just getting her to be able to recognize things. Have you read Oliver Sacks's book, *The Man Who Mistook His Wife for a Hat*? Oliver Sacks is a neurologist, and one of his patients was a music teacher who had a right-brain tumor, and he could describe things in detail with eloquent phrases and keen observations. He could describe them with remarkable precision, but he couldn't identify what they were; he couldn't ascribe a function to them. He did in fact try to lift his wife's head off her shoulders to put it on his own head. He thought her head was a hat."

"Yeah, I've read that book. Fascinating, isn't it?"

Michael nodded. "I want my lady friend to have some right-brain function. I want her to be able to recognize that you are you and I am me, and that's not an easy thing to do. I want her to be able to learn. If she's introduced to a new person, I want her to be able to separate that person's face from all the others."

"Even considering humans," Israel remarked, "not everyone can do that. Kurt Vonnegut, Jr., said he wasn't able to remember faces. He recognized people by their voices or the way they walked."

"That's a good idea. I'll work on giving her those functions too. Like I said, it's a matter of time." He paused, then said, "And I've got minions hidden away, working on this for me." Michael somewhat listlessly looked at the scattered parts on his work table, looked at his hands, and then said, "Like some lunch? I'm hungry. Let's go up to the hobbit hole."

They climbed the stairs, passed through the kitchen, and then, sitting across the table from Michael in the mansion's hobbit-hole dining room, Israel said, "I don't want to fall in love with her."

"With Gina? Seems you already have."

"I don't want to fall in love with anyone right now."

"What will be will be. Love is a good thing."

"What if I'm successful? What if I get back to Markus and save him? I'll branch off into another timeline, won't I? And I'll be gone from this one. What happens to Israel and Gina then?"

Michael looked gently amused, not concerned about the gravity of Israel's worry. "First of all," he said, "when I'm troubled by anything, I like to eat a grilled cheese sandwich and a bowl of tomato soup, so let's have some." He pushed a button on a remote control device and soon Jeeves came in wearing a new pair of pants, green this time. "Jeeves, my man, Mr. Green Jeans Jeeves, I would like two orders of my comfort food number one."

Jeeves recited, "Grilled cheese with onions sautéed until translucent or slightly browned, cheddar cheese and processed cheese in a two-to-one ratio, slices of bread dipped one side in melted butter and then browned with the cheese and onion combination melted under a lidded skillet. Anything else?"

"Very good, Jeeves. Two beers. And make it three beers and three sandwiches. Come join us."

The corners of a smile appeared on Jeeves's face. He turned around in military fashion and marched into the kitchen.

"Quick study, that man."

"He cooks for you too?"

"He likes to cook, and I pay him well. Who needs a wife, right? Jeeves and a robot. I'll be good with Jeeves and a robot. Now, as concerns you and Gina, remember whatever you decide to do, it's already happened, so don't feel so dearly responsible. You know what I mean? It's already done. Einstein, remember? Determinism."

"Maybe not if I make a new timeline. Maybe determinism wouldn't be the case in a new timeline."

"Ah!" Michael squealed. He nodded his head once and then

shook it. "Even then! Of course it would. Even a breaking-off point into another timeline would have to be predetermined. If it's going to happen, it's already happened. Don't trouble yourself with it. Enjoy it. If you branch off into another timeline, then the Israel you leave behind will have the same mind and body he has right now. He will love Gina just as much; she won't know the difference. Israel won't know the difference. It'll be okay."

"It won't be me."

"It won't be you? What do we mean it won't be you? Of course it will be you."

"Me without my spirit? Are there people walking around without spirits, Michael? Zombie people? Robots?"

"No." Michael laughed. "Not that I know of. Still thinking on it, to admit the truth." He paused and clearly started to think about something else. "Got to give her a name, and a voice. Hey! Do you think Gina would let me use her voice for my robot?"

"No."

"What do you mean no? You haven't asked her."

"No, Michael. You're getting too close. Back off. You don't want me fondling your robot's fake breast, and I don't want you using my girl's real voice. Okay?"

"Actually that's a good question, whether there are people walking around without souls." With his right hand, Michael stroked the left side of his face, pulling it a little, and then he pushed his hand up the right side of his face and around to the back of his neck. "There's certainly an enormous amount of energy beyond space-time, maybe a limitless supply of energy that could fill any void." He paused and looked directly at Israel. "Don't you think?"

"Spirits waiting in the wings, waiting to fill a . . . a . . . void?"

"Yes, sort of like baseball players in a dugout. Who's on deck? Next batter up. Or think of it like this: maybe each of us is like a drop of water out of an ocean."

"I really am a body snatcher when I time travel, aren't I? I push another spirit out of a body, at least during the time I'm there. Michael! What's going on here?"

Michael cleared his throat several times. "We are exploring a new continent, Israel, a new continent of the mind. You are our Leif Eriksson. Go bravely into that good night."

"Go bravely into that good night? Dylan Thomas." Israel sounded mildly contemptuous. "'Do not go gentle into that good night,' Michael. That's what he wrote. It was about death. He was writing about his father's deathbed. He wrote for his father to rage against it."

"But there is no death, Israel."

They looked at each other. A steady stare of realization comfortably embraced their minds.

"There's no escaping it," whispered Israel.

"There's no escaping it."

"Reincarnation without Nirvana! It doesn't matter what I choose to do; it's happened already. It's going to happen anyway, whatever I do. I'm just along for the ride? What kind of an existence is that? Where is the meaning? What about free will, Michael? I can't believe there isn't at least some chance of free will."

"I thought you thought like me on that: no free will. You and I arrived at that by different routes, but it was the same destination, right? You said you believed one event leads inevitably to another and another to another, to another and another; and I said the quantum guys argue against that idea. They say everything is a matter of probability, and every once in a while a low probability event will occur, maybe allowing there to be some influence by a person's selective observation. I can understand why you'd still be open to the possibility of free will, but even then, one event leads to another, and there might not be a whole lot of free will going into how we observe an event.

"Beyond that, and this slams the door shut on free will, I'm convinced that relativity trumps all of it." Michael drew on the table with his finger. "You see, relativity tells us the future already is there, all the quantum crap has been completed already, and you can't change it. You can't! And if you want something scary to think about, you're not the first one to live the life of Dr. Israel Newman.

Countless others have gone before you. Prove me wrong, Israel. Show me some free will. Make it happen." There was silence. "You can't do it. You can't prove free will."

Jeeves came in with the sandwiches and beer.

Michael continued, "Even if you're wildly successful and save Markus, relativity would say it already happened, and you're just experiencing it as you ride along the dimension of time."

Israel looked at Jeeves. "Does he know what we're talking about?"

"A little," answered Michael.

"Not much, but I'll figure it out," answered Jeeves.

"It's okay for you to talk in front of Jeeves, though. He can handle it. If Jeeves figures it out, he figures it out, and he probably will. He's a quick study."

With a tentative voice Israel said, "I ought to just enjoy it, watch the scenery as it flies by."

"Sounds like a good plan."

"For a genius, there's a lot you don't know."

"You're damned straight on that," Jeeves said.

Michael and Israel looked at him, and Michael said, "Welcome aboard, Jeeves! Here, just a moment. Beer is best drunk from a wine glass." He retrieved three plain wine glasses from a cupboard, poured beer into each of them, and set a shimmering amber glass in front of Jeeves and another in front of Israel. While still standing, he hoisted his own glass. "Cheers, gentleman. May we live in rib-poking bliss for the rest of our days, except on Israel only the ribs on his left side, for a while anyway." They drank some beer, and then, with his glass held close to his chest and looking directly at Israel, Michael said, "If, for whatever reason, you find yourself able to change the events of Markus's death," he pointed his glass toward Israel, "if you manage to keep him alive;" he moved his glass in an arc indicating all the space around him; "even if you start a new timeline, it won't be an act of free will. It already will be in the structure of the universe. Call it God's will; why not? Sure, why not? Call it God's will."

"Now you sound like a preacher."

Michael subtly shook his head from side to side and then tapped his temple softly. "Mathematics! Logic! Principle of relativity!"

Jeeves chuckled.

"What if I find myself in a new timeline, would this one disappear?"

"No! That won't happen." Michael sat down and drew on the top of the table with his finger again. "The universe is not centered on you, Israel; don't think that. Think like Copernicus. Your own world revolves around something else, something bigger than you." He leaned back in his chair, ran his hand through his hair, looked pleased with himself, looked at the ceiling, and yawned. "Not enough sleep last night." He looked at Israel. "All it would mean is that your energy, your awareness, is there in that other spacetime thread and not in this one." Michael stopped and then began again. "Or maybe . . . I don't know. If the physical universe divides, maybe the 'spiritual universe'" he made quotation marks with his fingers. "Also divides. Maybe there would be two different spiritual Israels or a dozen or a billion." He paused again. "At any rate things would be okay." His brow furrowed, and he looked at his hand drawing a pattern on the table. "I do wonder, though."

"Wonder what?"

"If your spirit landed in some other spacetime, and it didn't come back to this one, what would your body-mind here remember of your travel? Nothing, right? So as long as you remember something when you get back, I'll know it's the same good old you." He smiled.

Israel asked, "When the mountain jumped back and forth, in my mind, my observation of it, those were different timelines I saw, right?"

Michael nodded.

They tried to read each other's thoughts.

Michael continued. "What if there are already a number of pre-determined universes? That would explain the mountain jumping back and forth, but you wouldn't have control of it. The best you could hope is that you'll land in a predetermined universe in which Markus lives to be a hundred years old."

"Or maybe Einstein's structure of our universe doesn't apply to other universes."

Michael chuckled.

Jeeves chuckled.

Michael and Israel looked at each other again.

Jeeves looked concerned. "May I ask a question?"

"Certainly," answered Michael.

"Are you going to put a vagina in your female robot?"

Michael slapped a hand against his forehead and then covered his eyes with it. He spread his fingers apart enough for one eye to look first at Jeeves and then at Israel. "He fits right in, doesn't he?"

"I'm trying to have a serious discussion here." Israel didn't want to laugh.

"Jeeves," Michael said, "how much of that beer have you drunk? Many years ago, when I was still a kid, a Chinese fortune cookie informed me that very soon I would be able to accept it as perfectly all right and natural to play with myself."

"You're lying," said Jeeves.

"No, it was a very progressive Chinese restaurant."

"Listen, guys, it's been nice, but I've got to go." Israel stood up.

"Please sit down, Israel. We can be nice. Can't we be nice, Jeeves?" He raised his eyebrows.

"We can be nice."

Israel said, "Except now I can't talk about Gina. Not when the conversation has turned this corner. She's not a robot and she's not a . . ." He sighed. "God, you guys!"

"You want to know if Gina would be in the new timeline?" said Jeeves.

"Yes. Would Gina be in the new timeline?"

Michael swirled his beer in the glass. "I'm going to say probably. Because if the new timeline started just before you managed to save Markus, it wouldn't influence the occurrence of Gina in the world. She would be born and would be alive in it; that is, unless saving Markus had some link to an earlier event in the timeline. Or if you landed much earlier in a timeline, then who knows?" Michael drew with his finger some more. "Probably."

He tried to make a joke. "You would have to figure out how to get shot in the chest again so you could go to the hospital and meet her." He laughed. "You'll have to find some way to have psychological problems enough to go see Frank, get into the support group, and meet me. And I'll probably be the same berserk, abandoned jerk in the new universe as I am here in this one. I'll take you to Cutters again, get you shot in the garage, and everything will be rose petals. Hey! Do this for me: say hello to the me in the new timeline. Do it for me, won't you?"

Michael continued, "Also, think about this. What if you go back to yourself in the past, repeat exactly the same behavior, and Markus dies, and you join the group, and you and I meet each other, and you time travel again. This could become an endless loop going around and around."

"But the now-beacon helmet would pull me back, wouldn't it?"

"Ah! Yes, it would, probably. Yes, I'm certain it would. The energy is not bounded by spacetime. That's your safety net. Do you want to take another jaunt?"

Israel looked down at the table and slowly shook his head. "I'm not ready. The last one was too much. I wish I could forget things. Have you fixed it so that it will be only one life at a time?"

"I've fixed it."

"And it's safe. I've got a safety net. Ooookaaaaaaaay. I'll skip today, anyway. I want to be all in one piece tonight when I see Gina. She went to church this morning, and now she's at work. Tomorrow morning I'm going back to work myself, half days. And I want tonight to be wonderful. I want to show her how special she is to me. I've never met anyone like her, Michael. There's something magical with her. Let's take a break from time travel, at least for today." They sat quietly for a moment.

"You love her," said Michael.

"Can I have your chicken Riviera recipe?" Israel asked.

"Sure. Why?"

"I think Gina will like it. I'm going to make her dinner tonight. She's been the one taking me out. It's time I did something for her."

"In that case you need to know the secret ingredient." Michael whispered it in Israel's ear. "Just a dash of it."

"Comfort food number seven," said Jeeves.

They walked out into the foyer where they heard the music of Burl Ives. "To market, to market to purchase a pig. Home again, home again . . ."

"Thanks again for that," said Israel. "It's a nice touch."

"You are entirely welcome. It was the least I could do."

After Israel left, Michael and Jeeves looked at each other, and Jeeves said, "I guess I'll get back to work on quantum computing."

While driving to the supermarket and then home, Israel thought many things, but it bent his mind too much to think about time travel and multitudes of predetermined universes. His mind kept sliding back to Gina. *God, I want to fuck* . . . the thought of Michael's robot vagina soured his mind. *No! I want to make love with her. I want to love. How do I tell Gina about time travel? Flowers! I need to buy flowers.*

His cell phone rang; it was Michael. "How would you like to have your dinner over here? I would be delighted to be your cook and Jeeves could be your waiter, give you a chance to pay attention to more important things."

"Maybe. No. Then it would your gift to Gina, not mine. She'd decide she wants to make love with you instead of me."

"I could handle that."

"Michael, thanks for the thought."

"Maybe next time."

After Israel collected what he needed and drove home, and while he chopped carrots and peppers, onions and garlic, pausing frequently to allow flares of pain in his chest to subside, he wondered why he had not accepted Michael's gracious gift.

Gina was going to appreciate this meal.

Seventeen

GINA'S MARK

G ina drove to Israel's one-story house, a picturesque little dwelling with a white picket fence around it, a cottage feel to it.

Why did she love this man? Did she really know him? It felt like she knew him, like she always had known him. Wanting to be sexy for him, she wore red heels, fitted and stretchy black slacks, a thin black jacket that zipped down the front, and nothing underneath except a bra. She had thought about not wearing a bra at all, but her cleavage showed better with one, so she chose her sexiest red.

Watching closely for Israel's first reaction when the door opened, she was pleased that time stopped for a moment.

His eyes softened, and his voice was reverent. "You're beautiful."

She kissed him with soft lips.

Soft jazz was playing.

"I brought you some wine. Chianti classico. You said you were making red sauce, so this is right for red sauce, Italian."

"Yes. Perfect." He moved his left hand apprehensively to the right side of his chest.

"Would you like me to open it?" Gina smiled.

"Would you mind?"

"Not at all." She put her own left hand lightly on his chest over the wound and moved her thumb until she found the nipple beneath his shirt and gently stroked over it. "You sweet thing," she said. She smiled. "It's nice to be with you again."

Israel put his left hand over her left hand and pressed it against his chest. "You are amazing." They stood and looked at each other's eyes and then lips. They kissed again.

"Something's happening here."

"A little fast, don't you think?" Gina stepped back from him. She looked toward her right, into the small dining room decorated with candles, fine china, and silverware, flowers at the far end of the table. "This is lovely, Israel."

"For you."

"The colors all match. Are you certain you're not gay?"

"Uh? Yeah."

She put her hand on his crotch. "Definitely not gay." She tilted her face up to him and parted her lips a little. With a breathy voice she said, "Smear my lipstick."

As they kissed she felt his hand move to her buttock and squeeze and then pull her against him. She moved her own hand to the back of his neck and kissed him closer.

After a deep kiss and then a few more short intimate kisses, like shock waves after an earthquake, Israel said, "At this rate we're never going to eat."

"Man does not live by bread alone."

"No, definitely not. Vegetables are important. Man needs vegetables, lots of vegetables. And kisses. You are incredibly hot. I'm feeling loved."

"There's something going on between us."

"Gina, I don't have . . . I don't think I'm able to control my emotions with you."

"Good! I don't want you to control your emotions with me. Now lead me to the kitchen so that I can take a look at this wonderful red sauce of yours."

"Not mine. This is Michael Hannity's recipe, and actually this is the first I've made it, but it's amazing. Tastes almost as good as you."

"You're saying all the right things, sexy man."

While eating a romantic dinner by candlelight and speaking with soft voices, Gina rested her leg against Israel's. She slipped a foot out of its shoe and stroked his leg with her foot. They touched hands across the top of the table, fingers entwining, eyes meeting, lips anticipating.

Israel got a serious look on his face. "Gina."

"Yes?"

"This is going to sound funny." He sighed. "I know you're not a robot."

"What?" There was childlike laughter in her voice. "Sometimes you say the craziest things."

"I mean you have a soul. I know you have a soul, and I care about you." He looked sincerely at her. When I play with you, you're more than just a toy. I care about you."

She reached her hand across the table, and when Israel responded by putting his own hand next to hers, she turned his hand over and pressed her fingers against his palm and then stroked from his palm to his wrist. She did it a second time. "Maybe you're going to get lucky tonight."

"That would be so nice. There's something I'd like to do for you first though."

"Oh?"

"I want to learn how to give great foot massages, and I'm asking if you will let me practice on your feet."

"How sweet! Of course."

"Then we can have dessert."

"If we get that far," Gina said as a flirt.

"We could go to the living room where you can lie back on the sofa, but it would be better, easier, for me to massage your feet if your lie on my bed. It's higher, and you'll be more comfortable with your feet over the edge."

"Lovely!"

He already had placed a plastic tub next to the bed as well as candles. Soft music played. "Filling the tub with warm water will take me a few trips," he explained. "With this rib pain I can't carry the whole tub all at once, so I'll bring the water a little bit at a time with a watering can. It will be like I'm watering my favorite flower."

"I can help you."

"No. This is my gift to you."

"I'm your favorite flower?"

"You're my only flower."

She sat on the edge of Israel's bed while it took him several trips back and forth, and with each he inquired whether the temperature was right. He brought her a glass of wine and they talked lazily while her feet soaked.

"Lie back now." He wrapped her right foot in a warm towel, just out of the dryer. He dried her left foot with another warm towel and warmed olive oil in his hands before stroking it onto her foot, moving from toes to her ankle and then up her leg to her calf. He gently rotated her ankle and then flexed it and extended it. Rhythmically in little circles he massaged her feet, five circles in one place before moving to another, occasionally interrupting the circles to stroke in one place or another, toes to ankle, toes to heel, circles between the cords on the top of her foot, on the bottom of her foot, sometimes with his thumbs and fingers, and sometimes with his knuckles, strokes and circles on either side of her heel cord, gently rotated each of her toes and stroked each individually, giving each a little snap at the end. He rubbed the tips of her toes with his knuckles, and with firm hands starting at her ankle he stroked up and onto her calves .

Gina felt sensations not just in her feet. "This is nice foreplay," she said. *How comfortable do I feel with Israel? Pretty darned comfortable.* She unzipped her jacket and unhooked her bra; she touched her breasts.

He said nothing. After a while he wrapped her left foot in a warm towel and massaged her right. At the very end he said, "I'd like to try something. Tell me how you like it." He put her big toe in his mouth and sucked as he moved his mouth back on it, gently pulling. He did it again, stroking her toe with his tongue.

"Oh my god! Israel!"

"Do you like it?"

"I want you to fuck me."

"Maybe we can wait and have dessert first."

"Are you crazy? Timing, Israel! It's all about timing. Make love to me now. We'll talk about it over dessert later."

They made love, and they talked about it over dessert later, sitting naked at the kitchen table, and then Gina thought, *I wonder if he's good for more.* She stood up and walked around to his side of the table. "Pull your chair out from the table. I want to sit on your lap." She straddled him, facing him. Her head was above his. *He can crane his neck for once.* She clearly knew she was in dominant position, the one in control. She kissed his mouth as wet as she could, slow shallow tongue, relaxed mouth. She felt his penis grow and harden.

"My god!" he whispered. "What a beautiful kiss."

She straightened up, bringing her breasts closer to his face. "Suck my nipples. Will you do that for me, darling?" She softly moaned her pleasure for him. "Ah, that's wonderful." *I have control of him.*

Taking his head in her hands she kissed his mouth again, and then she said, "You sexy man." She kissed his mouth again. "I'm going to go into the bathroom and clean up a little. I want you to go into the living room, in front of the fire, and play with yourself. Keep yourself good and hard, because when I come back I want to sit on you. And I want you to talk to me while you touch me. Tell me you love me. Tell me I'm beautiful. Can you do that for your lady?"

"I can do that."

She kissed his lips, and then she kissed the front of his neck and sucked hard, leaving a purple mark where it would show. Israel didn't seem to mind. She said, "I'm sorry. I lost control. There's going to be a mark there."

"You branded me."

"I guess you're mine now."

They looked at each other's eyes.

She got up and went to the bathroom. It was pleasantly clean and fresh. She took a lipstick out of her purse, applied it, and was about to put it back into her purse but then decided no. She put it into one of the drawers.

She took a tiny vibrator out of her purse. Before opening the door she looked at herself in the mirror. *Okay, fate, here I come.*

The next morning she awoke beside a soundly sleeping Israel, and resting on her pillow was a sheet of stationery with a sonnet written on it.

To pluck of pleasure pleads to speak of suck
and glistening heat and salty tastes and clasps.
The softened swelling round and round to tuck
a savoring tongue and swallow richer gasps.
I taste your body's sweat and smell its sweet
perfume and spasm deep my breath's release.
I lose control of kiss and know the sheet
is tease, so tear it off and feel your crease.
I know that you and I are one, not two,
and lose myself inside your womb to seal
it into you and out of me, the spew
of spirit deep and trembling flesh to feel.
To be those hips and lips who move so sweet
we part and pierce and press in rhythmic beat.

Eighteen

NOT A METAPHOR

srael awoke alone in bed and looked at the clock. It was 8:10. Gina must have gone to work; she had been quiet when she got up. He smelled the fragrance of her pillow. He dropped back again and looked at the ceiling. He was not in control of his feelings with her.

In the bathroom he encountered Gina's single lipstick in his drawer, and he felt aroused by it. In the mirror he examined the hickey on his neck. How would he hide it? He smiled. If she really loved him she would have left some makeup in this drawer, some base color to cover up this hickey. He smiled. She wanted him.

After dressing he couldn't find his keys, normally kept in a precise spot on the top of his dresser. They weren't there. He found them in the kitchen holding down a note on his own stationery.

Good morning, sleepyhead, you sexy man! I loved last night. Don't take me for granted, darling, but are you ready for more? I love the way you did me, but it's about feelings. Don't take me for granted, please. This is a very big deal for me. It's suddenly a different world, angel.

Love, Gina.

Israel said out loud, "I didn't want to fall in love. I love her!"
He drove over to Coffee-on-the-Go.

"Haven't seen you for a while, sweets."

"A lot has happened, Sally. I got shot in the chest and I fell in love."

"You got shot in the chest? And you're out driving a car? You got a doctor's note says you can drive safely?"

"It's just a flesh wound."

"But you're in love. People don't drive safely when they first fall in love." As she leaned forward to hand him his coffee and chocolate treat, Sally showed her cleavage again. It was lovely cleavage, but this time Israel noticed her eyes, beautiful and blue; this time he saw sorrow in them. *Isn't there a place in the mind where Sally's eyes always are sorrowful?*

"How are you doing, Sally?"

"Can't complain."

Wouldn't complain. Why was she sorrowful? Would Israel ever know? When would he know? When would he be her, and who would be him then? No! This was crazzy. There had to be separation between people.

Unfamiliar thoughts erupted in his mind. *I am the spirit of soaring and suffering, one alone who has been divided. I yearn for the touch of wind on my face, and I feel it. I am the breath of love breathing upon me, a baby's giggle and the ear that hears it. I am the thirst for fruit of the vine and hunger for the pasty flesh of moistened bread. These pleasures are of flesh and of spirit. They are ignorant hypocrites who murder me.*

Israel shuddered in a brief, disoriented moment. How were people separate from each other, and how were they one and the same? Physical and spiritual. Man and God.

He drove to work, and with almost every person he met that day, almost every patient, he wondered when he would live as them, in their lives. He wondered about the obvious ways he was separate from them and the subtle ways of their shared existence. When he became them, who would be him? He felt enlightened but increasingly he was amazed by whether he really knew what that word meant. Oh, my god! When would he be Gina? He got an erection at the thought of her. Good thing doctors wear long white coats!

The day was speckled with episodes of lightheartedness. Sylvia Potter was a woman in her seventies who visited every third month for a refill of her pain medicines. Toward the end of her visit she told Israel, "Josephine still thinks you're eye candy."

"Josephine? Who's Josephine?"

"My cat."

"When has your cat seen me?"

"She's seen your picture."

"You have a picture of me?"

"It's on your flyer."

"Oh, yes. So you showed my picture to Josephine."

"Yes."

"And she thinks I'm good looking."

"Yes, but of course she's blind."

Israel broke out laughing. "Your blind cat thinks I'm good looking. Sylvia, you're precious." He hugged her.

Jerry Morris came in with his nearly lifelong struggle against joint pain. It started years earlier when he played professional football as a defensive back. He once intercepted Brett Favre. "The thing about that guy, he was fun to play with whether you were on his team or an opponent because he took risks. He played the game like when we were kids. You could intercept him, and a lot of us did, but he also could make impossible plays. He completed impossible passes, made touchdowns that left you standing there thinking how did that happen?" During a practice scrimmage, Jerry had sustained dislocation of a hip, disrupting its blood supply. "It was a legal hit." Thereafter the hip more or less crumbled, and he had a total hip replacement as a young man, and then the artificial hip dislocated. His other joints started to crumble as well, even without injuries, and he ended up having the other hip and one of his knees replaced, and then a shower of tiny blood clots traveled to his lungs and nearly killed him, prompting a workup that diagnosed a clotting disorder.

Jerry was like Sisyphus, the mythological king of Corinth who offended Zeus, and Zeus condemned him to roll a boulder up a hill in Hades, only to slip near the top of the hill and have the boulder roll back down. Over and over it happened for eternity.

In Jerry's case the boulder was the pain cocktail that he drank four times a day. He'd start with each of the four doses being fifteen milligrams of methadone, and each week the dose would drop by a tiny amount. Inevitably whenever the dose got down to about three milligrams, something would spring upon him, and one of his many pains would flare terribly. He'd be back up at fifteen milligrams again, bottom of his hill in Hades.

"Sisyphus is considered a hero by many existentialists," Israel told him.

"How's that?"

"He doesn't give up. His relentless pursuit gives his life meaning, even though he never reaches his goal."

"Yeah, well, I'm not sure that's the kind of meaning I want my life to have."

"In your case you keep weaning the medicine down, and that requires courageous determination. Even though these flares occur and your dose bounces up again, it bounces back up to only fifteen milligrams. If you hadn't been weaning the medicine down, your dose would have bounced from fifteen milligrams to thirty, and the next time maybe fifty. You've been victorious because you've kept your methadone down at reasonable levels. This is a good thing; it's success."

Jerry sat and looked at Israel. He was a smart man and understood the argument. Slowly he accepted it. "One of these days maybe Sisyphus will be able to roll the boulder up and over the top of the hill. I'd like to do that."

George Johnston came in, another physician. He had chronic pain. He worked at a different clinic and came for Israel's care in part because he wanted his colleagues to know as little as possible about his dependencies. He used very little opioid. The most bothersome problem in his life was his marriage. He and his wife had drifted apart slowly during the raising of their children who now were teenagers. His wife didn't know whether she wanted him, whether she wanted to stay in the marriage. George still loved her.

"It's not surprising your pain is worse," Israel told him. "You've got only so much psychological energy, and if you're using it all up on your worries, then you've got less to cope with your pain. And stress contributes to muscle spasm."

"I know, but what can you do about it?"

"Last time you were here we talked about how maybe you and your wife could start dating again. Have you done that?"

"Yes, we've done that, but a date isn't so much fun when the woman is lukewarm about you. Tepid! Every now and then she's ice. I do my best. I buy flowers for her, and I send cards in the mail, but she says I'm trying to manipulate her. After a while I realized these things seem manipulative to her because she doesn't feel the same love for me that I feel for her. My attempts annoy her."

"Manipulation really isn't such a bad thing, you know. It seems to have gotten a lot of bad press, but people change the world by manipulating it. It's a tool; that's all it is. When it's used to make good things happen, it's a good tool. So where do you think your marriage is headed?"

"I don't know. Lonely! I'm lonely because she doesn't love me. She's lonely because she doesn't love me. What will I do if finally, after all this time, she comes to me and says she has decided to stay with me? It will be like she's saying, 'I'm not all that into you, but I'll stay anyway.' How do I trust that?"

"Why do you stay with her?"

"There are two different worlds, Israel. She is in one of them and not in the other. Two very different worlds, separate, and they don't intersect. Does that make sense? I don't know how to say it differently. My problem is that I still love her."

Dr. Johnston sighed. "I had another killer day yesterday, worked from six thirty in the morning until seven thirty in the evening, nonstop. Ate an egg salad sandwich for lunch but was answering messages on the computer while I ate, so there wasn't a break.

Pretty grueling day! Driving home I stopped at Arby's and picked up a pecan chicken salad sandwich; brought it home and drank a beer along with it. That was good. But I didn't come home to a warm body and soft lips. Then I crashed, exhausted, found myself awakening on the top of my bedspread with my clothes still on, stuff still in my pockets, feeling the eternity of my loneliness. Funny to say it like that, huh? That's what it felt like. The quotation kept coming into my head, 'Maybe this is as good as it gets.' So I looked online and read lots of memorable quotations from that movie, really a great movie."

Israel nodded.

Dr. Johnston continued, "Some of us are more interested than others in contemplating what it all means, life. Some people need more than others for life to have meaning. We can't just let it be, can't just step back and enjoy it. Look what glorious fun it all is! Spirituality is that wonderful gift that allows us to construct scaffolding that supports a notion we are here to learn, each of us accumulating a unique batch of experiences to pour into the grand unified ocean of us all.

"I wouldn't have minded so much working my ass off for years, with sleepless nights, to pass a million different tests of my intelligence and character to get into a profession where I'm required to work my ass off and have more sleepless nights if I simply had managed to get that connection with somebody, that carrot I was chasing all along, the connection that never happened, even though a few times I thought it had, for a short time. Those several times that fooled me contributed to my sense of distrust, an interesting distrust, a distrust of my own ability to know what the fuck my experiences mean.

"I suppose the productive thing for me to do is dig myself out of my self-pity hole, build a ramp to get out and to another place where I accept my situation. Enjoying the good fortune of others is happier than resenting them for it, resenting life for it, resenting God.

"I'm tired. Chalk it up to that. I don't trust my hope. But it's okay because it doesn't make a difference whether I hope or not. It's not as though my hope, or lack of it, will interfere with any one or another path toward my destiny.

"I remember as a kid going sledding at a place about a half hour walk away from my home, and it was cold, and after a sledding awhile, day was turning to night. I began my trek home but was tired, and I wanted to lie down and fall asleep. Later I learned that falling asleep in the snow was how people ended up freezing to death. Well, I kept walking through a dreamlike state, a sort of exhausted trance in which I thought maybe in fact I was dreaming. I got home and took off my wet clothes, sat with my beet-red, nearly frostbitten feet next to the heating vent, waiting for feeling to come back into them, waiting while numbness turned to prickles to pin pricks to aching and finally to normal sensation. The best parts of that memory are the smells and sounds coming from the kitchen where my mom was preparing dinner. I would so love to eat at that kitchen table again."

Israel resisted the temptation to launch into his own thoughts on eternity. There just wasn't enough time. Ironic!

The rest of Israel's day was more of the same, a doctor's work life. People have problems and sometimes the problems get solved in ways less than satisfying.

At the end of the day, while he was completing his paperwork, he read again the summarized medical history he had reported about one of his more tragically stricken patients.

Melanie White has chronic pain with complicated medical and social history.

1994: Lumbar microdiskectomy L4-L5

1995: Repeat microdiskectomy

1997: Anterior interbody fusion of L4-L5 and L5-S1, complicated by a surgical nick of her bowel leading to emergent crisis, and then, three weeks later she was operated for sepsis, peritonitis and abdominal gangrene. Surgical wound was left open to heal by secondary intention. It took seven months to get rid of the infection.

2001: Abdominal surgery because of incarcerated hernia, re-quiring partial bowel resection. Two layers of mesh and prolonged recovery

2007: She refused to give her narcotic analgesic to her boyfriend who then beat her with a baseball bat. He abducted her and kept her in a cabin for a month, where he tortured her. He strangled her by dragging her across a room, pulling her with a belt tightened around her neck. She survived. The court moved her home to a se-cret location to protect her from a still-dangerous assailant who had made a death threat and would be getting out of prison soon.

This episode delayed discovery and treatment of rectal cancer, surgical resection and then chemotherapy complicated by residual, permanent, severely painful peripheral neuropathy.

Still suffers from post-traumatic stress disorder, afraid to leave her home and afraid to stay in her home. Recently she learned that her assailant was looking for her. He now is back in prison on a drug charge, but he won't be there forever.

She returned today because she is unhappy with the pain man-agement she received in another community. Brought a copy of a recent report and complained about the shabbiness of it. "He regur-gitated a fifteen -page document I had to fill out . . . and then he left most of it out . . . he spent five minutes with me." She pointed out the errors in his note.

Currently she is on disability. Earlier worked as a paralegal. Smokes sometimes, but not every day. No alcohol.

Israel looked at the ceiling. "Not fair," he said out loud, "unless . . . " Unless we all live the same lives, every one of us, the exact same lives; then it's fair, and then it's true karma.

A voice whispered in his head, *even for the least of my brothers.*

He searched the phrase on the Internet and got Matthew 25:31-45.

31 When the Son of Man comes in glory, surrounded by all the holy angels, then he will sit upon his thrown;

32 And all nations will gather around him, and he will divide then as a shepherd divides his sheep from the goats,

33 with the sheep on his right and the goats on his left.

34 The King will say to the righteous, "Come you who are blessed by my Father, and inherit the kingdom that was prepared for you when the world was made;

35 For when I was hungry you fed me; I was thirsty, and you gave me drink; I was a stranger, and you took me in;

36 You clothed me when I was naked, and when I was sick and cast out from the community you came to visit me. I was in prison and you visited me."

37 The righteous will ask, "Lord, when were you hungry, and we fed you? or thirsty, and we gave you something to drink?

38 When did we take you as a stranger into our home? or when did we clothe your nakedness?

39 When were you sick or in prison, and we came to visit?"

40 And the King will declare, "Truthfully I say this to you, Inasmuch as you have done these things to any of the least of my brothers and sisters, you have done it to me."

41 Then to the unrighteous on the left he will say, "Depart from me, you who are cursed, into everlasting fire prepared for the devil and his angels,

42 For when I was hungry you did not feed me, and when I was thirsty you left me parched.

43 I was a stranger, and you shut your door to me; I was naked, and you let me be naked; and you did not visit me when I was sick and when I was in prison".

44 And the unrighteous will ask, "Lord, when did we see you hungry and not feed you? or thirsty, or a stranger, or naked, or sick, or in prison, and did not assist you?"

45 He will answer them, "Truthfully I say this to you, Inasmuch as you did not do these things for the least of my brothers and sisters, you did not do it for me."

Israel said aloud, "Quaint, obsolete thinking!" Matthew

portrayed a lord who demanded humans to be merciful and benevolent to each other, but then the lord himself demonstrated
no mercy for those who were selfish. Those selfish souls he condemned were fragile and selfish because of causes and effects.
They had nothing to do with deciding how they came to be the
way they were. Determinism. Einstein. The future already is there
waiting for us. This story in Matthew made God a hypocrite, a parent who set a bad example for his kids. This story was written by
a righteous man certainly but at a time when justice was based on
the mentality of an eye for an eye and a tooth for a tooth. People
then had no idea, not really, no clue about the precise pervasive-
ness of cause and effect. They believed in atonement by revenge,
by getting even, by evening the score.

Many people still believed that way. Just like Matthew, they
didn't understand that Jesus was the goats too, not just the sheep.
He was the unrighteous as well as the righteous.

Israel was amused with himself. He was fighting God again. But
this was not God. This was Matthew's mistaken notion of God. We
all have mistaken notions of God. Matthew didn't know any better.
He lived at a time of history when he wasn't able to understand.

But Jesus! Jesus meant it literally when he said, "I was hungry
and you fed me." He meant it literally; it wasn't a metaphor.

Israel leaned forward with his forearms on his thighs, and he
looked at the floor. He understood this. He imagined Jesus inside of
him and made a sign of the cross on himself. He took the pendant
out from under his shirt, pulled it off over his head, and looked at
the cross Gina had given him. He was in each and every one of us.
In fact he was even inside selfish people who did not take care of
the needful; he was inside the unrighteous.

He drove over to Michael's mansion and immediately asked,
"May I use your computer for a moment?" He wrote a short email
to Gina.

I love you.
Things happen of course, cause and effect. It just happens that

I love you. I've been full of analyzing things, but this is something I don't want to analyze anymore. I just want to let it be what it is. I want to tell you that I love you, and I don't want to worry about how you might think maybe it's too strong for right now, that maybe things are moving too fast. I don't care. I don't want to think about how you might have some sort of psychological advantage over me because you know I love you. It just is. I'm not going to worry about it.

I love you.

He talked to Michael. "I'm ready."

"Ready to travel?"

"Ready to travel."

"What changed?"

"I'm not afraid anymore. Like you said, 'What will be will be.'"

"What if it's another wicked experience?"

"It won't be; I'm confident there's a purpose to all of this, and I've already learned the lesson of hell. I don't have to learn it again. And even if it is a wicked experience, so what?"

"So what? You don't want to be miserable again, do you?"

"Michael, we've gotten used to thinking it would be wonderful to live forever, but we seem never to consider that doing it might be wonderful only if everlasting life were granted on our own terms. What if the terms of eternity turn out to be something we never expected, something so perfectly and obviously fair that we can't dispute the creator's judgment? What if we were caught up in an eternity in which quibbling about our circumstances would be meaningless or even preposterous?"

"How do you mean?"

"I'm beginning to think that living all these other lives is inevitable. Each of us is going to do it anyway, some time or another. It's the karmic balance. Each of us will end up living the same lives, all of them, one at a time. That's what makes the universe fair. This spiritual time travel I'm doing just gives me a little control over when it happens, but it's going to happen anyway. These little trips

I've been making are like trailers to movies that are happening. Listen, it's not just about Markus anymore. I still want to go back to Markus, but now I want to be the other people too, live some of their lives in such a way that I hope I'll be able to remember more and more. I'm learning from this. I want to talk with Jesus again. I know you're a Jew, and don't take me wrong about this, but I think Jesus knows about this continuous energy that exists between particles of the universe. I want to talk with him about it."

Michael listened patiently, and then he answered, "Good enough for me. So tell me; what do you think about what I said before, that to change an event in a deterministic world you'd have to change the entire future? Why would a god do that for you?"

"How many billions of stars are there, Michael? How big is the universe? We already know God is bigger than we can imagine. So what makes us think we need to draw a line between what he can and can't be? How can we say he's bigger than we can imagine but no bigger than that? It's human pseudo-intellectual arrogance to put any limits on God. Why should any of us think we need to limit his creation at all? Maybe all things really are possible."

Michael nodded with a tilt and wiggle of his head. "When do you want to go?"

"No time like the present."

"As a matter of fact, all of the different times of the universe are the present." Michael chuckled. "Maybe that's a clue to entangled particles. What do you think?"

"I have no idea. You're the genius."

They walked up the stairs to the Mozart laboratory and the now-beacon helmet. Israel picked up the helmet, but then he stopped. "Not yet. I've got to talk with Gina about this first. I'll be back."

Nineteen

LOVE AT FIRST FIGHT

"So how did you expect me to react? This is insane."

"I'm not making it up."

"I'm not saying you made it up. I'm not saying I don't believe you. Frankly, my mother talks about this sort of thing too. It's not a new thing for me."

"It's not a new thing for you?"

"I'm saying it's crazy that you'd want to take that kind of risk, and you're giving me mixed messages. First you write me this charming letter about how you love me, and now you're telling me you're willing to give me up, you're willing to change the natural order of the universe, in order to save Markus. From my point of view, that's not good decision making."

"To save his life."

"See what I mean? You don't even know that you can do it. It's like you're willing to give me up on a whim. Don't you think I should reconsider how much emotion I'm willing to invest in our relationship?"

"It's not like that. If I can't save Markus, I'm not going anywhere. I'm still here."

"You're willing to give me up. What kind of a start to a relationship is that? I thought we had something here. Something was happening with us, something good."

"I love you."

"But only so far. You love me only so far. You're willing to let some other Israel have me, an Israel who looks and talks, and smiles, and kisses just like you. But it wouldn't be you." She paused. "I'm not yours to give away. I'm not your plaything. I'm not a prostitute."

"What?" He looked at the floor. "That escalated quickly."

"You might as well go. The damage is already done. At least now I know where I stand with you."

"No, I don't think you do." There was silence, during which Israel wanted to hold Gina affectionately close to him, wanted to feel her skin against his skin, her breasts against his chest. He wanted to feel the inside of her. Instead he was entwined in thorns. He began again. "Actually if I go into a parallel universe, I'd also stay in this one. It would still be me, my spirit in this body."

She looked at him, arms crossed, waiting. He pulled the cross out from under his shirt. "Thank you for this. I was looking at it when I realized we're all part of the same spirit. Jesus told me . . . this sounds crazy. The boy Jesus I told you about, no beard, not the storybook character; this was the real thing. He said he's inside us always. I love you, the same as I love Jesus. It's something to think about." He waited for her to respond.

"Jesus isn't going to give you a blow job. It's something to think about."

The two of them looked around at things, different things, occasionally at each other, but when their eyes met they quickly looked away again.

Finally Gina said, "Hold me, will you? No sex. Just hold me. I don't want to lose you."

"You're not going to lose me." Israel pulled her close to him. "I don't want to lose you either." He was aroused by her body against his.

"So what are you going to do?" Gina quietly asked. "What is Israel Newman going to do, Mister Gotta-have-it-all, even though he's already got the most loving and sexy woman he could dream of? It makes me wonder who I'm making love to when we have sex. Am I making love to your body or your soul?"

"Both."

"I want it to be your soul."

Israel pulled her closer and kissed her forehead. His chest no longer hurt. "My soul's not going anywhere, Gina. I love you."

She turned and looked at him. "Yes, it is. That's what we're talking about; your soul is going away." She wiggled a little against him. "Your body's nice though."

"Not as nice as yours."

Gina mused, "If Jesus is inside each of us, is it like he's making love to himself? Divine masturbation!"

They laughed.

"But if you time travel the way you say you do, then your soul does go somewhere. It goes into some other body in another time. You'd be the soul inside another body that's making love with somebody else. I don't know if I can handle that. I don't want to have to think about that."

"Maybe that's not what really happens. Maybe Michael has that part of it wrong. When I travel, maybe I'm just going into a cosmic awareness of all that is, the Akashic records; I go into a part of all that awareness. I don't myself really go anywhere."

"You mean the Akasha, from Sanskrit. Okay, so maybe we lift that out of Hinduism and make it Catholic, just for me, okay? because I've got to understand this from my point of reference. You're thinking it's the holy spirit?"

"Yes, that fits. You understand. And you never hear about it being spirits, do you? It's not plural. It's one spirit. One spirit in all of us."

"So you think it's the holy spirit who has been making love billions of times throughout history?"

He nodded. "The holy spirit experiences it, anyway."

"He must get exhausted with all that sex."

"Gina, you make me happy."

"People do other things to each other besides making love."

"Yes, they do."

"Why would God do that to himself?"

"Good question. Maybe he uses us to learn."

"You think God uses us to learn."

"Maybe. When we talk about a soul, about a spirit that's inside us, maybe we're really talking about God, not ourselves. People talk about their spiritual growth, but individual people grow in their physical bodies and minds. The soul isn't theirs; it's God's. Some people say that some souls are more advanced than others, but how does that make sense if we're all one and the same? To say one soul is more advanced than another is like the holy spirit saying one part of him is more advanced than another part. 'Look at my right foot. It's much more advanced than my left one. That's why I run around in circles.' That makes no sense. And it divides people. It's not right. There's no karmic justice in it."

"You said, 'Maybe.' I'm not fond of that very significant little word. It's not a word that turns me on, you know. It's a like saying 'Maybe I'll fuck you senseless for the rest of your life, and maybe I won't.' You're conjuring up excuses trying to get me to say, 'Oh, I understand, dear. Please do continue going to other bodies and fucking other bodies so that God may experience life and grow. Please do.' Sounds like a little bit of crap, if you ask me. Okay, so tell me, what do you think happens with God's spiritual growth?"

Israel imagined being on a tight rope, executing a risky balancing act.

Gina observed the slowness of his answer; it sounded tentative.

Israel said, "When somebody thinks their soul is more advanced than another, that thinking comes from a mistaken perception by their material mind, you know, the part of their mind that is anatomy and physiology, the cause-and-effect part. Maybe their physical mind is more enlightened than others, or less enlightened, but if they think it's their soul that is less or more advanced than anybody else's, then they're fooling themselves. They're confusing what is physical with what is eternal and spiritual. They don't understand that there's only one soul, the soul of God that is in each of us."

"You're sidestepping the issue. Let me make it clear for you.

I don't want you fucking other women, not here, not there, not anywhere."

"In Hindu they call it Brahman. Jung called it the oversoul."

"Jung has pretty much been discredited, you know."

"I know. That doesn't mean he wasn't right."

"And when you time travel you are able to experience a part of what that soul experiences in other bodies, but you don't actually live them."

Israel nodded. *Am I lying? I don't want to lie to Gina. I don't want her to hurt. I don't want to lose her.*

"You're sounding like a little shit. You're very cerebral about all this, but it doesn't excuse your sticking your dick into other women's pussies." She said it in a matter-of-fact way, as though she were studying for a college exam.

The comment completely silenced Israel.

"So how is that going to save Markus?" She had checkmated him.

They sat and cuddled silently awhile, and then Gina said, "I love you."

"I love you."

They kissed.

"This changes us," she said. "It changes our relationship."

"How's that?"

"I don't know; time will tell."

Israel felt a cloud passing in front of the sun. The sun was still there, but so was the cloud.

She put a finger on his shirt and stroked the nipple hardening beneath. She saw a lump getting larger in his pants and put her hand there. "Are you interested in some divine masturbation?"

The next morning before work, Israel wrote another sonnet:

I'm fairly certain that we do not choose
to love the ones we love, and yet we do,
love, I mean, selected by a muse
or many chemistries with causes true.

What arrow was it struck its mark in me
and pinned my heart to you in helpless mess?
My captive soul and I imprisoned be,
without the cage but captured nonetheless.
I had not even wiggle room nor clue
of what was happening. I know it's not
your fault that I got caught, and yet I stew
because it is your fault. You're just too hot!
And so I'll make the best of it, my dear.
It's by the star of love for you I'll steer.

Twenty

BELIEVE WHAT YOU WILL

"You told her that?" Professor Hannity asked with an air of incredulity, sitting across the table in his hobbit-hole dining room and behind a steaming cup of hot chocolate. "Fuck damn, shit shit shit. That's a good one. Priceless. It's one for the ages."

"What do you mean?"

"You don't believe that crap, do you?"

"Why not?"

"Only because of what you told me yesterday. You were talking about how you valued the role of karmic balance in the world. You called it fairness, remember? You told me about how each of us lives all of the same lives as everybody else, and that's what makes the universe fair. Remember? So now if it's God's spirit in everybody, and if there's no individual me spirit, then I get stuck being this schmuck. I don't like that. Super Schmuckman is all I'll ever get to be. What's so fair about that? I'll never get a chance at being Brad Pitt or Warren Beatty. I'll have you know I was looking forward to those lives. Paul Hornung is another. And if I think that someday I will be that bum on the street who's begging me for money, won't I be more likely to want to help him out?"

"Wouldn't you want to help him out anyway because he's God inside?"

"Yeah well, not so much."

"What?"

"So maybe I'm selfish, all right. Maybe I'm like Jacob, always trying to bargain my way through life. I keep asking what's in it for me. If I'm going to be Brad Pitt someday, then maybe I'm willing to be patient during this lifetime. If someday I'm going to be the bum on the street, then maybe I've got some generosity for him. That makes sense to me, and if all of us are in the same boat, then that's karmic balance, and maybe that would make me a better person.

"However, if it's God inside the bum, and it's only God; if it's never going to be poor defenseless me, then I figure God can fend for himself pretty damned well. He's got power and might. In that case I'll keep my bucks to pay for a large-screen, high-definition television because that's what God seems to want while living in my person." He took a sip of his hot chocolate, swallowed, and sighed loudly. "And other people think the same as I do. This is the way they think. You know they do."

Israel stewed about it and nodded his head.

"So, are you going to tell her?"

"Gina? That I really travel with my conscious soul? Not on your life."

"Why not?"

"Because she already knows it. She didn't believe a thing I said." After Michael stopped laughing, Israel asked, "Is it true? Do I really travel spiritually into those other lives? I actually become them?"

"You find that hard to believe?"

"I find it . . . I would think that having done this a few times I would know for sure what's happening, and I don't. One moment I'm sure I understand it, and the next I don't."

"That's okay. Life is like this. You don't necessarily have to understand." After a long moment of looking at each other, Michael asked, "Do you want to travel?"

"Yes, I do."

They walked up the stairs, and just outside the Mozart laboratory, Israel stopped and said, "Maybe it could go both ways; I mean one way or the other."

"What are you talking about?"

"Karma or God. Maybe the natural way of things is that we reincarnate over and over in all the lives of world history, but maybe a person could choose not to do that. He could choose to let God do it instead. You could just become part of the body of God, and he'd be the spirit in all those lives."

"All the bad lives anyway, right? Maybe he'd let you keep the good lives, and that would be heaven, something like that? You get to keep the heavenly parts?"

"Yeah, something like that."

"Sounds very Christian."

"It does, doesn't it?"

"Yeah, well, I'm a Jew."

"Not entirely. You're like Einstein, almost a Jew but not quite. You don't believe in free will, and Jews do. You're like Albert Einstein that way."

"So I am. Thank you for reminding me." Michael put a fatherly hand on Israel's shoulder. "Now for the truly awesome implications of all this: I dislike smugness in any form. I value humility. The blind faith of religionists bothers me. The nose-in-the-air superior attitude of blind scientists bothers me. A determined universe, as shown to us by Einstein's principle of relativity, must come into existence in its entirety, all at once, beginning to end. Past and present and future all coexist. Every breath of every person in all of history came into being in one instant, every heartbeat, every kiss, every song, every rifle fired, every step on the sands of a beach, every drop of blood spilled, every bolus of food tasted and swallowed, all of it from beginning to end came into being in one instant.

"There's a popular debate about whether Einstein did or did not believe in God. He once said that the main difference between what he believed and Judaism was that Jews believe in free will, and he was a determinist. He believed you can't have a personal relationship with God. That was Einstein."

"And you?" Israel asked. "Do you think you can have a personal relationship with God?"

"It's enough for me that the question exists. Many of our most accredited physicists explain that the existence of the universe can be explained without there being a God, and then they begin with the big bang, but this displaces the question. They don't answer what needs to be answered. The question is this: How do you explain the universe, all of it, coming into existence at once? All of it from beginning to end in one instant?"

They walked into the laboratory and over to the Paul-Hornung-now-beacon helmet. Israel said, "I wonder when I'll get to be Paul Hornung."

"Me first," answered Michael. "Sometimes I think this entire universe is simply a giant amusement park for a carnivorous lord with a gruesome sense of humor."

They studied each other's eyes.

God intended for it to be this way, or at least allowed it, all the good and all the bad, all the evil, the joys and the disappointments, all of it.

Michael said, "Look, the creator of the universe, I don't put any limitations or expectations on it, whoever he, she, it, they, or whatever it is. Call it God if you want, but it may turn out to be nothing more than a mathematical equation, a glorious mathematical equation. And I don't demand that it be all-knowing or all-powerful. It's not necessarily all good or bad. It just is whatever it is. That's what I believe. Would you like to travel?"

"Yes." Israel stared at the inside of the helmet. "I hope this time I live in a body that knows it matters what it does toward other people."

While Israel tentatively picked up the helmet, Michael busied himself with last minute checks on the calibration of his instruments, at one moment motioning Israel to wait as he repeatedly pushed a button aligning sinusoidal curves on a screen, at another slowly turning a dial until a light glowed and numbers appeared and advanced, stopping at forty-two. He turned toward Israel and rolled his hand in the air. "Let's get this show on the road."

Israel donned the helmet and the straps on his wrists and ankles and sat back in the recliner pilot seat.

Michael whispered, "And away we go." While watching Israel reclined in the pilot seat he wondered how long it would take before the lad realized he didn't need the device. It was his training wheels, this contraption. That's all it was. When would he learn to steer his travels?

He can do it; the lad's like us; he has the gift.

Minutes passed until the instrument sang its soft buzz and ring, and at the exact same moment, the universe considered whether or not to tear itself apart. Michael didn't notice the transient blip in the structure of the cosmos because there was no violence in it, the vast potential of a single moment struggling to find its way, all things possible in the collapse of a quantum moment. Is the universe like a biological cell dividing into parts moving along different paths toward different destinations? Is it like a new bud growing from the branch of a tree? Or are different paths considered and in the mere observance of them, a single way selected? Are there infinite numbers of universes or only one? Computer monitors of Professor Hannity's time machine made no registration of it, but at that moment the world selected what it would be.

Michael sang happily, "La la la de da dum; dum!" He paced slowly around the pilot seat, waiting and watching for Israel to sit up, and finally he did. "How was the trip, my friend?"

Israel appeared disoriented as he held up a hand. "Wait a moment. There's a lot of stuff in my mind; I want to hold onto it. There's a lot of stuff I remember this time."

Michael smiled.

Israel frowned. "Michael, do you remember Whitey Ford?"

"Sure. Pitched for the Yankees during the fifties, a great player."

"No, no, no. A kid you went to school with in Milwaukee. I had really blond hair, almost white. My real name is Will."

"That punk? Fuckdammit."

"Yes, I'm sorry about that."

"You were him?"

"Yes. I'm sorry my friends and I teased you mercilessly."

"And the couple times your gang beat me up?"

"Yes, sorry about that too. Honest! I'm sorry, and it's not just me, Israel, saying that. It's me, Whitey, saying that. I changed later in life, Michael. Something clicked in my head, and I changed." Israel looked around the lab, taking it all in, and then he looked at Michael. "What's this all about? I treated you like shit back then, and here I am becoming a close friend with you. Is that karmic balance?"

Michael suppressed the contempt he felt for Whitey, but nevertheless a trace of it could be identified in his voice as he answered, "Karma isn't about punishment, Israel, and by the way you're Israel now, not Whitey, so snap out of it. Karma is about learning. Look at me, Israel. Karma is about learning."

Israel shook his head a little. "I changed. I became a missionary in Haiti, taking care of kids in a Christian school. I taught English there, and we all took care of them, all their needs; we did that together; they had needs, some of them like you can't imagine. And then one day . . . Michael!" Israel's eyes widened, and his voice became slightly tremulous. "One day the ground shook. Earthquake! No escape from it. The roof collapsed on the kids and . . . oh, God in heaven! Where were you, God? I survived, but I was pinned under concrete that had fallen on me, and there in that darkness, in and out of consciousness. I heard the kids shouting and crying. Lots of them were hurt. Some were killed. I survived. I had crushed legs and then gangrene, and they amputated my legs below the knees. More than fifty thousand people died, Michael. Over a million people homeless. I've got to go back and help them, Michael. Help me go back. Why am I here? What am I going to do here?"

Michael waited for him to continue.

"They were going to teach me to walk again with prostheses, artificial legs. I was in Milwaukee where I could get better medical care. I was in a car, passenger in the front. This was some few months after the earthquake, and my thighs had been hurting for a couple of weeks. It was sudden, a pain in my chest, and I couldn't breathe. That's the last I remember. I must have . . . I must have died then; something happened that made me come here. That day was . . . when was it? The earthquake was January 12, 2010, so I must have died that spring. That's the last I remember."

Michael clenched his teeth. He cleared his throat. He studied Israel's face. *He hasn't been prepared for travel into the future.*

Realization slowly dawned on Israel. "That was how long ago now, Michael? When was the earthquake? It was January 12, 2010. How long ago was that? Let's see. Michael, what's the date today?"

Michael watched the curtain gradually lift from Israel's consciousness.

Israel said, "Oh, my god! Today is . . . it's September now, isn't it, two thousand nine. Michael! It hasn't happened yet. I've been to the future, Michael. It's going to happen, and we can warn people. We can tell them to stay out of buildings. This is a good thing. We can save people from a lot of suffering."

Michael studied his protégé. He had the gift but not yet an understanding of the universe, that it is what it is.

Michael said, "Israel, let's go down to the Hobbit Hole and talk about this. We want to be credible to the rest of the world, don't we? We don't want you to sound like another doomsday prophet. It's a delicate matter how to get people to believe you. Come on, let's go down and have a snack of some sort. Would you like another hot chocolate? A lemonade? Maybe a beer would be more like it. Come along, lad."

They walked down the stairs and to the right through the proscenium opening to the grand room that looked like the outdoors, through the circular door and tubular tunnel into the kitchen. Jeeves was there. Michael said, "I know just the refreshment for us, refreshing as can be. Jeeves, take Doctor Newman into the dining room and just sit with him. I'll prepare this myself, some tea with a twist of lemon. You two go into the dining room, and I'll be right in with it. Looking cognitively awkward, Israel nodded and walked through a circular door, out of the kitchen, and into the small dining room with its rich wooden panels. Jeeves followed him, leaving Michael alone in the kitchen.

The Mozart Lab is for physics; The Dungeon is my robot lab; and this kitchen is my potion laboratory. He whistled quietly as he went to the cupboard, pulling a chair behind him, and then he climbed up onto it, more easily to reach the very back of a cupboard where he pressed against a panel, and it opened for him. He took a small bottle of white powder from the secret cubby and closed the door again, carried the bottle, and set it down carefully on the counter. "Lemon tea coming right up." He poured the sparkling amber beverage into three of his mother's beautiful tea glasses and then put a pinch of powder in one of them, rubbing the tips of his thumb and index finger together. "With a twist," he chirped, and then he quietly sang, "Em-eye-see, kay-eee-why, la dee da dee dum." As he carried the refreshments into the next room he thought, *Israel's glass is the one on the right, the one on the right, on the right, on the right. Nice if he'll drink it without a fight, without a fight, without a fight.*

"Here you go. Have a Mickey."

Israel received the correct glass with a grave smile. Michael handed a glass to Jeeves. "Cheers, my friends."

Each tilted his glass a little toward the other, and then they drank.

"Interesting situation," Michael began, intending to allow a few minutes for the benzodiazepine to take effect, to calm Israel and make him more suggestible. "Jeeves. Dr. Newman has been to the future. The future is a scary place to go. There's so much responsibility attached to it." Israel looked at him. Michael continued, "We want to go about this right. Tell me, at this moment, do you feel more like Whitey or Israel?"

Israel waited a moment before answering, looked sorrowful, and then said, "Gina! I want to be with Gina." Israel was coming around.

Michael smiled. "Good good good. A little debriefing first. We'll get this planned out, how to go about things, and then you go to your woman. Good!" He watched Israel drum his fingers on the table. He was impatient. "So you're Israel now."

"Yes, but it's real, Michael. These memories are real."

"Of course they are. What about determinism?"

"What about it?"

"The future can't be changed. It's already there, isn't it?"

"But we can change this. At least some people will believe me. At least some people will be saved on that day because they'll listen and believe. At least some of them."

"Yeah, the kooks will be saved. The kooks will believe you. Do you want to save more than just the kooks?"

"You can be an asshole sometimes."

"No, actually I'm not being an asshole at all. I'm being a pragmatist. God's the asshole. Why the fuck does this sort of thing happen?" Michael watched Israel's eyelids droop slightly; his body slumped a little, and he leaned on the table. The medicine was beginning to work. "I'm worried about my friend, Israel. I'm afraid of what determinism means for you. The earthquake is going to happen, no matter what we do, and fifty thousand unaware people are going to die no matter what we do. While living as Whitey Ford, do you remember anything about somebody warning there would be an earthquake?"

Israel looked dumbfounded. "No."

"No, I didn't think so. Why not? Why wasn't there some doctor named Israel Newman warning the world about an upcoming earthquake in Haiti? Why doesn't Whitey remember that?"

Jeeves answered, "Because something silenced the dear Doctor Newman."

"No." Israel shook his head. "This clearly is a situation in which free will exists."

Michael nodded his head thoughtfully. "And maybe not." He sipped his tea. "I'm wondering if Doctor Newman got silenced by a motor vehicle accident or a cardiac arrest. Maybe his friend Professor Hannity talked him out of it." Maybe this dangerous idea could be hypnotized out of Israel's head.

They sat silently for a while, and then Israel said, "This is an experiment. We need to have courage enough to go through with it. I've got to do this. If I'm successful, then we'll know that free will exists."

Michael answered, "And you will be a hero and on the front page of every magazine at the supermarket."

Jeeves added, "You'll need a new wardrobe."

Israel was aghast. "No! Damn!"

Jeeves added, "And they'll want you to predict other future events."

"Yes." Israel sighed and took another sip of his spiked tea. "But I've got to do this. There is no choice for me. I can't choose not to do this. You understand that. Of course you do."

"An experiment?" Michael asked.

"Yes, an experiment."

"What about your life with Gina? That's going to get screwed up."

"I've got to do this."

"What about Markus?"

"This is the same thing as Markus, isn't it? It's on a much larger scale, but it's the same thing, an experiment of free will."

"That it is," Michael mused. He had intended to hypnotize the lad, and instead Israel was persuading him to play along. "You might die."

"I just don't see that happening, but even if I die, this is the right thing to do."

"The right thing?"

Israel looked at him serenely.

Michael answered, "I don't want them coming in here and tampering with the Mozart Lab."

"I'll just say I had a premonition. An angel visited me."

Michael shook his head. "You're going to look like a damned fool. What about your job? What about Gina? Can she put up with that?"

"I don't know. I don't have a choice."

Together they wrote a letter to the president of Haiti and a press release for the *Seattle Times*. On his way driving home, as he dropped the letters into a mailbox, Israel felt a vague shudder of disorientation.

Twenty A

THE SELECTED EVENT

I am Whitey Ford, reformed bad guy, recovering alcoholic, missionary, double amputee after being one of the lucky survivors of the earthquake in Haiti. I'm depressed, sitting in my car in a parking lot outside Froedtert Hospital in Milwaukee, out along Watertown Plank Road. I've got time before I go in for my appointment, just sitting here, pain in my legs that has been going on a couple weeks and won't go away.

This pain in my chest, heavy, can't breathe, my ears ringing loudly. Darkness.

Beyond spacetime and back into it.

Israel felt disoriented. *I exist. What am I?* He waited while the world congealed before him, until he could make sense of it and could think. There was a man with spectacles pacing around him, humming a song. Other music in the background. Israel sat up.

"How was the trip, my friend?" The bespectacled man was talking to him.

"Wait a moment." Israel held up a hand. "There is a lot of stuff in my mind: I want to hold onto it. There's a lot of stuff I remember. I want to remember it." *Am I Whitey Ford? No. I'm Israel Newman. But I'm Whitey Ford. No. Not here. Not now. My god! This is Michael Hannity, the same Michael Hannity, the Superboy kid.*

He asked the bespectacled man, "Michael, do you remember Whitey Ford?"

"Sure. Pitched for the Yankees during the fifties, a great player."

"No, no, no. A kid you went to school with in Milwaukee. I had really blond hair, almost white. My real name is Will."

"That punk? Fuckdammit."

"Yes, I'm sorry about that."

"You were him?"

"Yes, I'm sorry my friends and I teased you mercilessly."

"And the couple times your gang beat me up?"

"Yes, sorry about that too. Honest! I'm sorry, and it's not just me, Israel, saying that. It's me, Whitey, saying that. I changed later in life, Michael. Something clicked in my head, and I changed." Israel looked around the lab, taking it all in, and then he looked at Michael. "What's this all about? I treated you like shit back then, and here I am becoming a close friend with you. Is that karmic balance?"

"Karma isn't about punishment, Israel, and by the way you're Israel now, not Whitey, so snap out of it. Karma is about learning. Look at me, Israel. Karma is about learning."

Israel shook his head a little. "I changed. I became a missionary in Haiti, taking care of kids in a Christian school. I taught English there, and we all took care of them, all their needs; we did that together; they had needs, some of them like you can't imagine. I wanted to help them, devoted my life to it. It's what made my life worthwhile, my atonement. I know we can't really atone for our sins, Michael. Once something's done it's done, but we can learn from it to do the right things later. We can do that. We can do the right things and maybe be even better at it once we've learned what not to do."

Michael nodded his head. "We can do the right things."

"One day there was a loud siren and there were bells, and that's when I left and came here."

"What were the bells and siren about?"

"I have no idea. I remember right up to that moment, and then there's nothing. My memory abruptly stops. It's like anesthesia, when you get put to sleep for surgery; everything stops, and immediately you're waking up again, only this time it's into a different me. Don't know what the siren and bells were about. Did I die?"

"Maybe. You remember a lot this time?"

"Yes, a tremendous lot."

"Good! You must write it down."

"There's too much, Michael. I can't write it all down, but trust me; I remember. This is strange. Right now I'm . . . right now there's a guy named Whitey Ford working with kids as a missionary in Haiti, and I know everything about him, everything. I've got a scar on my left hand where I cut myself when a glass broke while I was washing dishes, and I've memorized that scar. It's like sins of my past I no longer do, but they've marked me. And I love the scar too, because it's me. I know that scar." Israel looked at his left hand where there was no scar. He whispered, "Damn! I'm going to have to sort all this out. I could go meet myself . . . him." A feeling of dread pervaded his mind. "Or maybe not. It would be too weird, impossibly weird." Having said this he felt relieved by the thought of never traveling to meet Whitey Ford in Haiti. Again he looked for the scar on his left hand, but it wasn't there.

Israel felt a tremendous loneliness and craving. "I want Gina," he said. "This is a turnaround. She told me she wanted me to be her anchor, but right now I need her to anchor me." It was as though the mere thought of Gina pulled him back fully into the life of Israel. "I need her, Michael. Right now."

Twenty-one

ENTANGLED SOULS

srael said, "Something has clicked inside me, and wanting to be with you has become the most important thing in my life. Gina, listen to me. This has happened fast. I want to be with you, and I don't want you to worry about . . . things."

"Things? You mean your sexual exploits in other lives? You're right about me worrying about things. I don't want to have to think about 'things.'" She emphasized the last word, and it was like she slugged him in the chest. "Tell me how to get 'things' out of my head when you make love with me."

Israel knew the answer in his heart and carefully searched for accurate words. "Making love with you subtracts the rest of the world. It goes away."

"Have you said that to the others?"

"No. This is an Israel-to-Gina comment. It's not a somebody else-to-somebody else comment. I am not Israel in those other experiences. I am Israel here with you."

Gina's demeanor softened. "That's meaningful," she said. "The soul, though, the soul is still meaningful. I still want your soul to love me."

"It does love you."

"When you're in those other lives?"

"How about when you're in those other lives?"

"I'm not in those other lives."

"You don't really know that. You can say you don't remember those other lives, but your soul is not confined. If not now, it will be later. Your soul will live forever."

Gina studied his eyes. "I like when we make love. It subtracts the rest of the world for me too. I want to be able to depend on this connection between us. We've just found it, and I treasure it. I'm jealous of it. How are you going to reassure me that this is a treasure for you too, and you're not going to let it go?"

"Make love with you a lot?"

"Stay with me?"

"Yes, of course. Stay with you."

"That's the right answer." Her voice softened. Gina put her hand on Israel's shoulder and moved it up onto the back of his head and neck, lacing her fingers into his hair. "I love you."

Israel simply nodded his head, not knowing exactly what he was thinking, not in detail, anyway, recognizing by way of feeling that he wanted this woman's hand to continue touching him, her body to embrace him, her mind to focus on him, and her presence to be ever closer. "I'm not lonely when I'm with you."

"When we make love the rest of the universe goes away. We purify each other that way. It's meaningful and needs to be repeated." She snuggled close to him. "Hold me. I want you to hold me." Their bodies together became the center of the universe, and each of them wanted to be closer to that very center.

Gina asked, "What about Markus?"

"I can't stop the past from happening, Gina."

"That's a change. You used to think you could."

"I know, but determinism; it's a real thing. What's done is done. Stay with me, Gina. Please! Just stay with me."

"You've got it." She kissed him, and he pulled her closer.

"You just might be the real deal," she whispered.

"The real deal?"

"My man, my soul mate."

"Soul mate. It's a real thing. My brother, Jeff, is psychic. He says souls tend to travel together in groups, life after life. This may not be the only life we've been together. We might have lived lots of other lives with each other."

"But we're not in some other life right now; we're here, lucky to have each other now. Stay in the moment with me, Israel. This is going to last between us, isn't it!"

"It's going to be forever."

Gina slipped her hand under Israel's shirt, launching a blissful cascade, each of them tasting and feeling and moving upon their object of affection, trying to crush away any distance that separated them. After making their craved and desperately needed love, they fell asleep together in Gina's bed surrounded by the happy softness of her room, absolutely refusing to part from one another.

Israel dreamed fitfully, images in black and white, several dreams beginning with one in which he was a Muslim in a Spanish inquisitional court, denying his own faith to save his family from being robbed of its home, to save himself from imprisonment or death. He claimed Jesus for his lord and savior, justifying his deceit by admitting the great prophet Jesus would indeed work with his own beloved prophet to save himself and his family. He prayed, *Please let them believe me.*

He dreamed of being a fourteen-year-old boy being ousted from the Boy Scouts of America because he confessed to being an atheist.

A dream then placed him as a prisoner in a death camp, in a work detail checking mouths of recently killed people, searching for gold in their teeth. He hauled bodies with a cart rolled on wooden boards laid over a barren, muddy terrain to a pit where he dumped the bodies into a mass grave. While doing this he saw on two of them the faces of Gina and Markus. The world abruptly collapsed on him with a silencing thud, replaced by completely black darkness, where a dog growled in absence of light, approaching until Israel could hear it breathing close to him. He awakened.

He lay trembling, sweaty, and cold. *Nightmare! It's not real.* He refused to believe it might be real. He looked at the digital clock, at the glowing numbers staring back at him: 3:16. *Damn! This isn't funny.*

He turned to look at Gina sleeping quietly beside him and watched the rise and fall of her chest. She was here with him, very much alive; her warmth and fragrance touched him. He put his face close to hers and purposefully breathed the air exhaled from her lungs. *I need you, Gina. Don't let them take you away from me.*

He rolled onto his back and meditated to fall asleep again, this time using Gina's name as his mantra instead of Markus.

He traveled beyond spacetime and back into it again.

The lives of servants are not as complicated as those we serve, and I am like a sister who never will have her own way. My happiness depends on the success of the family, and of course I have no say in that. Others in the family call me Amma usually, but sometimes Bat Sheva calls me Alitza, especially when I have made her smile.

I love Bat Sheva and wish to say that her manipulation of events has had its good reasons. She should not be condemned for what others have called sin.

I sit waiting with her while her infant son reclines limp and with shallow breaths in the quiet mournfulness of impending death. I want to make her smile, but it is impossible. People have called this child's misery the retribution of our creator's rage, but they are cruel. What sin has this helpless child committed? Did he even desire birth? Can a son's death atone for the sin of his father? These people avoid that question and say it is enough that he even exists; that is sin enough, they say. They are cruel.

Bat Sheva is daughter of Eliam, one of the king's thirty esteemed warriors, and Eliam is son of Ahitophel, a close advisor of the king. Our house is next to the king's.

"The king will have what he wants," I remember Bat Sheva saying. "The trick is to get him to want what you want him to want."

She was delightfully cunning then, and she will be again when her grief releases her.

It made no sense when her father gave her to Uriah, the Hittite; it made sense only in the ways of fathers and favors and agreements that are not shared with those of us they trade and sell. It is not for us to question such decisions, and in this way Bat Sheva is not different from me. I am her servant, but both of us are her father's possessions, and he does with us as he pleases. This is why I say I am like a sister to her, a sister who never will have her own way.

Bat Sheva is different. She is beautiful and born to parents of repute. Often I wish it were my clothing that was stroked away from my shoulders and my purity which was dismissed by the king. Now Bat Sheva has become important. She is both envied and chastised by the people. She wears colorful and finely woven cloth, and her breasts are touched by hands that are both strong and soft. Her neck is kissed affectionately by the king. When I think about this without dismissing my thoughts, I wish I were the king kissing her. She is beautiful, and I love her.

Uriah was rough, and I think he did not prefer women. He was gone always, off to war and his warriors. He preferred his men. Bat Sheva was left alone like an abandoned lamb crying to be embraced by one who loves her. She wanted to be kissed, and there is worth a woman can feel in the persuasion she exerts on the emotions of a beautiful man. Uriah was not beautiful, and he treated her as worthless. She could have no influence on him. People talk profusely about sin, but the law does not always tell the truth about it.

Long ago she persuaded me to bathe her on the roof of our house. We set up a screen so Bat Sheva could not be seen from windows of the king's house. She would appear to be modest, but modesty was just a tool for her, and lustfulness could be a tool as well. She observed that the king walked on the roof of his house during the early evenings, so astutely we set up the screen so that it hid her nudity from any of the king's windows but was low enough for him to savor it from that more elevated location. I complied with her ruse because I loved her, and I hoped she might allure a better life into hers, a life into her loins. And it was fun, but I was envious of her affection.

The king played his part well, ducking behind the low wall on top of the roof, and from there he watched discretely, which allowed us to pretend we did not notice him. We giggled, and the smile on Bat Sheva's face made her even more beautiful.

"Wash my breasts, Alitza," she commanded, and when I stroked her she put dreaminess on her face and closed her eyes lightly. She let her legs lie to the side, and I washed the insides and creases of her thighs. I felt my own loins moisten. She dared even to touch herself, and she sighed deeply and stretched her body into a graceful and inviting arch. How deliciously enticing she was! If only I were a man; I would have made love to her myself. While stroking her, my mind played a curious story of names. I wanted to call her Gina.

"It will not happen immediately," she said. "It takes a while for a good man's desire to overcome his sense of decorum. We must be patient and do this again after a few days of letting him wait."

I enjoyed telling her how beautiful she was.

It happened as she said it would, not right away. Messengers came to our house and summoned Bat Sheva to the presence of King David. When she returned to our house it was like the light of a soft sun shone on her, and the smile was in her eyes. "He wants me, Amma," she told me. "He asked me to sit next to him, and we shared small amounts of delicious food and drink. We ate from the same bowl. He told me I was beautiful and how he had longed to see me closer. Alitza! He talked about my eyes. He was patient about saying he wanted to kiss me. He waited until the drink had relaxed my posture, and then he kissed the side of my neck and stroked my arm gently, so that my clothing moved softly against my skin. He kissed my shoulder. He kissed my cheek, but I would not let him kiss my lips.

"'I am sworn to Uriah,' I reminded him. 'Alas,' he answered. 'That man is a lout. You are a treasure like none other. How can he resist you?' Alitza! He talked about me this way. I did not get up and leave him until he had touched my breast. I wanted him to feel the nipple so he would know I desired him, and then I left. He ordered two of his men to escort me home."

"Bat Sheva," I said. "This is exciting." I could feel excitement in my own loins just imagining it, but there also was pain of envy. "Now I think it will be necessary to stop bathing you on the roof of our house."

"No, no, a woman must be clean. We will continue, but of course with a higher screen. He will not see me, but he will know I am there, and his own imagination will topple him."

We smiled into each other's eyes, and Bat Sheva said, "Alitza, I love you." These words delighted my heart because this is what I live for, Bat Sheva's love.

In the days that followed she was brought back and forth to the king's house, over and over. She told me ways that he wooed her. He recited poetry and played music on a lyre and sang to her.

One night she confided, "The king has been inside me."

"You allowed him?"

"I kissed him in ways that he could not resist. Yes! It is I who wielded the sword in this battle, Alitza. I trembled at his touch, and when he pressed himself against me I unfolded for him, and he pushed himself into me, slowly at first, agonizingly slowly. Then, like the rhythm of a dance, like the drums of war, he exerted himself, and I moved for his better pleasure, and I moaned. I put my hands on his buttocks and pulled him relentlessly. After his body shook, he lowered himself on top of me, and I kissed and called him beautiful. I begged him to give me bliss like that again. I have coerced him with more than just my body, Alitza, and he will want more of me."

"But his seed?"

"Ah yes, his seed." She smiled then. "To bear a child who resembles David."

"But this is not righteous, and it's dangerous," I told her.

If it had been a countenance of forlorn resignation that I saw on her face, I would have thought she was helpless in this situation, that her honest love had ensnared her. Instead she said, "Yes, it is deliciously dangerous. How lonely will the outcast be, I wonder." She smiled. "David the king; he will lavish his affections on me, and my sons will be kings themselves."

That was then, and now I sit with her and her darling little dying king, even as she rocks back and forth whispering through her tears over and over, "I will have another. I will have another."

She looks at me with her reddened eyes, and she says, "Oh, Israel! Make love to me. I need you."

I kiss her lips.

Israel traveled beyond spacetime and back into it again.

He awoke with an erection. *What was that? A dream? A spiritual jaunt into another body?* Gina lay sleeping on her tummy beside him. He put his hand on her beautiful back and stroked slowly to her neck, then down again, feeling the contours of her shoulder blades, the small of her back, her buttocks.

"Mmmmmmmmmm." Sleepily she said, "That's nice. What are you doing?"

"I want to make love with you."

"Right now?" She paused and then said, "That's nice." She appeared still to slumber.

Israel moved over onto Gina's back, felt her warm smooth skin against his belly, her buttocks against him, and he moved on her.

"Let me turn over."

Israel lifted his weight from her and watched her sleepily turn onto her back with her eyes still closed.

"Okay, my love," she said, putting her hands on his arms without lifting her own arms, touching together the entire length of both their forearms. "Do whatever you want with me," she said, and then, "What time is it? I don't want to be late for work."

"There's time."

"Good. Okay, then do whatever you want," and she appeared to fall asleep again.

Israel entered her slowly and continued a slow gentle rhythm, and as he made love to her he heard in his mind the music of a lyre and the words of a song.

You are the one from whom my dreams are made.
Your kiss crumbles the rampart of my resistance.
Your embrace calms my soul's trembling.
Your smile brightens the delight of my own heart.

Twenty-two

ENTANGLEMENT QUARTET AND GRAVITY

srael sat at Kerry Park in the faltering glow of a twilight sky, with Mount Rainier far to the south, pink with sunlight spilled upon it by a sun still above the mountain's horizon, a sun that had just set below Israel's horizon.

> *I love them, Gina! Markus, broken dove,*
> *and physics out of my control compel*
> *me there to him. Each time I fail to tell*
> *a travel tale, must love disable love?*
> *It's no surprise we wonder if we're not*
> *alone inhabiting our precious selves,*
> *and maybe if a stubborn spirit delves*
> *enough he'll find the other minds his body's got.*
> *To each of us belongs the other one.*
> *If one of us rolls over while in bed*
> *together, then the other, as if led,*
> *will also roll. A kiss is more than fun.*
> *I'm stuck. I'm simply stuck. Nowhere to run.*
> *I'll go with it. I'll do what must be done.*

Gina sat on the balcony of her apartment rocking gently with an unfinished afghan in her lap and a ball of yarn beside her. She watched for the moon's appearance in a darkening eastern sky, wondering how much Israel honestly shared with her about his travels. Is it a lie when a lover choses simply not to tell?

Where are you, Luna, angel of the night
who gazes down upon us all the same
and sees us paired in love with ardent flame
of love's embrace, in passion burning bright?

She lit a candle and set it on a table next to her, watching for a clairvoyant whisper of the evening. Would the flame burn straight toward heaven, clean and pure, or would it wiggle in a breeze and yield smoldering ash into the air?

Luna, love, and candlelight adorn
my evening's reverie and show me wrong
from right. I sing a superstitious song,
I know, but sing it anyway. I'm torn.
It's both of us as one, belonging, wed.
Beyond what we control, we must not break
the spell that's captured us, for heaven' sake!
Do not escape this prison's heart or head.

Gina blew a gentle breeze of longing breath against the candle flame and watched it sputter like a lover buffeted by a kiss.

The many breezes on our lives provoke
our dodging love but do not mean it's broke.

She cupped a hand behind the candle's flame and puffed it out. A string of sooty smoke curled up from a smoldering black and orange wick.

Michael sat at his desk in the Mozart laboratory, occasionally drumming his fingers, tugging his hair, and sometimes shaking a fist in the air. He squirmed in his chair and scratched an increasing, itching soreness on his bottom.

> Expands! The universe expands with growing
> speed, accelerates right here in front
> of us, and we are unaware. A stunt
> of cause that challenges our need for knowing.
> Expansion pulls; inertial mass resists
> it. Heavens, then! That's it! It's simple.
> Lagging mass against a swelling pimple
> called the universe. My ass be kissed!
> A little secret now will be unfurled.
> There is no subatomic gravitit.
> Gravity is mass resisting it,
> the ever faster fester of the world.
> You fucking bastard, God! And you! You too,
> almighty Einstein! You shits! You two.

Jeeves sat in the Hobbit Hole dining room with a pocket watch in his hand, smiling upon the seconds ticking by.

> My struggling fellow travelers through time
> are quite beside themselves with wishes strong.
> Have patience, friends, for fickle life is long,
> and it will shake each tree you try to climb.
> We fuss about them, woes of weary quests.
> Can they be calmed, the many weary woes?
> Entangled particles, as lover knows,
> they move in correspondence with their guests.
> It all requires patience, dears; now hush.
> Don't fret about what you cannot control,
> but keep it close and watch it as you stroll
> along the path that's made for you. Don't rush.
> And as you doubt and reassess your learning,
> be certain that the answer's there worth yearning.

Twenty-three

THROUGH THE EYES OF A FISHERMAN

A flaxen net is cast upon a troubled sea
and snares a ripe community of fishes.
These slippery silvery souls for food so destined be,
a captive crowd for many morsel dishes.
A net upon our troubled sea, humanity,
invites, embraces souls, replenishes
and promises a frightening gift, eternity,
unwitting want of many mortal wishes.

My name is Daniel, son of Paul. Along with others I fish the Sea of Galilee, employed as one of the oarsmen in the boat of Simon, son of John. We call Simon Rock because he swims like a stone, and therefore we keep him at the center of the boat. He can be hardheaded too, another reason we call him Rock.

His father owns our boat outright, meaning we do not have to give extra of our catch to the counters, as the others must do who rent their boats from the syndicate. Simon the Rock must pay only the tax on our catch. How many fish is the tax? It depends on the counters; every day is different.

The boat is kept at Capernaum, a good place to live if you like eating fish. That's what there is to eat and usually a lot of it. We enjoy when a cook knows food can be more than just eggs mixed with fish sauce and milk. South of us on the shore, at the market in Magdal, one can purchase smoked and pickled fish. They are delicious.

With a full crew we have four of us oarsmen who do the rowing, and when there is wind in the right direction we work the sail. Four others tend the nets, and in one way or another we all do the fishing. Everybody helps with every job. It's a good crew.

We work along with a second boat owned by Zebedee and his sons, James and John. Drag fishing requires two boats.

In summer we fish at night when we can, when the moon is bright and the air is cool, when the sun is not hot on the water, and fish come closer to the surface. For a while hot weather has kept our catches small. When the water gets warm the plentiful small fish, sardines, swim deep where it is cooler, too deep for our nets. The larger fish enjoy the warm water, but when all of the lake is warm they scatter far and wide, to all locations, and we catch only a few at a time.

It is morning, and the sun has risen over the hills on the far side of the sea. We are tired as we finish our work, cleaning and repairing the nets, drying and folding them. The shore smells different in the morning than at night, and I like the morning smell because it tells me soon I will eat and sleep. This past night has not been good fishing. The water is warm and the plentiful fish are too deep, where it is cool.

We catch more fish in the winter when the water is cool, and the plentiful small fish swim closer to the surface. They can be caught using casting nets with lighter flax cords and a narrow weave with smaller holes. The edge of this kind of net is weighted with stones so that when it is thrown onto the surface of the water, the edges sink faster than the rest of it and circle under the fish, trapping them, and then we haul on the synch lines and close the opening as we drag the fish toward our boat.

Musht, the larger fish with a spiny dorsal fin, also are easier to catch in winter because they like warm water. During winter there are only a few places in the sea where water is warm enough for their pleasure, and because they go to those places, we know where to find them. Hot springs warm the sea, but only in a few places.

In the winter we travel south and spend weeks at a time because it is a long way to row, down near the new city, T'veriyah, built over the top of the ancient village of Rakkat. Herod Antipas calls his new city Tiberias, after the Roman emperor, and pours investment into it to make it special for visitors. He flatters the emperor and enjoys the praise he receives for the city. It is a jewel built with proceeds from selling fish he takes from the catches of all fishermen. Everything else gets taxed as well. Tiberius is not a Jewish city anymore. It is Rome's city. He is a sycophant to Rome and a parasite of all that is Greek. They are mostly Greeks who live there. Jews will not live in a city that has a cemetery within its perimeter, making it unclean. Bodies are buried directly into the earth, and not many Jews will live near such a place.

Now in summer all of the lake is warm, and the musht scatter. This past night we caught only seven, and the counters will take two or three of them, depending on deals made and the size of the fish. They take what they want. We caught a catfish too, but of course we threw it back because such fish are unclean. We might have sold it to the Greeks, but it is best not to touch those fish more than necessary.

This morning, while we clean and dry and repair our nets, not far from us a traveling preacher calls out, "Good news!" At first only a few listen, but more arrive later, a few at a time. He has a sense of humor and shows us how silly we can be.

Preachers come around, many with crazy ideas, many without another means of livelihood, and they live off morsels people give them. They are beggars who put more work into their begging than most. A man without skills can either steal or he can beg. If a man begs by preaching it is better when he has something to say and knows how to say it. Either way, preacher or thief, can such men be trusted? Some of them imagine themselves obscure prophets, hoping to make it big. Most of them preach about baptism washing away our misguided nature, and they tell us we must return to the faithfulness of our old ways, reminding us of the kingdom of David and a promise of its return.

I wonder if the kingdom of David was just as corrupt as ours is now. Memories are bad about other things; why not this?

They are mostly the same, these preachers, copies of each other, and it is easy to understand that they choose this way of begging because there is nothing else they know how to do or nothing else they have interest in. Some of them preach about throwing off the yoke of Rome, but they do it at their peril, behind closed doors. If they are caught it does not go well for them.

Around here they do not complain about the Greeks, not now that Rome has spoiled Greek lives as well. This is a way Greeks and Jews are alike. A lot of Greeks live here.

Today's preacher is different, refreshing, talking about a new promise given by Elohai, a covenant he calls good news. Like a child, he calls the holy one "Dad." I laugh. Dad! He is lighthearted and daring, this one, calling the great one "Dad." We listen to this preacher because he is funny and does not take himself so seriously. He knows he is a preacher and a beggar; knows his place and the role he plays.

He talks about wine. "It makes your body numb, numbs your weariness in the world. Nothing in earth or heaven makes you as drunk as Dad's wine. It is as potent as a new promise. Wine from grapes makes you drunk, and if you get too drunk you bump into things; you fall in the street and make a buffoon of yourself. Some of you want that," he says, and we laugh. "And all of you will want to get drunk on Dad's wine. You will bump into things you never bumped into before. Instead of falling down in the street, you will fall down in a new world, Dad's kingdom. His wine has life in it and is the key to the door of his house. Come be a buffoon with me. Get drunk on Dad's wine, and we will fall down together in the streets of heaven. Oh! But wait! What about the hangover?"

We laugh again.

He says, "I tell you truthfully: getting drunk on Dad's wine, there will be no hangover. Once drunk you stay drunk."

This preacher is funny. Dad's wine! The great one is a vintner.

He says, "Some of you will believe the new promise and drink Dad's wine. You will get drunk and become happy buffoons with me. There is more to the world than what you see, more to life.

"But some of you will not be able to believe. You are as sober as Pharisees. Have you ever noticed how sober Pharisees are? They don't get drunk. It only seems like they're drunk, sometimes."

We laugh.

"I'm sorry they will not get drunk on the new promise, but whether they believe or not is between Father and them. Let them be. Like the wine itself, believing is a gift from Dad. Nobody comes to the father except by the path he gives, and he gives it to everyone. What I tell you is, the wine is the path."

There are murmurs in the crowd.

He continues. "Everyone walks on the path, but only some see it. When you drink the wine you will see the path, but only some of you drink it. New wine cannot be contained by old wineskins. New wine swells as it ferments, and if you put new wine into old wineskins that no longer can stretch, they burst. Dad's wine swells and cannot be contained by the likes of Pharisees who are old wineskins clinging to old ways. They have no stretch left in them. You have met Pharisees who even look like old wineskins; no need to mention names."

We laugh.

"Their way of thinking will burst if they drink Dad's wine. They are constrained by meaningless rules. If they get drunk and see that everyone walks to Father, not just them, how surprised they will be! They will have to become something other than Pharisees. Might they fall down and be buffoons along with the rest of us? Old wineskin Pharisees fear dancing in the street because what if they fall down? Might they be mocked? But Pharisees are welcome. A new-wineskin Pharisee who gets drunk on the new wine will become a buffoon like us. Dad's buffoons!" The preacher walks back and forth, wobbling like a drunkard. "You laugh at me," he laughs, "but I see the path, and when others get drunk we laugh and dance in the streets of Dad's kingdom where we are not afraid to fall down."

He shakes his head. "Pharisees cling to old rules that shut them in a cage." He stops and shouts loudly, "Old wineskins cannot hold Dad's new wine. What are we going to do with old wineskins?" He cheerfully almost sings and almost dances. "We love them. The wine makes us so drunk we love everyone. Are you an old wineskin clinging to old ways? Are you a new wineskin? Truthfully I tell you that Dad's love is like new wine swelling to the extreme. It will pop out of your ears."

He stops talking and walks around a bit, puts his fist against his belly and burps, and then he begins talking again. "Every generation brings something new, and the young will teach the old even as the old teach the young. Dad knows all things in heaven and earth. Do not be afraid of new knowledge, for even the hairs on your heads have an exact number. Dad knows all things and reveals them to those who are attentive." He shouts, "What is this new wine? It is now and always has been, and it always will be love." Quietly he says, "Prepare yourselves for it, and the new wine will flow into you." He shouts again. "What is the wine? It is life." More quietly he explains, "The wine promises life, and if you get drunk on it you will see your life lasting forever. When you fall down in the street you will get up again. After you die you will be born again."

More people arrive, curious about the laughter and chatter. They crowd around so that only the very close can see him. One man pushes through the crowd and shoves the preacher. "Blasphemer!" he shouts. "Elohai is not a drunkard."

The preacher stumbles and almost falls. "Whoa!" He laughs. "Dad's wine has a powerful punch."

Simon the Rock runs to the preacher and tugs his arm to bring him to our boat. The preacher climbs into it like he knows already that this is what will be. I row him out a short way, just far enough that the water is too deep for the crowd to follow, and I anchor the boat. It is just he and I in the boat.

"A question has been raised," the preacher shouts to the crowd, "whether our father is a drunkard." He puts the back of his left wrist against his forehead and gently shakes his head. "Look around you at this world, at the crazy things that happen. Is there a better explanation?"

Some of the people are willing to laugh even at this daring blasphemy. Nobody leaves. He has captured their interest.

"I tell you most truthfully and solemnly that our father gives us his wine of love and life, so that when we get drunk on it we can bear the unbearable. Dad knows the troubles of this world and he gives you a tool to repair it."

He proclaims many things, as though he himself has lived in heaven and knows things the rest of us do not, as though he has sat at the breakfast table of the holy one. He is curiously bold and gently blasphemous. Who can know the holy one in the ways he says? The spirit inside us is holy, he says, a holy spirit, and I think yes, we all have this spirit. We have learned this before. What is special?

"You cannot run from the holy spirit," he says. "Dad is like a thief in the night who puts his hand into your pocket when you are unaware, but instead of your pocket it is your heart, and instead of stealing, he gives. If his gift frightens you and you reach inside to remove it, you learn that you cannot remove it because it is yours in heaven and cannot be touched by your hand in earth. Your spirit is in Dad's kingdom, and your hand is not."

He speaks in riddles.

"Do not be frightened because this is happy news. You will not perish. I have told you only a little, and there is more that I could say that would make better sense of it, but now you do not know enough to understand what I would say. You are not ready; you are unable to understand the things that would make Dad's promise more sensible. Therefore believe me, even if it is with faith alone, and you will be comforted by peace that surpasses all of what you understand. You do not have to understand all things. What I say is true. Many who come after me will speak to you of these other things that you now cannot comprehend, and when they come you will know you can believe them because they will speak with the

spirit of truth. What is revealed by them about the world will glo-
rify me, because everything they tell you about the world is Dad's,
and all that is Dad's is mine. The spirit of truth will guide you to all
knowledge, one step after another, and in this way the truth will
become known to you."

He begins to laugh and announces, "If you are new wineskins,"
and he shakes his head and laughs louder. "If you are new wineskins and old wine is poured into you, it will spoil and taste sour.
If you are new wineskins you will crave the new wine, the wine of
love and forgiveness and eternal life." He pauses and then adds,
"Whether you're an old wineskin or a new wineskin, either way,
you're a wineskin, are you not? Be good to your fellow wineskins."

At the end of his preaching I ask him, "What if you're a middle-
aged wineskin?"

He simply laughs.

I ask him, "Who are you?"

"I am Yeshua."

"Son of?"

He shakes his head. "Yeshua of Nazareth."

He does not want to share his father's name.

He says to me, "Israel, open your eyes and see."

Upon his saying it, doors swing open in my mind, and a whole
new world appears. I am Israel Newman, and I say, "Yeshua!"

"It is good to see you again, my friend." He laughs. "It amazes
other people as well, all of you who come to visit. Everyone who
visits me lives in amazement, like the punchline to a good joke." He
chuckles. "Everyone has questions too. All my visitors are amazed
and inquisitive. I ask you this, Israel, if it is not difficult to listen to
a story, why would it be difficult for me to recognize that it is you
who sits here in this boat with me? You are like nobody else, and
you are here before me like words of a story. On your forehead it
is written, 'Hello, my name is Israel.' And to this let me add, since
every moment is eternal, I have plenty of time to be with you and
with every other life who visits. Be amazed, Israel, just as I am." A
startled look crosses his face. "Hold on a second; there's another

soul on the line. Call waiting, you know." He teases me, pokes me in the chest with a finger.

"I do have a question."

He nods. "About three-sixteen?"

"Yes, how do you know?"

"It is one of those things, Israel. I'll tell you later. You are not ready to understand the answer yet, but it will come to you after a while. There will be a tremendous battle because of three-sixteen. Even in a large lake like this one, there are rivers where the water is different. Cold water flows as a river through a sea of warm water. So it is with the spirit. I tell you this now, truthfully; there are those who want to do away with me, and they will do whatever they can to exterminate me and memories of me, but of course they will not succeed. They cannot kill what is not of this world. They will kill only what is of this world, and they will think they have solved their problem, but no. They will go on their way because this world is all they see. They are blind to the rest. The spirit of truth, Israel! The spirit of truth is on its way. You are puzzled now, but you will know the answer to three-sixteen before you are done. I promise. Don't be afraid of dark dreams because they come from your own mind. You are troubled, but only because you are about to learn something new. After a while you will understand three-sixteen, and then you will ask 'Why did Father make it like this?' There always will be questions."

"I have had to be patient about a lot of things."

"Israel!" He laughs. "You have not been patient at all. That is why you are troubled. It is okay, my friend. I do not criticize you for impatience. Impatience is understandable, and it is its own punishment." He tilts his head. "You have another question, and it's about your son, Markus."

"Yes."

"It is a difficult road you will travel yet before this ache in your heart subsides. You must live as the world has been made."

I clasp onto what he says, *this ache in your heart subsides.* "What about Gina?"

Yeshua smiles broadly. "Gina!" He shouts. "Love is wonderful, is it not? Loving Gina is wonderful. She is the light of the world, Israel. And you are the light of the world. Each of you and every one of us is the light of the world."

"Do you always talk in riddles?"

"These are not riddles. You ask me about your future, and I answer that it already is. It exists for you. Your impatience makes it seem like these are riddles."

We sit in the boat and look at one another's eyes, and I realize there is nothing more comfortable than to have Yeshua share your soul.

He says, "Tomorrow is a special day here on the lake, this Sea of Galilee. Don't go yet; stay until tomorrow, and you will see a miracle written into the amazement of our father's world." He smiles broadly, raises his eyebrows, and nods his head. "Eh?" he says. "Tomorrow!"

I wonder; he talks to me as though I have control over when I come and go in these lives. So far I've seen no evidence of it.

The next night the moon is in the sky again, and stars. We fish by the moon's silvery reflection glowing on the waters, following us wherever we go, and it reminds me of eternal time and the constant presence of past and future. It reminds me that I am on a path myself, and maybe my life is like moonlight reflected on water with ripples and waves. I don't understand the meaning, but believing it comforts me, and even the depth of the sea is comforting, with all its mysteries, because it always has been here, always will be, and my life is like moonlight reflected on its surface.

The water is warm, and small fish swim too deep where it is cool; large fish are scattered around the lake, and we have no luck. Our cedar boats creak and moan like the cravings of our hungry bellies.

After the long night of toil without reward, we are cleaning and drying our nets in the morning sun, and Yeshua of Nazareth walks over quietly, this time without an entourage of listeners. "You have caught no fish," he says to us.

It is just a greeting, but it is obvious and unhappy that we have caught no fish, and I find his statement annoying.

Simon the Rock answers, "Yes, it gets this way in hot weather. The water gets warm and fish hide in the cooler depths."

Yeshua nods. "Then if the water gets cooler, they would rise to the surface over the deep waters."

This comment irritates Simon. "The man talks as though he knows fishing," and of course Simon does not yet know what I know about Yeshua. "Many people think they know how to do things they never have done." Simon thinks this preacher never has fished.

Yeshua puts his hand down into the water and remarks, "This water does not feel so warm to me. Maybe it is cooling off. Touch it."

The water is cold!

"Go and fish the waters over the deep right away." he says, "Fish while the fishing is good."

Yeshua's face looks amused, like an uncle who has given his nephew a gift.

Simon goes over and shows the coolness of the water to Andrew and Zebedee, James and John, and they look startled and hopeful. Our workers are weary after the night's unrewarding toil, but Simon tells them they will be paid double, and we push off.

First we try a casting net, and as we pull it toward the boat we recognize the resistance caused by a heavily laden net. A few of us laugh. We bring it alongside the boat and see that the net is full with both small and large fish. It is an amazing catch. The boat tilts when we try to lift the net into it, and a couple of snapping sounds alert us that the flax cords cannot withstand the weight. We open the mouth of the net a little, and some of the men reach with their hands to pull fish into the boat until the catch is lighter on the net and we can heft it safely. We lose a few of the fish this way, but what is to worry with a catch this large?

Simon signals to the other boat that we should work together with a drag net. Zebedee nods his understanding. We bring our boat around while the other holds its position, and as we move through the water, at first fast and then slower, we oarsmen strain against the weight of another large catch. All of us are chattering and laughing because it has been a long time since fishing was this much fun.

Again the net is too full and we must haul fish into the boat with our hands. The net still is heavy with fish even after we have filled both boats as much as they can be filled without drawing too deeply in the water. We drag the net slowly behind us and haul the fish to shore.

The sun is high in the sky behind a large cloud when we arrive, and Yeshua sits on a stone, drawing with a stick in the loose earth. As we approach him he looks up and laughs. "How was fishing?"

Simon answers, "The cool water made a difference. How did that happen?"

Yeshua shrugs his shoulders playfully.

Simon asks him, "Who are you?"

"My name is Yeshua of Nazareth."

"That is your name, but I want to know who you are. Who is this person called Yeshua?"

Yeshua looks over at me. "Your man here, Daniel, knows who I am. Daniel, do you want to tell Simon the Rock who I am, or shall I?"

"You are gracious, Yeshua, but that is for you to say."

He laughs; he always is laughing. "What fun is that? Let me start you out. If I am a letter written by one to another, who is writing the letter, and what does it say?"

"Do you always talk in riddles?" Simon asks.

"The letter is from Dad, and it says, 'I love you.'"

Simon asks, "How did you make the water cold?"

"Do you say that I made it cold? Truthfully I tell you it was going to be cold, even from the time the world was made, maybe because Dad wanted to surprise and startle you into believing. If you think of it as a miracle, then think of all things as a miracle, because all things are made just as this was; one thing is as miraculous as another. If I knew about it before you saw it happen," Yeshua looks at me, "it is because of things you are not ready to understand. The spirit of truth someday will explain it. Can you see the future, Daniel?"

First Yeshua and then Simon look at me. Yeshua says, "There is power in that, Daniel. Everything is a miracle, and miracles are made by our father."

Twenty-four

LOVING YOU IS WONDERFUL

srael awoke to the sensation of Gina stroking him, which quickly oriented him to place and person. "That's very nice." He was still half asleep.

"You like that?"

"Yes. Keep doing it."

"Have you been dreaming?" Gina spoke softly, hypnotically. She was gentle and warm "Where have you been?"

"Fishing."

"Fishing? Did you have any luck."

"Exceptional luck."

"Lots of fish?"

"Tons of fish, literally tons of fish. We couldn't get all of them into the boat, there were so many."

"Oh? Who was in the boat with you? A girl in a bikini?"

Her comment woke Israel all the way. "No, no girl; a bunch of guys. It was a big boat. Not a single guy was wearing a bikini. Once it was just one guy. He wasn't wearing a bikini either. You'll never guess who it was."

"Why? Do I know him?"

"Yes, you do. It was Jesus."

"Jesus? Oh my god! What was that like?"

"You were right. He wouldn't give me a blow job."

"You asked him that?"

"No, of course not. Didn't even think about it. Not that there's anything wrong with that." Israel smiled and waited for Gina to comment, but she didn't. He continued. "I asked him about you, and he wanted me to let you know that loving you is wonderful."

"You asked him about me?"

"I asked him about you."

"And he said loving me was wonderful?"

"*Is* wonderful."

"How am I supposed to be angry at you when you tell me this?"

"Why would you be angry with me anyway?" Israel pushed Gina onto her back and lay atop her. "Loving you is wonderful," he said, and as lightly as he could, he touched her lips with his own. "Loving you is wonderful."

"You've been time traveling."

"I don't have much control over when it happens now. It just happens. I don't need Professor Hannity's lab anymore."

"I know."

"How do you know that?"

"You change moods abruptly. You change conversation topics unexpectedly."

"I've been doing that?"

"Jesus said he loves me?"

"He said it's wonderful to love you."

"Maybe you're just crazy. Maybe you're not traveling at all. You just have a vivid imagination."

They looked at each other's eyes.

Gina put her hands on Israel's bottom and pulled him toward her. "I want to be your woman, Israel, your only woman."

"You're my only woman."

"Make love to me. I want you inside of me."

Twenty-five

THE DAWN OF CONTROL

There are many stories in a lifetime, all interconnected, and many points at which the telling of them might begin.

One story began the day Israel and Gina visited the Seattle Art Museum when in the American section looking at the wondrous painting by Albert Bierstadt, *Puget Sound on the Pacific Coast*, a yearning filled Israel, and he became aware that at a deeper, almost subliminal level, his mind labored over what colors to mix next for the painting in front of him.

"Gina," he said. She was not far away. "Gina, come over here, please."

Gina came over, took his hand and cuddled his arm, relinquishing her hold of it only when Israel put it around her and pulled her close to him. "I need you," he said to her.

"I need you too."

"Look at this painting."

"It's huge. I like how the waves look translucent. And the details; you can even see seaweed floating in the water."

"Yes. It was better for public display that way, better for charging admission." He smiled. "It gives you a feeling of actually being there."

"Well, yes, but actually it doesn't look like any place I've ever been."

"No. Maybe it looks like a place you would like to be, maybe like heaven."

"I've never thought of heaven being this dark or this powerful."

"I remember painting this, Gina."

Gina exhaled, turned toward him, and put her face against his chest.

"Just now I remembered selecting colors, mixing colors for this painting. I was thinking how people have criticized me for unnatural colors, for inaccurate scenes. Some of them, though, some of them realized I was painting beyond the scene. I was painting inspiration. God's world is more than just what we see with our eyes; it's what we see with our imagination."

With her face still against his chest, Gina shook her head ever so slightly.

Israel said, "I remember things in this other life, Gina."

"You scare me."

"What? Scare you? What is so scary?"

"I don't want to lose you. I find myself wondering. Are you crazy? Are you suddenly going to realize you're in love with someone else and stay with her? Leave me? Or him?"

"No. No." Israel put both arms around her. "You are the person I'm pinned to, for all eternity. You and I find each other over and over again. Anybody else has been only a mistake until I find you. You! You're the one."

"Oh my god," she whispered.

"Oh my god!" He laughed, and with that little interchange Israel continued mistakenly to think Gina was more comfortable with his travels, more accepting, than she really was.

Gina remained quieter than her heart needed her to be because she hoped over time either she would get used to it or Israel would get tired of it.

Later the same day, as they were strolling through Pike Place Market, Israel stopped to admire some tie-dyed shirts, and Gina moved a couple of booths farther on.

Israel briefly studied the woman behind the shirt table. She had straight blond hair, glasses, and a nice figure. She had four piercings in her left ear with pretty little rings, and she wore a shirt with an unusual organic pattern, a splattering of colors, mainly greens and browns with accents of red and blue and orange. Israel recognized her shirt, remembered having been the artist who made that design, the methodical laborer of hundreds of ties, just so, and dyes carefully applied. He remembered having loved that shirt and wearing it often. He was fully aware of his mind sliding into what he thought might be an hypnotic trance, but he was fully aware of it happening, aware of the rest of the world receding behind what seemed a theatrical scrim. He told the woman, "What a lovely shirt you have on."

She smiled. "Yeah, this is my favorite. Thank you."

"Are you the artist?"

"Uh-huh." She nodded. "I did all of these, me and my man."

Israel's eyes met hers, and he realized he was looking at himself. He was in the woman's body looking at himself. His left knee ached and he was bearing weight mainly through his right leg, using the left leg mainly for balance.

He was then in his own body again, Israel's body. He struggled against a temptation to allow relinquishing his grip on the structure of the moment, either to fall deeper into the trance or to reveal what had just happened. He tried it again and made it happen. He was inside her body with the aching left knee and wearing the beautiful shirt, and then he shifted back into his own body and was looking at her. Back and forth like a see-saw. He said to her, "Your knee hurts. Are you okay?"

She looked at him with a puzzled expression. "How'd you know?" She said it with a quiet curiosity, searching for a deeper connection, trying to understand how the man in front of her knew about her painful arthritis.

Looking intently at her, Israel noticed a little orange heart-shaped fleck at the bottom of her otherwise gray left eye.

He said to her, "It's the way you're standing. I'm a doctor. You're protecting your left leg by not putting weight on it." He held out his hand. "I'm Israel Newman."

They shook hands.

"I like your shirts. They're nothing short of miraculous, really."

She smiled in response, and the spell on the two of them ended. She quickly forgot about it, but Israel did not.

She answered him, "I'm Susan Andresen. I'm glad you like my shirts."

With the see-saw interaction fully over, he looked at Susan's eyes again and noticed the orange heart-shaped fleck was gone. *It's not on her eye; it's in my mind, an indicator light on a panel inside my mind.* He purchased one of her shirts.

He walked quickly on, catching up to Gina. He put his hand on her back and caressed it first with the palm of his hand and then with the tips of his fingers, making it a loving scratch of her back and shoulders.

"That's nice," she said, and she leaned against him.

He put his arm around her and turned her to face him, pulled her close to him, enjoyed the feeling of her breasts against his chest, needing to feel her breasts against him. He scratched her back some more.

"This is even nicer," she said.

He kissed her mouth passionately, with all the world and humanity around them, pressed her firmly against him. After the kiss he said quietly and intensely, "I need to make love with you."

She smiled at him and put a hand in his hair.

He said, "I mean it. I need to make love with you, right now. Let's go to the car."

The car was parked on level C in the garage beneath Cutters, very close to the place where Israel had been shot, a place now enshrined with emotions of a new love. Israel put the back seats of the car down and forward, so that there was room in the very back for them to recline, and under a blanket they took off each other's clothing, kissing various parts of each other's body. After a while, and after she begged him, he entered her, and while they made love he allowed himself to be fully aware that sometimes he was in Israel's body and sometimes in Gina's. He took control of it.

Twenty-six

ANOTHER TIME LINE

"I can do this." Israel sat with Michael and Jeeves in the Hobbit Hole Dining Room. On the table in front of him was a brown sweater.

"How do you know?" asked Michael.

"Each of the times I moved from myself into another body while having some control of it, there was some material thing that triggered it. First it was the painting, then the shirt, and then Gina. I just knew how to do it, kind of like riding a bicycle, like first learning how. It was impossible over and over again, and then, just like that," he snapped his fingers, "suddenly it's easy."

"But you haven't made the trip yet," Jeeves observed.

"No. It's scary. It's going to happen, and I needed to come talk with Michael about it."

"Hey! I'm an important guy all of a sudden."

"Um. Not all of a sudden." Israel put his hand on the brown sweater. "I was at Nordstrom buying this sweater when Sonya went into labor with Markus, and I've associated it with his birth. I was wearing it the day I got the telephone call that Markus was dead. I took it off and never wore it again. I'm going to use this sweater to focus my travel. I can do it."

"Of course you can," Michael agreed. "Still, it's a pretty tall order."

"I know about the letter upstairs in your desk in the Mozart

Laboratory." Israel waited for Michael's eyes to indicate he understood what was being talked about. "I wasn't snooping, wasn't getting into drawers or anything. You left it out and I read it. I wrote
that, didn't I?"

"I think so. I think it was you. Honestly I don't know for sure."

"I can do this. I'm going to make it happen."

"When and where? Right now and here?"

"Let's go up to the lab."

"Do you need the lab?"

"It can't hurt, a little boost, an easier target for returning if
things don't go well."

"I want you to wear the number five jersey."

"Really? That's priceless to you."

"Yes, it is, except you were going to wear the sweater."

"No, I'm going to hold the sweater. I'll put the sweater back on
after my successful mission."

"Here we go." Michael put his hand on Israel's shoulder as they
followed Jeeves, who opened doors for them and led the proces-
sion up the stairs.

The foyer reverberated with music, Beethoven's majestic *Ode
to Joy*, a premonition of success. "Thanks for that," said Israel.

"Thanks for what?"

"The music."

"What music?"

They entered the Mozart Laboratory and listened to *Tempo di
Menuetto*, from *Sonata K.303*, as Israel donned the number-five
jersey and the now-beacon helmet and reclined in the chair at the
middle of the room with his brown sweater lying on his belly. "I'm
ready."

He felt the coarse texture of the sweater as he meditated, sub-
tracting all else from his mind, and it was not long until he traveled
outside of spacetime and back into it again.

Day 1
I sit up in bed. I am Israel Newman, and I remember. I look at

the clock calendar. Three sixteen a.m., Sunday, February 10, 2008. What the hell? Three sixteen again! Must have something to do with my destiny. Wow! I am going to save Markus.

I have to be careful. Everything I do differently from before will change history. It will set me off into a different time thread, or will it? Determinism! I can't change the future. Or can I? Have to be careful. First things first.

I sit down and write a letter to Professor Michael K. Hannity.

Dear Michael,

I am writing to you first, before doing anything else, because I don't know how my actions will change the future. I want you to know that I have succeeded. I have time traveled to where I need to be, and I remember. I remember everything, Michael. It is possible.

You have not yet met me. You will receive this letter before we meet. You and I will meet, Michael. You are instrumental to my having gotten here. We have to meet. Otherwise I wouldn't be here.

My god, Michael, I am about to launch into another timeline. What does it mean? You have successfully made it possible to travel spiritually to different locations within the same timeline, but what about different timelines? It must be the same thing, right? Different particulate timelines would be connected by the continuous energy, wouldn't they?

I sit and think, not knowing what to say next. Finally I just write *Thank you.* I don't sign the letter. The letter on Michael's desk was not signed, so this closing is the right one. For a moment I think, why not? Test the concept of free will. No. My entire quest here, to save Markus, is a test of free will. Stay with the program.

I must mail the letter before I do anything else.

While driving I notice there is no pain or tightness on the right side of my chest. I haven't been shot.

The letter gets put in the mailbox, and I stop at Safeway to pick up a newspaper. I purchase a copy of the *Seattle P.I.* How about that? Haven't read a *P.I.* for a long time, not since they stopped printing it in March of 2009. I scan the news. Hollywood writers reached tentative agreement with major movie studios. Mike Huckabee won the Kansas Republican caucus and the Louisiana primary. John McCain won the Washington Republican primary. Barack Obama won the Democratic caucuses in Washington, Nebraska, the U. S. Virgin Islands, and the primary in Louisiana. I laugh a little song, "I know who will wi-i-i-in."

Make a note to self: remember to sell stocks in September before the collapse and buy gold. There you go. This is going to be fun. Outstanding!

The task before me, the important task, is to wrest Markus away from his mother and hold him secure and safe until after the twelfth. I'll offer her some incredible deal she can't refuse, tickets to something magnificent, and I'll take care of Markus while she's doing it. I look through the Arts and Entertainment section for ideas. Jill Scott will be singing at the Paramount. *Mame* will be playing at the Fifth Avenue Theatre and *By the Waters of Babylon* at the Seattle Rep. Any of those might work.

Hey, what's this at The Kirkland Performance Center? *The Moscow Circus.* That's it! That's even better. I'll buy four tickets and give them to her. She can take Markus herself and one of Markus's friends and a parent of the friend. That's it! Eureka!

I'm about to buy the tickets, but then stop. Markus is too young to enjoy the Moscow Circus. It might even scare him. Won't work; back to plan A.

Mame? What's at The Village Theatre in Issaquah? It's a bit of a drive for her, but that's okay. What's showing? *Barefoot in the Park.* Which will be more likely to snare her? I choose *Barefoot in the Park,* call, and I'm lucky and get two tickets only seven rows back. Great!

It's always scary to call Sonya. Which of her personalities will answer? I hesitate, but not long. First ring on the other end; second ring; third; fourth; answering service. I say, "Hi, Sonya. It's Israel. Listen, I've got two tickets to *Barefoot in the Park* at Village Theatre in Issaquah. Actually you have two tickets. They're at will-call in your name. I just wanted to do something nice. They're for the show on Tuesday night, 7:30. I'm taking Tuesday off from work, and I'd love to take care of Markus for the day. Here's an idea. If you can get off work early I'll throw in for an early dinner at that little restaurant adjoining the theater, okay? What's it called? Fins. Fins Bistro. Take your best friend. It's on me. Call me."

Day 2

It's Monday, February eleven, early in the morning; haven't heard from Sonya yet.

I call work and tell them I'm sick.

What's in the news? Obama won the Maine caucus. Pattie Solis Doyle resigned her position as campaign manager for Hillary Clinton. It's going to be a rough road, Hillary. Another suicide car bomb in Iraq. Bomb scare at a Norwegian oil rig in the North Sea.

I think about Gina. I wonder what she's doing.

I call Sonya and leave the message again. Is she ignoring me because she hates me? Or is there some legitimate better reason why she's out of reach? I'm scared. Anxiety is setting in. Depression, like I remember it, is scratching its claws on the door I managed to close not long ago.

Day 3

It's Tuesday the twelfth. I couldn't sleep last night; nerves. Still nothing from Sonya. Damn! What to do? What to do?

Call in sick to work again. "I'm a mess," I say.

I *am* a mess.

Time drags by. Time flies by. Too slow; too fast. God! Do something. I read the news but can't keep my mind on it. A giant ferris wheel in Singapore; famous paintings stolen; Democratic primaries in D.C., Virginia, and Maryland. What the hell? I'm going nuts.

I call Sonya again, leave another message.

It's three o'clock. It's three thirty. It's four o'clock. Markus got/ gets run over at seven this evening unless I do something. I'll drive there. Where was it? Damn! Where was it? Calm down. I wish I had some lorazepam. Calm down. Keep your mind straight. Think.

It was south of here; east of Renton; out a ways on—what was the name of that major road? A Polish name. Proski? It goes by Valley Medical Center. It goes by there. Okay, I'll drive there. I've been there. I'll remember when I see the landmarks, but it was so long ago. Eons. My god! How many lifetimes ago was it? Go. Go. Go!

I turn off the car radio. Can't stand music right now. Happiness isn't happy at this moment; it's torture. Happiness is torture. Sadness is torture. Everything is torture.

Rush hour traffic. Everything is slower than I'd like. I drive south on I-5, north on 405 and south on 167. Sign for hospital, first exit, turn left a couple of times, up a long winding road. Look for street names, 43rd Street SE. Carr Road SE. Keep driving. The road becomes Petrovitsky. That's it, the Polish name. Keep driving. Where do I turn? It was to the right out here. It was countryside, a short steep slope down and then turn right, and then back up a steep winding hill. Where is it?

I'm running out of gas, running on empty. Drive up a steep hill, and suddenly there's a gas station on my right. I drive in there. I fumble with the credit card but manage to get it stuck in and pulled out quickly. I think of Gina. Damn it! Markus!

It's starting to get dark. I drive east, come to a short steep downhill to a stoplight. Ahead I see a large above-ground pipeline extending diagonally on the right side of the road in front of me, and I remember it. I've seen this before. Yes! I'm on the right track. I turn right. The road winds upward but not as steeply as I remember it. Keep driving. Nothing looks familiar. Was it a fence or a wall? The property had a fence or a wall. Trees, of course. Everywhere there are trees out here. Nothing, nothing, nothing. Look for Sonya's car. It was—what was it? Red. No, burgundy.

Nothing looks familiar. I drive back and forth on the road awhile. Did I turn wrong? Maybe it was left? I remember the pipeline. I was on track up to that point. I'll try going back, turning left at the light. Time is getting short. Drive faster.

Down the road to the light. Stoplight red. "Fucking goddamn it to hell anyway." There are no cars, so I drive straight through the red light. Ahead and up the winding road, steeper, more promising. Forty-mile-an-hour speed limit; I'm driving fifty, fifty-five. Out on the flat. Estates. A road branches off to the left and then upward to the right. Do I take it? I don't know, don't remember. Did I drive up a hill like that? I don't remember, but maybe. Where the hell is it? Down the other side of the hill, there's a highway, Renton to Maple Valley. I've driven too far. I drive across the highway and turn around again, back up the hill, across the top of it.

I'm driving fast. The world is a blur in my vision, in my mind. A deer! I swerve and miss the deer. A tree! I swerve and miss the tree, but I'm off the road and deeply mired in mud. Damn! I'm not hurt. It's 6:48. I get out and walk. It's raining. It's cold. It's dark.

Markus, where are you?

I walk and I walk, and after a while I look at the time on my cell phone. It's 7:01. My legs become as heavy as lead. My feet are cold and muddy. The world around me, wet and cold and dark as my soul. A car drives by, slapping water off the pavement and buffeting me with a windy cloud of spray. I stagger and put my hand down to sit, instead of falling down at the side of the road. I sit in my wet, cold, dark soul, now and then repeatedly buffeted by grimy clouds of mist lifted off the road by cars whose drivers are too busy to stop. I'm one of the lost people that life passes by.

In the distance I hear the siren of an emergency vehicle.

Will this new timeline continue? Will I repeat the next few years of my life knowing what will be? My time away from work? Frank and the support group? How will it feel to meet Michael again? Get shot again? Gina? Will Gina be as lovely? I weep. This is not a happy loop in Einstein's predetermined universe.

Or will the Mozart laboratory call me back mercifully? Maybe, but this timeline of course will continue whether I'm living it or not. Of course it will. I feel pity for this body and mind I'm in, for all those whose awareness will live like this. Is it just going to be me? How many others? The thought of it staggers my mind, and I feel my mind putting its hand down to sit instead of falling at the side of this timeline, just like I reached to sit beside the hard, real road that stretches beside me.

I sit, absolutely drenched and dirty, at the side of the road, without ambition enough to stand up and walk back to my car. After a long while my cell phone rings. "No-o-o-o-o-o-o-o-o-o-o-o-o-o-o-o," I moan. I can't make myself answer the damned stinking phone.

Twenty-seven

A FORGOTTEN MEMORY

Michael and Jeeves watched as simultaneously with the hum and the ring of the instruments, a pained expression burst upon Israel's face.

"Oh no," Michael quietly said. "It hasn't gone well."

Israel sat up from the chair's reclined position, opened his eyes, and looked around the room, and then he closed his eyes and sat silently. He clutched the brown sweater on his lap.

"Is he all right?" Jeeves asked Michael as he began to move toward Israel but stopped when Michael gripped his arm.

"Not yet," Michael said. "Leave him alone for a minute. He needs to adjust."

Minutes seemed long, and then Israel said, "I need to go back."

"A trip now?" Michael asked. "Are you sure? You've told me you've noticed that your mood influences your trip. Is this the mood you want to be in when you travel?"

"Maybe we should find out what music is playing in the foyer."

"There shouldn't be anything."

"Yeah, I know."

Tempo di Menuetto continued to play in the laboratory.

"My favorite," said Israel.

"Yes, it's quite beautiful, isn't it? It's not long enough."

"Do me a favor and play just that piece over and over until I get back."

"You've got it."

"This time I've got to go further back in time. Give myself more time. Now I know I can do it. I've just got to go and get the job done."

Israel traveled beyond spacetime and then back into it.

This time when he arrived earlier into his own life, Israel was not as aware of his mission as he had wanted to be. He was not aware of being a visitor in his own body.

I am Israel Newman. You'd think I'd know how to avoid situations like this. I mean, psychology is a large part of my work. I'm a pain management specialist, and really, psychology is everything in that specialty. People tell me I'm good at what I do, so how did I let my own wife slip away from me?

Already I know the answer. I tell it to my patients all the time. You need to control your own behavior, but you can't control others. That's one of the secrets to happiness. Stay in control of your own behavior, and do your damnedest to avoid controlling others. That's key. I'm not happy.

Even before Sonya left me, tension was as palpable as a blanket full of burrs. I admit that I don't have enough insight how I might have behaved differently with her, avoided this situation. Neglect! That must have been it. My wickedness was that I neglected her. Damn! Too bad you can't go back in time and do it all over again. Hindsight is twenty-twenty. No, that's not it. I want that to be it, but it's not. She called me jealous. From my point of view it's more like insecurity and pride mixed together. I don't want to play the fool. I just want truth and reassurance that everything's okay. Jealous? It's not like if I had searched her cell phone calls or hacked her computer email. Maybe I'm not cut out for a lasting relationship.

Except with Markus. I'm cut out for a relationship with that little guy forever. He's with Sonya now, and I need to talk with her about having more time with him. It's like she guards him from me, and for what reason? She tells me mixed things about it. First she says he cries because he misses me; then she says he's afraid of me and doesn't want to see me. Afraid? This makes no sense, except maybe it makes sense if he's afraid that she will leave him too, like she left me. Maybe he's afraid she'll leave him when he's here with me. Three-year-olds are attached to their moms.

Sonya says these things to me because she wants me to feel guilty. She wants me to think it's my fault.

I get my courage up to call Sonya on the phone. It's always a mind game with her, an emotional labyrinth with no exits, only booby traps. I say one thing, and she makes it mean something else.

The phone is in my hand, and it rings. I answer it.

"Hello?"

"Hello. This is Sonya." She sounds agitated. "How are you?" She doesn't want an answer.

"I'm fine. What's up?"

"Have you gotten the letter from my lawyer yet?"

"What are you going to do me out of this time?"

"Just sign the letter, okay? It's got Markus's best interests in mind."

"Markus's best interests? Like seeing his dad once in a while?"

"He gets confused when he visits you. Right now he needs stability, and he has that here with me."

"I want to see Markus."

"Just sign the paperwork when it comes, okay?"

"So what's the paperwork all about?"

"I want to have full custody of Markus."

"No."

"Markus needs stability in his life. He needs to be calm. I don't want him to get worked up like he gets after he's been with you."

Because he wants to stay with me. "He needs his father to participate in his life." There is silence. I'm waiting for an answer, dreading whatever the shrew comes up with. "Sonya?"

"Yes?"

"A boy needs his father." Again silence.

Finally she speaks. "You're not his father."

I am stunned. It takes a moment to realize that she's trying, psychologically, to throw me off a precipice and strike me hard on stony ground. I feel the numbness that precedes pain. "What?"

"You're not his father."

"Of course I'm his father."

"On paper."

I want to call her bluff, but it erodes my composure to ask, "Who's his father then?"

"Nobody you know."

"Can I know his name?"

"It's not his name that's important; it's his cock. And he doesn't have any of that Charcot-Marie-Tooth shit like you do. You don't have to worry about it anymore. Markus will walk without a limp."

What a bitch! "I don't believe you. You just want to hurt me."

"I'll send you some of Markus's spit. You can do the tests. He's not yours."

"He is mine. I'm the dad."

"Not anymore."

"I've got a better idea. Let Markus come over this weekend. I can manage getting his spit myself."

She hangs up. Time passes. Lots of time passes, weeks.

It's Tuesday evening, February 12, 2008. The telephone rings.

The chasm into which I've been thrown is wide and deep, with a hard rocky floor against which I've been dashed, and there are no handholds or footholds on the face of the cliff I must climb.

Suddenly Mozart's *Tempo di Menuetto* played boldly in Israel's ears, persistent and beautiful, unrelenting.

Michael looked intently at Israel. "Good or bad?"

"Markus." Israel put his head in his hands. "Markus is my son."

"Yes, I know. What happened?"

"I was myself. Sonya told me Markus was somebody else's."

"What?"

"Somebody else's sperm, Michael. Not mine."

"What the fuck?! Fuck-fuck-fuck-fuck-fuck-shit-dammit."

"Right! You couldn't have put it any better."

"Does this change things for you?"

"It doesn't. Markus is my son."

"Of course he is."

"He's my son because I love him. Everything else is circumstance. Markus is mine because I love him."

"Are you angry?"

"Yes."

"Good. You should be. What can I do to help?"

"Just be my friend, okay?"

"Okay. That's easy. Tell me what hurts more, your ex-wife talking like a witch or getting shot in the chest?"

They laughed a little.

"Do you want to try it again? One more trip? Try to rectify the mess?"

"Can't do it right now; too much pain, too much self-pity." Israel looked at the floor and whispered, "Too much ego."

Michael walked with Israel to the guest room that had become Israel's room, his home away from home, his fortress of solitude. After Michael left him alone, Israel wrote his thoughts into another poem, a sonnet.

No longer will I wrest to know the how
or why of swinging tides of happiness.
The many times ago with strains and stress
I strove to understand are done for now.
Do not think deep on this, but rest assured
you'll feel the joy of life from time to time,
the smiles sweet of gentle touch or rhyme,
or screams erupted, thrill of thrills endured.
And sadness too will hamper you, and fear,
and angst and anger, hate and love, the rest.
You'll know them all, emotions dread and blessed.
You'll know them all and live the laugh and tear.
For if it be for joy we yearn, the goal,
then faith, with courage calm, sustains the role.

Twenty-eight

DEEPER IN DILEMMA

Feeling quite over her head in the complexity of her new love, Gina wondered how long she would have to tread the deep waters of dilemma. She had known Israel so short a time, but from the beginning something about him compelled her as though they belonged with each other. His voice, his mannerisms, the breadth of his spirit, all of it seemed both familiar and astonishing. When she was with him it seemed as though for the first time in her life she knew herself fully. The connection was there, and when they made love she lost herself in something grander that blended them together. She couldn't explain it with any more detail than that. She loved him, but she found herself asking questions about the meaning of love. What kind of love requires what kinds of behavior? What kinds of trust?

Even before the craziness of Israel gallivanting around time and space like a lunatic knight errant, a Don Quixote on an impossible quest, Gina herself had problems with trust. Could she trust him?

Professor Michael Hannity called her on the telephone. "Hello, Miss Gina," he said. "I'm calling to tell you that Israel Newman, right now, is in sort of a mess. He took a couple of travels. I know you know what I'm talking about, right?"

"I know what you're talking about." Gina felt herself building a wall of resistance to defend against what the goofy professor would tell her next.

"He took a couple of travels back to save his son, Markus."

She felt a rush of anxiety, an unstoppable locomotive approaching, bearing down on her. There was an edge in her voice. "And how did he do?"

"Not so well, I'm afraid."

She felt relieved. She searched for the right thing to say. "He must be disappointed."

"To say the least; he's despondent, depressed even. His ex-wife told him some things he didn't know, or maybe he just didn't remember, and she reminded him. She told him—hey, I don't know if I should be telling you all this stuff, but he loves you; you should know that. She told him Markus was somebody else's son."

Quietly and thoughtfully she said, "Oh my god!"

"So he's not doing well. I put him to bed here, gave him something to help him sleep. Sometimes medicine is okay. Like in times like this."

"Yes."

"Would you like to come over and be with him? I think he'd like that."

"Yes, certainly. I'll be right over."

Professor Hannity made sure she knew how to get there, and just before hanging up, he said, "It's almost Halloween. Halloween is fun. I'm going to have a Halloween party, maybe cheer Israel up that way. Yes! It will be an open-house, throw-caution-to-the-wind, dress-up costume Halloween party. Tell your friends, Gina. Invite your friends."

Invite my friends? Sure! Certainly! That's exactly what I'll do. She put a filter on her irritation and answered simply, "Okay. You can give me the details when I come over."

"Right-o!"

As she drove her car to a brand new destination, not knowing what awaited her, she felt a haltering enthusiasm. *What have I gotten myself into?* She slowed her car because of a bicycle directly in front of her, in the middle of the street. *Don't you know I'm irritable right now? I could decide it's worth my while to run you down.* "You knucklehead!"

The man on the bike signaled a left turn, and he turned.

"It's a damned good thing." *Good thing he turned left; made some sense of this asinine situation.* A minute later the driver's door of a parked car swung open, and she swerved her car to avoid knocking the door off and sending the clueless, careless, dumbass perpetrator of the *open- door policy* from here to kingdom come. *The world is full of booby traps!* She slowed her car way down. *Be careful. I'm in control here. I'm not the crazy one(s), Israel and his insane friend, the professor. Stay in control. Really! They can't hurt me. I'm whole. Just like everything else, they are an appendage of my life, and I'm complete all by myself.*

At the front door of the professor's mansion was a sign that read *Ring the doorbell and hope for the best. If you're Israel, then press your thumb against the reader, and the door will open.* She pressed her thumb against the little screen, and nothing happened. She pressed the doorbell, and immediately the door was opened by a man who was neatly dressed in dark blue trousers, black shoes, white shirt, and a golden brown corduroy vest. "Good day! Ms. Provetti, I presume? I am Professor Hannity's valet, Reginald Pear. You may call me Reggie. It's my pleasure to meet you. Your appearance is every bit as stunning as the professor and Dr. Newman have described."

Startled by his compliment, Gina's disposition softened. "Thank you."

"Please come along, Ms. Provetti; I'll show you to Dr. Newman's room."

Dr. Newman's room! He has a foothold in this place. She looked around at the foyer with its high ceiling and crystal chandelier, the magnificent stained glass windows at the top of the first flight of stairs, the large rooms on either side of the foyer, noticing how sparsely furnished they were. "What a beautiful home."

"Yes. Someday the professor may even find a use for it." Jeeves smiled, turned in crisp military fashion, and walked with a symmetrically even, elegantly paced gait to the stairs and then up the stairs. "Your Doctor Newman is a charming man. The professor is quite fond of him." He paused, and when Gina said nothing, he added, "And though I've only just met him, and even if it is not my place to say, I also regard him as quite a cut above the rest."

"Yes," Gina responded. "There is much in him that a person cannot help loving."

Jeeves turned briefly to smile at her. "He's having a rough go of it at the moment."

They climbed the stairway up to the stained glass windows and then up another short way toward the right on the side opposite the Mozart Laboratory above the foyer. When Jeeves stopped and knocked on a door, no sound escaped from within. "He will be delighted to see you." He opened the door himself, at first just a crack, and then a little more.

Twenty-nine

SON OF MAN

Israel put aside the sonnet he had just written and found himself craving the peacefulness of escaping from ego. He meditated, not with the intention of traveling but fully aware it might happen. He just wanted to escape. Focusing on a single sound in the room, the soft whirring, breathing sounds of the computer next to his bed, he eliminated awareness of his senses of touch, vision, taste, and smell and then he eliminated sound as well and was left with the ringing in his ears, *tintinnabulation of my tinnitus*, and finally he eliminated that sound as well. He floated in a vast ocean of being, of being nothing more than life itself.

He was unaware of the opening of the door to his room.

He floated in the vast ocean, and, quite independent of his control, he was swept along in a current he didn't resist. He trusted and found it irresistible to travel beyond spacetime and then reenter it.

I am. Who am I? I don't know who I am. The room is spinning. I look at the floor because it doesn't spin so much, but it spins and nauseates me, and I don't want to vomit. I look up and to my left. It is James on my left. James will know who I am. "James?" I say. "James, I say."

He looks at me. His eyelids are droopy, but he doesn't look as drunk as I am. He still laughs at jokes that I have a difficult time hearing. I can't even hear them.

Who am I? "James," I say. "Who am I?"

He looks at me and laughs.

I ask him again, "I mean, who am I?"

"Does it matter?" He laughs. "If I tell you, will you remember? Maybe we shall wait until morning, and then I will tell you. It will save time that way. I will have to tell you only once."

"But I will be nobody between now and then."

"And that is how it should be." He laughs.

"I know I am not Judas; he does not get drunk. Peter does not get drunk either. Maybe I am Yeshua. Yeshua gets drunk."

With his mouth James makes a sound like he is passing gas, and then he says, "I don't think so. Yeshua gets happy on wine, a little loose, maybe, sometimes, but he doesn't get sick. Let's see now, who around here gets sick on wine? That would be a clue."

"Andrew gets sick, and Thomas."

"Yes! Maybe you are one of them."

"Maybe I am one of them. I could be Thomas or I could be Andrew."

"You have drunk too much wine."

"Yes, I have. I agree with you."

A servant comes into the room. "Is there one among you who is called Yeshua of Nazareth?"

Yeshua is at the other end of the table on which I lay my head. He says, "I am Yeshua of Nazareth. Do you have a message for me?"

"I do. There is a woman outside asking for you. There are two men with her that call themselves your brothers."

"Oh, they do? Who do they say their father is?"

"They did not tell me. I did not ask them. Is that what you would like me to do?"

"No, it is not necessary. Would you ask the woman who my father is?" Yeshua watches the man react as stone would react, without expression at all. The man stands like stone, and Yeshua says, "She would answer that I am the son of God, but then are we not all sons of God? Truthfully I tell you I am the son of man, but my father is not the man who sired the two men who accompany her. So how are they my brothers? These men here with me, these men sharing wine with me, these are my brothers. This causes you discomfort, but I beg of you, go to the woman and tell her I am here with my brothers already, drinking wine with them. Tell her I am the son of man."

I am glad to have heard this, but nausea is getting the better of me. "I need a pot, James." He gives me a pot, and I vomit into it two times.

"Now you are a new man," he tells me.

"Yes, that helped. I am a new man now, like Israel will become a new man. I am a new Israel. I am a new Israel man."

"Mister new man, you are still drunk," James tells me. "Take the pot out and dump it. Do that for the rest of us. After you dump the vomit, you will be a new man."

The ringing in my ears is louder than the world.

Israel again was swept into a river within the sea of spirit, beyond spacetime and back into it.

I am Tom, son of Harel, and I live in Nazareth. I kick the dust into straight lines in front of me as I walk toward the home of my friend Yeshua. He sits in the front of it with his back against the wall and his head down, resting his face on his hands.

"Yeshua!" I call.

He looks up at me; he has been crying.

"What is wrong?" I ask.

He shakes his head.

"I'm your friend," I tell him. I put my hand on his shoulder.

He breathes deeply and says, "My mother will not tell me who my father is."

"Is it not Yosef?"

He shakes his head.

"My mother and father told me your father is Yosef."

"They think you are too young to know the truth."

I frown, feeling it in my eyebrows. "They have lied to me?"

"Aha!" Yeshua laughs. "Parents do that. They think it is because of love that they lie."

"Who is your father, then?"

"I do not know."

"When you ask your mother, she must say something. What does she say?"

"She tells me that God in heaven is my dad."

I do not know how to respond.

Yeshua continues, "She says this because she is ashamed of how my life began. She thinks she does this out of love for me, calling me the son of God. She thinks that telling me this will help me to see myself as being like everybody else, because we all are children of God, but we all are children of man as well. By doing this she denies me."

Yeshua says a very strange thing, and it seems like someone else saying it, but it is him. "Whoever knows the father and the mother will be called the child of a whore."

He is Yeshua again, and he says, "I am a good person."

He takes my hand and puts it on his chest.

"Does my heart not beat?"

"Your heart beats, Yeshua."

"I am son of a man. I want to know who my father is."

"I must ask my parents. If I ask them straight out they will learn how much I already know, and then they will not lie to me about it."

He nods. "Yes, ask them. They have less reason to push me away from themselves than my own mother." Yeshua draws with his finger in the dust beside him. "She will call me Yeshua, son of God. If you love me, Tom, do not deny me the way she does. Call me Yeshua, son of man, and then I will be like you and everybody else."

"Then you are son of man," I tell him, "and I am son of God. We are the same." I put my arm around his shoulders and shake him a little."

He laughs, and there is ringing in my ears.

Israel was pulled into a stream of the spirit out of spacetime and back into it, into his room in the mansion of Michael Hannity.

He murmured, "Yeshua is psychologically screwed up too, just like the rest of us."

He did not hear the door of his room softly close or the footsteps in the hall walking away and down the stairs.

Thirty

DO NOT DISTURB THE NEED TO BE DESIRED

Gina stopped partway down the stairway at Michael's mansion to admire the stained glass windows with sunlight behind them, dazzlingly brilliant and intricate, emitting prismatic schisms of color splayed across the walls and steps of the stairway. *With such beauty in the world we can choose to be happy.* She slowly walked down the rest of the stairs feeling glamorous.

Just as she put her shoe on the floor of the foyer, Jeeves met her.

"Are you leaving so soon, Ms. Provetti?"

"Gina. Please call me Gina."

"Yes, Miss Gina. Was Dr. Newman in a surly mood? You're leaving so soon."

"He will be okay. I didn't want to disturb him, not now. Do you have any stationery?"

"Yes, of course. Follow me to the study where you will find a pleasing selection from which to choose."

She followed Jeeves and sat at an antique French provincial writing table. "How lovely," she said, running a hand along its woodwork. "Is it a family heirloom?"

"Not my family's. Next time I run into the professor I will point out to him there is information about his furniture about which he brazenly has left me uninformed."

Gina smiled. "You're a funny man."

"Thank you. Are you going to write a letter to your grandmother?" He seemed quite serious, not a hint of a smile.

"Eh, no. I would like to leave a short message for Dr. Newman. I mean Israel. Now you've gotten me talking overly formal."

Jeeves smiled. "Do put it in an envelope and seal it. If you leave it there on the desk, I will deliver it to the doctor after you have left. That is your intention, is it not, to make a point so valid and strong that you will not accept any argument from him in return?"

Gina looked at Jeeves without responding.

"I approve," he said, and there was a twinkle in his eyes.

Gina found off-white paper with subtle and pretty embossing of interlocking hearts. She wrote, *Dearest Israel, It appears I am in competition for your soul.* No, that statement wouldn't do. She crumpled the paper and put it into her purse. She began again. *Dearest Israel, I still have rights to your body, and I'm claiming them. You are mine. Call me and invite me to accompany you to the Four Seasons Hotel for dinner and dancing and a private party in your room upstairs, underwear optional. As long as I am in your life, you can choose to be happy.* She put on fresh lipstick and kissed the paper, leaving an imprint, put the paper in an envelope, and sealed it.

On her way out she was met at the front door by Michael. "Gina!" he smiled. "So good to see you. Would you join me for a cup of tea in the Hobbit Hole?"

"Israel has told me about your charming home within a home," she answered, "and another time I would very much enjoy seeing it and spending time in conversation with you. At the moment I do have things I need to do."

"Another time then."

"I left a letter for Israel on that beautiful writing table."

"My mother's. And her mother's."

"With such beauty in the world we can choose to be happy."

"Yes, we can."

"Goodbye, then. Tell Israel I love him."

"That I will do, and don't forget the Halloween party. Details;

there must be details. Yes!" He whispered behind his hand, "Fuck yes."

Gina closed her eyes and opened them again in a slow, pretty blink that calmed her anxiety about allowing herself to get pulled deeper into what was becoming a messier, even if entertaining, relationship. Israel had friends with colorful personalities.

"Let me think now," said Michael. "This year Halloween will be on Saturday. Perfect! First we will have a dinner here with the principals, you and Israel and my parents. Gina, my parents will be here." Behind his hand and quietly he said, "Holy fucking shit, my parents will be here." He wagged his head back and forth, noisily wiggling his lips, and then he said, "Excuse me. My bad manners are under control now. No more surprise words, no. But on Halloween, maybe there will also be a surprise guest, hopefully, if all goes well. We will begin dinner at six, and we'll have guests start arriving at seven thirty. Guests! We need to invite guests. Do you have friends who would like to come? Tell them. As many as you want; just let me know for planning purposes. There will be food and decorations and libation. Tell them to wear costumes."

"I'll tell my friends."

"Good!"

All smiles Gina walked out to her car, got in, started it, and then sat for a solid two minutes. What the hell had she gotten herself into? She wanted to jump his bones. Why? Because she loved him. Why did she love him? Because he loved her. She knew he loved her. He loved his son; he loved her. Why couldn't he have them both? "God? Are you listening? Why can't Israel have us both?" *I'm an idiot. Fools rush in. That's me, a fool in love.* "Damn it!"

She drove to Victoria's Secret. *I'll make his prick so hard he'll faint because there won't be blood left for his brain. Go down fightin', girl.*

She arrived home with her new weapons of love, and as she was putting them into a lingerie drawer she was interrupted by a call on her cell phone. It was a familiar voice that she hadn't heard for many months, but not so many months as would have allowed it to lose an emotional purchase on her. It was the voice of Randy Shephard, the man who dumped her half a year earlier.

"Gina," it said, touching her in parts of her being where she no longer wanted it to touch. "I miss you terribly. I've learned a lot of things since we broke up, things I needed to learn, about how much you meant to me, how much you mean to me. I know I handled it poorly. I was a jackass, I know. I know I was. I've learned, Gina. You're the most perfect woman I've ever known. I want to get together and talk about us again. We were great together. I know that now, better than I ever did before."

Gina listened to him and didn't say a word until he stopped talking, and then she simply told him about the Halloween party at Professor Hannity's mansion. A split second after she pushed the button to end the conversation, her mind exploded. *Why did I tell him that! Crap!*

Thirty-one

THE HALLOWEEN PARTY

O ur souls continued to march through time.
Israel was unable to control the destination of his many travels, realizing the reason had become his preoccupation with himself, his inability to relinquish ego; but travels continued by a force separate from himself. He continued frequently to awaken in the night with his bedside clock staring the puzzle at him: 3:16.

Gina made love with him, and when, because of his depression he was a bit slow to arousal, she was proficient. He realized his love for her was more selfish than he wanted it to be.

It would be the second Halloween since Markus died; he would have been five years old, and the day triggered Israel's grief.

Wanting to lighten the heaviness of Israel's burden, Michael had planned a party on that ghastly night. Jeeves would hand out candies to trick-or-treaters during a raucous open house, and he invited four people to sit with him for dinner before the party. They sat in the intimate dining room of his little hobbit hole within a mansion.

Gina and Israel came as Marilyn Monroe and Abraham Lincoln. Israel tried to remain statesmanlike while Gina kept flirting and teasing him with a breathy voice. "Happy birthday, Mr. President."

Recently arrived from Milwaukee, Michael's parents were dressed like the cartoon characters of Boris and Natasha, like little old wrinkled versions of Boris and Natasha.

"Has to get Moose and Squirrel, Dahlink."

"Yeah, yeah. Later in our bedroom. Not in front of the kids."

Michael sat at the end of the table dressed as himself, Kal-El. He looked like Superman without the cape, and he sported muscles enough to fill the costume. A Lois Lane robot sat in the chair to his left. She spoke and moved sometimes according to Michael's directions on a console, but she also was capable of injecting comments independent of his will. He enjoyed being surprised by her, but hadn't yet perfected the technology for giving her complete independence.

"I love you, superhunk. Fly me to the moon."

"I'd like to fly you to my fortress of solitude for a little one-on-one entertainment," answered Michael, putting on his best Groucho Marx impersonation, raising his eyebrows and wiggling an imaginary cigar.

"That's my fortress of solitude you're talking about, superhunk, and don't be getting presumptuous about it, or I'll cut you off."

"She loves me." Michael winked. His antics were just creepy enough to fit Halloween.

Michael had placed elegant wood-framed chairs in the room, upholstered with a new-age, durable and easy-to-clean material called plastic, black and orange, of course, and whenever somebody squirmed on them they made farting sounds.

At one point during a break in the conversation Michael said, "Some people tell us that when there is a period of silence like this, an angel has passed between us. Angels are spirit, of course, and so you can't see or touch them, but somehow you know they're there." He squirmed in his chair, and a noise erupted. The group laughed.

"It's so nice your parents are here," said Gina, and then she looked at Israel and said, "I have an announcement to make. My mom is coming to visit for Thanksgiving; I'm excited that you're going to meet her, Israel. You two are going to love each other; I just know it."

"As I've said before, you can fool some of the people some of the time."

"Cut that out."

"Of course I'll like her; she made you, right? How could I not like her? But how do you know she'll like me?"

"Actually you're a lot like each other. You both have deep compassion. You are going to be a big hit with her. She's wanted me to find a guy like you for a long time, and now lookie here. Voila!" Gina's effervescence was like bubbles over champagne. "She is such a charitable person, always giving herself to others, sort of like a not-so-famous Mother Teresa. She just told me that right after New Year's she's going to go to Haiti to help teach poor kids at a mission school."

A dark shudder shook Israel's body. He had no idea why he felt pale and silenced by dread. He looked at Michael.

Michael was looking back at Israel with quite a blank expression, and then he turned a smiling face toward Gina. "How lovely! What a wonderful person she must be. Please tell her that she has won Professor Hannity's first annual Halloween jackpot, a two-week, all-expenses-paid vacation to the Bahamas, but she has to take it between January fifth and nineteenth."

Gina stared at him incredulously.

"Actually," Michael said, "I've already booked a room there for myself, but something has come up, so I want to give it to your mom. Please tell her. Bring her around to meet me when she visits for Thanksgiving. Please. I want to do this."

"You're an angel!"

Michael smiled and nodded acknowledgment.

"Israel," said Jor-El, "tell us something funny about your patients."

"Something funny?"

"Yes! People are funny. You must have amazing material."

"Well, just yesterday a guy told me he had to quit taking gabapentin because it made his nipples hurt, so I asked him if maybe he was being visited at night by the Nipple-tweak Fairy. This was the first time I had met the guy, so he didn't know me, and his wife was right there. Neither one of them laughed at my joke, so I got real serious, just as serious as they were, and I told them, with the most instructive demeanor I could muster, that there is no such thing as a Nipple-tweak Fairy."

"You call that funny? I can be funnier than that with my pants falling down."

"He's right about that," chimed Lor-El. "When his pants fall down he's quite funny. I speak from experience."

They laughed.

Lor-El said, "How about this? I'm thinking I'm going to start believing this twenty twelve bunk about the Mayan calendar and the end of time. Two years from now. it's going to work like this. Some fat-assed tycoon oil magnate is going to drill an oil well in deep water, probably the Gulf of Mexico. It's not a good idea. The damned thing will spring a leak, and they won't be able to stop it, so it will leak forever until, when will it be, September or December of 2012? It will fill up the oceans with oil until there's this one great big giant oil slick. The smell will be atrocious." She fanned her face with her hand and scrunched her nose. "All the countries of the world will hate the United States, just because it's the country everybody loves to hate. It's like the New York Yankees that way. Even the United States will hate itself. People will hold national self-hate events, with cake and ice cream and petitions to screw some poor bastard in Washington who has no control of it in the first place. Americans! We're all the same! It will be in September of 2012, September or December. It doesn't matter. Then some goofus will light a cigarette and throw a lit match into the water, and *poof*!" She snapped her fingers. "Just like that the oceans will be ablaze all over the globe. It will look like a giant Weber grill when Jor-El used to start the charcoal with gasoline instead of the starter fluid you can get at the grocery store. There will be methane explosions like nobody's business. Never mind global warming; this will consume oxygen in our atmosphere, and we'll all suffocate, like people did from the bombs over Tokyo in World War II. Jor-El will be the first to go because he's been asking for it a long time. Already his lungs are going, from asbestos exposure. Ha ha; not so funny." She looked around the group.

They looked back at her like they were waiting for a better punchline.

"From the moon," she exclaimed, and spread her arms up toward the ceiling. "The spectacle will be glorious. Looking up in the moon sky, there will be a beautiful burning Earth. An astronaut up there is going to wonder what the hell! Can you imagine how it will seem to him? He'll realize he's the last living human in the universe, and his own days are numbered."

She sang, "Goodbye to all the bakers; goodbye to all the priests; goodbye to all the wild lands and all the wild beasts. Goodbye, beloved darling, the pretty girl he fucks; he's feeling awfully lonely now 'cause damn, this really sucks. Goodbye to all his family; goodbye to all his friends; goodbye to God's creation, 'cause this is when it ends."

She looked around at the others. "Oh, don't be so glum," she ranted. "It's a Halloween story, for god's sake. Have some fun with it. Just think. There's an astronaut up on the moon who suddenly wants to kill himself. Acute depression! He picks up a moon rock and pummels his helmet with it repetitively, trying to break it, because he wants to die quickly, put himself out of misery, but the helmet won't break because it's manufactured from the latest and strongest materials made from, you guessed it, oil. Think of the irony."

The room was silent. Nobody squirmed in a chair to make a farting sound.

Michael said, "Ladies and gentlemen, I give you my mother," and he smiled at her, not in a condescending way, although there was memory of condescending smiles of the past, but this one had warmth in it, of acceptance and realization and amusement.

Jor-El said, "It makes no sense to talk about some topics. Other topics, it takes no sense to talk about. In general takes-no-sense topics are more fun than makes-no-sense topics. Your mother is a pro at doing both at the same time."

"Ladies and gentleman," said Michael, "I give you my father."

Jeeves's cheerful face poked in through the door. "The first party guests are arriving, professor."

Michael announced, "And with that they all got drunk and had a merry time."

As the party swung to a crescendo of playfulness, Gina became more and more gregarious and outgoing. Quite convincingly she donned the stereotyped personality of the on-camera Marilyn Monroe. She flirted and flashed her cleavage and ran her hands down her sides and onto her thighs. She blew kisses.

Israel watched with some irritation; it bothered him. *Maybe she drank too much wine.* He did his best to armor himself with thoughts of spirit over matter. *At some time I am her, and sometimes I am them.* This thought worked well enough, for the most part, until a tall, slender man appeared, a handsome and dashing man, and Gina spent a disproportionate amount of time with him. Her flirting and laughing did not seem as innocent with the attractive man who was dressed as a vampire and acted like he would bite Gina's neck. She moved away just enough that he did not kiss her, but she appeared to enjoy his flirtations. She scolded him with smiles.

Israel tried to remain nonchalant, but it was a self-conscious nonchalance. He focused his eyes on the bubbles in his beer, on the wallpaper. He spent more time than necessary appreciating the details of guests' costumes. He did not follow when Gina accompanied the stranger to a different room. Wanting not to appear glum but believing he could not refrain from it, he retreated into the hobbit-hole dining room. It and the Mozart Laboratory, and the stairs to the basement were the only locations in the house that were locked and strictly off limits to partygoers. Israel had an approved thumbprint and iris for entry. In a cupboard he found a bottle of Scotch whiskey. *Thank you, Michael.* He poured two fingers of it into a glass and sat down at the table. He sipped it slowly. *God, why do you afflict me? Did you make us this way because you like surprises?*

A few minutes after he finished the whiskey in his glass, Gina entered the room. "Israel, I've been looking all over for you. Is something the matter?" She sat down beside him.

She pretends she doesn't understand what's going on. He nodded. "I'm sorry. I'm not as enlightened as I thought I was, not as enlightened as I want to be. I still get hurt."

"What are you talking about? Who hurt you? Is this about Markus?" She sounded sincerely concerned.

A flash of lightning in his chest caused him to take a short gasp. *She won't volunteer an acknowledgment of her part in my bad mood until I embarrass myself by confessing my jealousy.* He shook his head and closed his eyes lightly.

She put a hand on his shoulder and stroked up to the back of his neck. "You know that guy who came dressed as a vampire? He made a pass at me. He pushed himself on me and kissed me, even though I tried to push him away."

Tried to push him away. Tried! She kissed him. A thought erupted in his mind, a remark made by one of his medical school buddies. *Nobody gets seduced unless they want to be seduced.*

She continued, "I told him I have a guy, and I'm in love with my guy, and then I couldn't find you."

"Yes, well, you know, Gina, it's Halloween and everybody has gotten a little drunk and they let themselves do things they normally wouldn't do." He sighed. "In a way people become a little more revealing of themselves that way. The alcohol and the party atmosphere remove their inhibitions. They're not as responsible as they normally are."

He felt Gina recoil, as though she had been slapped. There was silence. Israel squirmed in his chair. "There goes another angel," he said. The comment did not break the tension between them.

Gina pressed one of her legs against his. *Under the table!* He wanted this touch from her, but it was a trigger for memories of infidelity.

Gina stroked his hair and said, "Let's go to your room." She stood up and pulled his hand. "Come on, Mr. President. Show this girl a good time."

When Israel stood up, she pressed her body against him and kissed him enthusiastically. She tasted like wine and lipstick. She led him out of the room, and as they climbed the stairs, she pulled his left arm around her and put his hand on her breast. They entered his room and locked the door.

Gina turned her back toward him and pulled her hair up with her right hand. "Unzip me."

He unzipped her dress and pulled the top of it down. Standing behind her, he slid his hands lightly down the front of her shoulders and chest. He stroked his fingers in wide circles around her breasts, making the circles smaller and smaller until his middle fingers were on her nipples. They were hard, and he pushed them slightly inward and swiveled them.

Gina leaned back against him. "Mmmmmmmmmm."

"You're so fucking hot," he murmured in her ear. "You're so beautiful." He cupped her breasts and lifted them slightly so that they pointed more, and he felt her erect nipples between his fingers. Relaxing his hands, the fingers softly squeezed those sensitive parts.

Gina moaned again and laid her head backward against his shoulder, turning her face to the side so that they could kiss lips.

Israel was a prisoner of his own mind and the impact of previous experiences upon it, though. He was blind even to the clarity of Gina's having chosen him. It might have been different had he known the whole story, that the stranger was not a stranger. He didn't have that crucial piece of information. His thoughts exploded. *Not about sex my ass! It was the other guy who aroused her, and now she's— Is this the right thing for me to do? If I don't make love with her, what will she do? She said she's not a sex junky who's in need of a fix. What's going on right now?*

He dropped his hands. "Gina, I can't. Not tonight."

She looked surprised. "Why not? What's wrong?"

"Sex is sex, right? But I thought sex between us was supposed to be about love, not about sex. That's what you told me back at the beginning. Sex for us was going to be about the love and not about the sex itself." He paused to collect his thoughts. "Each of us has our limitations; I know that. We all have frailties. Really, I understand that. Causes and effects, right? It's just that I'm not . . . it's not clear to me what sex would be about tonight."

"Don't you love me?" Gina looked genuinely hurt. She turned to face him.

"Yes, Gina, I love you."

"What is it then?" There was an edge to her voice.

He rocked slightly sideways, back and forth, and then he said, "I'm not sure I'd be the guy who's in your head tonight."

She got angry. "I'm not going to put up with jealousy, Israel. I promised myself I'd never get entangled with a jealous guy. I'm not going to live with that."

"You talked with Michael, remember? You learned the scoop about me when I was still in the hospital."

"But I'm not your ex-wife. I don't sleep around."

"I didn't say you did."

"But it bothered you that I had a little bit of fun tonight, at a costume party on Halloween, playing the part of my character. You were hurt by that? I didn't do anything wrong."

Israel rocked slightly forward onto his toes, then back again. "You're right. You didn't do anything wrong."

"But you don't want to make love."

Yes, I do. "No, not tonight."

"Because you're jealous."

"Okay."

"Okay?" She yelled, "No! Not okay." She pulled her dress back up over her front and clutched it there with her left hand. "You're an idiot, Israel. Worse than an idiot, you're a jealous idiot intent on ruining the best thing in his life. I'm loving and I'm sexy and I love you. I chose you. You don't even see it. You're a blind jealous idiot. Is this the way you treat women you love? You treat them like tramps? Not tonight? Okay, you're an idiot."

She turned and stormed out of the room without asking Israel to zip her up. He watched her bare, pretty back exit through the door.

What was that all about? He realized more had happened in that interchange than he understood. *Maybe I'm too much of an anchor for her.*

Thirty-two

ONE, TWO; BUCKLE MY SHOE

uddenly the room became truly his own, a small section of a primitive community cave, individual and lonely, a parcel of space demarcated by a border of stones. Clashing with Gina had filled it with the spilling of his soul. He protected himself by retreating behind the stone wall of his intellect.

With uniquely patterned warps and ripples, each of us is a carnival mirror reflecting distortions of the world, each silly one of us seeing something different. What's real? Matter or spirit? The particulate world doesn't change. It was, is, and always will be what it is, but the spirit living within it does change. So what's real? The world? Or the many different perceptions we have of it? Every experience is as real as any other and can make us and others appear to be beautiful, bland, or ugly.

He slowly paced, and a remembered thought emerged from an earlier epiphany. When faced with a problem they cannot solve, many people will blame someone else; not all people do, but many. He sat down and wrote another poem.

This trouble is of trouble's trade,
and I'll not let it tarnish me.
Triumphant whole of spirit made,
as such cannot divided be.
For having been the slayer's sword

and having by the sword been slain,
am I to dread the angry word
or fear a promise or a pain?
It's true that ache of heavy heart,
of broken love's abandoned soul,
is different from the severed part;
and yet there too, I've paid the toll.
To know that what will be has been,
like yesterday so certainly,
will be again, again and then
a bittersweet eternity.
Oh, bittersweet eternity!
It's now my turn; I cannot run.
Thy kingdom come. Thy will be done.

He walked over and locked the door to his bedroom, methodically tended to his hygiene, and crawled into bed. There he meditated, hoping to find a time in his mind before he was belabored with sorrow. It had to have been before Markus died, before Sonya betrayed him. Would he find the happy memory in his early days with Sonya? Even those days, that once were happy, now were burdened by what followed them. *When was I happy? With Gina, but still clouded by the loss of Markus.*

There are moments when complete joy touches us. It might happen upon the birth of a baby or the singing of a choir; it might be something planned or a surprise, a first kiss. When it happens, whether by a touch of God's mind on ours or just the collusion of a trillion particles of a subatomically structured universe, it is special, and we bless ourselves by taking notice of it, by allowing it to caress the loneliness of our bruised spirit. In these moments of joy we become aware we are not alone. In fact the idea of loneliness fades away completely because joy connects us to the rest of life; and for those who are able to believe it, joy manifests the very essence of the cause of existence that dwells within each of us.

What of those times when there is not joy, when we cannot see it lying beyond the horizon? Is it fair at these times to believe that survival alone is enough? And if it is true that survival is enough, what is that bit of courage clinging to survival even in the darkest hour, knowing that joy will blossom again? Is it faith that moves us from one moment of joy to the next? Then faith must be the substrate of existence that makes survival possible, and joy is what makes it worthwhile. Entwined with this is sorrow, often knotted with joy, and together they are a tear that flows down the face of God.

Israel had lived long and often enough to know that joy would thrive again, if not in this lifetime then in another. He prayed. *Father, come into me so that I may understand you better. Jesus, come into me so that I may be more like you.* He fell asleep clinging to survival with his expectation of future joy.

Until an unrelenting headache pestered him, he slept soundly and did not want to allow it to awaken him, but it swelled in his awareness until he could focus on nothing else. It pressed steadily and strong. His ribs no longer hurt.

He crawled out of bed and put on a pair of pajama bottoms and slippers, clambered down the stairs, and found Michael in the kitchen with a cup of coffee and a computer screen open to the *Journal of Theoretical Physics*.

Michael looked up. "Good morning, sleepyhead."

"Sleepyhead? It's six thirty."

"Excuse me, but I've been up an hour and a half already. Don't get me wrong. I'm not scoffing at what you doctors keep telling us. I am absolutely certain that sleep is every bit as important as you say it is, but I can't sleep very long with Mom and Dad in the house."

"You're stressed?"

Michael nodded.

"Why are you stressed?"

"It happens, and I'm not going to fucking swear about it."

"Why does it happen?"

Michael shook his head and waved the question away with a hand. "It happens."

"I see you're drinking some diarrhea water." Israel pointed to the coffee.

"You want some?"

"Yes, I do. With this headache I could use some caffeine." As he poured a cup, Israel said, "Great party last night, by the way."

"What happened between you and Gina?"

"I don't know. I mean I could say that she flirted too much with a guy and it bothered me. I could say she got angry with me when I let her know it bothered me, but there's more to it than that, and I don't understand it. I don't know why she acted the way she did and why I acted the way I did. On deeper levels it's a mystery." After a pause he added, "Determinism."

"Determinism doesn't explain it."

"No, but it helps to accept it."

"She left the party alone last night; called a cab and went. Maybe you should call her."

"Maybe I should. I don't know what I'd say."

"Maybe saying nothing would be saying too much, more than you want to say."

"Michael, let's talk about something else."

"Okay. What'll it be?"

"How about a trip?"

"You don't need the lab anymore. You can do that on your own now."

"Not so much lately. I'm too caught up in my own problems now to do it on my own, I'm thinking maybe I can do it with the help of the Mozart Laboratory."

"A trip now? Are you sure? You've told me you've noticed your mood influences your trip. Is this the mood you want to be in when you travel?"

"Maybe we should find out what music is playing in the foyer."

"There shouldn't be anything."

"Yeah, I know. It was quiet just now when I came down."

They climbed the stairs slowly, awash in the prismatic light through the windows that sprinkled all around them, and when they arrived at the Mozart Laboratory the music playing, once again, was Mozart's *Tempo di Menuetto*.

"My favorite."

"Mine too."

"Yes, it's quite beautiful. I wish it were longer. It's a good omen that it's playing now."

Israel tried to travel but without success.

Thirty-three

FORGIVENESS, RESTORATION, AND JUSTIFICATION

After a lonely and unsuccessful Sunday, Israel looked at his Monday schedule at his clinic: November 2, 2009. He wrote on it, "Call Gina. Tell her I know I need to change."

Albert Ronald Bormann came in; he used his middle name, Ron. He was the last patient of the morning, put on the schedule in an urgent appointment because of recent apparent suicide attempt by overdosing on his medicines.

"Twenty-nine tablets isn't suicide; it's a headache." Ron laughed, but there was no humor in it.

"It worries me," Israel answered.

"I don't want to commit suicide." Ron was devoutly Catholic and believed suicide was an unpardonable sin. "I don't want to go to hell and be with my father." He had been horribly abused as a child. "I'm absolutely certain he's there."

It was a long appointment. Israel allowed Ron two oxycodone tablets per day and wrote prescriptions for only one week at a time.

The first patient after lunch was an older man, dressed beautifully in dark golden corduroy trousers and a light-green collared shirt with the two upper buttons unfastened, showing a silver chain around his neck. He wore a textured light brown jacket. His hair was as white as snow, long and fastened in a ponytail down his back as far as the shoulder blades.

When the interview arrived at social history, the man said,

"I'm afraid of people who love me." This statement grasped and elevated Israel's attention, and he looked more searchingly at the man whose eyes were mixed green and brown with flecks of gold. One of the flecks of gold in the lower left iris was shaped like a heart. The man continued, "When love enters into it, somebody's going to get hurt." The man paused a moment to collect himself. "My wife and I argue with each other. We're always arguing. Last Passover they kicked us out of our retirement condo because of it. Two months ago she said I abused her, but I didn't abuse her. She abused me. She slapped me, and my glasses went flying across the room. She hit me, and then she called the police, and when they came out they took me to prison instead of her." The man shook his head looking at the floor. "But I have a good lawyer who helped me get out without any lasting blots on my record."

Israel felt himself pulled out from his body by an irresistible force, out of himself and into the being of the older gentleman, his patient, looking at the face of Doctor Israel Newman, whose brown left eye had a green heart at its bottom.

"Israel," the doctor said. "Life is about forgiveness. Forgiveness is the solution."

"Yeshua?"

"Day after day my patients and I talk, and one day one of us said, 'Have you ever noticed that people don't get along with each other?' We laughed at that, and it launched me into a cascade of thoughts leading to this interesting word: forgiveness, a term appropriated but not owned by religions. Despite cosmologic distortion of the meaning of the word by Christianity, it can be studied as a psychological rather than a religious concept."

"Are you not Yeshua?"

"It's important to recognize forgiveness means different things to different people. As a physician, every now and then I find myself helping patients to forgive themselves for not being able to forgive others. Many suffer because they think it's a sin not to forgive. Observing others struggle with this concept has shaped how I think about forgiveness.

"Whether or not to forgive is a personal choice and is best decided without the supernatural influence of divinely decreed rightfulness or wrongfulness. Ultimately forgiveness is a constructive selfish act, benefitting the person who forgives at least as much, and often more, than the person who is forgiven. In fact sociopaths tend to be interested in forgiveness mainly to the extent that it may make their future infractions successful."

Israel was unable to decide who was inside his body talking to him in the other body, and his natural distrust welled up in him. Whoever the spirit was, it was inside of him, part of him. He wanted to challenge it. "What is forgiveness?" he asked.

"Long ago I began to counsel patients that forgiveness was important if they wanted to continue a relationship with the one who hurt them; otherwise it was not as important. I decided to modify and expand it. Forgiveness is the willingness and ability to take an experience of having been hurt out of the emotional territories of their minds and make it purely a cognitive memory. It's the ability to think about it without allowing it to hurt. We can forgive without forgetting, and in this way forgiveness resembles the process of grieving. Of course some people are more able than others to do it. Forgiveness is, at least in part, the cure for grief, grieving for the loss of something important. We learn to detour around the emotional content of loss."

This explanation made sense to Israel. "Forgiveness is the cure for grief?"

"In part. Sometimes grief is caused by something unseen, unknown. Who must we forgive, then? Mother Nature?" The soul in Doctor Newman's body laughed. "God?" He paused, looked down at his hands, and drew with his right index finger on the top of the writing table in front of him. "This is a clue perhaps for what things cause us to feel a need to answer the question in our hearts, whether to forgive. We ask ourselves this question because of our resentment about wrongs done, wrongs that have caused grief, that have caused loss of something, particularly loss of something valuable in a relationship."

"Who are you?" Israel asked.

"The soul in Doctor Newman's body," came the answer. "There are at least two independent decisions to make in the process of choosing whether to forgive. Do you want to continue the relationship? Do you want to set aside the emotional torment a wrong has caused? These are two separate questions, and you can choose neither or both or just one or the other.

"Restoration of a relationship requires more than just forgiveness. Restoration requires forgiven people to acknowledge the forgiveness and accept it. Forgiven people must understand what the behavior was that caused the hurt, what their role was in it. They must commit themselves to work diligently not to repeat the harm, which restores the relationship, especially if people talk with each other about it, let each other know what they are doing and why it is important to them.

"Justification! Justification is even more than forgiveness and restoration. How does one take away the harm done? How does one make a life as sturdy and strong as it once had been? It is not always possible. Can one put a severed limb back on a body? Sometimes. Now sometimes, but it hasn't been always so. Can a dead person be brought back to life?"

The Doctor Newman body tapped on the knee of the man within whose body Israel found himself. "Smile." The doctor grinned. "Now I will take you on a fascinating whirlwind of a journey, and you will learn from it. Listen to me; I'll tell you this now about what you will learn. It is the behavior of one person to forgive. Restoration requires the participation of two or more people. Justification requires action by the cause of existence. Are you ready for it?"

Israel didn't answer.

"Take my hand." Just as a parent takes the hand of a child, the Doctor Newman body took the hand of the man within whom Israel resided. "Here we go."

Together they traveled beyond spacetime, and Israel heard his own voice say to him, "We will meet again soon enough; I am always with you." The other spirit then seemed to leave, and Israel reentered spacetime.

Thirty-four

JUDAS ISCARIOT

I am named after Judas, son of Mattathias, a priest who lived two hundred years ago and launched our uprising against the Seleucids. They had desecrated our temple with their many idols and sought obliteration of our belief in the one true God. They would kill us all or make us Greek. Antiochus IV Epiphanes dispatched evil on the holy ones of us, gathering together the women whose baby sons had been circumcised. He killed the babies, hung the corpses around the necks of their mothers, and then executed the mothers as well. Against such horror we revolted.

Judas, my namesake, was the general who defeated the Seleucids, even against vastly superior forces. Judas outwitted them and came to be called Maccabeus, which means *the hammerer.* He restored purity to our temple in Jerusalem, and from the day of that new consecration, every year we have celebrated the eight days of Hanukkah, which means *dedication*. We dedicate our temple and ourselves to the one true God.

With victory came a pact with a devil that later bit us in the ass like a sneaky little dog. Judas Maccabeus made an alliance with Rome, and Rome has become the dog who bites our ass.

I am Judas Iscariot. I work with a band that eventually will overthrow our obsequious government and its unholy alliance with Rome. Like Judas Maccabeus I will regard it an honor to die in battle. For now we act in secrecy, taking what our enemies unwittingly give us. We are thieves and assassins, but we are not indiscriminate. We select our marks carefully.

Rome is the sneaky little dog, and Pilatus is the dog's piece of shit who rules as prefect of Judea. He has announced his job is to keep peace, and his idea of peace is Rome's idea of peace. As long as taxes flowing to Rome are sufficient, there is peace. He rules with terror, once infiltrating our markets with mercenary traitorous Jews, and one of them instigated a riot, and then all of them came out with their sticks and beat innocents to remind us we must be peaceful or suffer consequences.

A while ago a preacher came to one of our meetings and coerced me into changing my ways, at least for a time, into following him. I look at him now across this table prepared for seder.

He was brought to our meeting of revolutionaries by one who raved about how this Nazarene, Yeshua, performed miracles and how an increasing number of people were developing affection for him. He would be good for our cause, people said, except we were assassins and he preached nonviolence, so we began to think about a two-pronged attack.

He came to us and said, "You plot and wait for governance that already is in your midst. Father's kingdom is here now. Open your minds to it."

I was the one who answered, "Rome suppresses us, steals from us, beats us down if we complain. How can you help us cast the Romans out of our home?"

"Rome is a problem for you only because you want more than you have been given. Truly I tell you that you can live well with even less than you have. Desire less for yourselves, and you will be happier."

His comment angered me. Piss on that, I thought. "My purpose in life is to fight for Jewish freedom."

"In Father's kingdom the Jews are free now."

"I do not feel free."

"If you instigate violence, the people of Judea will suffer."

One of the others, a man called Thomas, asked, "How does a person come into your father's kingdom?"

That is when I realized, rather than us bringing him into our fold, he would bring at least some of us into his. As it turned out, he wanted me because I was able to read and write, and though I was too violent for his tastes, he trusted me.

He answered the question, "You already are in our father's kingdom. See it by opening your mind."

I enjoyed my companion's response. He said, "If the kingdom is mine right now, then it is mine to lose," which is how we feel. He said more. "So how will that happen? How will I get thrown out of the kingdom? I'll get thrown out because my sins will stink up the place like many farts and belches, like rotting fish. The righteous ones will throw me out on my putrid behind."

Yeshua laughed. "All are sinful, friend. Everybody farts and belches. If one of the hypocrites tries to throw you out of what they claim as their own house, how surprised they will be to learn that you have landed with your putrid behind still in Dad's living room. If people get ejected because of sins, then nobody will be left, and what kind of party would that be? I tell you truthfully, listen; the problem with Dad's kingdom is you cannot escape. It is like prison that way. You may deny your presence in it, but you would be deceiving yourself."

Thomas, behaving like a bargaining Jacob, said, "I like this idea. I can get away with all sorts of abuses and abominations, break the law. I don't have to be good."

"You are an amusing lad. Obeying the law is a way of opening your mind to see the kingdom, a way of making your life in the kingdom happier." Yeshua picked up Thomas's knife and poked at the air with it, brandished it. "It is like this: to be good at something you must practice. An assassin practices with his knife until he wields it perfectly without even thinking about it, until movements become memorized by the muscles themselves. Everything becomes just right, and then, when everything is perfect, he kills with skill. Our father's kingdom is like an assassin who kills with skill. It comes from practice, except you must practice the things that are in his kingdom, so your happiness can grow. Be righteous always, and practice the law. Otherwise you will not feel Dad inside you. He will be there, but you will not know it."

Conversation continued. For every question Yeshua had a good answer, and over time, he persuaded me to walk with him. He needed someone who could read and write so that scribes would not cheat his little band of brothers, and I offered my service. He needed someone to manage a budget for his group, and I did that task as well. I have been his scribe and treasurer, a lovely job that has earned for me the suspicions of all his other followers, who sometimes make themselves mean and stubborn. Yeshua is the one who trusts me, and now I watch him prepare his mind for the seder. He sits alone and meditates.

I have not relinquished my knife, still hidden beneath my clothes, there if I need it. A man can both smile and frown at the same time, and I think Yeshua's response was because of my knife. He does not talk with me about it.

People have come to him. Yeshua talks about loving everybody; everybody matters, and lonely souls looking for love find their way to his doorstep. That is my Yeshua. Everybody matters, even women. There are many bad husbands and many bad wives, and sometimes they are better off parting ways. The problem for women is they don't have a good way to earn money enough to stay alive. Divorce ends their lives. Where do they go? They come to Yeshua. That is the way it is. Men put demands on their wives that women do not meet; men beat their wives as they have a right to do within reason, and wives take an indefinite trip away from home. Some of them have come to our group for assistance, and their husbands have not been pleased with us.

Husbands have gone to the Pharisees, who are righteous for the sake of righteousness, righteous according to the law and not the heart. Once the Pharisees came to us and complained for the husbands whose wives had left them. As is their way, they tried to trap Yeshua with scriptural argument. They always seem to get their way when they argue scripture, but that is not what happened when they came against Yeshua, who knew righteousness by the law just as well as they did, and unlike them he also knew righteousness with his heart.

The Pharisees asked him, "Is it lawful for a man to divorce his wife for any and every reason?" They tried to lead him into a trap, because the law says a man can divorce his wife, but a woman cannot divorce her husband. How could a woman divorce her husband? He owns her; she doesn't own him. Heaped on top of that fact, her needs are provided by her husband, so why would she want to leave him? But some women would rather die than stay with their husbands, and that happens. Too many women have been abandoned by frivolous husbands, have struggled in poverty, and died.

The Pharisees asked this question and watched as Yeshua stirred the soil with a finger as he said, "Have you not read that in the beginning the creator made them male and female?" He put his index fingers side by side, and he bounced them forward like a couple of people joined together. "For this reason a man leaves his mother and father and unites with his wife, and the two become one."

The Pharisees seemed not to understand. They waited with furrowed brows.

Yeshua's face expressed amazement and awe. He laughed. "Do you not understand? They become one; they copulate." He laughed some more. "Therefore, what God has joined together has become one being, and it cannot be separated by man."

I also laughed, because the Pharisees did not understand that Yeshua was teasing them. He was being sarcastic. They were blind to it because they thought in terms only of the law and not of the heart.

In their blindness they asked, "Then why did Moses declare that a man could give his wife a certificate of divorce and send her away?" They were hypocrites. By saying this they put Moses above God, but they couldn't see it.

Yeshua told them, "Moses permitted you to divorce your wives because you were a bunch of whiners, but it was not like that from the beginning. Moses had to keep peace among a throng of complainers, men like you." Yeshua shook his head slowly like an older brother trying to keep a younger brother out of trouble and said, "I tell you, anyone who divorces his wife and marries another has committed adultery. I'm sorry to tell you this, but you will have to answer to Father, not to Moses." He watched them react, and he added, "Except when a wife has been unfaithful." He shrugged his shoulders. "Then you cannot blame the man for divorcing her." He said it because the law allows a man to have an adulterous wife stoned. He was telling the Pharisees that God's love is better than man's laws.

The Pharisees fidgeted and said, "Women stay with you. How is this respectable? They are not yours. You do not own them. They are not men who can live of their own free will. They belong to their husbands."

Yeshua wagged a finger in the air. "Things do not stay the same. These women walk with me," he put a hand over his heart, "and after a while in my presence they transform into men. I have seen this with my very own eyes. My disciples have seen it too. We have women here who have become ha'adam." Yeshua used a word that meant two things, both *men* and *human*. He confounded the dullards.

They meandered away, complaining that Yeshua had not argued in fairness, had not adhered to legitimate argument, because they wanted to argue strictly using Mosaic law. They were like Shammai, and Yeshua was like Hillel. That was my Yeshua, whom I love.

After that scene with the Pharisees, we sat together as a group drinking wine and telling jokes. Is it blasphemy to ridicule the law? After all, Moses is not God. A few of us spoke in mock protest. If there cannot be divorce at all except for infidelity, then anyone would be a fool to get married. Why enter a trap from which you cannot escape? My beloved Yeshua, who had drunk a little too much while laughing along with us, said, "There are a lot of fools, then, because there have been a lot of marriages. Not everyone gets married. Even from birth there are men who have no interest in women, and there are men who are castrated for various reasons. Some men deny themselves for religious reasons. Truly I tell you, marriage takes balls. Some men have them and some men don't."

We all love this man, Yeshua. Sometimes he has called me Israel, and I have wondered about that. Why? Once I corrected him. "My name is Judas."

He answered, "Yes, so it is. A day will arrive when you remember that I called you Israel, and on that day you will marvel about it. Each of us is Israel."

"You speak in riddles again."

"They only seem like riddles, and sometimes such seeming riddles are the only way."

One day Yeshua was approached by the family of brothers who heatedly disputed shares of inheritance after their father had died. The family requested him to decide which brother should receive what, based on how well each had cared for his father during his illness. Yeshua put on a startled look and said, "You want me to divide this estate among you?" He turned his head to the side and downward, as if in deep thought, and said to himself almost in a whisper, "But I am not a divider." He turned to the rest of us, his followers, and he asked with amusement, "I am not a divider ,am I? Am I a divider?" He faced the family and answered them earnestly, "I am sorry, but I am not a divider. If you want to be happy, give all the inheritance to those in poverty and be satisfied with what you already have."

Later he said to the rest of us, "When I no longer am among you, people will change who I am, will make me who they want me to be. They will make me a divider who judges who will be saved and who will not. Truthfully I tell you I will not divide you. I ask you a question. Will the world and all the people in it be saved? To answer this question I ask you another question. Do you know me? If you know me, then you know our father, and you will know the answer."

When we arrived in Jerusalem the first time it was not Passover. Many of us marveled at the temple, how grand it was, finding it hard to believe the size of the stones used to construct it. Many people came and went, purchasing items for *korbanot*, sacrificial offerings. Wealthy ones bought a sheep or a bull, which pleased the *kohanim*—the priests—because not only did the considerable money spent for such an offering go into the temple's coffers, but also after *shechita*, the ritual slaughter, only some parts of the animal were burned on the altar, while the other parts were cooked and eaten by the worshiper and shared with the kohanim. It was a party.

Worshippers with less money purchased doves or grain or wine or incense. These items were good enough for God, of course, but not so delectable for the kohanim. It was not a party.

Inside the temple the kohan prayed, "Accept, lord our god, the service of your people, Israel, and the fire offerings of Israel, and receive their prayers with favor. Blessed is he who receives the service of his people Israel with favor."

We watched the people coming and going.

Yeshua asked us, "Did you know that John the Baptizer despised the kohanim?"

This observation puzzled some of us.

He continued, "His father was a priest. He could have been a priest himself and lived a comfortable life, but he chose not to. Why do you think that was?"

None of us answered.

Yeshua asked, "What is the purpose of korbanot?"

One person in the group responded, "We are to realize that we ourselves deserve to die for the sins we have committed, but the animal dies in our place."

Another man said, "When we sin, it is the animal in us that has done it, separating us from our true spiritual selves. When we burn the korbanot, we burn away this part of our nature."

"This is what korbanot used to mean," answered Yeshua. "You are not children anymore. Think deeper." He then said to me, "Judas, what is the purpose of korbanot?"

I felt uneasy because already the others resented me. I was the pragmatic one instead of the dreamer. I answered, "Commerce.

The kohanim sell merchandize for profit, and their income is taxed by the government. The kohanim and Herod and Rome all are quite happy with this arrangement."

He smiled at me. "Are your sins so severe that you deserve to die for them?"

"Me? Maybe. I've been a very bad man from time to time."

"What about Matthew? Does he deserve to die for his sins?"

"He was a tax man. He is lucky nobody has killed him already."

The men laughed.

"What about poor Philip here? How severe are his sins? If he cannot afford to purchase a korban, should we put him to death?"

"No, Yeshua. He has done nothing to deserve death."

"You are saying that Philip does not need to purchase a korban." He stroked his beard. "Let us consider this. Korbanot is sold here, and that makes it easier for pilgrims who otherwise would have to carry it with them, a more difficult package for travel than just money. This is convenient for them, yes? A wealthy man purchases a bull every couple of weeks, and the Kohanim appreciate him because he shares his wealth with them. If this man wishes to discuss with the Kohanim an idea he has for proceedings within the temple, will they listen to him?"

We answered that they would.

"There also is a poor old woman who has little or no money at all. She combines her own money with that of an acquaintance, and together they purchase some kernels of wheat. As a portion of all she has, she sacrifices more than the wealthy man who buys the bulls. Will the Kohanim listen to her?"

We answered that they would not.

"This is the way of the temple. Is it this way in our father's kingdom? Do wealthy people have more influence on Dad than the poor?"

We answered that our father listens equally to all people who pray earnestly and truly from their hearts.

"You tell me that this majestic temple does not resemble Father's house." Yeshua nodded his head. "I thought as much." He walked to one of the tables where money was traded for korban, and he said to the clerk, "Tell me what you have here."

The clerk showed him, and then Yeshua asked, "Do you think our father will be more pleased with me if I purchase a sheep or if I purchase a stick of incense?"

The clerk answered, "Either will satisfy him, but if you wish to please him very much then the sheep is the way to go. However, you look like you do not have the means to purchase so expensive an animal. May I suggest a dove?"

Yeshua smiled at him gently. "Do you mock our father's temple?"

The man acted perplexed and said nothing.

Yeshua said quietly, "I see. That is just the way it is." He hefted the table over onto its side, causing coins to spill on the floor. The noise of it startled the crowd, and all the people stopped and looked. He said to them, "The smell of burned korban is not what pleases Father. This shanty is not Father's house. It is large and heavy and does not resemble the eternal. It will crumble, and in very short order I will rebuild in its place a true temple, inscribed on your hearts, living in your souls." He left and we followed him, leaving behind the startled eyes and ears.

This behavior of Yeshua's was too bold because Pilatus had eyes and ears everywhere. It surprised me that Yeshua was not seized on the spot, but then it was not Passover week, and sometimes eyes and ears are lazy. The clerk rushed at Yeshua, but I stopped him, and the rest of our men gathered quickly around. This was why Yeshua escaped.

I confess they have come to me, operatives of the Maccabeans, and they brought messengers from the Kohanim who were displeased with Yeshua's teachings even before this. Caiaphas was furious and looked for a traitor among our group to catch Yeshua in a crime so he could be shown to be a fraud. Kohanim knew my history of deceit and said I was the correct man to do this deed.

I would not deceive Yeshua, so it rakes my skin to know what has happened since then.

To these messengers I answered, "Why would I do that? Who

are the Kohanim to me? They want to use me? Tell them I am not their tool." I wished to say, but did not, that Yeshua had power because he was chosen by our father to be a great prophet, and they have no power to match the creator. He is not a flash in the pan, as they imagine him to be. Why would I choose to be with them, a losing Goliath, when already I am a companion of David? Why would I throw in with them whom I have hated from the beginning? Instead I said, "They chose a soft life for themselves, the Kohanim. They wear comfortable clothes and eat delicious food. How unlike John the Baptizer they are! He wore a shirt made of camel hair, purposefully to irritate his skin and remind him of his humility. Tell the Kohanim that Yeshua is their camel hair, to irritate their skin and remind them of their own humility." This comment would infuriate them, yes. I knew that, and I wanted that. "I do not tell Yeshua what to do. I am not the boss of him. He is the boss of me."

They did not listen. "Encourage him to break the law for the good of the people. The good of the people, Judas! He will do this. Then Caiaphas will get what he wants, and Pilatus will do the rest," they said and left.

Pilatus would do the rest.

I told Yeshua that monsters hide in the shadows and will jump upon him when they can.

"Yes, they will," he answered. "I know the where and when of it. Do not resist events that befall me because they will happen just as they have happened since the beginning of time, and if one day the powers of heaven change it, it will not be this time. It is because of this that Father chose to live in me, and because of me, in you as well. Do not interfere with what happens. Instead be faithful to the way I show you." This is all he said at the time.

This knowledge stabs me in the heart. I would rather die in battle like Judas Maccabeus. Secretly I arranged for acquaintances to follow Yeshua and protect him.

That was then, and now is now. We have been in Jerusalem, and it is Passover, with crowds of people all over, allowing only standing room. One must push to move on the streets, and assassins lurk in such closeness.

Arrangements were made to celebrate the first day of unleavened bread, when the Passover lamb was sacrificed. We came here, just outside Jerusalem, and rented an upper room in a man's home. Jerusalem is so crowded that private homes have become inns.

When we first came into the room and removed our outer garments, Yeshua decided he would wash each of our feet. After he finished he said, "Now we are all clean." Thaddaeus came in after tending to the donkey in the stalls below. Yeshua said, "We are clean except one of us. One of us is not clean." He laughed and cleaned the feet of Thaddaeus as well.

Earlier today most of us stayed in the room, out of the hot sun.

Yeshua sat in a corner and prayed, and when I looked at him I heard his voice inside my head. *Father, I have made you known to the humans you took from the world to give me. They were yours and you gave them to me. Everything you have given me to share with them proceeds from you. I have taught them what you taught me, and they believe it. I pray for them, not for the part of them that is in the world, but for that which is in them that is yours and which you entrusted me, because they are yours. I am no longer in the world, but they still are. I will come to you, but they remain here. Keep their minds true to you so they may experience oneness with us. While in the world I have shared with them what is not in the world, but now if the world hates them because of me, because they no longer belong to it, protect them if it is your will. Entrust them to share with others what you first gave to me. May they all be one as you are in me, and I am in them. Make them completely one so the world will recognize that you sent me. Before the foundation of the world we were, and now they also are.*

I moved closer to him, and when he opened his eyes I asked, "What does it mean?"

"Someday you will understand. You are a new wineskin and are able to understand."

Commotion erupted in the streets, and Philip ventured out to learn what it was.

From that moment Yeshua wore a cloud over his head. He looked solemnly at the floor and then at various ones of us. When he looked at me I could hear him thinking, *This I will do for you.*

Philip returned and announced, "There has been a riot at the temple. The Romans have beaten many and have imprisoned many. Pilatus declared this is a warning against further violence, and he will crucify the captives, saying they are criminals against the government."

"What?" I shouted. "This is outrageous."

"Why was there a riot?" Bartholomew asked.

"People protested commerce in the temple. There was pushing and shoving, and tables were tipped over. Pilatus was ready with thugs in the crowd, and they made the ruckus into a catastrophe."

"Don't they know Jews argue with each other?" I said. "This is what a Jew does. The Roman bastard has blood lust and needs to be assassinated. He will bleed us into submission, the bastard."

"Bastard?" Yeshua asked. "You are a hothead, Judas."

"Guilty as charged."

"The people know I am in the city, and they repeat my teachings. Now what will happen to them?"

We were silent.

"I am responsible for this, am I not? What will happen to me?"

We realized what he was saying. "No!" we said.

"I must give myself in exchange for the innocent."

"You are the innocent one."

"I cannot go directly to Pilatus, because he would take me straightaway and crucify me along with the rest."

"Stop talking like that."

"This requires negotiation between worldly powers who will listen to each other."

We were silent.

"For the same reason I cannot go myself directly to the Kohanim. There must be negotiation. One of you must go to the Kohanim to tell them I will offer myself in exchange for the many who now are condemned. Caiaphas is the only one who will be able to persuade Pilatus he may have both his blood lust and peace during Passover, but only if he makes this trade. Otherwise there will be more riots. He may slaughter the responsible one."

"No!"

"One of you must go to the Kohanim. Caiaphas will do this." Yeshua looked directly at me.

Yeshua looks at me. Here I am now as he looks at me, his eyes stabbing my heart. I swallow painfully on the memory of my own words, *to die honorably in battle*. No!

He says, "We must not bring calamity against this home of our guests, so several of you will come with me, and I will await my captors at the Garden of Gethsemane."

We argue against Yeshua.

He quiets us for Seder, and when we are quiet he says, "*Ma nishtana ha lyla ha zeh mikkol hallaylot?*" (Why is this night different from all other nights?)

We answer that this is the night we Jews fled from slavery in Egypt.

He plays the role of the youngest child, asking the four questions that the rest of us answer. At the time of the first cup of wine, Kiddush, he also plays the role of our father by telling the story of the Exodus, and so, on this night, he makes himself both the father and the son.

Each of us dips a vegetable into salt water, reminding us of the tears of our slavery, and on this night we truly wet them with our own tears. So it goes through the steps of the seder, but I cannot keep my mind on it because of what Yeshua will command of me. We drink the second cup of wine, Maggid, the cup of the Messiah.

After the last piece of unleavened bread, our dessert, the Afikoman, the last morsel we will eat at this meal, Yeshua departs from the seder. He says, "Thank you, Father, for the gift of this bread." He breaks it and says, "This is the body of the lamb sacrificed so that Father's children will live. Eat it."

We eat the bread.

At the third cup of wine, the one for redemption of the dead, he thanks God for the wine and says, "This is blood that was shed by the sacrificed lamb of God, painted on the doorposts of Israel so her children would be spared death. Drink it."

We drink the wine.

"Do this for me." He requests, "Whenever you eat this bread and drink this wine, remember me, that I sacrificed myself so others will live. This is the blood and body of those who have sacrificed their lives so that others will live."

We are stunned. It is blasphemy and it is truth.

We drink the fourth cup of wine, meant for taking the redeemed into the world to come.

When we finish, Yeshua says, "Now one of you must go to the Kohanim."

Simon the Stone asks, "Must it be me, Master?"

And the others rapidly follow, all at once, "Must it be me?"

I am silent, because I know it will be me.

Yeshua says, "The man who does this for me tonight will be repudiated by the world. They will say even that I cast him into hell and that it would have been better for him if he never had lived. This is the ignorance of the world. You must remember that none of you belong to the world anymore. You belong with me in our father's house. I will not drink or eat again until I am in Father's kingdom, and there I will drink new wine." He nods his head toward me.

"Must I do this?" I whisper.

"Go. Do what you must do."

I leave like a man slapped by his lover. Shadows dart away from light; they swell and shrink and dissipate. I stumble through the paths of night and count my steps. My past spits me out, and my future swallows me.

As I approach a light, I cannot see
the shadow close behind and creeping up
on me, contracting as the light comes near.

Or, better said, as I come near the light,
the shadow shrinks until, when I am at
the light, it disappears inside of me.
I wonder when the light will shine completely
through and quench the shadow, drive it from
me. Light is life, and then, with shadow deep
inside of me, I die. I cannot live
without becoming dead, opaque until
I die myself, and in my death allow
the light to shine completely through my soul.
As I pass the light and move away,
the shadow springs again from me and grows.
It points, but not to where I have to go;
instead it moves in arcs of my despair.
The light and my despair come with me as
I go to my appointed destiny,
and if I die, then sorrow disappears.
They put into my hands a bag of coins
and thank me for my duty, done, for doing
right in shadows looming dark behind
the ones who block the light. Oh, how did I
arrive in this unholy place? Oh, why
is this, this bag of coins I carry with
me in my hands? We stumble forth; they know
the path and drag me with them, helpless me.
They pull and push, and I, I count the steps.
I watch the back of him who walks in front
of me and blocks the light. How long have I
been here and watched that back? It always has
been here, has never gone away, and I
have always seen it take me where I told
the priests to go, to where the son of man
and God would be. They cannot see the light
that shines from him because they live in shadow,
blinded by the things within this world

that block the light. I kiss his pretty cheek.
"Betrayal with a kiss?" he says to me
and then embraces me. There is a brief
dispute, a skirmish, and he stops it short.
"Do not by sword invite your own demise,"
he says. It then gets dark because they take
the light away. I can no longer see.
At this unholy, holy place I fear
my future hates me, spits me out as well.
My past and future both despise and will
not have; there is no other place for me
to go. A rope and branch that hang above
a hill. I will no longer block the light.

Thirty-five

BEYOND SPACETIME

Within the structure of this world, one thing follows another, but beyond spacetime the beginning and the ending are in exactly the same place. They are singular. The beginning cannot be divided from the ending.

Maybe this is not for me to understand.

In this world are good and evil, and they can be accepted in their entirety or not at all. There is no pick and choose.

Who is Yeshua?

I am within everyone.

Everyone?

This I can, and this I do. In this way I am not alone, and you are not alone.

Why is there evil in the world?

Because the world is whole and cannot be divided.

Why must Yeshua die?

He chooses to do this, and I am within him, and then because of his love for others, I am in them as well.

Can one man alone bear the weight of all creation?

He is not alone. I am within him.

Can I be with him also?

You already know that you are with him, so what do you mean?

I want to bear some of his pain, along with him.

You are unable to bear it unless you are him.

Then make me him; I cannot bear that he must bear it.

I am the world and what is beyond the world.

Then I am part of the world and part of what is beyond the world. Let me bear a part of Yeshua's pain.

I give you an infinitesimal fraction so that by your witness of it, you will have a tiny understanding. This is a terrible gift, and you will not tolerate it unless you remember that I abide in you.

Israel Newman's mind erupts with thoughts and experiences, beginning with a single voice: *Father, if it be your will, then let this cup pass me by, and then* there is another: *Forgive them, Father, for they do not know what they are doing,* and then there are two thoughts simultaneously: *I commend my spirit into yours. It is finished.*

Three simultaneous thoughts appear: *Some of my fingernails grow faster than others. She walks toward me in her dress of corn-flower blue, and never before have I seen such beauty. Tonight after I have teased him with kisses he will imagine he has captured me and I am his prize, but when I beg him to kiss my breasts, he will become mine; I will own him.*

There are five more simultaneous thoughts: *The termite crawls into one of the many holes, and I remember Mother inserting a long, skinny stick for the insect to climb onto. Some things young-sters must learn for themselves. I ache and want to call my mother to lament how much I miss my deceased father, for she, best of all, will understand, but I cannot call her, for she now also has died. I suddenly realize I'm picking a scab on my arm, and I didn't realize it until just now. Leave it alone. Screw the bastard; he wants to play hardball with me? Fuck him.*

There are then eight simultaneous thoughts: *I shot myself in the eye with my pee. I love him; I love him; I love him. I recline next to her sleeping body and breathe her breath. Please forgive me. Let me die; I want to die. Spare me; don't let me die. I'm just messing with your mind. She tells me how handsome I am in my new suit. I thank her, and as I walk away a series of little farts erupt from my ass, one with each step.*

Next there are thirteen simultaneous thoughts: *I'm not so spry on my feet anymore and slip on a wet leaf and fall hard; my hip hurts too much to move; a man comes, and I tell him I need help; he grabs my pants by the pocket and rolls me over to take my wallet. I scream. I am inside of you. I feel him inside of me. I feel her tighten on me. This we have in common. Why do you say that? Why would you say something like that? It isn't true. That hurts. God. that's good! Do it some more. I think if you keep killing it, after a while it will stay dead. I have dreamt that your lips are lovely to kiss. She kisses my lips, and they are no longer mine; they are hers. It's too painful; I can't do this. There! I can see the baby's head!*

There are twenty-one simultaneous thoughts: *Gorgonzola and pear and a glass of pinot. In and out, and my back hurts; I hope she comes soon. It was well worth the wait. I waited too long; missed my lucky break. Money means nothing to me. Got to put food on the table. Cancer! Make me laugh. There's a knock on the door. Paralyzed? Forever? Where are all the nice guys? More than one hundred thousand people have been killed by the quake. More than a million have been killed by the war. God, no! He eats my baby. Seven severed heads roll out on the dance floor. Just get him to commit; sign the damned paperwork. Let the buyer beware. I had no idea what I was signing. He could take the fun out of the second coming of Christ.*

There are thirty-four simultaneous thoughts, then fifty-five, eighty-nine, one hundred forty-four. It is miraculous that Israel understands and is able to make sense of it all. Until it becomes unbearable.

One of the thoughts is this: *Because light travels at the speed of light, time stops for it. Light never ages.*

Another thought is this: *I am reading this here and now, and I know that the spirit is inside of me here and now, and I am not separate from it.*

He finds himself kneeling in a stable looking at a swaddled baby laid in a manger with his mother watching over it. There are others kneeled in the stable. He asks the woman, "Who is the child?"

"His name is Yeshua."

From the baby itself, though it did not open its eyes or speak, Israel heard the voice of Yeshua. "Israel! I was killed and I died and now I am born and live again."

Thirty-six

MARKUS

Israel was pulled beyond spacetime again by a power other than his own, and then he reentered it.

I Marky.

Bahderdahly good.

Mommy: love, warm, soft, kisses, cuddle, smile, food. Want Mommy, love.

Daddy: funny, strong, tickle, play, ice cream. Daddy gone; miss Daddy. Sad.

We drive Kristeen visit.

Kwuk!

Cut tree good. Cow!

Kristeen fwend, play, laugh. Kristeen naughty.

Happy birdy cake. Sing happy birdy to Kristeen.

Play. Big ball. Get ball Marky. Downhill go follow. Ball big not lift. Push ball up hill Kristeen help.

Daddy voice. Marky. Laugh. Look, Daddy. No, Daddy. Sad.

Fall down.

Ball roll downhill follow. Push ball up.

Voice say, "Marky, sit." Daddy voice. Where Daddy? "Sit, Marky!"

Marky sit. Car go whoosh! Down crash tree go pow!

Marky kie. Mommy come lift Marky. Mommy kie.

Thirty-seven

A NEW TIMELINE

Israel found himself driving his car on a country road in the dark, disoriented and not recognizing where he was or why he was there. Mixtures of different lines of thought made little sense to him.

He drove back and forth on the road awhile. Had he turned wrong? Maybe he should have turned left instead of right when he saw the pipeline. He was certain he had been on track until that point. He drove back to the traffic light. It was red. He felt the need to be urgent, looked all directions, and seeing no other cars, drove through the red light, straight along the road in a direction that earlier would have been a left turn. He drove up a fairly steep hill, winding first to the left and then around to the right before straightening out again. It looked more promising, as there was some familiarity of scenery at the top of the hill.

Time was getting short, and he sped up, but his mind seemed blank and hyperaware of being blank. *Time is getting short for what?* He slowed his car to a stop. *What am I doing here? Where am I? Am I going crazy? Timeline craziness? Timeline craziness!*

A car's lights shined in his rearview mirror. *Einstein.* He drove his car forward and onto a narrow shoulder of the road, stopped, and turned on his warning lights. *I'll remember if I just give myself time to remember.*

He sat in his car at the side of the road for a few minutes. A deer walked slowly across the road. *Déjà vu.* A memory was triggered and slowly congealed in his mind: *I'm driving faster. The world is a blur in my vision, in my mind. A deer! I swerve and miss the deer. A tree! I swerve and miss the tree, but I'm off the road and deeply mired in mud. Damn! I'm not hurt. It's 6:48. I get out and walk. It's raining. It's cold. It's dark. Markus, where are you?*

Markus!

Israel looked at the clock on his cell phone. It was 6:55. Anxiety deluged him as though a dam restraining it had broken. He felt his heart turn over, and there was a stab on the right side of his chest where a gunshot had . . . no, not in this timeline. A flood of anxiety immobilized him. "Oh, my God! What do I do?" He wept. *Einstein's predetermined universe. Will the Mozart laboratory call me back, mercifully?*

A car drove by fast in a cloud of windy spray, and he felt his own car buffeted.

His cell phone rang. "Hello?" he answered with a whispered croak.

"Hello, Israel? This is Sonya." She sounded anxious but energetic. "Sorry I didn't get back to you sooner. We were away for a while, and you called my land phone. We then had to run out to a birthday party, one of Markus's friends."

"Markus! Is Markus okay?"

"I suppose you can hear I'm kind of excited right now. Yes, Markus is fine. We had a scare, though."

"A scare?"

"Yes. Geez! Don't let this upset you. Marky's okay. He and I were just scared and crying for a while."

"What happened?"

"A parked car, on a hill, rolled down. Brakes went out or something." She paused, and with a tearful voice she said, "It just missed Marky."

"He's okay, though?"

"Yes, he's okay. I think it scared me more than him."

Israel laughed.

Sonya asked, "Israel, are you okay?"

"Me? Yeah. I'm great. Couldn't be better. No, I'm crazy. But great. Really, I am."

"What's so funny? What are you laughing at?"

"Life. I'm laughing at life."

"I don't know what there is to laugh at. Your son almost got crushed by a runaway car, and you're laughing."

"Yes, I know. It's crazy, isn't it? Just for this moment, Sonya, I'm crazy, good crazy. I'm trying to figure stuff out. Nothing's wrong. Markus is alive and healthy; he's healthy isn't he? Life couldn't be better, Sonya."

"Well, he's exhausted. I'm sure he'll sleep all the way home."

"The world spins on us, Sonya. It's a strange world, and we just figure it out as we go along, right? We take it moment by moment, and we figure it out. Listen, Sonya, this is going to sound strange, my asking this, but at the moment my mind is, only momentarily, my mind is kind of completely goofed up, confused. Can you tell me, and this is a serious question. Are we married, you and I?"

"Israel! Have you been drinking? Are you on drugs or something?"

"No, I . . . think it's my headache. Migraine. Strange things happen with headaches."

"No, Israel. We are not married. Not anymore, sweetheart. I'm sorry."

Israel laughed again. "But Markus is all right. He's safe and sound."

Sonya laughed. "He's the loveliest little boy. I just adore him."

"I need to see him." Israel cried. "I need to see him as soon as possible. Please let me see him soon again."

"Are you all right, Israel? It sounds like you're not doing so well."

"Honestly I'm doing very well. Just emotional."

"Come over tomorrow. We'll eat cheese pizza and drink chocolate milk."

Thirty-eight

IS THIS HEAVEN?

Israel passed through the months.

Markus was playing with his cars on the floor. "Hi, Daddy."

Together Israel and Markus built a wall across the hallway with blocks Israel earlier had made by inserting one milk carton into another. Israel pushed Markus in his pushcar, crashing into the wall and breaking it down. They laughed and built the wall again.

Thirty-nine

IS THIS HEAVEN?

srael wanted to meet with Michael Hannity and drove over to his mansion. It looked the same from the outside except there was no tiny screen outside to read his thumbprint and unlock the door. He knocked on the door with its clapper that was green with patina. Soon there were footsteps on the other side, and the door opened.

It was Jeeves. He smiled. "Sorry, we don't accept soliciting at this address."

"No, no. I'm not a solicitor. Please let me explain. I'm—"

"Doctor Newman. Please come in. There are things on which we must catch up."

"You know who I am?"

Jeeves laughed. "We have known each other a very long time. Come in."

As Israel stepped across the threshold into the expansive foyer, he said, "Then you must think my behavior right now is, eh, how do I want to say this? It's unusual."

"Not at all. You've been through a lot, Doctor Newman. Would you like some afternoon tea? Come along this way. We'll go to the Hobbit Hole."

Israel followed Jeeves along the familiar path through the large room on the left, with the carpet that looked like a spring meadow, to the round door and tunnel, through the kitchen to the richly wooded, intimate dining room. There were the busts of Einstein, Plank, and Maxwell. There was the photograph of a little boy wearing a Super Boy outfit.

"Not much is different," said Jeeves. "Have a seat. I'll return shortly with the tea and something scrumptious."

Israel sat. The chairs had fabric, not the squeaky plastic he remembered from the Halloween party. He looked around the room. Everything else was entirely familiar.

Jeeves returned with a platter upon which were two bottles of local brew, Alaskan Amber, and a couple of packages of Twinkies. He set them down on the table. "Tea can refer to many things; I would say anything amber and liquid. Does this give any clue to who I am?"

"To who you are?" Something lodged in Israel's mind. Some day he would share Twinkies and beer with someone.

Jeeves poured the beer into glasses and then he poured a few drops to make a tiny puddle on the tabletop. He sat down, opened a package of Twinkies, and took a bite. "Enjoy these while you may. Only four more years of Twinkies. At the end of 2012, Hostess will go out of business. Of course it will be only a little while. Twinkies will return." Jeeves put one of his fingers in the tiny puddle on the table and drew symbols with it. His movements were completely familiar.

"Yeshua!"

"Sort of. I'm Jeeves at the moment, but spirit as well; it's hard to tell us apart sometimes. What you do with any of my brothers you do with me." Jeeves smiled.

"Aren't you still back in Nazareth?"

"Of course. You already have experienced this, Israel. Every point in time contains within it all eternity. It can be this way because spirit travels beyond spacetime. You have done this many times before, and right now, are you not also in the Garden of Gethsemane, betraying me with that silly kiss on my cheek?"

Israel was stunned. "Oh, my god!"

Jeeves laughed, "Oh, my god! Oh yes, Israel! We are a pair, are we not? Let me tell you another thing. Even as all eternity is contained in every point of time, the entire universe is contained in every point of space. It is made like this. Think of entangled particles. Think of multiple universes."

"Am I going crazy?"

"No, you're drinking a beer and eating Twinkies with an old friend."

"It was going to happen on Mount Rainier, though."

"Give us time."

Israel was at a complete loss for words.

The two men sat together quietly, aware of a clock ticking in the room.

"Where's Michael?" Israel asked.

"At work."

"He's working?"

"Chairman of the Department of Physics."

"At the U-Dub?"

"Yes indeedy."

"Wow!"

"He's in better control of himself here in this timeline."

"This is good. I can hardly wait to see him."

"I look forward to introducing the two of you."

"He doesn't know me here?"

"No. Not to worry. He will very much enjoy your telling your tale. He is just as tuned to timelines here as where you were. The two of you will be best friends."

"Tell me about Gina."

"Gina is here."

"How can I meet her?"

"That is for you to figure out. She doesn't know me, so it is not like I can introduce the two of you."

"But you can be anybody."

"Be patient, Israel."

The clock in the room made a whirring sound, and Israel looked at it. The time was 3:16. He shot his gaze to Jeeves. "What does it mean?"

"What have you thought it to mean?"

"It's a message, something to do with John 3:16."

"For God so loved the world that he gave his only begotten son to die for us, that whoever believes in him will not perish but have everlasting life."

"Yes."

"If I were to tell you that 3:16 has come into your life no more frequently than any other combination of numbers, what would you think then?"

Israel sat in silence, not knowing how to answer.

"It would mean that you are preoccupied with John 3:16, don't you think? Tell me why you're preoccupied with it."

"It divides people into those who are saved and those who are not, those who are loved and those who are forsaken."

"But can't everyone choose to believe or not?"

"No, they can't. The world is not constructed that way."

Jeeves smiled with amused warmth. "So you are saying I'm not a divider."

"Yes!"

"You're correct, Israel. I am not a divider. You have been able to experience the lives of many people, and you know that some believe and some don't. Did I value any of them less than the others? No. It is the spirit inside that I love, is it not? Do I love the carriage or the riders in the carriage?"

"You love them both."

Jeeves laughed. "Yes, Israel. I love them both."

"Why did Yeshua have to be crucified?"

"He chose to be heroic. This is why I chose to live in him first. There are many others who also have been heroic, and I have lived in them also."

"You have lived in everyone?"

"Yes."

"Why?"

"The world was made, and I watched as it grew and expanded. It was wonderful and horrible at the same time. Upon its completion I decided to live within it. I chose Yeshua first because of his love and courage. I tell those who listen to him that the holy spirit will come to them, and the holy spirit is me. I live in everyone. Whatever you have done even to the least of my brothers, Israel, you have done not only to me but also to yourself."

"Holy god."

"Thank you very much." Jeeves laughed.

"You laugh a lot, Yeshua."

"Jeeves, you mean. Is there anything better to do? Laughter bolsters our courage."

"Why did you choose to enlighten me?"

"You were ready for it. Not everyone is ready at the same time. You are a carriage in which I enlighten souls."

"I love you."

"I love you."

They looked at one another. Israel said, "I see a tiny heart-shaped fleck of color in the bottom of your left iris. I've seen it in Michael's left eye as well."

"Amusing. It is the way you have come to recognize my presence. The fleck is in your own mind. By the way, I see it in your left eye as well, because I am able to be you, looking at you. It is charming, Israel."

"What does it mean to be the Christ?"

"To be the Christ? The chosen one? The anointed one? This was the Greek distortion of the Jewish concept of the messiah, was it not? The messiah was to reestablish the independence of the nation of Israel, to restore justification of the nation with God. Is this what Yeshua did?"

"No."

"The Greek concept of Christ, given to us by Paul, was that Yeshua paid the price of the sins of all mankind by dying. It says to us that because God became alive in Yeshua, Yeshua was able to do this. From your understanding now, is this what Yeshua did? Did Yeshua need to die for there to be justification of all humankind with me? This is an ancient concept of atonement by death.

Am I that ancient, Israel? It is sadly silly. Yeshua died because he chose to do it, or Pilate would have killed many innocents. It was a very human act of love and courage. Yeshua is amazing, which is why I chose him first. The Christian church grieves the death of Yeshua by making it part of Father's design for salvation. They make it Father's requirement for salvation. Thereby they relinquish the responsibility for a human act of brutality. They say God intended this as a gift to humankind. It's all very psychological. It's social and old."

"The creator made it this way."

"The creator! Puzzling; isn't it?" Jeeves paused, and then he asked, "Am I this Christ?"

Israel was afraid to answer.

Jeeves continued, "It is not true that a person must believe any one way or another to be saved, so I am opposed to this concept of Christ. I love all people regardless of what they believe. Each of them lives, and I am in them. I am who they are. If I were a divider, then I would be saving parts of myself and casting other parts into the rubbish heap. Is that what I do, Israel?"

"No, it is not."

"You will live in heaven and in hell, Israel. Everyone will live in heaven and in hell. I am sorry that souls must live in hell, but the structure of the universe is that both heaven and hell exist, and if one experiences one, then the other as well. Karma is about learning. You and I together will choose your next life. Behold what a vast menu there is from which we may choose. Father's house has within it many mansions. Look at the world, Israel. Eventually you will be all of it, and in fact since beyond spacetime there is no space and there is no time, already you have been all of it. Most people are aware of only one life at a time, and you are aware of a few lives, but you are all of it, just as I am. Be kind to others, Israel; it is how you make heaven."

"There is free will then."

"There is and there isn't. You are not yet ready for this knowledge. It will come to you later. You are mine, Israel." Jeeves was stone faced. "I am in all of what exists." It was clear he would not say more about the subject.

"I'm glad for that." Israel tapped the long finger of his right hand on the table. "You didn't exactly answer my question."

Jeeves shook his head. "No, I didn't. You are mine."

Israel said, "It seems there are at least two dimensions of time. In spacetime there is the one that relentlessly progresses in the forward direction. But beyond spacetime there is eternity, and it doesn't move at all. It just is."

Jeeves smiled. "Eternity! If you think even more about it, Israel, you have experienced eight of the dimensions of the universe, four of spacetime, and four beyond spacetime. There are others. The spirit of truth will teach you."

Jeeves offered more. "About 3:16, think about First Corinthians 3:16. Do you not know that you are the temple of God, and that the spirit of God dwells in you?"

Israel asked, "Is the Bible the word of God?"

"You know the answer. Are you confirming it? Every word ever written or said was caused before the beginning of the universe."

"So much has been evil."

"So much has been good. Like other writings that have been ascribed authority, not just the Bible but also the Bill of Rights, and there are many others, they are tools that can be used for either good or evil. When people use them, they show us who they are."

"You mean how they were made to be."

Jeeves smiled. "You understand."

This comment caused silence.

After a while Israel said, "An angel has passed."

"You are an angel, Israel."

"Angels have needs and desires? There is another thing then, if this is going to be heaven for me. Gina."

Forty

IS THIS HEAVEN?

Israel ached to be with Gina, a woman he loved in another timeline, and he labored for a strategy to meet her again. He eschewed the idea of resembling a stalker, but nevertheless he parked outside her apartment building, hoping to see her coming or going. It never happened.

There was a yarn store on the top of Queen Anne Hill called Hilltop Yarns, and he went there over and over, hoping to meet Gina. What would he say if he ran into her? He went to other yarn shops and never encountered her.

He went to the Puyallup Fair and stood in line forty-two minutes without seeing Gina before climbing into the slingshot seat. It sat two at a time, and a young girl named Emily sat in the seat next to him. Up into the air they flew. It was exhilarating and over too quickly.

He drove over to Issaquah and talked to people about paragliding. Maybe he would do that.

One day he visited So Much Yarn, a store on First Street, not far from where he used to attend support group with Frank Linder. She was there! His heart did a flip-flop. He lacked nerve enough to approach her, the consequence of which intimidated him. So much depended on doing it right. What would he say? His preparation wasn't adequate.

A man approached her, tall and slender, good looking. Israel remembered him, the vampire guy at Hannity's Halloween party. He walked to Gina, and they talked quietly and urgently about something. There was anger. Gina stood tall, did not look at the man, and she moved quickly, abruptly. The man put his hand on her shoulder, and she shrugged it away. He tried to touch her again, and she grabbed his hand and threw it aside.

What should Israel do? He was encouraged by Gina's anger, but this was not the time to introduce himself.

He watched them intermittently, not to draw attention to his interest, but there was commotion enough to interest other customers as well. It did not turn into an altercation that required outside interference. Gina turned and briskly walked out of the store. The man trailed after her.

Israel went to the Husky versus Trojan football game and looked for her, but she was not there. There were two empty seats in the midst of Trojan fans, and he sat in one of them, imagining her presence. The Huskies won again.

A year later, one day in November 2010, there was a dry day interlude in the wet weather, so Israel took Markus and his friend Nicholas to a playground on the north end, top of Queen Anne Hill, the corner of Third Avenue West and Howe. Both boys were six years old. He pushed them on the swings and on a red and white merry-go-round there. "Faster," they shouted, and he pushed them faster until they could barely hold on. He thought of God spinning the earth at breakneck speed, and he was amazed that gravity holds people on. *It holds us on, but it doesn't. Time and time again we fly off the earth and out of the world.*

The boys ran to a little sandbox at the south end of the playground. There was a stone ledge there, part of a landscape retaining wall, and Israel sat on it to rest and watch them play.

An older woman was sitting on the same ledge. She said, "That one in the red shirt, he's yours, isn't he? He looks like you."

He turned his face toward her but didn't really look at her. He answered, "Yes, he's mine." He thought about a small birthmark on Markus's right forearm. It was exactly the same as one on his own forearm. *He's mine.*

The woman said, "He's beautiful, a gift from God."

A gift from God, she says. "Yes, he is." He felt this fact deep inside.

She said, "Ultimately we cannot really earn anything for ourselves. Everything is a gift from God."

He looked at her. She spoke as if she had things she wanted to say, things she thought she had authority to say, and Israel was only beginning to realize something was extraordinary about her.

"A gift from God." He nodded. "Yes, that's for sure."

"What is his name?"

"Markus."

"Mark us," she said. "It's a good name. And his friend?"

"Nicholas."

"Where is Markus's mother on such a fine day?"

"She could be doing any of a number of things. She lives her own life now."

"You're a single father?"

"That I am."

"Do you still love her?"

"Markus's mom? I don't know. Yes, I guess. I mean once you love someone it never really goes away; does it? Maybe it does in some cases, but it's always there. The past is always there. Anyway, it doesn't work between her and me anymore. We don't get along. Let me say that differently. We get along but only by not being married to each other. Does that make sense?"

The woman sat quietly for a while, and then she asked, "Are you looking for a wife? Could you love another woman enough to give it a try again?"

What a bold question! She was nosy, this old biddy, but she was pleasant, so he answered, "Yes, but I'm not actively looking. I've got so many other things I need to do; no time to search for love, you know? Don't get me wrong. My eyes are open, and if someone comes along who knocks me off my feet, I'll take notice." He admitted, "In fact I'm in love with a woman already, enough that I can't get her out of my mind. I should say that I loved her once upon a time, body and soul."

"Somebody other than Markus's mother, I take it?"

"I met her after Markus's mom and I split. It's not adultery."

She didn't say anything.

He continued. "I understand that sometimes a marriage is intolerably unhappy, and then divorce can be an appropriate choice, but I wouldn't want to make my marriage unhappy by falling in love with someone other than my wife. Having a family changes the way a man ought to think. If I'm married and I'm going to stay in the marriage, then it would be no fun to fall in love with someone else. You see what I mean? Why would I do that? Why would I put myself in a situation like that?"

"You've thought about this subject. You've got a lot on your mind, answering questions I haven't even asked." She fumbled around in her handbag a moment and then looked out across the baseball field. "You're a faithful man."

He had to think about it. He sat awkwardly back against the stone wall, sighed, and then as though he were hypnotized and without a filter on which thoughts he shared, he confessed, "No, I'm not. I'm faithful only to a point. I betrayed Jesus. Actually it was an act of faith. You can't have any idea what I'm talking about."

"We all have betrayed Jesus," she said.

"No, you don't understand. I am the one who's responsible. I am the one who handed him over to the priests and the Romans. I'm the one. I am Judas Iscariot." *Why am I saying this? She's certain I'm crazy now.*

"We all have," she answered. "We all have handed Jesus over to the priests and the Romans. We all have pounded the nails in his hands and feet. Love doesn't mean a person is perfect." She paused, and then she added, "There are many of us who have traveled, Israel."

The hairs on the back of his neck stood up. He shivered. He looked closely at her face and noticed that her green eyes looked quite familiar. There was a fleck of blue at the bottom of her left eye, and it was shaped like a heart.

She remarked, "We all have handed Jesus over to the Romans."

Israel was dumbfounded. He looked at her while she watched him, and then she asked, "What do you think about evil in the world?"

Who is she?

"Evil just is. If we didn't have evil we wouldn't have goodness either. They are part and parcel of the same universe. They come along with each other. Let me see if I can think of an example." He scraped his right foot against the ground. "Competition; it's both good and bad. Because people get competitive, each one wanting to be better than everybody else, we end up with better products. Life is better because people compete. But you take that same competitiveness and put it into the heads of drivers on the road, all trying to get to their destination faster, and you end up with people driving crazy, getting into accidents. Good and evil; I guess it depends on context, among other things." He felt intelligent and satisfied with his answer.

"Ah!" She rocked slightly forward and backward. "I can give you another example. You know how youngsters can get into trouble, teenagers and kids in their twenties? They ignore that little voice in their heads that says 'Do that and you're going to regret it.' They ignore the voice, so they do those things anyway. To the rest of us it seems like they don't think about what they're doing, but they do think about it. They know the risks, but they're thick skinned and take the risks anyway, risks that we older folks would never dare." She looked askance at Israel and said, "They are young wineskins." She smiled. "Some kids get into trouble with drugs and sex and the law, but every now and then one or two of those brilliant children take a risk that changes the world. They become entrepreneurs with new and glorious ideas because risks don't intimidate them. Look at Bill Gates, the risks he took." She nodded. "I do wonder, though, why God made it that way."

"Maybe he likes to be surprised. Maybe he doesn't have complete control."

They watched the boys playing, and then she asked, "What do you think about jealousy?"

"It has its place."

"Perhaps it has its place, but you are not as jealous a man as you think you are. You have changed, and that might have to do with self-confidence." She waited for him to respond, but he remained silent. She continued. "What do you believe about forgiveness?"

His heart was pounding. Seriously he wondered who she was. Was she testing him? He answered, "Forgiveness means we decide to do things that allow a relationship to continue even after we've been wronged. It doesn't mean the wrongs have disappeared because they haven't, but it means we won't let the wrongs get in the way of things that are more important to us."

"Is it necessary to forgive?"

"Some people are unable to forgive."

"What happens to them?"

"Often they are lonely."

"You and I understand things much the same way; so how do you solve a problem like the role of God in our lives?" She smiled and didn't wait for an answer. "It's a different world you live in now, Israel. In a previous world you met her, and the two of you were nearly perfect for one another. You fell in love. In this present world you will fit each other even better."

He looked at and tried to study the woman.

She nodded her head at Markus. "He's a gift from God. Tell me one thing that is not a gift from God."

He didn't answer.

She said, "Next week is Thanksgiving. Markus will be with his mother, I take it."

"Yes."

"Come and have dinner with my daughter and me. She will understand because I'm always picking up strays. Forgive me for being an incorrigible matchmaker, but you see, a half year ago my daughter split with a man who made her unhappy. She's delightfully bright and playful. Ahem! And she's beautiful and sexy." She raised an eyebrow. "All her life she's been that way, except with him. She was not herself with him. Come and dine with us, chat, and be happy. Everything is a gift from God, you know."

Israel did not answer.

"Let me introduce myself," she said. "I am Sophia Provetti, and my purpose in life is to make others happy. That is what I do, as simple as that. Come and meet my Gina. You two will make each other gleeful; this is something I know. I've seen it." Sophia waited to make sure she had Israel's undistracted attention, and then she added, "Israel, have no doubt about it. I have seen it in my travels. It is the reason I came here today, to do what I can to assist with unraveling the future story." She paused and then laughed. "And to meet you, of course."

Forty-one

PROPHESY FULFILLED

During the first July after his twenty-first birthday Markus wanted his dad to accompany him for a long hike on Mount Rainier. They stopped to rest at a place with a beautiful view. Markus dropped his backpack to the ground and took from it two bottles of Alaskan Amber and two packages of Twinkies. He handed one of each to Israel and said, "It's good to be with you again, my friend. Let's chat awhile."

AFTERWORD

A long tradition exists in literature for names of characters to tell us something about them. How we love Dickens's choice of the name Scrooge! The name Prof. Hannity was chosen to accentuate his brain's proclivity to default toward objectionable verbiage. But look at his other names! Michael means "resembles god." Kal-El means "voice of god." Israel Legato Newman means "struggles with god, progresses smoothly, new man." One may point out that his travels were not so very smooth, that here were lots of bumps and potholes on the way, but it was within and through the continuous, smooth part of the universe that he traveled, beyond the particulate construction of spacetime.

My son, Joshua, shared with me his amusement that Reginald Pear objected to the name, Jeeves, given to him by Michael, but nevertheless every body continued to call him Jeeves, even the narrator of the story. The possible exception was Gina. I have talked with Reginald, who let me know that secretly he was complimented by the name. His annoyance was a put-on. Jeeves is the name of an admirable character whose council constantly was sought by others in the series of stories written by P. G. Wodehouse. You will enjoy reading them. They will tickle your soul and put a smile on your face. Wodehouse was a master of phraseology.

Things have changed since the events of this story in 2009. The Red Robin Restaurant closed, where Gina and Israel ate dinner after the football game. Hilltop Yarns closed, one of the stores where Israel looked for Gina. The gas station where Israel stopped on his first, unsuccessful venture to save Markus no longer exists at the southwest corner of 140th Avenue and Petrovitsky. A bank is now at that location. Alaskan Viaduct, just west of the parking garage where Israel got shot, was torn down in 2019, replaced by an underground tunnel. In 2009, responses on Facebook occurred above preceding posts, and now they are below. The colors of the merry-go-round at the park where Israel met Sophia might have changed; I don't know because I haven't returned there, but in 2010 they were in fact red and white.

Also since 2009, doctors and pharmacists, insurance companies and governments, all have become stricter and more restrictive concerning the availability of prescription opioid medicines, and there continues a debate on the rightness or wrongness of how zealous the war has been against the overuse of opioids. Certainly we want to use them as safely and as effectively as we can.

The Cutters Bay House restaurant is a choice place to visit. In this story I characterized it as glass and brass and class because I liked the rhymes. Actually there is not much brass there. There is more beautiful wood than brass. Yes, there is plenty of glass and class. To the best of my knowledge there never has been an assault in the parking garage beneath it, where I park my car when visiting. It is one of my favorite restaurants.

In my own life, 3:16 kept appearing. I awoke countless times in the middle of the night at this exact time. It haunted me. What did it mean? Was it a warning? It was in my mind of course, and at least in part as a product of my disbelief of free will, I interpreted the occurrences of 3:16 as having been placed at the moment of, and existing since the beginning of spacetime, urging me to write this story. It was a push for me to get it done. Consistent with that hypothesis, I now awaken in the middle of the night at other times as well; I say with a wink and maybe a little heart-shaped patch of blue at the six o'clock position of my otherwise green-brown left eye.

CPSIA information can be obtained
at www.ICGtesting.com
Printed in the USA
LVHW011805100220
646430LV00002B/81

9 781977 215369